SHERIDAN LEE

WOUNDED SOUL

by Sheridan Lee

For Jay-Maree

You're a *must* have in life. Love you, Jesus Freak.

ACKNOWLEDGEMENTS

I crafted *Wounded Soul* from the concepts in my brain, but Jeanette Cameron's expertise, dedication, and steadfast belief in me revolutionised this story. Thank you, dear friend, for continuing this journey with me. I praise God every day that I hitched my wagon to your star.

Many thanks to Cynthia Hickey and Winged Publications for adopting me as one of your own. I've enjoyed getting to know my fellow WP authors.

An enormous, gushy thank you to the beautiful readers who've gifted me with their heartfelt messages about my first book baby. I hope you enjoy this next trip to Tellarine, hanging out at Benanu's and revisiting my beloved Jacobsens. I write these stories for you.

My endless gratitude to Dad and Mum for, yet again, supporting me in my writing endeavours, and the squishiest of hugs to my amazing Mr Wonderful and our five awe-inspiring girls. You six rock my world and give me the biggest high.

And thank you, Heavenly Father, for loving me. You've blessed me beyond measure.

GLOSSARY OF AUSTRALIAN WORDS AND PHRASES

ATAR – Australian Tertiary Admission Rank
Dim sim – a small steamed or fried Chinese-inspired dumpling-style roll filled with meat and vegetables
Dunny – toilet
Garbo/Garbologist – a tongue-in-cheek reference to a garbage collector
Like the clappers – very fast or very hard
Ning nong – a fool, idiot
P-plater – a new licenced driver with a provisional licence
RACV – Royal Automobile Club of Victoria
Skerrick – the smallest bit
Squiz – look or glance
Stubby – a small squat bottle of beer
Thongs – flip-flops
Trackie daks – Track pants
VCE – Victorian Certificate of Education

CHAPTER ONE
Decisions

I shifted against the cold leather backrest of my bedroom desk chair and fidgeted with the edge of the pine desk. Maybe I was destined to be a garbologist after all.

"What's your score?" My cousin Anna Beaufort lolled on my crumpled doona in her fluorescent green shorty pyjamas, phone in hand.

"Still logging in."

Our thirteen years of State-mandated education had concluded a few weeks ago, and our VCE and ATAR results had released online at seven o'clock this morning. Anna stayed the night so we could check our scores first thing, but we had stayed up late talking and slept through our alarms.

Flutters danced in my midriff with each keyboard press. I wiped my clammy hands along my pyjama pants legs and steadied my laboured breaths. Had I earned an acceptable tertiary admissions rank for my first preference journalism course? I wrinkled my brow. I hoped so, although life tended to happen regardless of my plans.

Anna squealed. "Eighty-six point seven five!" She bounced on the bed, her messy mousy-brown hair jolting against her shoulders.

"Top fifteen percent, baby! I knew you'd ace it. Well done!" I grinned at my cousin before reverting my gaze to my laptop. My stomach clenched. Would my score be as spectacular? An image of future me, trucking the streets of Tellarine in grimy overalls with my long brunette braid poking through the back of a baseball cap, filled my mind. "Do they make overalls for tall women? Or would I need to buy men's clothing?" One of several downsides to my six-foot frame.

"Huh?"

"Nothing." The screen transformed and opened my results page. I scanned the webpage in search of the all-important number. My eyes bulged, and I gasped.

Anna padded to my desk and leaned against my back. "What did you—"

We screamed at my laptop showing my score of 95.70.

"Diana Nicole Jacobsen! That's amazing!" She wrapped her arms around my shoulders.

Tears pooled in my eyes. Journalism, here I come.

My bedroom door slammed against the wall, and Dad appeared, his wide-eyed gaze aimed at me. He scrunched his brow. "Everything okay?"

Anna thrust her arms in the air. "Diana's a genius!"

I snorted before turning my laptop toward Dad.

He inhaled a sharp breath and peered between me and my computer. "Wow." A huge grin spread across his face. He laughed, pulled me from my desk chair, and hugged me. "So proud of you, Princess. You worked hard for this."

I pressed against his warmth, enveloped in his woodsy cologne, and closed my eyes. Dad smelled like home. I pressed my lips together and fought against the burn in my eyes.

He kissed my temple. "Want to call Victoria?"

I pulled back and nodded.

Dad yanked his phone from his back pocket, dialed, and connected to speakerphone.

"Hey, handsome."

"Hey, beautiful. I've got some excited teenag—"

Victoria gasped. "How'd you go, girls?"

Anna leaned against my side. "Really great, Aunt Vicki. Eighty-six point seven five."

"That's wonderful, Anna! I'm so proud of you. Congratulations."

"Thanks."

"How about you, Diana?" Victoria asked.

I grinned up at Dad. "I did okay."

Anna elbowed me. "She did better than okay. Tell her!"

Victoria laughed. "You had me worried for a moment. What's the verdict?"

"Ninety-five point seven."

Victoria squealed an ear-piercing scream over the phone.

Dad winced and Anna snorted.

"Oh, sweetheart, that's brilliant. You're brilliant." Victoria sniffed. "I expected nothing less after the remarkable work you've churned out the last two-plus years, but still"—her voice wobbled—"so proud, Diana."

Would Mum have said the same if she still lived? Tears leaked from my eyes, and I swiped my fingers against my cheeks. "Thanks, Victoria. For everything."

More snuffling sounds emanated from the phone. "These pregnancy hormones have me blubbering. Sorry."

Anna and I snickered.

"It's okay, beautiful. I wouldn't have you any other way," Dad said.

Victoria snorted. "What, fat and pregnant with your larger-than-average child?"

"Exactly." Dad grinned.

"Ugh, enough, you two." I narrowed my eyes at Dad, poked out my tongue, and grinned. "Madison, Grace, and Gabby are coming over this morning to help pack more boxes. Are you okay with us tackling the kitchen and family room areas, Victoria? Or would you prefer to be here to help?"

"I trust you. Most of the items are from before I moved in, so you might be the best person to decide what to keep and what to donate."

Warmth spread through my chest. "Okay. Thanks."

We said goodbye and ended the call. Dad pulled me in for another hug. "So proud, baby girl."

My chest expanded. "Thanks, Daddy."

"I guess we should dress and get to work," Anna said.

Dad stepped toward my bedroom door. "I'll be heading out in about half an hour. There's leftover pasta in the fridge and bread in the pantry. See you tonight."

"Bye," Anna and I said.

Dad pulled the door closed behind him before Anna and I dressed and tamed our hair.

My phone beeped from my bedside table. I glanced at the text and groaned. So much for promises.

Gabby: Sorry but I gotta ditch. Mum needs help here. Hope you get stuff packed. Hopefully see you at Mad's Christmas party tonight?

"What?" Anna leaned against my arm and snooped at the screen. "Oh. I'm sure Maddy and Grace will still turn up and help."

I glanced around my barely packed room, sighed, and typed a reply.

Me: Hope everything's okay with you guys. And, yes, I should be there at some point. See you tonight.

Anna nudged my arm. "C'mon, let's eat, then get busy."

♥ ♥ ♥ ♥ ♥ ♥

"Oh. My. Goodness. What the bajinks is this?" Madison Taylor scrunched her pert nose and widened her hazel eyes, her gaze focused on a once-furry, mangled-looking orange-and-red object in her hand.

I lay a newspaper-wrapped photo frame in the box at my feet and trudged across my faded lounge room carpet. "Where'd you find it?"

She gestured to the odds and ends cupboard no one had opened in years, underneath the board game shelf.

I grabbed the soft toy from her fingers and squinted. "What the bajinks" was right.

Grace Robinson leaned against Madison's arm, her cropped dark-blonde hair falling across her cheek. "Could be a *Fraggle Rock* plushie?"

Madison snorted. "A *what*?"

"*Fraggle Rock*." Anna pulled a book from the nearby bookshelf and slid it into a box. "A Jim Henson puppet-type show—like *The Muppets* but totally different—from the eighties. You never watched it as a kid?"

"An eighties TV show? No. I didn't watch lame-o stuff like you and Di." Madison raised her brow at Grace. "Or you, by the sound of it."

Grace giggled. "You're the only one of us who hasn't watched it, so maybe—"

"You're the lame-o, Mad," Anna said.

"Whatevs." Madison scrunched her nose and turned back to me.

"So, what're you going to do with it? Save it to frighten your future kid?"

I chuckled and rotated the not-so-plush plushie in my hands. A faded white tag bore Mum's name—Debbie—in a childlike scrawl with jumbled uppercase and lowercase letters. My throat tightened. "It was Mum's."

"Oh." Madison dropped her gaze.

I rubbed my free hand across my chest. If I had known packing up the contents of my childhood home would turn into such an emotional experience—Dad had left everything untouched since Mum died when I was six—I might have waited for Victoria's help. She had a way of helping me process things like this. Probably because she had unpacked an Airbus-sized load of luggage over her abusive ex-husband and deceased children. A true example of how to live a Christ-centred life.

Anna stepped close and clutched my shoulder. "Maybe put it aside to sort out another day."

"Good idea." I dropped the toy into the deal-with-it-later box.

Grace cleared her throat and redirected her attention to the cupboard she was emptying. "Anna, have you decided yet if you want to go to uni?"

I returned to the shelf and grabbed another photo frame. Mum and toddler me.

"Thinking I'll submit the Arts degree preference but will defer it for twelve months to see if I want to commit to paying back thousands of dollars to the government for the next two decades of my life."

Madison's chuckle echoed in the cupboard into which the top half of her body had disappeared.

"If you're not sure, then it makes sense to think about it," Grace said.

"I'm not like Diana in wanting to do something since I was tiny." Anna huffed a laugh. "Not that Di's ever been particularly tiny."

"Funny." I wrapped a gold frame in newspaper. "I can't help it if I know what I want." To write and make you proud, Mum.

Grace hummed. "Which university are you thinking?"

I stowed the packaged photo frame in the box. "RMIT Melbourne. The city campus so it's easier to catch public transport."

Madison's laughter reverberated in the cupboard. She leaned back and fluffed her light-brown hair. "You know Andrew's planning to go to RMIT in the city?"

My cheeks warmed. Andrew Daley, the cute nerd of our class, had harboured a crush on me for years—I was pretty sure he had liked me since Year Seven—but my insides never flipped around him. Not once in my six years of secondary school.

Anna giggled. "Looks like she knows." She narrowed her eyes at me. "What happened when you two spoke after the English exam?"

I groaned. "He asked me out again, and I turned him down. It got a little awkward, but I think he'll get over it like he usually does."

Anna pursed her lips. "Hopefully."

I taped closed another box and carried it to the nearby pile of sealed boxes.

Grace dropped a weighty box on top of the one I had deposited. "Do you feel a bit sad about leaving the only place you've ever lived?"

"A little." A lot. I glanced at the open lavender curtains and sighed when the vivid memory of Mum sewing them invaded my thoughts. "Dad's turning it into a rental property, so it's not goodbye forever."

"But it's not like you could come over here any time you want, either."

"True."

An alarm blared in the corner of the room. Madison jumped and raided her backpack. "That's my cue to head off and help Mum with the par-tay preparations."

Grace turned toward Madison. "Do you need extra help?" She pivoted back to me. "You'd be okay if I helped her?"

Why not desert me too? I could totally pack this stuffed-to-the-gills house in six weeks all by myself. Ugh. I affixed a smile. "Go help Madison."

"Thanks." Madison and Grace disappeared through the front door.

Anna bumped my arm. "Don't worry. I'm still here."

But not for long. Just like me. I offered my cousin a smile before glancing around the messy room. Soon I would abandon this house and close the door on my memories associated with Mum. A betrayal my heart struggled to accept.

CHAPTER TWO
Party on a Hill

I tramped along Madison's driveway beside Anna, sweat trickling the back of my neck after the short walk from my place. Despite the summer heat having decreased several degrees after today's scorcher, the early evening temperature was far from mild.

"You going to be okay?" Anna glanced at me.

"Ah huh." I rubbed my aching jaw, sore from grinding my teeth while I packed up more memories. Why had I promised to attend this end-of-school-slash-Christmas party when all I wanted to do was crawl into bed and cry?

Muffled base vibrations from upbeat music magnified with each step closer to Madison's front door, pulsating the porch steps under my feet. A soft breeze swirled through the leaves of two tall eucalyptus trees beside the house, and tinsel danced in its fixed position on the verandah railing.

"Might want to smile." Anna reached for the front door handle. "Shake it off for the night and deal with all the stuff rotating in your head tomorrow."

I nodded and followed her indoors. The not quite ear-splitting croon of Bing Crosby's *White Christmas*—the bassy remix version—welcomed us along with the delights of refrigerated air. I heaved a sigh and enjoyed the cool caress along my bare arms and legs.

Anna linked her arm through mine. "Did you bring your swimsuit?"

"I've got my period, so I can't be bothered." Not after today's physical and emotional toll.

"Fair enough." Anna nodded toward the kitchen. "Looks like

Keanu's in charge of drinks."

We stepped toward the spacious kitchen with white marble benchtops and smudge-free stainless-steel fixtures.

"J-Bird. Anna." Keanu Everton's familiar, mischievous dark eyes glinted above his signature smirk and dimpled chin.

"K-Man." A soft smile drifted to my lips. Keanu and I had been friends since Primary School.

"I assume you two did well with your ATARs?" He widened his eyes.

Anna grinned. "Of course, we did." She hip-bumped me. "This genius here blew my decent score out of the water."

I bit my bottom lip and shrugged.

Keanu chuckled. "As I expected. Well done, ladies."

A smile slipped to my lips.

"We're here for a drink." Anna tilted her head. "What've you got?"

Keanu eyed my cousin. "I could make you a cocktail." He turned and captured my gaze. "And there's water and soft drinks too."

I eyed the alcoholic and non-alcoholic beverages cluttering the island bench. My gut churned. "I didn't think Mrs. Taylor would allow alcohol since not everyone's eighteen yet."

"A few people brought their own." Keanu shrugged and nodded toward the deep sink filled with ice and beer cans. "Didn't think you'd want a stubby."

I shuddered. No thank you.

Keanu pointed to a set of six liqueurs in small bottles. "These are mine. Thought I'd practice my cocktail-making skills on the friends I know are legal age."

Anna chuckled. "You and your barkeeping skills."

Keanu straightened and extended his chin. "The sooner I learn, the sooner Dad'll share the responsibility of running Benanu's."

I smiled. "Considering it's named after you and Ben, it makes sense you want to be involved." Keanu's older brother, Benson, had moved to Melbourne a few years ago to study medicine and never looked back.

Keanu harrumphed.

"Okay, so what cocktail will you make me?" Anna perused the available options.

"Wait and see." Keanu handed me a bottle of water. "Madison, Grace, and Gabby were outside the last time I saw them."

I narrowed my eyes. "She talking to you again?"

Keanu grabbed a stainless-steel shaker and dropped a few ice cubes inside. "Gabby's still being weird, but she did kiss me earlier, so I figure it's a good sign." He filled and shook the metal container, then poured the liquid into a fancy glass.

"I guess so." What would I know, having never dated a guy, let alone kissed one? Well, other than the time David MacLeod had kissed me, but Keanu said his jerk-iness disqualified him from being my first *real* kiss.

Keanu slid the glass across the counter to Anna. "Enjoy."

Anna sipped and wrinkled her nose. "Uh, what is this?"

"It's a Summer Treacle."

"It's kinda bitter. Yet sweet." She sipped again, curled her lip, and shuddered.

Keanu extracted the glass from Anna's hand, poured Coke into a tumbler, and added a splash of something from his liqueur collection. "Here."

Anna sipped and smiled. "Mmm, rum and Coke. Thanks."

Keanu tasted Anna's rejected cocktail, squinted, and muttered something about practice.

Anna grabbed my hand and dragged me through the back door. We stepped into Madison's oversized yard, sporting a rectangular in-ground pool, a covered barbeque and dining space, and a huge patch of grass farther down the block, where a few youths played a round of cricket.

I squinted from the glare of the setting sun and turned toward Anna.

Someone pressed against my back and covered my eyes. Gabriella's staple perfume wafted to my nostrils.

"Hey, Gabby."

Gabriella huffed a whine and removed her hands.

I turned, shielded my eyes with my hand, and smiled at her pouty expression.

"How come you always guess, Di?"

I suppressed an eye-roll. "Because you're the only one of my friends to still play this game and you're wearing your usual perfume."

She crinkled her nose. "Nuts. Wanna swim?"

Anna leaned closer. "Diana's on her period."

Gabriella raised her brow at me. "Since when has that stopped you?"

I shrugged, grabbed Anna's cocktail, and grinned. "I'll watch your drinks."

We ambled along the paved pathway and unlocked the pool gate. Madison and Grace splashed in the deep end with a few other girls and guys from school. Looked like a game of Tag.

I settled at a nearby table and reveled in the cold metal seat beneath my bare thighs.

Anna stripped to her swimsuit and left all her belongings beside me.

"Have fun." I watched Anna dive into the pool and sighed. Would it be rude to read a book on my phone? Victoria had suggested I might like Agnes Canestri's latest *Laws of Love* romance. Something about beautiful European locations and a swoony guy with delicious dark stubble. I suppressed a snort. Would I ever understand Victoria and her stubble obsession? Probably not.

I sipped water and observed the pool fun and games for five minutes before I slipped my mobile phone from my shorts pocket. A message alert flashed.

Dad: Is ANNA STAYING ANOTHER NIGHT? UNCLE CHRIS WANTS TO KNOW IF HE'S COLLECTING HER FROM MADISON'S LATER.

Me: LAST I HEARD HE'S GETTING HER, BUT IF HE'D PREFER NOT TO COME INTO TOWN AND YOU'RE FINE WITH IT, ANNA AND I CAN WALK BACK HOME?

I rolled my lips together and tapped my fingers on my thigh.

Dad: BE HOME BY MIDNIGHT OR CALL ME IF YOU THINK YOU'LL BE LATER.

I grinned at the screen. Another win for adult independence.

Me: OKAY. LOVE YOU.

Dad: LOVE YOU TOO, PRINCESS. HAVE FUN.

I typed a quick message to Anna.

Me: IN CASE I FORGET TO TELL YOU, YOU'RE SLEEPING OVER ANOTHER NIGHT. ;-)

Shrieks and laughter blasted from the pool, and I glanced up. Gabriella and Madison sat on two different guys' shoulders, and my friends hit each other with fluorescent pool noodles.

I chuckled, glanced around the yard, and spotted Andrew walking toward the pool. "Hey, Andrew!" I stood, tucked my phone back in my pocket, and waved.

Andrew stopped, straightened, and approached me. "Diana."

"How's it going?" I grinned at him. "Did well with today's results?"

He cleared his throat and nodded, his sandy-blond hair skimming his eyebrows. "I did."

I furrowed my brow. Was that all he had to say? "That's, ah, good." I scuffed my thongs against the pavement.

Andrew blinked. His hazel eyes seemed distant, almost icy. What had caused his reticence?

I angled closer. "You okay?"

He leaned away. "Fine." He cleared his throat again. His jaw tightened, and he gazed at the pool.

I bit my lower lip. "You planning to swim?"

Andrew nodded. "You?"

"Not tonight."

His shoulders eased.

Was he relieved I had decided not to swim?

Andrew eyed me, then nodded toward the pool. "Okay, well, see you around."

"Yeah. Bye." I watched him saunter away. My chest ached when he offered Anna and Grace a beaming smile.

Andrew lifted his T-shirt over his head and dived into the water.

I flopped onto the hard metal chair and observed my friends in the pool. Andrew seemed his normal, friendly self now. An uncomfortable, cold sensation bloomed in my abdomen, and I crossed my legs. Had I hurt Andrew when I rejected him last time? What had changed? Any other time he had hinted at asking me out, I let him down in my usual—and I had thought gentle—way, and our friendship never changed.

Andrew lifted Grace onto his shoulders, and she squealed. Their laughter pealed over the continual low thrum of music.

I grimaced. Maybe it was best I had vetoed swimming. The awful niggling in my gut dug deeper.

🖋 🖋 🖋 🖋 🖋 🖋 🖋

16 December

Sorry if this ends up on the depressing scale of my usual writing, Mum. It's been a big day and I really wish you were here to help me through everything. All this sorting through stuff, packing, and tossing things away is turning me into an emo teenager. It's draining.

In the good news department, I did really well in my end-of-year VCE results today. I'm 20 points over the asking ATAR for the RMIT journalism course, so be proud of me. I'm embarking on the ambitions you nurtured in me as a little kid, the dream to write.

If only you were here to cheer me on. I feel like my connection to you is about to be severed with just over six weeks until we move. Writing to you gives me a semblance of peace, but in other ways I feel like I'm betraying you with this house move. Is that crazy? Anna thinks I'm crazy to think so, but Aunt Rebecca's still alive and loving her daughter. Not that you don't love me, Mum. I'm sure you do.

As an added bonus to this delightful day, I've also messed up my friendship with Andrew. Wish you could share your 'how to interact with boys' secrets. Or any secrets, really. That drunk driver dealt me a crappy hand when he took you from me. Stupid, drunk P-plater.

I miss you.

CHAPTER THREE
A New Season

A week later, Dad, Victoria, and I entered the Morgans' kitchen. I called Victoria's cousins "uncle" and "aunt" out of respect and because they were closer to Dad's and Victoria's ages. They also happened to be pretty cool.

I slipped onto a bar stool. "I had so much fun tonight. It was out of this world. Thank you."

Dad pulled Victoria against his side and rested a hand on her growing belly. "You deserved it, kiddo. Vue De Monde served some great food and views."

Victoria snorted. "Great food and views? Really, Nicholas? Tonight was a culinary experience few achieve in this life."

He kissed her temple. "Glad you both enjoyed the hit to my wallet."

Uncle Steve entered the kitchen. "Who hit your wallet? Can I join in?"

Aunt Stacy waddled in, a few steps behind her husband. Wow, she looked ready to pop baby Morgan any day.

Victoria hip-bumped Dad. "You gave it up of your free will."

"That's what she said." Uncle Steve dodged Aunt Stacy's punch to his shoulder. He raised his hands in surrender, laughing. "Okay, okay. I was joking."

Aunt Stacy huffed. "The cop humour never ends." She turned toward me. "You had a great night?"

I kicked my legs out and grinned. "The best."

"Speaking of the best …" Uncle Steve eyed his wife. A silent question passed between them.

Aunt Stacy nodded.

"Stace and I were thinking about this afternoon's discussion regarding Miss Diana here and university."

My ears pricked.

"We'd love to have her move in to our spare room."

I sucked in a sharp breath and stared at the Morgans.

Uncle Steve turned to me. "Isn't your first preference at RMIT's city campus?"

I nodded to the beat of my thudding heart.

"What do you think?" Uncle Steve glanced between Dad and Victoria before his gaze fell to my widened eyes. "Can you survive living here with the soon-to-be-four of us?"

A laugh bubbled in my chest. "I reckon I can survive"—I turned to Dad—"and assume Dad'll be happy to tuck me away safely in the home of a cop and a lawyer." I raised a brow and turned back to my uncle-in-law.

Uncle Steve's blue eyes sparkled. "Stace and I thought that might be the case." He turned toward Dad. "Nick?"

Dad grinned, stepped forward, and clapped Uncle Steve's back. "Too right. Thanks, Steve. Stacy. Victoria and I appreciate your kindness, hey, my love?" Dad looked at Victoria.

She beamed. "Of course." Victoria reached across and hugged her cousins before resting an arm around my shoulders. "You'll get to help with Toby, and once baby Morgan comes along, I know Stacy will appreciate an extra set of hands."

Aunt Stacy nodded with a tired smile and pressed her palm over her basketball belly. "I'll love your company especially when Steve works, and Toby will appreciate your hugs. He seems to love those."

Bubbles danced in my chest, and I held back a shriek. My favourite three-year-old boy on the planet had stolen my heart the moment his little face had peeked out from behind Aunt Stacy's skirt two years ago, when we first met in Tellarine.

Thank you, God, for fulfilling my accommodation requirements before I even contemplated the need.

"I look forward to it." Aunt Stacy yawned. "But for now, I need to sleep. Nick, can you collect the charcuterie platter first thing tomorrow for the family Christmas gathering?"

"Sure."

Aunt Stacy turned to me. "I'll need your help wrangling Toby while Vicki and I prep things. That okay?"

"Of course. It'll be great practice for me."

She smiled and yawned again. "Thanks. Not sure why I volunteered this year. What was I thinking?"

Uncle Steve chuckled. "You've plenty of helpers, and you know Mum will be by to boss everyone." He winked.

Aunt Stacy sighed. "Thank God for your mother." She yawned again. "Night, all."

Uncle Steve escorted his pregnant wife up the staircase.

Victoria rubbed Dad's hand pressed against her stretched belly. "Will you be up much longer, Diana?"

I glanced at my bed, an air mattress tucked near the couch in the adjacent family room. "Probably should sleep if I'm on Toby duty tomorrow."

Dad and Victoria bid me goodnight and disappeared up the stairs.

I padded into the downstairs powder room, changed into my summer pyjamas, and brushed my teeth. After tucking my worn clothes in my backpack, I grabbed my phone, switched off the kitchen lights, and dropped on the plush couch under the muted light of the overhanging lamp. "Please be awake, Anna," I whispered.

Me: HAD AN AMAZING NIGHT OF FANCY FOOD WHICH ENDED WITH AN OFFER FROM THE MORGANS I COULDN'T REFUSE.

I yawned, switched off the lamp, and slid into my temporary bed. A text message toned.

Anna: WHAT OFFER?

I grinned and tapped the glowing screen, my face possibly worthy of a creepy horror-movie scene. Not that I knew much about horror movies since I refused to watch them. I shuddered and pulled the thin sheet closer.

Me: ACCOMMODATION ONCE I START UNI! I'M SO EXCITED!

Anna: WOW! THAT'S AWESOME! ONE LESS THING TO THINK ABOUT.

Me: NOT THAT I'D THOUGHT OF IT YET.

Anna: I CAN HARDLY BELIEVE THAT WHEN YOU AND AUNT VICKI ARE SO ORGANIZED.

I laughed.

Me: OKAY, GOTTA SQUASH MY EXCITEMENT AND GO TO SLEEP. I'M ON TOBY DUTY TOMORROW. SEE YOU CHRISTMAS DAY! XX

Anna: LOOKING FORWARD TO SEEING YOU IN TWO DAYS. GIVE

ME ALL THE GOSS THEN. NIGHT.

I dropped my phone onto the plush carpet beside the bed, closed my eyes, and soon fell asleep.

I swiped my forearm along my damp hairline and stretched my weary back. Cleaning Day officially sucked more than yesterday's Moving Day. *If only you were here, Mum.*

I glanced around our modest bathroom—which paid homage to the eighties with its apricot-and-beige floor and wall tiles, bronze-tinted shower glass, and apricot vanity atop wood cabinetry—and stared at the tiny beige bath. Memories permeated my conscious mind. Mum flicking warm bath water on my face while I giggled and splashed. Standing on the soaked bathmat wrapped in a huge, fluffy towel, shivering, while Mum rubbed my back and shoulders dry.

I blinked against the burn in my eyes, retrieved the old toothbrush, and returned to the cramped shower cavity. Back to reality.

I scrubbed the top shower tiles and hard-to-reach places someone of my height found easier. Silly me, volunteering for the "tall person" jobs.

A throat cleared behind me.

I turned and affixed a smile I hoped appeared genuine. "Martin. What's up?" Dad had hired a local cleaning team which Martin managed.

He surveyed my work. "You sure you're not interested in joining my cleaning team? We could do with a long-legged lass." He winked and chuckled. His deep-set eyes sparkled.

A sincere smile laced my lips. "Like I said, I start uni in four weeks, and I don't need a holiday job."

"Too bad." He nodded toward the doorway. "The team's all done. Would you like to do a final inspection before we leave?"

"Great." I downed my work tool, shucked my gloves, and followed Martin around my childhood home.

Fifteen minutes later, we stood on the verandah near the open front door.

"You happy with everything?" Martin glanced inside my now-empty house.

A middle-aged man hauled a vacuum cleaner and mop through the doorway and nodded in farewell.

I smiled at the man before reverting my attention to Martin. "Everything looks great. Thanks."

A young lady exited the house and passed a clipboard to Martin. "Can we head off to River Street?"

Martin nodded. "See you there." He set his blue-eyed gaze on me. "Nick said you'd sign and pay?"

"That's correct."

He retrieved a pen from his shirt front pocket and extended the pen and clipboard to me.

I signed on the dotted line. "Let me duck inside for my wallet." I jogged back to the bathroom, grabbed my wallet from my small backpack, and returned moments later. "Is cash okay?"

Martin grinned. "Cash is perfect."

I counted out several hundred-dollar notes Dad had given me and handed them to Martin.

He tucked the money into his pocket. "Great doing business with you and Nick. All the best with your studies."

"Thanks." I watched him descend the steep verandah steps, turned, and re-entered the house. A house filled with a lifetime of memories. I ground my molars. My chest squeezed, and tears slipped down my cheeks. *Am I deserting you, Mum?* Would my final steps out the door sever my connection with her? With my past?

I palmed my wet cheeks, returned to the bathroom, and completed my scrubbing tasks. Moments after I removed my rubber gloves and bagged the cleaning gear, my phone rang. I scrambled to extract it from my backpack. "Hello?"

"You all done, Princess?" Dad's voice echoed in my ear.

"Almost. Martin and his team left about ten minutes ago." I zipped my backpack and slipped it over my shoulders. "Do I need to drop the house keys at the agent's office?"

"I left my set with Miranda this morning and said the house would be ready for viewing tomorrow." Laughter warbled in the background. "Will you be home soon? Matt and Belinda brought over a heap of food for dinner, so I've told Chris and the gang to join us, and we'll have a barbeque."

I smirked at the strange turn of events. Less than a year ago,

Uncle Matt—a name I still struggled to use after six years of calling him "Mr. Briggs" at school—had rivalled Dad for Victoria's affections. Now he was engaged to Victoria's best friend, Aunt Belinda, and the men were close confidants. Weird.

"Diana?"

"Sorry. I'll be home within the hour."

"Great." More chuckles bellowed. "I'm proud of how you've stepped up and helped manage the move while I've been busy finalizing the house build and working and Victoria's been taking it slower. Your assistance has been invaluable."

Heat infused my skin and warmed my face. "You're welcome." My voice cracked. "See you soon."

"Bye, Princess."

I pocketed my phone, exited the bathroom, and stepped into my empty bedroom. Martin's crew had done a remarkable job erasing the carpet indentations where my bed and desk had rested for almost two decades. The walls were brighter without smudges, the window free of streaks. A heaviness pressed against my shoulders. The lavender curtains were all that remained of my connection to the room. "Help my heart, Father. Help me move on," I whispered.

After shuddering a long breath and running my fingers along the doorframe, I trundled down the hallway, muttered my farewell to each room I passed, and descended the stairs. I entered the empty kitchen, with its unadorned benchtops and spotless sink, and gazed out the window into the backyard. More memories crept to the edges of my mind, taunting me with long-forgotten happiness. Reminiscences I had locked away, precious keepsakes of my childhood.

Dark red caught the corner of my view, and I leaned forward against the stainless-steel sink. Mum's favourite rosebush. My chest clamped, and I closed my eyes and downloaded my last memory of her.

Wide cocoa-coloured eyes and pink lips curved into an affectionate smile, her long brunette hair plaited over her shoulder, and her T-shirt smeared with dirt. She had shown me how and where to cut a rose from the bush. "It's always opportune to give a little prune," she had sung before snipping and inhaling the rose's fragrance.

I never forgot her words despite her life being severed the next day.

My vision clouded. I slipped from the kitchen, unlocked the back door, and stepped into the summer sunshine. The deep, heavy scent of the standard rosebush triggered more recollections, and tears trailed my cheeks.

I twisted to unzip my backpack and retrieved a pair of scissors. "Forgive me, Mum, for not using secateurs." Breathing in the delicious perfume, I avoided large, sharp thorns and clipped several long rose stems. I kneeled and lay the velvety flowers on the yellowed lawn, wrapped a rubber glove around the base of the bundle, then locked the back door for the last time.

A soft afternoon breeze cooled the dampness at the back of my neck. The cool change had arrived.

I retrieved the rose bundle, glanced around the yard, and walked toward the side gate. More tears ensued. "Goodbye, Mum. Forgive me for leaving you."

CHAPTER FOUR
Adulting

"I'm going to miss you so much." Victoria crossed the paved driveway of our new house, wrapped her petite, strong arms around my waist, and heaved a quiet sob.

The wind triggered goosebumps along my arms, and I held onto her, fighting back tears. The overcast sky seemed to share our collective mood.

Her swelled stomach pushed against my side, and my unborn sibling kicked my hip.

I laughed. "I think the watermelon's going to miss me too." I bent down and kissed the curved mound hidden beneath Victoria's dark-blue maternity shirt. "You be good for your mummy, and I'll see you in two months, okay?"

Madison opened the driver's door of her red Ford Fiesta.

Dad stepped forward and wrapped his arms around his wife. "You girls, drive safely."

"We will, Mr. Jacobsen." Madison climbed into her seat and closed the door.

With a final kiss on my parents' cheeks and a brief wave, I collapsed on the passenger seat. "You crammed a lot of stuff in here."

Madison buckled her seatbelt. "I played car boot Tetris to fit your suitcase. I'm so glad I asked you to measure it yesterday cos if it'd been any bigger, I would've emptied the entire car and started again in your driveway."

I surveyed the house which had been my home for less than a month and sniffed. What a whirlwind time of unpacking, new furniture deliveries, and settling into my new space. The final preparations in the nursery for the newcomer remained, little things Dad and Victoria would do together.

Madison pointed to her mobile phone in a centre-console cup holder. "Can you go to the music app and Bluetooth it to the car, please?"

I grabbed her smartphone and used her outstretched finger to unlock it. "Looking forward to living in Clayton?"

Madison shrugged. "Kinda. I'm nervous about attending Monash Uni. I hear it's huge, but I'm glad to have close accommodation. Mum's all sad about it, but now Grace's agreed to live in the other room, I'm more excited than I was."

"It's crazy to think we're old enough to move places and live hours away from our families, don't you think?"

"Yeah. I do."

Several hundred kilometres and a few hours later, we pulled into an empty non-permit parking bay two streets away from my city home. Madison helped me unpack, and we spent the evening with the Morgan family.

Aunt Stacy yawned and padded to her lounge room rocking chair. "I'm so glad you're here, Diana. Toby's been talking incessantly about you."

Uncle Steve deposited little Ella Mae in all her five-week-old glory into Aunt Stacy's arms. He kissed his two girls before disappearing down the hallway.

I straightened where I perched on the couch beside Madison. "I'm excited to be here."

Madison leaned forward. "You have a beautiful home, Mrs. Morgan."

"You're welcome anytime, Madison. And please call me Stacy."

Ella rooted around at her mother's chest before settling at drink number seventy-two for the day.

Aunt Stacy closed her eyes. She looked a fright, with dark rings under her eyes and her usual neat hairstyle resembling a bird's nest. "We can talk about household responsibilities when I'm more awake." She opened her eyes and grinned goofily at her newborn daughter.

"Sure. We'll head up to bed now." I stood, and Madison

followed. "Night you two."

"Night." Aunt Stacy closed her eyes again.

Madison and I headed to my bedroom, where Uncle Steve had set up a mattress on the floor for my friend, and we readied for sleep.

Madison exited the ensuite and slipped into her bed. "Doesn't this feel eerily familiar?"

I lowered to my bed. "How so?"

"This is like all the times you stayed at Nan and Pop's with me during the school holidays and we'd giggle under our blankets on those lumpy mattresses Pop'd pull out for us." She sighed and grinned. "I loved those nights sprawled across their family room floor."

"Me too." Madison's grandparents had adopted me, so to speak, as another grandchild after Mum died. I had spent a lot of time at their restaurant or at their home when Madison stayed with them. "But this really isn't similar at all … unless your mattress is lumpy." I nestled into my comfortable bed. "Mine's perfect."

"Same."

We talked and laughed long after midnight. A final night of "childhood" together.

Madison departed just before midday the following morning.

I hugged her on the footpath outside her car. "Sorry I can't help you unpack at your end. Call me when you want to catch up, okay? Uncle Steve said he'll get another single bed in my room so you can stay anytime you like."

She squeezed me with similar fervour, stepped back, and climbed into her car. "Looking forward to seeing you soon. Love you."

"Love you too."

The next few days were filled with keeping Toby entertained and cooking family meals before I switched into school mode. I loved assisting Aunt Stacy with the children during the day.

I entered the lounge room after tucking Toby into bed.

Uncle Steve caught my gaze from his armchair. "Any chance you want to quit your studies and be our live-in nanny?"

I chuckled and curled up on the couch. "Don't think Dad or Victoria would be very happy with me … or you!"

He waggled his eyebrows. "They'd get over it."

Aunt Stacy huffed a tired laugh from her rocking chair, where she nursed Ella. "No, they wouldn't. Nick would have you in a headlock, and Vicki would bust your face before you finished the announcement. Let's just enjoy Diana's company while she's under our roof."

"You win, darling." He winked at his wife and turned to me. "So, tomorrow's Orientation Day? You excited?"

I clasped my hands together. "I s'pose?" I had pushed away the nerves all day and intended to stick to the plan. I would deal with it tomorrow.

"It's a big change." Aunt Stacy played with Ella's tiny fingers. "Although your school was pretty big on the scale of secondary schools, RMIT is immense."

Uncle Steve leaned forward. "You have our numbers if you need us."

"I know. Thanks."

Aunt Stacy squeaked a long, loud yawn.

I pressed back a smile.

Uncle Steve stifled a yawn, peeked at Ella, and chuckled. "Bubkins is sleeping. Let's get her to bed, and perhaps we can get some extra shuteye too."

Aunt Stacy bowed her head in a slow, weary nod and stood.

Uncle Steve supported his wife's shoulders with his arm while Ella slept, still and quiet, against her mother's breast.

"Night, Diana," Uncle Steve whispered.

"Night." A slow smile played on my lips, and I imagined Dad and Victoria experiencing similar fatigue and joy in the coming months. Foaming effervescence eddied inside my chest. Not long and I would be a big sister! Well, I had three younger stepsiblings through Victoria. Children who would never grow up.

I rubbed my chest and whispered a prayer for my parents and their unborn little one. I looked forward to holding that precious baby and watching him or her grow.

Less than a decade had passed since Victoria birthed her youngest, Ryan. But almost two decades had elapsed since Dad held me as a tiny baby. Would he be out of practice? Probably. I smirked and ascended the stairs to my room.

Had Dad and Mum been joyful when I was an infant?

I stumbled and grabbed the doorframe. Where had that thought come from? Shoring my steps, I shut my bedroom door and closed my eyes. How had my parents responded to my arrival? They had both been young and newly married. Had they been afraid? Anxious? Or excited like I was for this baby?

I opened my eyes, pulled out my desk chair, and eased onto the seat.

1 March

Hey, Mum, it's time for another round of Twenty Questions with your darling daughter. Or at least a moment for me to contemplate stuff.

I wish I could ask you if you were happy when you discovered I existed. Was I a surprise or a planned event? Were you giddy with joy and hormones after I was born? Did you grin sleepily like the Morgans? My strongest memories have you smiling a lot. Especially when you jotted down the silly, made-up stories I dictated to you, and you proclaimed me a writer. But the passage of time could've helped you overcome your early fears. Concerns I'm sure many new parents must deal with.

Dad says I was a welcomed addition to your family but shares nothing more. I wish I knew the "more". Your true thoughts. Anything about how you felt as you looked down the barrel of parenthood and sacrificed your body to incubate your baby.

I suppose it doesn't really matter now, does it? Even if you struggled to love me then, you love me now. And I will spend my days making you proud.

I promise, Mum.

CHAPTER FIVE
Outsider

"**Student card, please.**" A squinty-eyed RMIT staff member stared up at me over her slim computer monitor.

I slipped the card from my wallet and surrendered it.

"Have you completed the 'How2GetStarted' and 'How2GetAhead' online sessions?"

"Yes."

"And you want a physical tour instead of the virtual campus tour?" She raised a brow.

I scuffed the toe of my right sneaker against the hard flooring. "Ah huh." I had already completed the online tour but wanted one in person. The city seemed ginormous and labyrinthine when I travelled alone.

"I've booked you in for the next session." She returned my student card, raised her chin, and nodded toward the door I had entered minutes earlier. "Meet out front in an hour. I also suggest you book an appointment with the Student Connect team to confirm your tech needs."

"I will. Thank you." I shoved my card and wallet into my backpack.

"Anything else?"

Apart from a way to settle the nerves swirling in my tummy? I pursed my lips. "Do I just keep walking down Bowen Street for the Orientation activities?"

"Yes, follow the noise. You should find plenty of people about to help." She offered a quick smile. "Next!"

I clutched my backpack strap over my shoulder, nodded at the short guy waiting behind me, and ventured outside. Laughter and chatter filled the street as people milled past in groups or straggled by in ones and twos. Smiling students with multiple ear and face piercings. Dreadlocks, shaved heads, short bobs, and long plaits. Kaftans, short skirts, cropped tops, and tattoo sleeves. Ripped jeans and T-shirts, trackie daks and thongs.

My stomach dropped. I glanced at my simple attire—bootleg jeans, V-neck T-shirt, and Asics sneakers—and tugged on my long, neat braid. Did my outfit scream "country bumpkin"? Or would I fit in at this big city university?

After setting an alarm on my phone for fifty minutes' time, I set out for the social clubs' hub. When I had perused the RMIT website, the literature society and Christian Union groups had interested me.

I weaved through the decent-sized crowd, where a mishmash of perfumes, overpowering cologne, and traces of cigarette odour, invaded my nostrils. I spotted signage for the literature society and approached with a smile.

"You look well read."

I turned to the young man near the literature sign. Was he a member?

He raised a brow.

"Do I?"

His cheeks lifted with an attractive smile. "You do."

I pressed my palm over my belly. "I like reading. And writing." *Nice going, Diana.* Warmth heated my cheeks.

"It's a great group. We have casual game nights and catchups, writing competitions, and a monthly read." He leaned closer. "That tends to be more of a traditional or classic read, but members often break into smaller groups and choose a contemporary read as well."

I peered around and noticed a small group of girls whispering nearby. Maybe fellow bookworms?

"By the way, my name's Byron."

"I'm Diana."

He grinned. "A goddess of the countryside."

"Pardon?" Were my country roots so obvious? I clutched my thighs and silently rebuked my burning cheeks.

Byron grinned. "Not much for Roman mythology? You're missing your bow and arrows and your golden cloak." He perused my outfit and smirked. "I think you'd look great with purple half-boots, but you might want to skip the bejewelled belt."

I shook my head and grinned. "You know a heck of a lot about Roman goddesses."

"Always been fascinated with mythology."

"Nice." I glanced at the signage beside him. "So … if I wanted to join, how'd I do that?"

He handed me a pamphlet and leaned closer. "It's pretty basic. Just go to this link and join through the RMIT MyApps Portal."

I stepped aside. "Th-thanks."

He nodded and winked. "Hope to see you there."

I dropped my gaze, stepped toward the group of girls, and waved. "Hi. Are any of you members of the literature society?"

All of the girls nodded.

A slim blonde with crazy-tight leggings raised her eyebrow. "Enjoy your encounter with Byron?"

My face warmed.

The blonde giggled. "He's the reason I joined."

Oh? Were they dating?

A petite girl with a short ebony ponytail and bright red lipstick nodded. "If an intelligent guy like him reads and joins the society …" She shrugged and grinned.

I scrunched my brows. "Yes?"

Two girls wearing matching white tank tops—one with caramel tones and blonde-streaked dark-brown hair, the other sporting an elaborate network of hair beads in her jet-black locks—snort-laughed.

The blonde leaned closer. "It means you're guaranteed to have sex with a guy who possesses a working brain."

I parted my lips and a strangled "oh" escaped.

"He's actually not too bad in bed," she said, "but I think he's better at conversation."

I stared. Why was she telling me this?

"I'm in it for the reads." White Tank Top with Blonde Streaks jutted her chin.

Her tank top twin elbowed her. "Not the prescribed monthly reads, though. We formed a smaller informal group for spicier reads."

My insides froze. "Spicier?"

The petite girl yanked her phone from her pocket, swiped the screen several times, and turned the device in my direction. "Like this.”

My pulse thudded. I stared, wide-eyed, at the book cover with its hunky hero wearing a fully unbuttoned shirt and loose necktie, his shiny, tanned torso on full display. Spicy. “I get it now.”

She swiped her screen again. “Although I prefer paranormal romance.” She thrust another book cover toward me with a different shirtless man on the cover, this time paired with a gothic-looking, leather-clad woman. Both carried spear-like swords.

“Looks … interesting.” I squeezed my backpack strap against my chest.

“Epic sex scenes too.” She tucked her phone in her pocket.

I nodded toward the other social hubs. “Well, thanks for chatting. I appreciate the insight.” I stepped back. “Have a great day.”

“You too.” The blonde saluted a wave.

I walked a brisk pace to a space I had seen on my way from the Morgans’ and wilted on a low concrete wall outside a quiet building. Was this to be my life for the next three years? Spending time with sex-obsessed young people and hearing intimate stories in casual, group settings?

Really, Lord? Of course I knew students at Tellarine Secondary slept together. But it was never so … blatant. Or commonplace.

How would I fit in here without compromising my values? I closed my eyes and thought of Mum. Her applause after every story I had made up as a kid, her encouragement to write. I inhaled and opened my eyes. I needed to push through this discomfort and come out on top. No matter what.

“Not again.” I stared at the RMIT map I clutched, squinted, and glanced at the room numbers in front of me. Panic ratcheted in my chest. How long would it take to familiarise myself with this huge facility?

“First day for you too?”

I lowered my gaze to a pretty, petite blonde with beautiful blue eyes and perfect teeth. She wore jeans and a bright-pink top underneath a fitted black leather jacket—the jeans and jacket I later discovered were wardrobe staples—and carried a stylish black leather tote. Her head almost reached my shoulder, even with wedge-heeled shoes. Her smile dazzled.

I wrinkled my nose. "Yeah. Think I'm lost."

The pretty blonde extended her hand and extracted my map. "Lemme see."

I pointed to one of the circled rooms.

"You're headed where I'm headed. Just down the hall."

"Oh. Cool." We wandered past a few rooms before stopping outside our destination. "You're a journalism major too?"

"Yup." She straightened and extended her hand. "I'm Tara Roberts."

My chest loosened. "Diana Jacobsen." I shook her delicate hand.

She tilted her head. "You're tall and intimidating."

I smirked. Seemed her petite frame housed a bold, straight-to-the-point woman. "You're short."

Her eyes widened along with her smile.

"Love your jacket."

"Thanks." She grinned. "Wanna sit together?"

My stiff shoulders eased. "Yeah."

I followed her into the lecture hall, where we located two seats in the back half of the room.

Tara slung her tote bag off her shoulder. "I've never looked like the yokel I am."

I stumbled against my seat. She was from the country too? I sank to my chair and eyed my new friend. "Do I look like one?"

She scrunched her brows. "A yokel?"

I pursed my lips and nodded.

She narrowed her eyes and scrutinised my outfit. "A virgin? Yes. A yokel? Nope."

I choked on my saliva and coughed. What the haystack?

She laughed, glanced around the large room filling with students, and waggled her eyebrows. "Let's show these city slicker journo wannabes how it is."

"Thank you, Tobes, for my beautiful birthday song." I grinned across at my parents, on the opposite couch, while I clutched my phone to my ear with my left hand and balanced my sleeping nine-week-old baby sister against my chest with my right arm.

Dad and Victoria had welcomed Jasmine Sienna Jacobsen to the world on the first of May—all nine-and-a-half pounds of her. I arrived home earlier in the week for the July semester break and stole cuddles with my tiny sister in-between catchups with school friends still in town.

Anna chuckled on the couch beside me, balancing our half-eaten plates of dessert in each hand.

Wish I had more limbs so I could scarf down the scrumptious vanilla-and-strawberry sponge cake. Aunt Belinda had dropped it over earlier in the day on her way to visit Uncle Matt's family in Melbourne.

"I miss you," Toby whispered over the phone.

My heart cramped. "I miss you too, sweet boy. Have a good sleep, and I'll see you in eight days."

"Kay, Di-Di. Happy nine teeth!"

"Nineteenth," Aunt Stacy said in the background.

"Dat's what I said, Mummy. Nine teeth."

I quelled a laugh.

A sigh echoed over the phone. "Bye, Di-Di. Luff you."

"Love you too. Sleep well." I blew him kisses and disconnected the call.

"Steve and Stacy are raising such a beautiful boy." Victoria snuggled closer to Dad.

"They sure are." I retrieved my plate from Anna, balanced it on my lap, and speared a strawberry half. Delicious.

"Babies look good on you." Anna smiled at me with her hand poised around her empty cake fork.

I kissed the crown of Jasmine's head and breathed in her baby scent. Almost as yummy as my dessert. I stuffed a final forkful of sponge cake into my mouth.

"You do look sweet together." Victoria turned in Dad's arms. "Don't you think, Nicholas?"

Dad kissed his wife's brow and aimed a piercing gaze at me. "They do." *But no babies for you,* his eyes appeared to warn.

I swallowed the last of my cake, repressed my smile, and nodded to Dad. Message received.

Anna grabbed my empty plate from my lap. "I'm sure

Andrew'd be more than happy to fill the relationship void and fulfil his ultimate dream. What do you think, Uncle Cole?"

"Anna!" I threw a damp baby burp rag at Anna's head. Why did she have to bring Andrew up? My gut coiled.

She cackled.

Dad narrowed his eyes at Anna. "Who's this Andrew fella, and why's he dreaming of my daughter?"

Warmth pooled inside my chest. I had missed Dad's protective instincts while battling the emotional hazards uni life offered.

Anna smirked. "Andrew Daley. He's been head over heels for Di since Year Seven. And he's a Christian."

"He also snubbed me at Madison's Christmas party, remember?" An image of Andrew's borderline icy stare filled my memory, and I swallowed back a lump in my throat. Frosty claws cooled what warmth remained in my chest.

She turned to me. "I'm sure he'd get over it if you were interested—"

"Which I'm not," I whispered.

Anna raised a brow. "What's he studying?"

I pursed my lips and squinted at the ceiling before looking at my cousin. "Before school finished, he'd mentioned a double degree in Aerospace Engineering and Business Management at RMIT."

Victoria slipped from Dad's arms and reclaimed her daughter with a besotted smile. "Andrew's a lovely boy. He'll do well if he keeps his head in the books like he did for VCE." She returned to the cushion next to Dad, baby in her arms.

Dad wrapped an arm around Victoria's waist. His tight jaw relaxed, but his gaze still pierced my own. "RMIT? Is he at your campus?"

I shrugged. Although I had kept my eyes open for Andrew—and approximately twenty-seven conversation starters tabled in my brain should we ever cross paths—I had not seen him. "We haven't come across each other if he is." Maybe he had avoided me.

"Hmm." Dad cleared his throat. "If you came across him, would you want to spend time with him?"

I glanced at Jasmine while she fussed in Victoria's arms, rooting about for her beloved booby. "He and I were great friends at school, but … now I've no idea." And for some reason, this fact niggled at the back of my conscience.

Anna snorted. "He would."

Victoria chuckled, and Jasmine thrust her tiny arm out before resettling with closed eyes.

I huffed a laugh. "Anyway, I've no intention of breaking the guy's heart again on a whim." I squinted at my cousin. "You know that."

Anna sighed. "Live a little. If you see him at uni and he returns your smile, maybe it's a sign you should … explore something."

Dad growled. "Don't listen to your cousin. Do what you believe is right." He flared his nostrils. "And whatever you do, don't explore anything."

I laughed out loud, slid beside Dad on his free side, and encased him in a hug. "I love you, Daddy. I promise, no exploration."

Victoria and Anna's laughter reverberated the room.

I placed a gentle kiss on Dad's cheek and wiped my fingertips along the frown lines on his forehead.

"That's my girl," he said.

CHAPTER SIX
Responsibilities

"Will you be home for dinner tonight?" Aunt Stacy leaned against the kitchen island bench and poured milk onto Toby's cereal. She bounced Ella on her hip.

The cheeky little six-month-old slapped her mother's chin.

I held back a laugh and rescued the milk carton. "No. I, ah, have dinner plans with Tara." After depositing the milk in the fridge, I collected the bowl of milky cereal and placed it in front of Toby. "Here you go, cute stuff."

Ella extended her arms toward me.

I grabbed her with a giggle and a grin.

"I'm so glad you're getting out and socializing." Aunt Stacy toed the tiled floor. Her smile wavered. "Steve and I feel bad your commitments here might be interfering with your social life."

I opened and closed my mouth and pressed Ella closer. Should I share about my job interview later? *Not yet.* I dialed up my smile. "It's fine. Really."

"But you'll be home tomorrow night, won't you?"

"Of course. I wouldn't miss taco night."

Tuesday was taco night at the Morgan residence. Uncle Steve loved cooking and entertaining, and every second Tuesday Aunt Stacy worked long, hectic hours, so it worked out well. Aunt Stacy also seemed to enjoy her husband parading in his "Kiss the Cook" apron when she walked through the door.

Her eyes brightened. "Good. Steve'd be beside himself if he didn't have an audience."

I pulled a crazy face at Ella and was rewarded with an infectious giggle. "Tara said she might be over. I think she wants to be here for

Ella's first Taco Tuesday."

Aunt Stacy laughed. She reached across for her daughter and popped her back on her hip. "This little missy's going to have fun tomorrow, aren't you, my darling?"

"She bettah noh frow av-cado like sh'did da punkin," Toby said around a mouthful of cereal.

I smirked.

Aunt Stacy met my gaze with an amused expression before turning to her son. "That's why you need to set the example so Ella knows how to eat properly."

I eyed little Ella and imagined her mid-throw, green goop smeared across her highchair tray and squashed in her hair. I snickered. Tomorrow night would be a blast.

"Okay, Mummy."

I kissed Aunt Stacy and Ella. "I'll see you two at your midnight feed."

"Bye."

Toby peered up at me.

I hugged him tight and kissed the top of his head. "Be good and help Mummy."

"Uh huh."

I shouldered my bag, walked out the front door, and hightailed it to the nearest tram stop. Flopping onto the metal bench seat, I blew out a breath. My chest tightened. I hoped I got the casual supermarket job later today, then I could talk with the Morgans and re-jig the calendar. I had moved to South Melbourne five months ago and disliked feeling like a freeloader. My interview with the manager was booked for five o'clock.

Uncle Steve and Aunt Stacy had held fast to their adamant declarations my contribution in the house and with the children were more than adequate to pay for rent and food, but I needed more independence than my government-issued Youth Allowance payment. Dad and Victoria offered to send money each month— which I appreciated—but I wanted to prove to my parents I could look after myself.

This job would be a step in the right direction for my growing independence.

♥ ♥ ♥ ♥ ♥ ♥

I groaned and squinted at my bedside clock. Two past seven. "Oh no!" I launched from my warm bed and scrambled into some clean clothes. How had I not woken to my alarm? I had arrived home after everyone else had gone to bed and studied until after midnight, but my body clock usually kicked in by six-thirty.

I fumbled with my hair, tucked the supermarket uniform shirt into my backpack, and rushed down the stairs.

Aunt Stacy, Toby, and Ella dined at the kitchen table.

"Morning." I guzzled a glass of water and grabbed a banana and a muesli bar.

"Morning. Why're you rushing?" Aunt Stacy asked.

I halted and stared at the table. Aunt Stacy wore one of her many power suits, which meant … no! "You're working today?" My voice croaked.

"Yes. It's my Tuesday on." A single crease marred her forehead.

My heart's frantic pace somehow picked up more speed. How had I mixed up my fortnights? "I'm sorry, but I've gotta go, like, now."

"What?" Aunt Stacy sprang to her feet. "But I'm leaving in twenty minutes!"

I cringed and clutched my swirling stomach. My first work shift started in twenty minutes, and arriving late was not an option. Blood roared between my ears, and I shook my head. "I'm really sorry, but I've gotta go."

Aunt Stacy's eyes widened. "But I have court this morning. I can't be late."

I stepped closer to the doorway, my trembling body ready to collapse on the tiles yet bolt out the front door in the same breath. "I can't be late either. I'm sorry for the mix-up." I rushed from the house, bile singeing my throat and tears stinging my eyes.

All through my work shift—including a serious information dump and training session on the cash registers—Aunt Stacy's wide eyes and flustered expression tormented me. How had I screwed up my weeks? When the manager had offered me the job yesterday afternoon and asked whether I could start this morning, I had accepted the opportunity without hesitation. I was convinced I was available. Seemed a thirty-second calendar consultation would have saved me from an awkward conversation when I returned home.

I scanned a box of nappies and placed it next to the accumulated groceries of the animated mother across from me. "That'll be two hundred and thirty-one dollars forty-five, thanks."

The woman crooned to her toddler strapped in the trolley seat, pulled her phone from her hip pocket, and tapped her payment.

I smiled and handed her a transaction receipt. "Have a great afternoon."

Someone touched my arm. "Time to tap out, newbie."

I turned and stared at a girl with tons of makeup and bleach-blonde hair in a messy bun.

She raised a thin brow. "Melody said you might need help with the transfer."

"Thanks." I watched her log me out of the system and log herself in and committed the process to memory.

"I'm sure you'll get the hang of it soon enough."

"I will. Thanks." I nodded and headed to the staff area, where I grabbed my belongings, changed out of my uniform shirt, and caught the tram for my afternoon class.

"You sure you want me here for this?" Tara strode along the footpath beside me. "I can easily head back to uni and see if that hot med student is still at the library. He looked like the kind of guy I'd get more bang for my buck."

Tara and her obsession with men. I suppressed an eyeroll and glanced at her. "You'll be the perfect buffer." Other than knowing I needed to apologize and tell the Morgans about my new job, I still struggled to find the necessary words to avoid confrontation. Memories of my explosive argument with Dad a few years ago about a dumb guy still sparked a whirlpool of nausea any time I thought back on that disastrous evening. Thank God Victoria had been home and able to help me see reason after I had fled the house. My poor dad.

"And it's Taco Tuesday." Tara chuckled. "I don't want to miss Ella and her glorious mess."

We entered the house and dumped our things in my room. I stared at the staircase from my bedroom doorway, gripping the door handle, and expelled a breath.

Tara touched my shoulder. "Don't make this worse than it is.

Just apologize for this morning and tell them about your checkout-chick work. It's only two five-hour shifts a week. Surely they can work around it."

I inhaled a long breath. "You're right. Let's do this."

We wandered downstairs to the sounds of life in the kitchen.

"Hey, Steve." Tara bounded in, arms waving, and squatted to Ella's level where she chewed toys on her playmat in the adjacent family room.

"Evening, Tara." Uncle Steve lay down his knife and stared at me. "Diana."

My insides shrivelled. Was he mad at me? "Hi."

He raised a brow and crooked his pointer finger.

I swallowed in an effort to relieve my dry throat and stepped closer.

He lowered his head and laid his palm on my shoulder. "What happened this morning?" His soft timbre seemed free from judgement.

The tightness inside my abdomen unfurled a smidgen. "It was a stupid mix-up. I'm so sorry I messed things up for Aunt Stacy." I dropped my chin and bit my bottom lip.

Uncle Steve released my shoulder and inched my chin up with his finger. "It's okay. I was able to high-tail it home and drop the kids at Mrs. Jennings, who was, thankfully, available."

I grimaced. Just what a busy Sergeant needed.

"But it would be great not to have to deal with scenarios like this in future if possible."

I nodded and clasped my unsteady hands together. "I need to discuss something with you and Aunt Stacy. Can we speak later tonight?"

He smiled and nodded. "Of course." He returned to his chopping station. "How about you and Tara set the table."

Tara and Uncle Steve carried the conversation throughout dinner. Aunt Stacy had smiled at me when she came home but had refrained from talking much at the table. Maybe she still needed to decompress from her busy day? I hoped work was the reason for her silence, not this morning's mishap.

Tara and I cleared the table and stacked the dishwasher.

My chest squeezed with each repetitive motion. Would this conversation be a breeze like Tara believed? Or would the addition to my weekly schedule make waves within this time-poor household? I hated to think a few extra bucks in my pocket would rock the familial boat, but this was what people my age did. Studied and worked. And I knew I could still fulfil similar hours of child-minding if I pushed my homework time to later in the evenings. *Help me say the right thing, God. Give me the words to—*

Tara whacked my shoulder. "I said, 'See ya,' ya doofus."

I sucked in a breath and scanned the quiet room. "Where'd everyone go?"

"They're putting the kids to bed." Tara scrunched her brow. "You said bye to the munchkins and even blew kisses."

I did?

"Where's your head at?"

I shrugged. "I'm a little—"

"Nervous." Tara stretched onto her tiptoes and hugged me, angling her mouth as close to my ear as her tiny frame could manage. "Stay focused, tell them everything, and move on. Got it?" She dropped to her usual level.

"Got it." I escorted her to the front door, shivered in the wintry evening air that prickled goosebumps along my arms, and returned to the kitchen. Hot tea would go down a treat.

Halfway through my pouring boiling water into three white mugs, Uncle Steve and Aunt Stacy entered the kitchen.

"Why don't you let me finish this," Uncle Steve said.

Aunt Stacy nodded toward the lounge room.

"Okay, thanks." I settled on the couch near Aunt Stacy's rocking chair and clasped my clammy hands.

Aunt Stacy nestled onto her recliner, sighed, and levelled her grey gaze at me. "Care to explain this morning's jumble?"

I lowered my head, my chest tight. "I'm really sorry about what happened. I mixed up my weeks."

"Clearly."

"My blunder was unintentional, I promise."

"I understand things happen." She sighed again. "But can you appreciate the difficult situation you left me in? I have a reputation to uphold as a barrister, especially as a woman and mother. This case has been a challenge from day one, and I needed a focused, clear head, not stress over the children. And Steve? The poor man deserted his post mid-duties, which looks very unprofessional for a

Patrol Supervisor. With the possibility of promotion to Senior Sergeant in a few years' time, I only hope there's no backlash with the higher-ups."

My cheeks burned along with my stomach lining. "I'm sorry," I whispered.

Aunt Stacy sighed again.

I had never heard her expel this much air after one of our rare jogging sessions.

"I know. I forgive you, but you need to understand the seriousness of our positions."

I lifted my head and met her gaze. "I understand. Truly."

Uncle Steve set a tray of drinks and biscuits on the coffee table before plopping in his armchair.

"I'm glad that's settled." Aunt Stacy reached for her mug and sipped.

Uncle Steve smiled at me. "You said you wanted to talk to us about something?"

"Yes." My dry throat constricted. I grabbed my tea, gulped a mouthful of hot liquid, which scorched on the way down, and shuddered. I held the hot cup on my knee. "The reason for this morning's mishap was because … I have a job."

"What?" Aunt Stacy straightened.

"Just a casual position at the local supermarket. Two five-hour shifts a week."

Aunt Stacy huffed. "At the supermarket? Why would you take a job which has no bearing on your future career? How will this benefit your pathway to journalism?"

I shrugged. The thought never crossed my mind. Had I made the wrong decision?

"I thought we talked about this? You do the work of an au pair in exchange for accommodation and board, and Steve and I are happy to give you a little cash—"

"But I shouldn't be paid for doing my part." How could they think I deserved pocket money on top of free food and lodging? I gestured around the room. "I live here rent free when a room at a place like this would otherwise set me back a couple hundred dollars a week. My help with the children, cleaning, cooking, and laundry is only enough to cover my board."

Throughout my childhood, Dad had been busy with work, and

one emergency call-out could mean the difference between having clean underwear and dinner versus the contrary. It was best to do things myself. Getting paid to be an active member of a busy household was bogus.

I shook my head. "I can't have you pay me as well."

Uncle Steve leaned forward. "When are these shifts?"

I squirmed against the plush couch seat. "Tuesday mornings before uni, then alternating Saturday and Sunday afternoons."

"Why would you commit to working on Tuesdays? And Sundays?" Aunt Stacy's voice trilled. "What about church?"

I stiffened. "I attend church in the morning."

"But then you're limited to when you can socialise after church. Or attend night meetings."

I arched my brow. When was the last time I had hung out with city church friends? *Never.* I needed to check out the Christian group at uni this week. Hopefully it fit me better than the literature society.

"We should do our utmost to keep Sundays free of work." Aunt Stacy raised her chin.

I scoffed. "Then why do you sometimes pore over your files on a Sunday evening? And Uncle Steve works nights some Sundays?"

She narrowed her eyes. "Because, as you stated, it's *some*times. Usually a refresher before a court case the following day." Her jaw hardened. "Steve's overnights occur once a month, sometimes less. And his shifts start at ten PM. Not fortnightly on a Sunday afternoon."

Why was Aunt Stacy being such a pain about this?

Uncle Steve cleared his throat. "Did you have any suggestions how we can work this within our busy schedule, Diana?"

I inhaled a deep, cleansing breath and smiled. "I do. If Mrs. Jennings is able to take the children on Tuesdays instead of Wednesdays, I'll push my Wednesday morning study session to Tuesday and Wednesday nights, then I'll be free to look after the kids. Since you guys rarely need me on Saturday or Sunday afternoons, if you need me, then you can just book your date nights for times I'll be home."

"And if Mrs. Jennings isn't able to accommodate us?" Aunt Stacy's icy tone grated against my skin.

I squeezed my mug, grateful for the solid object between my hands. "Then I'll work something out."

She shook her head. "I just don't understand why you'd do this behind our backs instead of being forthcoming. We could've discussed this beforehand." Aunt Stacy rubbed a hand across her heavy-lidded eyes.

I clenched my jaw. Was she always this accusatory? No wonder Aunt Stacy was a sought-after barrister.

"What matters is we can move forward together," Uncle Steve said, his deep voice a tad louder than normal. "I'll speak with Mrs. Jennings when I drop the children off tomorrow morning, and we can go from there. Agreed?"

"Agreed," Aunt Stacy said, her voice less frigid.

I nodded, stood, and gathered all the mugs on the tray. "Night." I strode to the kitchen, added the dirty dishes to the dishwasher before anyone followed me, and escaped to the solace of my bedroom.

✒ ✒ ✒ ✒ ✒ ✒ ✒

28 July

I'm so upset right now, Mum. Sorry if this turns into a rant.

I have a new casual job at the supermarket. Yay, me. A job I thought was a good idea. A little money, a place I can meet new people. Isn't that what nineteen-year-olds do? Assert their independence? But now I'm wondering whether I was wrong. Not about my independence, but the job itself. Should I have searched for a job of some kind in journalism? Something to help me advance in this arena? I just don't know, and I wish you were here to help me navigate these foreign waters.

And Aunt Stacy? What is her problem? Am I impacting her precious, important life and family in a way she doesn't appreciate? Why doesn't she trust me and my choices? Haven't I proven myself over the last five months? One slip up and strike? I don't need her lectures.

I could do with some advice. The only woman I've spent any time with on a daily basis is Victoria, and she's so different to Aunt Stacy. But I don't want to get her and Dad involved in this. I need to stand on my own two feet.

Did I do the right thing?

CHAPTER SEVEN
Reconciliation

"Do you require my services tonight?" I stuffed the last of a banana in my mouth and filled my water bottle from the countertop kitchen filter.

"Pardon?" Aunt Stacy lifted her head from the papers she read at the island bench.

"Do I need to be home later?" *Please say no.* The Christian Union at uni had an event on tonight. Avoiding Aunt Stacy was an added bonus.

She offered me a small smile. "No. Go have some fun."

"Will do." I stuffed my water bottle in my backpack and exited the room.

My shoulders eased the moment I stepped through the front door. No wonder my friends at school with parent issues had often escaped their homes. Living with someone who doubted me ached deep within my chest. The past two weeks had been a challenge.

I loped into class and dropped in my usual seat beside Tara. "Want to go to a Christian Union function with me later?"

Tara snorted. "Wanna go jump off a cliff? Cos I think I'd prefer that to your freaky Jesus stuff."

I hid a smile. It was worth a try.

"Actually, I'd prefer to jump that guy." She pointed toward a student across the room.

"Of course, you would."

Tara snickered.

While the guest lecturer shared his passion about photojournalism and how images can enhance a news story, my mind wandered to my end-of-day activity. I had enjoyed meeting some of the Christian Union members last week and was assured tonight's gathering would be larger and well attended.

I leaned against the seat back. Would I find someone tonight I could relate to? A friend like Tara but someone who shared my faith and moral standards. I pressed away a laugh. Madison, Grace, and Anna's faces filled my mind. Madison had always been the crazy one back home, pushing boundaries with boldness and panache—other than when it came to guys. She believed the Bible when it said to keep your secret garden locked until marriage—but Tara had outdone anything "crazy" Madison ever accomplished. And then some.

Andrew's face filtered into my memories. I rubbed my hand across my mouth, and my shoulders slumped. I had kept my eye out for him at the last event but never saw him. Or maybe he saw me and bolted. I inhaled a slow breath. Sometimes I wished I had tried to explain my situation to Andrew, how I never felt any … zing between us. Never stared at his lips in that creepy teenager love-obsessed way. And only checked out his butt because my friends pointed it out.

Would a guy *want* to date a girl he knew was with him for his friendship and no other reason? Surely lack of attraction was a dealbreaker. But what did I know? Other than a harmless crush here and there, I had never been drawn to a guy. Not the way Dad and Victoria were pulled together with invisible magnets.

I wanted magnetic-force, gravitational-pull attraction. Suction-lips-for-life love.

Tara poked my shoulder. "Oy, you coming, or what?"

Huh? I surveyed the room. The lecture hall was half empty? Where had the last ninety minutes gone? I bit my lower lip. How had I daydreamed through an entire session? Zoning out during important training was unlike my usual studious self. My future journalistic career was on the line. *Not good enough, Diana. Get it together!*

I scrambled and packed my things into my backpack, my hands tremoring with each motion. "Can I get your notes?"

Tara smirked. "Already emailed them to you. Figured you were in la-la-land since you stared at your laptop, sans the usual typing."

I relaxed my shoulders. "Thanks, I owe you."

"Then do me a favour and don't ask me to your weirdo event

again." She descended the steps.

I followed not far behind, heart heavy and prayerful for my friend.

She waved. "Enjoy the weird-fest, see ya tomorrow."

"Will do, bye." I meandered along several buildings to the area I was informed the fun would start.

A woman a year or two older than me— slightly taller than Tara—with freckles, mousy-brown hair tied in a tight ponytail, and a smile warm enough to melt through a snow-capped mountaintop greeted me. "Welcome!" She tilted her head. "Were you at last week's CU catchup? You look familiar."

I stepped closer to allow a guy to slip behind me. "I was. My first visit."

Her smile stretched. "And what did you think?"

I nodded a few seconds longer than a normal person. Awkward. "Seems like a good fit for me."

"I'm glad." She waved at a passer-by before lifting her gaze back to me. "Do you go to church?"

"I do." I raised a brow. "I assume you do too?"

"Correct." Her warm brown eyes sparkled. She extended her hand. "I'm Lacey Spencer."

I enveloped her small palm. "Pleased to meet you, Lacey. I'm Diana Jacobsen." I released her hand and glanced around the small room. "I guess I'll find a seat."

Lacey pointed toward a chair draped with a black overcoat. "Feel free to sit by me. I'll be over in a few minutes."

"Thanks." A smile slipped to my lips as I padded the hardwood floor and occupied the seat beside Lacey's belongings.

Three hours flew by before I knew it, my heart soaring with the time. I bade my new friends goodnight and travelled home on a high of uplifting conversations and good old-fashioned fun.

I sucked in a long breath, retrieved my house key from my coat pocket, and slotted it into the front door deadlock. With a careful turn and push, I opened the door with a soft click, the almost noiseless action something I had practiced over the past fortnight. Now to tiptoe to the stairs past the creaky section and sneak into my room, unheard.

"Diana?" Uncle Steve's voice called from somewhere inside.

Busted. My shoulders sagged.

He stepped around the corner and leaned against the archway leading to the family room and kitchen. "Can we chat for a moment?"

I dumped my backpack at the foot of the stairs.

He ran a palm over his scruffy chin.

I pressed my lips together, nodded, and followed him into the empty formal lounge room. Was it so serious we needed to use this room?

Uncle Steve parked on one end of the couch and patted the cushion beside him.

I lodged on the edge of the seat.

His blue gaze penetrated my face. "Is there something I can do to help you move past the unfortunate kerfuffle from two weeks ago?"

My face heated.

"You're polite yet withdrawn, and I'd like to put an end to it." He pulled the ridiculous-looking face he used to extract a giggle from Ella.

I choked back a laugh.

"Enough of this pussyfooting around. This is your home, and I hate to think you feel awkward here."

I swallowed the lump in my throat. "She doesn't trust me," I whispered. "Even after proving my character and choices for months, I know this was a black mark against me."

Uncle Steve furrowed his brow. "Not true. A woman like my feisty wife doesn't let any old yahoo tend to her children."

That thought had never occurred to me. I chewed the inside of my mouth.

"Don't confuse trust with disappointment." He touched my upper arm. "Stace was disappointed, but I suspect more at herself than you."

I wrinkled my nose. "Why would she be disappointed at herself?"

He scraped his palm along his rough jaw. "Cos she feels the pressure to be perfect and knows she overreacted with you." He beamed a smile. "We love you and enjoy your company."

My chest eased. "And I love you guys and the great life you've afforded me here."

He nudged my shoulder. "So, d'you think you can do this old

man a favour?"

Old man? Uncle Steve was barely Dad's age! I chuckled. "What can I do?"

He nodded toward the kitchen and family room. "Clear the air with my beloved? Then she can cease her self-flagellations and pay more attention to me." He winked.

Laughter burst from my lungs. I enjoyed the lightness inside. "Now?"

"Please."

I leaned across and planted a kiss on Uncle Steve's unshaven cheek, the sensation against my lips reminiscent of kissing Dad. I missed everyone in Tellarine. The next three weeks until mid-semester break could not come fast enough.

Uncle Steve escorted me to the family room, where Aunt Stacy nursed Ella for her final evening feed. "Need me here?" he whispered.

I shook my head.

He leaned over his wife and daughter, murmured something about sweet loving in Aunt Stacy's ear—to which she snort-laughed and blushed—and disappeared.

I cosied on Uncle Steve's armchair.

"I'm sorry about everything."

I whipped my head up and caught Aunt Stacy's stare. "You stole my line."

She chuckled, her chest shaking and interrupting Ella's supper.

The little darling whacked her mother's collarbone with a pudgy palm.

I hid my smile behind my hand.

"But I am sorry about the awkwardness of the past fortnight." Aunt Stacy smoothed Ella's hair with a finger. "I overreacted and—"

"It's okay." I sighed. "I withdrew from our usual banter, and I'm sorry too."

"And you withdrew because …"

I tugged on the hem of my shirt. "I thought you no longer trusted me."

Aunt Stacy's brows drew together. "No, sweetheart. I trust you." She glanced at her feeding baby. "I trust you enough to leave my precious little people in your capable hands." She raised her gaze to my face. "I apologize for giving you that impression. You're trustworthy and wise beyond your years. Despite all you've been through, you're a level-headed young lady." A soft smile brightened her features. "You should be proud of who you are."

The backs of my eyes tingled. "Thank you."

Aunt Stacy lay her hand on my shoulder. "We love you very much. Don't doubt it."

"I won't." My voice rasped.

"Thanks for coming to speak to me. Not everyone would be as brave." She huffed a soft laugh. "Particularly the new clerk at chambers. Not sure how long he'll last."

"Poor guy." I grinned and brushed aside a tear.

Ella grunted and slapped Aunt Stacy's shoulder.

"I'll leave you to it." I stretched and rotated my aching neck. "Goodnight."

"Night. Sleep well."

For the first night in half a month, the possibility seemed achievable.

Mid-semester break came and went in a flash of babysitting gigs, where I hogged Jasmine and her hugs like the last copy of a romance novel in a bookstore.

One afternoon—after spending the morning hanging out with Keanu at Benanu's—I returned home to Victoria slumped on the lounge room floor, her red, puffy eyes aimed at the muted television.

My heart thundered, and I sank beside her, wrapping my arms around her slight body. The moment thrust me back in time when I had found Victoria in tears in the cereal aisle at the local IGA supermarket. At the time, she mourned the birthday of her deceased daughter. I racked my brain and calculated whether today was the anniversary or birthday of one of her lost children. Nothing came to mind. "What's up, beautiful mumma?"

Victoria rubbed her nose in a loud sniffle.

I stretched toward the coffee table tissue box, pulled a wad of tissues, and stuffed the bundle into her hands.

Victoria offered me a watery smile and wiped her eyes. She nodded at the television flashing Netflix promos. "It's just …

they've done another *Downton Abbey* on me." Tears trickled down her face. She shook with another sob.

I rubbed her back in slow circles. "What d'you mean they've done another *Downton Abbey* on you?" I had binge-watched the television series with Victoria over the summer holidays and had fallen in love with the characters, but I had never collapsed on the floor in tears over the show.

Victoria shook her fist at the screen. "They killed him. Just like they killed Matthew Crawley!"

Huh. When Victoria blubbered again, I retrieved my phone, held her with one arm, and sent out an SOS.

Me: YOU NEED TO ARRANGE A DATE NIGHT WITH YOUR WIFEY ASAP. SHE NEEDS TO GET OUT MORE.

Dad replied a minute later.

Dad: OKAY.

Me: I'M SERIOUS. I CAME HOME TO HER SPRAWLED ON THE LOUNGE ROOM FLOOR IN TEARS OVER THE DEATH OF A FICTIONAL TV SERIES CHARACTER.

Me: STILL NOT SURE WHICH SERIES, BUT IT'S AS BAD AS MATTHEW IN DOWNTON ABBEY. YOU KNOW HOW WELL THAT WENT DOWN. EVIL WRITERS.

And they *were* evil writers. Who cared if the actor had no desire to sign another contract? The viewers wanted more of the Crawleys!

Dad: THAT'S REALLY BAD. MUST BE THAT SHOW ABOUT CALLING HEARTS OR WHATEVER IT IS. SOME JACK FELLA'S BEEN GIVING ME A RUN FOR MY MONEY. I'LL BOOK SOMETHING FOR TONIGHT.

Dad: CAN YOU WATCH JAZZY?

Dad: PLEASE?

Victoria's sobs had slowed to an occasional hiccup.

Me: OF COURSE. I'M HERE FOR ANOTHER 4 DAYS IF YOU WANT TO GO OUT EVERY NIGHT.

Dad: THANKS.

Me: ANYTHING TO HELP. LOVE YOU. COME HOME SOON … PLEASE!!

Jasmine was set to wake any minute and looking after her would prove more difficult if her mother was a mess on the carpet.

Dad: WILL KNOCK OFF EARLY AND BUY FLOWERS.

Me: AND LINDT CHOCOLATE.

Dad: DONE.

I peeled Victoria off the floor and plopped her on the couch with a cup of hot chocolate. High-fiving myself for my marriage-counselling skills, I checked the freezer for breast milk. Yep, I rocked it today. After a rough August with the Morgans, I appreciated the win. Call me the best daughter and sister in the universe.

CHAPTER EIGHT
Building Bridges

"Ugh. This blows chunks."

I laughed at Tara's flair for the dramatic. We were ensconced in the university library at our laptops, surrounded by books and papers, studying for our final assessment task. "You'll be fine."

"Before or after I throw myself off that balcony over there?" She pointed past my shoulder.

I squelched a smirk and blinked at the screen. Journalism Law and Ethics. Tara was right when she said this subject sucked all the happiness from one's soul.

"Now that's what I'm talking about. Hello, Mister Morning Glory."

I turned in the direction Tara stared, gasped, and almost slipped off the hard chair. "Andrew!" I untangled my crossed legs, stood, and waved at him like a moron.

Andrew stopped in his tracks, and his eyes widened.

I offered him my biggest smile. *Please talk to me.*

His Adam's apple bobbed.

Seconds seemed to pass at a glacial rate. My pulse points vibrated throughout my entire body, my heart verging on cardiac arrest.

Andrew turned and closed the gap between us.

Thank You, Jesus! I gripped the back of my chair with quivering fingers.

"Diana." His hazel eyes assessed me above the uncharacteristic scruff covering his jaw.

I shuddered a breath, willing my heart to slow. "How are you? It's been ages!" Since the terrible Christmas party conversation eleven months earlier, to be exact.

"Busy. You?"

"Yeah, busy." I eyed him from head to toe. "You look … great." And he did, which was bizarre. When had Andrew ever looked "great" to me? I palmed my thigh and nodded toward his chin. "Forgot where your shaver was?"

The corner of his mouth wobbled. "Doing my part for Movember."

I stared longer than I should. Andrew appeared older and strangely appealing with his neat, trimmed beard. I restrained myself from dragging my fingers against his long stubble and stuffed my hands in my pockets. "I like the face fuzz. You should keep it."

He scraped his hand along his jaw. "I might."

My smile trembled. I lowered my gaze to his broad chest—had it doubled in size since I last saw him?—and noticeable biceps.

Stop checking him out! What was wrong with me? Had I belatedly reached the part of puberty where girls noticed guys? And Andrew of all people.

"Care to introduce me to your friend?"

I turned and noticed Tara had slipped from her seat and stood beside me. "This is Andrew, an old school friend of mine." My stomach tightened. Were we still friends?

Tara extended her hand toward Andrew. "Tara. Pleased to meet you, Andrew." She turned to me. "Geez, Di, where were you hiding this delicious hottie?"

I widened my eyes at her.

Andrew huffed a quiet laugh.

My face heated, and I inspected the floor.

"Busy tomorrow night?" Tara nudged my arm. "I planned to drag this one around on a pub crawl to find her a guy so she could loosen up."

"Tara!" I lifted my gaze to Andrew's. "She wishes I'd go home with a guy. But you know me."

A sudden softness filled his eyes. "That I do."

Tara elbowed me, hard. "I wish you'd let your morals slide. You've been so stressed recently and really need to get laid."

I whacked her arm. "That's not a slide of morals! That's … that's complete annihilation!" I narrowed my eyes at my pushy friend. "I don't understand one-night stands. How do you gain true fulfilment like this?"

Andrew cleared his throat. "I agree. Life's much easier when we keep it simple. One woman for life works for me. Well, that's the plan, anyway."

Tara laughed. "What, no 'try before you buy'? Good luck with that. You and Di are cut from the same cloth." She shook her head and surveyed Andrew. "Which works out well. Waddaya say? You up for a Friday night of fun?"

His probing gaze evaluated me for several seconds.

I counted my breaths.

"I'm game."

Yes!

"Great." Tara stared at me and raised her manicured eyebrow.

"What?"

"He's your friend. Do you have his number?"

I squinted at her.

She shook her head and sighed. "His *phone* number? Seriously, I think you're a lost cause sometimes."

Something undiscernible flickered in Andrew's eyes.

Did he think I was a lost cause too? A tight ball formed in the pit of my tummy. Was our friendship irredeemable? I handed over my mobile phone, and Andrew recorded his number.

"My job here's done." Tara gathered her belongings. "See you tomorrow night, Andrew. Bye, babe."

"Bye." I turned to Andrew, my throat tight.

"Tara's an … interesting character."

I watched the back of my dear, but sometimes misguided, friend disappear through the library door. "She's gorgeous, just a little lacking in the area of relationships, especially the God kind. I'm the light in her world and don't intend stopping, even though she throws men at me left, right, and centre." I sighed. "It'll be nice spending an evening with a guy who's not trying to ply me with alcohol and pick-up lines."

Andrew raised his hand, flat palm facing me like someone pledging a vow. "I promise not to ply you with alcohol and pick-up lines." He shrugged and dropped his gaze. "Been there, done that."

My smile evaporated. Not that Andrew had ever tried to ply me with alcohol, nor did I recall him using a pick-up line on me, but knowing I had hurt him, hurt me.

Andrew tipped his head forward and stepped back. "See you tomorrow night."

"Bye."

I skimmed through my wardrobe and flipped past clothes before returning to the first outfit.

Tara lounged on the spare bed in my room. "What's the deal with you and Andrew anyway?"

What *was* the deal? Andrew was … well, Andrew. Why was I second-guessing myself all of a sudden? He was my friend. Kinda. But I planned to have a declaration of friendship by the end of the night.

I lifted my chin, pulled a purple, short-sleeved silk blouse from its hanger, and lay it against my nicest black pants. "Too much?"

Tara gestured for the blouse and rose to her knees. "You want to be more casual. What about this blouse with your skinny jeans and cute ballerina flats?"

"Perfect. Thanks."

Tara searched for said shoes under my bed.

I stripped down to my purple laced underwear and pulled on my jeans.

"So? What's the go with him?"

I rubbed on some deodorant, sprayed a little perfume, and fanned my hands at the base of my neck. "He's just a guy I know from school. You know what it's like."

Tara pushed me onto the side of my bed and thrust my shoes at my hands. "No. I don't. And don't give me the old-friends-from-school routine. Andrew's hot, and you know it … don't you?"

I slipped into my shoes and reached across for my top. "He's had a crush on me since Year Seven." I unbuttoned the top two buttons and slipped the blouse over my head. "He's a great guy, but—"

"What?" Tara dropped onto the bed beside me.

I shrugged into my shirt and buttoned it. "I may be keenly aware he's stacked on some muscle in the past year, but … it doesn't feel right."

She bunched her eyebrows together. Lines creased her

forehead, giving her a cute bulldog look. "You do realise you can have fun? Why not get a steamy kiss in celebration of your hard work this year, and leave it at that?"

I stood and straightened my blouse. "I can't. I refuse to play with a guy. Especially Andrew."

Tara retrieved her leather jacket and purse from the spare bed. "I'm just saying it's—"

"I know what you're saying, but it's not for me. I … I—"

"What? You're waiting for"—she scrunched her nose like Ella had just filled her nappy—"Mr. Right to sweep you off your feet?"

Was I? A small smile lifted my cheeks. "Maybe."

Tara grabbed my bag and thrust it against my chest. "Mr. Right lives in those novels you read, not in real life."

"Not true." I knew several examples of Mr. Right finding love in Tellarine. I would hold out for my own true love.

I switched off my bedroom light and bounded down the stairs, Tara following behind. "See you later, Uncle Steve!" I waved as we left the house.

Tara, Andrew, and I hung out with a few friends at a pub Tara chose in the city. Deafening music overpowered most conversation, and the smell of beer, sweat, and aftershave filled the crammed venue. Laughter sporadically pealed above the pulsating music and my friends' loud discussions.

I observed Andrew throughout the evening, having never been in a social setting like this together. He fascinated me. He was fun and at ease regardless of whether a girl tried to make a move on him or one of the guys chatted about whatever it is guys talked about.

Andrew had also seemed to thaw as the evening progressed. His eyes twinkled for the first time in forever. But I still had not found an opportunity to address the elephant in the room and apologize.

My jeans back pocket vibrated, and I withdrew my phone. *Madison.* I beamed, handed my water bottle to Andrew, and slipped through the crowd to a quieter corner. "Hey, Maddy! What's up?"

"Sounds like some party over there. Where're you at? I'm in the city with Grace. Thought we could crash at your place tonight?"

"We're at Young and Jackson. Corner of Swanston and Flinders streets. If you hurry, we should still be here, but Tara looks antsy to leave."

"Stall her for ten minutes, okay?"

I laughed. "You know what she's like, but I'll try. See you soon!"

Tara squirmed through the crowd and slid her arm around my waist. "Ready to go to the next place?"

"Give me ten minutes? Please?"

Tara pouted. "Fine."

I returned to Andrew, nodded my thanks, and reclaimed my water. I stepped closer to speak into his ear.

His body radiated heat against my bare arm.

Stop noticing things about him! I shook my head to clear the haze. "That was Madison Taylor. She's on her way with Grace Robinson."

Andrew's eyes brightened. "Haven't seen them in almost a year. It'll be nice to catch up."

"You and Grace'll have plenty to talk about, I'm sure." Though Grace never said it, I always suspected she crushed on Andrew.

He squinted. "She barely spoke to me at school."

"Grace's studying Engineering at Monash."

He stared at me with wide eyes. "Really? Quiet little Grace is going to be an engineer? Impressive."

"Top of her class last semester."

"Cool."

I sipped my water, whispered a prayer, and plunged off the cliff in my brain. "I'm really sorry about how I handled our conversation after the English exam. I've never really had an opportunity to explain."

He pulled away and studied me with a probing gaze. His broad chest reverberated a deep sigh.

My lungs squeezed.

Andrew ran a hand through his hair. "Don't apologize. I don't need an explanation." A soft smile crept to his stubbled face. "What's done is done." He stretched out his hand. "Friends?"

My chest loosened. "Friends." I slid my palm against his large, muscular hand, and my stomach flipped. Uh oh. I extracted my hand from his warm grip and stepped back.

Andrew raised a brow and smirked. "You've officially been friend-zoned. Welcome to the world of random messages at one in the morning about hot girls, study frustrations, and endless pics of empty coffee cups. You've been warned."

Laughter bubbled inside, and I chuckled. "I look forward to sending you journalistic gems about stuff like the Tasselled Wobbegong, how Sparklemuffin and Skeletorus were discovered, and which cricket player has the nicest butt. It'll be fun."

Andrew grinned and sipped his beer.

Someone grabbed me from behind and whirled me around. "Diana!" Madison said. "Ooh … is that Andrew?"

Andrew smiled at Madison and her gaping mouth.

Grace snuck up next to me and offered Andrew a timid smile.

I wrapped my arm across her shoulder and spent the rest of the evening with my friends at various locations, my heart lighter than a feather.

✎ ✎ ✎ ✎ ✎ ✎ ✎

3 November

Mum, you're not going to believe it! Well, maybe you will. I not only feel like I aced my final assessment task for the year, but I reconciled my friendship with Andrew tonight! Okay, it was technically last night since it's three past two in the morning, but it's still tonight in my head.

Is this what winning in life looks like? Finally finding myself in a happy place everywhere I look? Loving my time living with the Morgans, enjoying my casual job, finding my feet with my studies, and now swimming in healthy friendships. Not to mention all my loved ones back home in Tellarine.

Life is, dare I say, as perfect as it can be. The only thing that'd make my life blissful is having you by my side. And maybe a handsome guy with dark stubble … yeah, I think I might've turned to the Dark Side. Something else I now have in common with you.

I love you, Mum. And I miss you every single day.

CHAPTER NINE
Ensnared

"Who recommended this sandwich bar?" I trudged along a muddy path with Tara on a cold, overcast winter's day in late June, questioning my sanity with each step.

She nudged my arm and led me into a laneway. "Does it matter?"

"I'd like to know." My mind drifted away from my hunger pains to the promised inexpensive, delicious sandwich which would keep starvation at bay for my train trip home. First semester of my second year at uni was now done and dusted, and I looked forward to time with Dad, Victoria, and Jasmine.

Over a month had passed since Jasmine had squished my face with her pudgy little hands. I missed her, amazed how fast she grew. Victoria messaged me photos and videos each night, the latest showing how my fourteen-month-old sister climbed out of her cot. I had giggled, wide-eyed, when I played the footage the first time and laughed imagining Victoria hiding her phone in Jasmine's room to catch the little jailbird in the act. My heart swelled with memories of cuddling Jasmine, tickling a path under her chin while she giggled and squealed.

Tara laughed and tugged me down another laneway overgrown with weeds. "Let's call him Zeus. The Greek god doppelgänger with curly blond hair I went home with last night."

"Zeus?" I always imagined the Greek god Zeus had dark hair.

Tara's body vibrated with stifled laughter. "I don't remember his name, but the man was the god of thunder in the sheets. If you know what I mean."

No. I don't. I lifted a silent prayer for my friend. "You know there's more to life than sex, right?"

She turned and raised an eyebrow. "Like what? Books filled with pious romance, like the stuff you read? Pfft. Give me a real flesh-and-blood man over your fairy tales any day of the week."

I eyed her before I dodged a puddle. "For your information, your lover-boy Jamie Fraser was a figment of Diana Gabaldon's imagination written on paper decades before he was ever on your TV screen."

Tara glided over a muddy patch. "But a hot Scot turned him into a tangible man. I'd prefer to watch that man strut his stuff onscreen than read the books." She huffed. "I mean, have you even *seen* the size of the *Outlander* book series? It'd prop open an entire floor of hotel room doors!"

My cheeks heated. I had watched several episodes of the TV show with Tara last year, but it was too much for my virtuous mind once we reached the wedding episode.

We exited the dark, dank alley, and the laneway opened to a single shopfront hidden behind Queen Victoria Market. Sammy's Sandwich Bar appeared fresh on the outside, with white painted bricks, light-grey window panes, and a sea-blue door. A bold blue-red-and-white sign filled the window, a happy man grinning with a delicious sandwich in his hand.

My mouth watered.

Tara eased the door open, and we stepped inside. The dark interior contrasted its bright facade.

I furrowed my brow and surveyed the cramped, dim room, filled with scratched inky-wood countertops and aged bench seats. My pulse spiked, and a shiver shot down my spine.

We needed to leave. Now.

Tara scanned the sandwich menu and create-your-own price lists above the front counter.

I leaned closer to her. "I don't feel good about this place." I hoped the shop attendant was out of earshot.

"It's a sandwich. Live a little."

I bit the inside of my cheek. My heart thudded against my ribs.

Tara approached the man behind the counter and announced her order with a confidence I lacked.

The man penned her transaction and handed her a bright-red numbered ticket. "Through to the next room for payment and collection, thanks."

Tara thanked him, flashed a smile over her shoulder, and waved to me. "Hurry up and choose. I'll see you on the other side."

I perused the menu with hands gripped together. My appetite had disappeared. I mulled over ideas while my mind battled against a nagging internal alarm. This was a sandwich shop, not some Melbourne gangland front for amphetamine trade. An eerie inkling of being in the wrong place at the wrong time loomed, but I huffed a breath and pushed aside the persistent thought. Tara was right. I needed to loosen up.

I nodded and flashed a hesitant smile. "I'll have a salami-tomato-cheese-lettuce-and-mayonnaise sourdough sandwich, please." I hoped the sandwich would remain edible until my appetite reappeared—most likely with a vengeance—on the train later this afternoon.

His unsavoury attention skimmed my body and returned to my face. Something glinted in his eyes.

I shivered.

Average in height with dark features and broad shoulders, the man looked about two or so years older than me. But his biceps and torso unsettled me. Too buff, like a bodybuilder on anabolic steroids.

I stiffened.

He flashed a toothy grin and handed me a red ticket. "My favourite. Through to the next room, lovely."

An unpleasant tingle shuddered down my spine. I strode under the archway Tara had disappeared through moments before into another darkened space. My breathing hitched. Was this business struggling to keep its lights on?

A short, young man prepared sandwiches behind a tall, dark wood counter. Several men milled about in the waiting area.

My hands itched, and I fidgeted with the hem of my top. I glanced around the room, searching for blonde highlights. Where was Tara? My pulse ticked up a notch. I spotted the ladies' bathroom and walked over to a man in his late-twenties to early-thirties near the bathroom door.

He had a gorgeous shock of auburn hair, firm pecs underneath his taut grey T-shirt, and a firm-fitting pair of Levi's plastered to his muscled legs. Taller than me too and, on closer inspection, bore the face of a model.

I approached Cute Auburn Model with all the confidence I could muster. "Excuse me. Did you see my friend head into the bathroom? A pretty blonde wearing jeans and a black jacket." I lifted my hand to my shoulder. "About this tall."

He squinted at a bulky man to my left before turning to me. "Yes, I believe she did."

"Thanks." I entered the bathroom in pursuit of my friend. "Tara?" I scanned the room but the cubicles were empty. A shadow lengthened across the floor from behind, and I turned. "Tar—"

"Sorry, beautiful." Cute Auburn Model lunged and jabbed a syringe into my neck.

I squealed as the hot sting of the needle and the coolness of the liquid assaulted my body.

Evil Auburn Model covered my mouth with his large, rough palm and grabbed me around the waist.

My heart pummelled my chest cavity, a painful punch with each beat. An uncontrollable urge to shake, scream, and run overcame me before a heaviness weighed my limbs. My mind clouded. I struggled to breathe, to think. Struggled to *be*.

My attacker dragged me to the end toilet cubicle, his hard body strong against my weakened frame.

Adrenaline hammered through my veins. My breaths shallowed, and my eyesight blurred.

He reached for an obscured door in the disability-friendly toilet cubicle and hauled me through, closing the door with a click.

Help me, God! Please! I stared at the barren white space ahead—a stark contrast to the dark sandwich-ordering areas—with several grey doors and a long corridor leading to who-knows-what terrifying places. Men of a bulkier, taller, meaner-looking persuasion than my captor passed by. One grizzly-looking character stared from beside a closed door.

My captor leaned closer, his breath hot against my ear. "I suggest you don't scream." Mint wafted with each word.

I blinked away tears.

He gestured toward the excessively tattooed stare bear ten metres away. "That big guy loves screamers. Turns him on, so keep your mouth shut."

My insides shriveled. I nodded under his hand.

Evil Auburn Model half-dragged, half-assisted me to a small

storage room across the open space. He closed the door behind us and grabbed something from a shelf.

I stared at his back, trembling. How had I ended up here?

He turned and pushed me face first toward the door.

My cheek and nose pounded against the cool wood.

In one swift motion he pulled my arms behind me and zip-tied my wrists together.

Pain scorched my wrists and tingled my palms. My chest seized. A second zip sounded, a second cable tightened into place. I muffled a scream, desperate not to attract the attention of the sadistic potential rapist on the other side of the door.

He flipped me around.

I hit the back of my head against the door. Stars flashed before my eyes, and my skull throbbed an incessant beat. Heat flushed my body, followed by sweat across my forehead and under my arms. Wooziness mingled with light-headedness, aggravating my stomach.

"Sorry, didn't mean that," he said, his voice gruff.

I refocused my eyes and slowed my breaths. *Do not faint!*

He removed several items from a shelf and shoved them into a black backpack.

A desire to strangle this pig of a man vibrated in my chest. I shook my head hoping to dispel the haze in my brain. "S-sorry? Sorry!" I hissed. "You ap-p-pologise for hitting my head"—the floor seemed to dissolve beneath my feet, and I slammed against his side—"but not for …" What was I saying?

He shoved me upright.

"For jabbing me in the …" My head flopped to the side. I flexed my slack muscles and concentrated on lifting my head up. *C'mon body, work with me!* "In-n n-neck an' abductin' me?" My words slurred.

Something flickered across his face before he clenched his jaw. Steel replaced his soft features. "If you wanna get out alive, I suggest you shut up and listen to everything I say. Understood?"

I slid to the floor. Tears overflowed my cheeks, and I shook with my face on my knees.

Evil Auburn Model squatted in front of me and lifted my head with gentle fingers. "Sorry, beautiful, just doing my job." He tucked the centre of a clean rag into my mouth, wrapped the corners around my head, and tied a hard knot at the back of my neck.

My lips chafed, and the sensitive corners of my mouth stretched and pulled. I had a sudden affinity for horses subjected to bits. And criminals held in handcuffs. Although handcuffs were sure to be looser than these cable-tie cuffs. Were my wrists already slashed and bleeding?

"We need to leave. Now." He threw the backpack over his shoulder, pulled me up, and opened the door. We re-entered the open space, where I could see the door leading back to the bathroom.

Where were we going now? To meet Tara? My breaths accelerated, and the room tilted. How could I escape these awful men? And why had I not studied to be a ninja? Those skills would be great to have. Or superpowers to zap the floor with lightning from my fingers. My feet slipped, and my attacker tightened his grip on my arm. Whoa.

The sadist approached us with a laugh. "Have fun in there, Loser? Looks like a feisty one." Drool pooled at the corner of his mouth. "Lemme have a turn."

My insides somersaulted, and bile burned my constricted throat.

My captor laughed a bitter, haughty laugh and squeezed my bottom.

I flinched inside. *Scream! Kick up a fuss!* But my voice and body refused to budge. Tears moistened my top lip.

He pulled me hard against his body.

I breathed in bold, sweet, and spicy cologne mingled with sweat … delicious. *No!* I wanted to kick and push away from his firm chest. Instead I pressed into him. The cable ties scratched his side, and friction burned my skin. This syringe-wielding ninja wrapped around my waist was safer than the hulk of a brute salivating in front of me.

"This one's all mine, Corey. She'll be a good ride." Evil Auburn Model pulled down my mouth gag.

I gasped for air—

He fused his mouth to mine in a savage kiss.

I froze. He tasted like peppermint. Peppermint and power. My paralysis gave way, and I chomped hard on his lip, drawing blood and a curse from him.

He smothered a cry and raised a hand toward my cheek. His

torso heaved on every breath.

My lungs seized, and I cowered. Blood thrummed in my ears, and my pulse thundered in my neck. My chest burned, and my bladder begged to empty its load down my legs. I prayed my brain cut off that particular signal.

My captor's hand stilled. He closed his eyes, inhaled a sharp intake of air, and wiped the back of his hand along his mouth. His eyelids fluttered open while blood smeared across his five o'clock shadow and bloodied his jaw.

My heartbeat doubled, and my mouth dried. I shook my head. Could I blame my foggy brain for the flare of warmth spiralling down my spine? Handsome and brutish, he now resembled a Scottish Highlander from Tara's TV show. I squeezed my eyelids closed, denying the fight between revulsion and attraction. I needed my head checked.

Corey snarled a frightening, gravelly laugh while my captor retied my mouth gag.

I glared at my handsome kidnapper. God, help me.

In one violent motion, Corey clutched my left breast with an animalistic growl.

My nerves exploded, and I screamed behind the cloth.

My captor punched Corey's hand away, his jaw rigid and eyes alight. "I said this one's mine. Back. Off."

Corey's crazy eyes gleamed. "You and your schoolgirl fetish. I hope you get as much as you give."

Evil Auburn Model tightened his grip around my waist and dragged me down a hallway.

Silent tears coursed my cheeks, blurring my vision. It seemed we travelled through twenty different corridors, but with my hazy head it may have only been five. What did it matter when my life was in danger?

A few minutes later, I was pushed through the doorway of a heavy, squeaky metal door. A cold gust of fresh air lapped against my arms, and the bright sunshine pierced my eyes. I squinted. Where was he taking me? What would he do when we reached his destination?

She'll be a good ride. His words echoed in my head. Sweat oozed from every available pore I possessed. I murmured a prayer. God would send someone across my path and rescue me. I blinked tears from my vision and focused on my surroundings. I needed to escape.

We stood in an expansive gravel car park with trucks and utes lined up for hundreds of metres. My captor dragged me to a muddy grey VW Amorak and opened the passenger door. He threw his backpack into the passenger footwell, then shoved me inside.

I fell on my left shoulder and hissed against the pain zinging down my arm. The door whacked my bottom, pinning my forehead to the centre console. I planted my left foot on the floor to right myself.

My captor filled the driver's seat and slammed the door. He reversed the vehicle, and its backward motion pushed my rear end against the glove box.

I hit the back of my head on his left hand, gripping the gearstick. The sudden motion loosened my mouth gag.

Evil Auburn Model swore. Loud. He wrenched his hand from under my head and shifted my shoulder so my head rested on the seat. Seconds later, he drove off like a man running from demons. Not a bad assumption after my recent taste of hell.

The ute halted a few minutes later. A huge sigh siphoned from my warden. "I'm going to sit you upright. Don't head butt me. Or bite." His voice rasped, his previous harshness nowhere to be heard. He slid closer in his seat, his thigh jammed against the centre console, and placed cautious hands around my waist. His intoxicating cologne permeated all the air I breathed.

I clenched my teeth.

He turned my body so my back rested against the passenger door before he pulled me into a seated position, my hands pinned behind my back. My head spun less than before, the haze in my brain floating away with each breath.

I focused on his unreadable expression.

He remained close, his torso leaning over the centre console, arm resting near my thigh. Heat billowed off his skin like concrete on a hot summer's day.

I arched my brow. How could he act like a pirate one minute and a saint the next? I turned and stared out the window to my left, sucking in large, deep breaths.

"We need to hurry," he said in a soft, low voice. "Look at me."

I had no desire baiting him so I turned.

His face was drawn, almost pained. "You need to listen. This's extremely important, you hear?"

My eyes watered. I nodded and focused on his face. The extreme burn in my wrists numbed me to all other pain.

My confusing captor retrieved a USB drive from his jacket pocket and held it up. "Once you're untied, hand this over immediately. You'll know when. This'll help the police find your friend."

What?

I creased my brow.

He wanted to help me? Why?

"It's important to hand it over and tell the police this'll crack the Black Dagger case." His gaze searched mine before glancing at my pants. "I'm gonna put this in your pocket now." He leaned closer and pushed the flash drive deep into my jeans pocket. His fingers warmed the cotton against my thigh.

Tingles danced down my leg. What was wrong with me?

He removed his hand in slow motion, then stared into my eyes.

My breath hitched, and my pulse raced.

His glazed dark-hazel eyes were edged with an exquisite ring of sapphire.

I squinted.

Were there tears in his eyes? How was this possible? I was the captive.

His intense scrutiny triggered warmth in my cheeks. Captor or not, his potency wrapped around my chest. What a twisted fantasy! Was this what people meant by Stockholm Syndrome?

His full lips curled into a boyish smile. "You're gorgeous."

The heat in my cheeks intensified, and my heart whumped.

I had to be sick. Damaged in the head.

Yes, my body had to be sick and damaged to respond like this.

"You're inexperienced with men, aren't you?"

What kind of question was that? My cheeks flamed.

His eyes darkened. "Stay that way. Save yourself for a man who gives you his all … h-his life." His voice croaked.

The air thinned, and I heaved my breaths.

Why was he acting … human?

A heaviness in his voice called to my soul. Other than Dad, no other man had spoken so directly, yet with such conviction, to me. I could almost imagine my nameless bandit ... cared?

He leaned closer, hesitated, then stretched forward, and kissed my lips.

My chest jolted. Softness and warmth in the midst of terror, a slight metallic edge mixed with peppermint freshness. A kiss I imagined Mr. Darcy shared with Lizzy. All gentleness and propriety.

Apart from the whole hostage-scenario thing.

Gosh, I needed to have my head read, pronto. And what was with me being kissed by jerks?

But ... *was* this man, with soft lips and firm yet gentle hands now holding my face, truly a brute?

I pressed closer.

Fireworks burst behind my closed eyes.

He moaned and wrapped a firm arm around my waist.

I parted my lips and allowed the sensations blooming under my skin to take control. My skin pulsated with each gentle caress, melting my insides until my hunger intensified.

Holy guacamole. We had somehow tapped into a deep current of connection. My mouth craved the kiss of a man I barely knew, a man I had hated moments before.

I was definitely sick.

Our face-to-face session ended when my captor slash best-kiss-of-my-life broke free from my fevered lips. His chest heaved in tandem with mine, both of us breathless. Whatever had passed between us was more than physical. It was almost ... spiritual.

His tender gaze stroked my face before an impenetrable wall of detachment slid into place. "I need to put the gag back on. Remember Black Dagger."

What?

Oh. Yes. *Black Dagger.*

I nodded, kiss-drunk from the nameless stranger.

He tightened the gag with more care than the first time and started the engine.

Moments later, we stopped in a laneway next to the North Melbourne Police Station. He pulled his phone from his pocket and sent a quick text, then reached over my lap for the bag at my feet, unzipping and removing a handgun from the backpack.

Adrenaline shot through my bloodstream, and my eyes widened.

My muzzled noises filled the cab while he checked the gun and loaded the chamber.

"I'm not going to hurt you, beautiful. Especially after that parting gift. Trust me and follow my lead." He leaned forward, tucked the gun into the back of his jeans, and stepped from the vehicle before opening the passenger door and assisting me through the police station entry.

From this point, everything happened in slow motion. He pulled the gun out and pointed it at my right temple. Onlookers' screams echoed inside the foyer, my own shouts muffled in my mouth. People scrambled from the room or dropped to the floor. Colours flashed across my vision, and blood pumped in my ears. Police officers removed guns from their holsters, uttering unknown words.

The cool steel on my temple shook, and I squeezed my eyes shut. Warmth spilled down my pants leg. Pressure from the gun barrel vanished, along with the press of his chest at my back.

I opened my eyes and turned.

His lips now wrapped around the metal, his blue-rimmed gaze cloudy.

I screamed behind my gag. Heat stung my eyes.

With collective tears, he released my waist in a final squeeze and pulled the trigger, shattering my eardrums.

CHAPTER TEN
Reverberations

"Diana?"

I opened my eyes and scrunched my face. My head throbbed, and my ears rang. My right ear pulsated, dulled to softer sounds.

A female police officer crouched in front of me.

Her auburn hair glinted in the fluorescent lights, and I was thrown back to another head of auburn hair with striking hazel-and-sapphire-rimmed eyes.

My stomach dropped, and I searched the unfamiliar room, starting with the brown tweed couch underneath me. I blinked as a ticking sound grew in volume.

Near the open doorway, the seconds hand erased time on a wall clock. Time I wished to reverse and delete. But my mind re-played his final moments.

Widened eyes and stiff legs.

Thinned lips stretched around metal.

I clamped my eyes tight, trying to quash the memories.

Grooves etched into his forehead, creases around his eyes.

A final, pained glance before he shuttered his lids and pulled the trigger.

Warm brain matter and flesh splattering my face and tangling in my hair.

My insides heaved, and I dry retched.

Stop.

Please stop.

"Diana?"

I opened my eyes. An uncontrollable sob inside my chest surfaced.

The officer rose from her haunches, grabbed a glass of water from a nearby table, and helped me sip.

The cool liquid soothed my parched throat. I wiped tears from my cheeks. "Wh-where am I?"

"Still at the police station. I'm Constable Lissing. You've been in a daze the past two hours." She glanced at my lap.

I glanced down and realised my hands shook. Bandages covered my wrists.

"Another female officer and I cleaned you up as best as we could and have contacted your parents. It's a good thing you had your driver's licence and credit card in your jeans pocket."

A good thing. Dad had drilled the habit to keep my ID and an emergency credit card tucked into my pocket while I lived in Melbourne. I had remembered the cash to buy lunch but forgot my phone. One less thing to have lost in the mess of today.

I peered at the oversized navy-blue tracksuit pants I now wore and lifted my gaze to the Constable, her features grave. Of course, I knew the answer but needed to ask the question. "What happened to … to … him?"

Constable Lissing drew in a deep breath. "He died at the scene. How did you know the offender?"

Dead. How could he not be? But why had he done what he did?

I cleared my vicelike throat. "He a-abducted me from a sandwich shop. Near the Queen Vic Market." I scratched my temple. My head hurt. "It doesn't make sense," I whispered. Why had he grabbed me? And lied about Tar—Tara! My pulse quickened. "My friend Tara was with me." Burgeoning tears overspilled.

Constable Lissing nodded. "What happened to your friend?"

"I … I don't know. They must have her. The buff, scary men." The sadistic guy's face infiltrated my mind. I shivered and covered my mouth with my hand. "He might have her."

"Who might have her? Diana? Who has your friend?"

Memories jolted in my brain, and I delved into my front pocket. Ow! My bandaged wrist screamed from the fast movement. Oh, right. I wore different pants. "My jeans pocket! Oh no, I—"

"The flash drive?" Constable Lissing sprang and retrieved my credit card, driver's licence, and the USB drive from the table.

"Yes!" I clutched my things. "Here. Take this." I dropped the technology into her outstretched hand. "He said it related to … to

…" I growled when his words escaped me.

Constable Lissing occupied the couch cushion beside me. "Take a deep breath in and slowly breathe out. Allow your mind to calm. Breathe in and out. In. Out."

I breathed as instructed, and my body relaxed, releasing my memories. The phrase I needed leaped into my short-term memory, and I almost laughed. "Black Dagger. He said it related to Black Dagger." Would it really help Tara?

The Constable's eyes widened, and her face paled. She rose and walked to the doorway. "I'll be back shortly. Why don't you use the blanket at the end of the couch and lie down for a bit?" Whatever I had said meant something.

"Wait! Please." I scraped my bottom lip between my teeth. "Can I … am I allowed to know … his first name?" I wiped my palms on my knees. "I just think if I have a name, maybe I can…" I shrugged.

"We haven't identified the offender yet." She pursed her lips. "But we should know soon. Get some rest." She disappeared down a short corridor.

I'm not going to hurt you, beautiful. Especially after that parting gift.

I gasped, and tears brimmed my eyes. This had been his plan all along? A suicide mission? My chest burned, and wetness trickled down my cheeks. Had he been so desperate, death was his only option? I shuddered a breath, and pain banded across my chest. My heart broke for the auburn-haired boy on a suicide mission. One which had intersected with my life. Had he saved me from a worse fate? A sheep dressed in a wolf onesie?

My teeth chattered. I grasped the woollen blanket, shook the fabric out, and lay it along the couch. Too short a sofa for me to lie with my legs extended, I lay in a semi-foetal posture, comforted in my curled-up side position. I now understood why victims in movies rocked themselves into a ball. I slid underneath the weighted blanket, positioned the couch cushion under my aching head, and closed my eyes.

Darkness descended inside and overcame my desire to think, the pull of sleep lulling me from my uncertain reality.

♥ ♥ ♥ ♥ ♥ ♥ ♥

"Diana, darling. Wake up, sweetheart." Victoria's voice roused me from a dreamless sleep.

My eyelids fluttered, and I squinted at the bright surrounds of the simple station room.

Dad and Victoria came into view.

I yawned. "Hi."

The ghost of a smile lifted the corner of Dad's mouth. Wetness shimmered in Victoria's eyes.

"Where's my Jazzy bear?" I shifted and groaned.

Dad lunged forward and assisted me into an upright position on the couch, his firm hands steadying my shoulders.

My adrenaline spiked, and I fought the impulse to shake him off.

Victoria claimed a place on the couch beside me and wrapped an arm behind my back.

I stiffened, my breaths shallow. *Relax, Diana.*

"Stacy's watching her for us," Victoria said. "She was playing with Toby and Ella when we left, possibly ransacking your bedroom in search of Sissy Di-Di."

I sighed, releasing the tension from my shoulders, and imagined Jasmine searching for me under my bed and in my wardrobe. My aching heart squeezed.

Dad pulled a chair from the nearby table to the couch. He lowered onto the seat and cleared his throat. Pain flickered in his dark-brown eyes. "You gave us a huge scare, Princess. I was going to call in a favour from Steve if we were pulled over for speeding."

Victoria pursed her lips and nodded. "Your father did some low flying today."

I dropped my gaze, clasped my hands together, and squeezed my fingers between my knees. "I hope you didn't drive like a complete maniac with my sister in the back seat."

Victoria huffed a laugh. "We didn't travel that fast, but it was close." She brushed a hand across my brow and kissed my forehead.

I pulled away, hard. "I-I haven't showered yet. There might be … bits on me still."

Tears sparkled in Victoria's eyes. She reached out and squeezed my hands, now fisted in my lap.

Dad's jaw stiffened. His chin vibrated. "What sick scumbag

abducts a girl, then paints his flipping brains all over her at point-blank range?"

"Don't say that," I whispered.

His mouth slackened.

"That so-called sick scumbag saved my life." *He ruined it too.* I swiped tears from my face with tingling fingers. "Today really sucked." My hands tremored, and a sharp pain twisted in my chest.

"I know." His deep voice cracked.

Vibrations jolted my entire body, and I crumpled onto Victoria's lap with a keening wail.

Victoria wrapped a firm arm around me and stroked my hair. Each gentle touch extracted my anguished cries. Tears, snot, and saliva saturated her pants leg while my sobs drained me.

"God promises new mercies every morning," Victoria whispered. "Today may have been horrid, but tomorrow's a new day."

My cries subsided, and with a sigh I grabbed hold of the promise. A new day would dawn.

Someone tapped the doorframe, and I glanced up.

Constable Lissing focused on me. "Just checking on you."

I sat up and wiped my palms across my face. "Thanks."

She glanced between me and my parents. "Did you need anything?" She nodded to her left. "Bathroom break?" She widened her eyes ever so slightly.

I furrowed my brow, snuck a glance at Dad and Victoria on either side of me, and nodded. "Yeah."

"Want me to come with you?" Victoria asked.

I shook my head. "I'll be fine."

The Constable smiled at my shellshocked family. "I'll escort her."

I stood and followed her down the corridor.

Constable Lissing paused outside the ladies' bathroom door and monitored the empty walkway. "His name is Pierce," she whispered.

Pierce. I had shared an amazing, shameful kiss with Pierce. My skin heated. "Thank you." I stepped into the bathroom on unsteady legs, unsure whether to be thankful or regretful for this new information.

♥ ♥ ♥ ♥ ♥ ♥ ♥

"This might sting a little." The nurse at St. Vincent's Hospital wiped the damaged skin around my wrists.

I hissed against the burn and squeezed away my constant tears. The smell of disinfectant nauseated me.

Victoria squeezed my knee, her sweet smile anchoring me in the midst of the bright, noisy emergency room cubicle. Dad stood near the foot of my bed, rigid and alert like a sentry on duty.

"The officer who initially treated your wounds did a great job." The nurse narrowed her eyes, turning my wrists over and under. "You have a type-two skin tear, but with your age and history of good health, you're low on our risk assessment."

"And that's a good thing?" I stared at the red raw rings with slight skin flaps where friction had worn through layers of skin.

"It is." She dragged a narrow metal-and-plastic wheeled cart to the side of the bed, ripped open a package, removed a sterile gauze, and attended to my wounds. "You'll need to come back in a few days' time for redressing, so please keep these dry."

"Okay."

She covered the mesh dressings on each wrist with another layer of bandage and smiled at me. "And as long as infection doesn't set in, these should heal nicely."

"What about scarring?" Victoria arched her brow.

Scarring? My throat dried. "C-could I have scars?"

The nurse pursed her lips. "From my experience with trauma like this, I believe you should heal without issue. There's always the possibility of scarring, but in your case, it would be faint and, hopefully, unnoticeable."

Victoria shared a glance with Dad. "Not noticeable like surgical scars."

"Correct. That's why we avoid using sutures in this type of scenario."

"Good." Victoria's shoulders seemed to ease.

The nurse glanced at Victoria and turned back to me. "Any more questions?"

"Not that I can think of." My brain hurt from thinking. And fighting the exhausting flashbacks.

The nurse filled out some paperwork and handed me the documents. "Then you're free to go. Get some rest and take care,

Diana."
"Thank you," I whispered.

CHAPTER ELEVEN
Inside Out

I glanced in the police station bathroom mirror and splashed cold water on my face. The refreshing coolness did nothing to ease my climbing nerves and churning stomach. "I can do this," I whispered. What alternative remained? I needed to tell the officer *everything*.

Ripping a few disposable hand towels from the wall, I dabbed my face, muttered a heartfelt prayer for strength, and exited the ladies' room.

"Ready?" Uncle Steve nodded toward the small office where I had been giving my witness statement for the last hour. Just over twenty-four hours had passed since Pierce destroyed my life.

I nodded and returned to my chair in front of the desk Officer Shultz—whose rank I had forgotten immediately—still rested behind.

Uncle Steve closed the door and hunkered on the seat next to me.

Officer Shultz puckered his lips as he reviewed his laptop screen. "Okay. The last thing you said was, 'He slipped a USB into my pocket and said to tell the police that this would crack the Black Dagger case.'" He lifted his head and regarded me. "What happened next?"

I glanced at my lap, where my hands were balled together. Heat rose to my cheeks.

"Take your time," Officer Shultz said.

I squeezed my eyes tight and relived the bittersweet memory of our kiss. Our deplorable, delectable, peppermint-flavoured physical exchange.

Uncle Steve pulled my hand into his.

I glanced at him. Tears pooled in my eyes. "You still promise not to tell Dad and Victoria?"

Uncle Steve's eyes softened. "I promise I won't disclose a detail unless you give me permission." He released my hand.

I abhorred the idea of sharing every minute detail of my encounter with my parents, so at Dad and Victoria's request, I allowed Uncle Steve to accompany me to the station. I found his presence comforting, and after living under his roof for over a year, I believed he would keep my story confidential.

I glanced at the leafy green plant in the corner of the room. "He kissed me."

Officer Shultz tapped the keyboard. "With aggression like the previous occasion?"

"No." I snuck a furtive glance at Uncle Steve, his features unreadable, although a permanent line had creased his brow all interview. "This was different. The … the kind of kiss you don't want to end." My face burned. Why had I admitted this out loud? "A … goodbye kiss of sorts."

Officer Shultz hummed. "And after this?"

I furrowed my brow. "He reminded me about Black Dagger, re-tied my gag, and pocketed the gun."

"Did the offender ever mention his involvement with Black Dagger?"

"No. Nothing like that. But he made sure I knew exactly what to say, that it was important." I licked my lips. "Can I assume my friend Tara is now mixed up in whatever Black Dagger is? Do you have any information about her yet?" Was she still with those men? Had they hurt her? Or worse? I muffled a cry behind my palm. My pulse escalated, a perfect match to my quivering hands.

Officer Shultz steadied his gaze on me. "We're actively following all leads to find your friend."

I gritted my molars. This was the second time today an officer was unable to tell me anything about Tara's whereabouts. "But surely you know something. I … I'm worried about her."

Uncle Steve touched my shoulder.

"As this is an ongoing investigation, I can't share anything. I'm sorry." Officer Shultz cleared his throat. "After the reminder, what happened?"

I sighed. "He assisted me into this police station, and I'm sure there're plenty of witnesses to tell you what happened next." I slumped against the seat back, exhaustion taking its toll on my mind and body.

"Let me print this off, then you can have a read and, if you're happy with it, sign off on it." Officer Shultz stood and exited the room.

"You did great."

I turned to Uncle Steve. "You say that to everyone giving statements?"

His soft chuckle loosened a level of tension in my chest. "Maybe. But in this case, it's true."

I rubbed my eyes. "Once I sign this thing, can we leave?"

Uncle Steve smiled. "I believe so, and I'd love to escort you home."

I lay on my bed in the same crumpled hoodie and leggings I wore yesterday—and slept in last night—staring at the bland white ceiling. City sounds leaked through my closed bedroom window, vibrant Melbourne life despite the chilled early-afternoon temperature outside. I wiped away a tear tickling my earlobe, thankful to hear white noise once again instead of the constant ringing in my ears.

I sighed and wished everything else could revert back to "normal" instead of Victoria and Aunt Stacy whispering in soothing tones, fluttering over me on my bed or the Morgans' couch. I could cope with Jasmine and Ella climbing onto my lap for endless hugs and Toby displaying his Duplo creations. But Dad? He had hovered like I was a helpless newborn—letting me out of his sight only when I needed to use the bathroom or get dressed—until Victoria and Stacy's friend, Amber Jones, had given him some work updating her kitchen. Something about new white goods to match her sexy marble benchtop.

Someone tapped against my closed bedroom door.

I grumbled, accidentally bumped my wrist on the bed, and hissed. The nurse had said, while changing my dressing this morning, that the pain should diminish over the next week or so. I stared at my new, thinner wrist coverings and wheezed a breath. Over ninety-six hours since Pierce upended my world and shattered every fragile, tenuous, and untethered part of me.

"Diana?" The door squeaked open. "You awake?" Aunt Stacy stepped into the room.

So much for pretending to nap. I lifted my blurry vision and met her scrutiny.

She furrowed her brow. "I know you're tired after your appointment, but I need to make you a little more presentable." She grasped my hand and assisted me upright. "Steve just called. He'll be here in a few minutes to take you to the station."

I thought my witness statement was all the police required? "Isn't he at work?"

"Yes, which makes me more curious." Aunt Stacy extracted a clean long-sleeved top, a pair of jeans, and socks from my chest of drawers, piled them on my rumpled bed, and located my favourite canvas shoes under my bed.

I nodded at the pile of clothing. "Thanks."

She smiled and stepped toward the door. "I'll leave you to it."

I fumbled my way into my clothes and pulled a comb through my hair. After I looped my long locks into a messy topknot, I plodded down the stairs and slumped on the couch.

"You're up, sweetheart." Victoria smiled from the floor where she played with Jasmine and Ella.

The little girls squealed and leaped onto my lap.

I wrapped them in my arms and squeezed them both to my chest.

Victoria laughed. "A-plus for enthusiasm, but take it easy, little ladies."

Jasmine sandwiched my cheeks between her plump hands. "Play?"

Uncle Steve stepped through the archway in his operational winter uniform, including his navy-blue cap bearing the Victoria Police badge atop a strip of Sillitoe Tartan.

"Daddy!" Ella tore away from my arms, planting a sharp kick to my gut in the process, and launched at Uncle Steve's legs.

He lifted his daughter with an effortless sweep, grinning, and kissed her cheek. "Hey, Muffin."

Ella's little brow creased. "Daddy play horsey?"

"No, baby, Daddy's here to take Diana to the police station." He lowered his gaze to me, his blue eyes indecipherable.

"Everything all right?" Victoria glanced between me and her cousin.

"Yep." Uncle Steve cleared his throat. "Ready?

I kissed Jasmine's dark curls. "I'd better go."

We exited the house and strode to a shiny squad car.

I regarded the late-model SUV. "Is this an official visit? Should I be worried?"

Uncle Steve smiled and opened the passenger door for me. "Detective Calhoun asked me to escort you to the North Melbourne station." Detective Calhoun oversaw the Black Dagger investigation.

Did the detective require more information from me?

We travelled the brief drive in silence, my insides tossing the entire car ride. Once we reached our destination, Uncle Steve signaled to the unfamiliar officer manning the front desk and discussed something in low tones.

"This way." Uncle Steve accompanied me to the office room I had given my witness statement. "Just sit tight, and I'll see if the detective's ready for you." He closed the door.

"Okay." My voice squeaked, and I hunched against the seat. Everything in the room appeared the same apart from the missing laptop. I fidgeted my fingers and fought against the memories.

The kind of kiss you don't want to end.

Heat spread to my cheeks and neck, and my throat thickened. I closed my eyes and pressed my fingertips to my lips. Soft, dewy warmth. Rasping prickles from his rough stubble. Peppermint with the tang of blood. And the augmenting heat zapping in my core, the most frightening part of all.

"Miss Jacobsen?" Detective Calhoun's deep voice catapulted me to the present.

I turned to Uncle Steve and the detective who stood near the now-open doorway and covered my fiery cheeks with my palms.

Uncle Steve occupied the seat beside me.

The detective rounded the desk and dropped to the chair. "I've asked you to come in today because we have news about Tara."

I gasped and glanced at both men. "Did you find her?"

Detective Calhoun pressed his lips together. "Through the

information stored on the flash drive you provided, we were able to trace her location."

My heart rebounded inside my ribcage. "Y-you found her?"

He nodded. "Yesterday afternoon."

"Thank You, God," I whispered. Tears sprang to my eyes. "May I see her?"

The men glanced at each other. Something passed between them.

Detective Calhoun cleared his throat. "Tara sustained some injuries and spent overnight in the hospital but is here with her mother in another private room down the hallway."

"Tara's here?" My pulse thumped.

He nodded. "Her mother wants to speak with you."

Tara's mum? I furrowed my brow. "Am I able to see Tara too?"

He exhaled a long breath. "She's endured a significant trauma. I can't guarantee she'll want to see you."

I nodded, leaned forward, and wrapped my arms around my waist. *Please help her get through this, God.* My eyesight blurred.

A few moments later, Detective Calhoun ushered a petite, middle-aged woman into the room before the detective and Uncle Steve exited.

I stood and offered a soft smile to the lady with a cute blonde bob and button nose, similar to Tara's. "Hi, Ms. Roberts."

She stared back with red-rimmed eyes. "Diana." Tara's mum wrapped her arms around me. "Thank you for bringing my baby home sooner." She squeezed me and stepped back. "And, please, call me Alannah."

We lowered to the available chairs.

I brushed aside a tear. "How is she?"

Alannah's chin trembled, and tears trickled down her face. "Not good." She shuddered a sigh. "I hope she gets through this. My girl's strong, but I'm not sure she's strong enough for this. Only time will tell."

Please help my friend, God. My lungs cramped. I balled my shaking hands in my lap.

Alannah lay her hand over mine. "And you, love? How are you?"

"I … I don't know," I whispered. Compared to Tara, my ordeal must have been a drag in the park.

She stroked my tense fingers. "You'll get there, I'm sure."

With Jesus, I was sure too. I met her gaze. "Are you taking Tara home to Swan Hill?"

Alannah nodded. "Once we complete her statement, we'll head home. The police said we can communicate over the phone should they need us."

"I'm sure she'll appreciate a familiar place to … rest." Another reason I wanted to go home to Tellarine as planned.

"I've suggested she take a leave of absence from RMIT." She wiped away another tear. "This is going to take more than the remaining holiday break for her to recover."

I nodded. Uni was the last thing on my mind at the moment. "May I see her?"

She pressed her lips together and scrutinised me. After a moment, she nodded. "Come with me."

I followed her down the short hallway to a room with its internal window shutters drawn.

Alannah approached the closed door. "Give me a minute."

"Okay." I waited in the hall inspecting the carpet, my hands in my pockets.

"Come in," Alannah said.

I stepped into the small room, closed the door, and stifled a gasp.

Tara perched on a chair near a desk with rigid shoulders and a straight back. A small bandage covered one side of her neck, and thick white dressings coiled her wrists. Sallow cheeks, pale skin, and vacant eyes focused on the wall completed the bleak picture.

Tears tracked my cheeks. I inched closer, brushing my fingers along my wet face.

Tara raised her head and met my gaze. The first flicker of emotion shadowed her features, and her eyes clouded.

I dropped to my knees and wrapped my arms around her waist.

Her sobs vibrated through me, matching my own. What had she suffered during the three longs days of her captivity?

My breaths quickened, and I held her tighter. "I was so worried." My voice sounded thin, strained.

Tara pressed closer.

We remained in this position for who-knows-how-long until a warm, firm hand touched my shoulder.

I twisted and met Uncle Steve's intense inspection.

"Tara needs to complete her statement so she can go home."

I nodded and turned back to my broken friend. "Stay in touch?"

"Okay," she whispered. Her mournful eyes pierced my heart.

I stood and kissed her forehead. "Love you." After another silent prayer for my friend, I followed Uncle Steve to his vehicle, my insides splintered.

CHAPTER TWELVE
A Brief Intermission

Victoria rested her hand on my shoulder. "Are you all packed?"

"Yes." My luggage had remained packed since—*stop*. I fingered Aunt Stacy's pastel-coloured, crocheted blanket over my legs and stared at the landscape painting on the Morgans' lounge room wall, avoiding Victoria's gaze.

"Would you like a cup of tea? Or hot chocolate before we depart?"

"No thanks."

Six days had passed since our worlds disintegrated. Six whole days of dizzying blurs and fractured snapshots.

"You haven't eaten much today, sweetheart. How about a sandwich?"

My eyes widened, and my stomach churned.

Victoria's face paled. "I'm sorry. I didn't think." She covered her mouth with her hand.

"It's okay," I whispered.

"I'm sorry." Victoria cleared her throat. "What about some fruit? Or veggies and dip?"

"Veggies and dip sound nice." My chest loosened when she smiled. "Thanks."

Victoria stared at me for a long second, sighed, and walked into the kitchen. My family still tiptoed around me, careful not to upset the basket case I was and spiral me into another sob fest. Aunt Stacy had passed on information for a city therapist, but I wanted to go home to Tellarine for the semester break as planned. I had my twentieth birthday to "celebrate" tomorrow ... and a life to re-establish.

I checked my phone for messages. Nothing from Tara. Still. My shoulders sagged, and I thumbed the phone screen. Two days since I saw her and she travelled home.

What demons was she wrestling right now? Would she want to hear from me? My chest squeezed, and I expelled a shaky breath. Her lack of reply to my text message yesterday might be her answer.

I stared at our message thread and bit my lower lip. We were comrades-in-arms in a way, battling the after-effects of this ordeal. A phone call would show my support.

I pressed the screen with a clammy finger and dialed Tara's number. Straight to voicemail. I cleared my throat. "Hey, Tar, it's me again. I, ah, just wanted to let you know I'm thinking of you and praying for you." I squeezed my phone against my ear and wiped away tears. "Love you." I disconnected the call, lay back against the couch cushions, and closed my eyes.

I've suggested she take a leave of absence from RMIT.

Alannah's words sprang back to my memory and bounced around my brain. That seed dropped into my subconscious, ready for when I dared contemplate the future.

On returning home, my efforts to re-establish my life were thwarted. Flashbacks battered me without a moment's notice and froze any ability to form a sensible thought. By the time the mid-term break drew to a close, I still favoured the comfort of my bed.

"Princess?"

I startled and dropped the book I stared at. My heartbeat and pulse skyrocketed.

Dad and Victoria huddled on the end of my bed.

How long had I zoned out for?

"Come here for a moment." Dad's voice echoed in my quiet room. He patted the bed, his smile welcoming.

I climbed from the covers and nestled between them.

Victoria cleared her throat. "Dad and I think you should consider taking a twelve-month leave of absence from your studies. It'll give you space to heal."

I glanced between them.

"We'd love to have you here with us, and you know Jazzy'll think all her Christmases have come at once if you lived here for a year." Dad winked.

The urge to smile for the first time in weeks tugged at my lips. I leaned into Dad's shoulder.

He wrapped an arm around me before he kissed the top of my head. "But you're an adult and need to make this decision for yourself. Victoria and I will support you however you decide."

I bit my lower lip. "I-I've been thinking something similar."

Victoria leaned in and squeezed my knee. "So you'll think about it?"

"Yes. I'm almost … excited by the prospect." I smiled. "And the irony of excitement over my life being put on hold isn't lost on me."

Dad and Victoria chuckled, and the sounds cocooned me like a warm blanket.

"You'll need to decide before Friday," Victoria said. "The RMIT admin team need to transfer you to next year's classes instead of failing you for not showing up after Tuesday."

"I'll give you an answer tomorrow."

✒ ✒ ✒ ✒ ✒ ✒ ✒

12 July

I've put off writing this entry for several weeks now, but it's time I shared with you. Since my last rant about the pressure of meeting my final assessments for the semester, my life has taken a twist in the wrong direction. In many ways I wish you were here, Mum, but I'm glad you're not able to witness the mess I am.

I made a really bad decision. I didn't listen to the unsettled voice inside telling me to leave and have paid the consequences with my soul. Not in an eternal life way (don't worry, I still love Jesus and hope my heart fills to overflowing with His love like yours did) but I feel like my innocence is gone. Is that cliché?

I was attacked by a man. Drugged and bound. I've never felt such dread before, Mum. In that moment when I realised what was happening, I was so afraid. My faith seemed to fly away as fear strangled me. I'm not sure I even prayed. I hope I did, but some of my memories in that heat of panic still escape me.

Since I'm writing this, you know I survived. But I'm petrified I'm forever changed on the inside. And on the outside if my wrists scar. And the worst part? I can't erase his kiss from my brain. He kissed me, and it was the most amazing feeling I've experienced. Maybe my heightened emotions added to its impact, but I'll never forget that intimate moment. I hate myself for it because it's just so … wrong.

I'm scared, Mum. Scared of where to go from here. Of the choices I need to make, and the boldness I'll need to pull out of thin air to take those steps.

I wish I could hug you.

CHAPTER THIRTEEN
Undercurrent

A week later, I was still a semi-vacant blob on my bed. A sudden pang for familiar company and comfort whacked my chest. I retrieved my long-ignored phone, scrolled through the plethora of unanswered texts from friends at university—except for Tara, who had sent a one-word reply of "thanks" last week—and typed out a message.

Me: HEY. ANY CHANCE YOU'RE HOME? I NEED A K-MAN HUG.

Barely thirty seconds passed before a message sounded on my phone.

Keanu: YOU STILL IN TOWN?

I sighed. It was nice to know I was not town gossip. Yet.

Me: LONG STORY SHORT I'M ON A LEAVE OF ABSENCE FROM RMIT.

Me: CAN YOU COME OVER?

I missed my friend. The last year and a half had been filled with studies and homework, and my messages to Keanu had become few and far between.

Keanu: BE THERE IN 30. WANT ANYTHING FROM THE BAR?

I huffed a breathy laugh at the inside joke. I had never consumed alcohol with Keanu—or anyone else—and he thought it funny since he lived and breathed his role at Benanu's.

Me: ALCOHOL TO DROWN MY SORROWS?

Keanu: THAT BAD?

Keanu: SEE YOU SOON

Me: THANKS XX

Tears pooled in my eyes, and my breaths hitched. I slid under my purple-and-lemon doona and snuggled into the covers.

I woke to a gentle knock and subsequent creak of my bedroom door. I must have dozed off.

"Diana, darling," Dad whispered.

"Mmm, yeah?"

"Keanu's here."

I rolled over to face him.

"I told him you were resting, but he was adamant you'd asked him to come over. Is this true?"

I sat up, rubbed my eyes, and nodded.

Dad grunted. He narrowed his eyes and stared at me. "You know I like the boy, but—"

"I want to talk to him." I huffed a breath. "It's not like we're going to do anything inappropriate."

His eyes flashed.

"C'mon, Dad."

He grunted again. "I'll send him up." Dad turned to leave.

"Promise me you won't threaten him or punch his face in?"

Another grunt met my ears.

"And please promise you won't hit the roof if you happen to find him here in the mornin—"

"Diana." Dad's controlled, low tone warned against argument.

I had pushed his overprotective-father buttons, but I needed his trust. "Promise me. We're not going to make out or anything stupid like that." Dads could be so annoying. "Please. Give me a little length on that tight leash you're holding."

He rubbed the back of his neck. His shoulders dropped, and the fire in his eyes disappeared. "I promise I won't punch his lights out, knock his block off, or threaten him bodily harm."

I smiled and blew him a kiss. "Thanks. Love you."

"Love you too, Princess." He smiled, turned, and walked down the hallway.

Minutes later, a large shadow fell across my bed. I glanced up at Keanu leaning against the doorframe, his broad forearms flexed across his chest.

"Nice room, J-Bird."

"Thanks." I patted the bed next to me. "Wanna sit?"

Keanu's gaze darted from me and back over his shoulder. "You sure ya dad won't kill me? Mr. J. looked ready to throw my butt outta the house."

"You're fine. Dad promised not to harm you, so you've a free pass. You're the first guy in my bedroom." I smiled. "Super special."

He walked into my room—his steps seeming to falter—and closed the door. "Super special, like the pizza yer dad'll make outta my face."

I snorted a laugh and patted the bed. "No wonder I love you. You're so much fun." Melancholy pressed hard against my chest. "I need some fun," I whispered. "I want to move on with my life."

Keanu lowered onto my bed and opened his arms.

I crawled onto his lap and snuggled in, my eyes stinging.

He wrapped his strong arms around me and rocked back and forth. His familiar scent embraced me.

Tears rolled down my cheeks. Deep sobs quivered in my throat and racked my body in shudders. Bone-deep despair seeped into the marrow of my soul and multiplied its cells of sorrow.

Keanu held me close.

"I'm sorry." My voice cracked with another sob.

He kissed the top of my head and squeezed my knee lightly.

"I want to move on to … to live my life without constant memories. I want to be happy. I want …"

"What?"

I choked on thick tears. "I want to be *me*."

Keanu cupped my jaw, raised my face, and surveilled my eyes. "What happened?"

My throat dried under his intense focus. "Promise me you won't get upset."

He clenched his jaw and ground his teeth, then puffed out a breath. "Not sure I can do that."

I pouted and widened my eyes.

He sighed. "Okay, I promise."

"You need to stay calm when I tell my story. I can't have you losing it and punching the wall or breaking my bedroom window—"

"How bad is it?" He furrowed his brow.

I shrugged. "Pretty bad … not as bad as it could've been." Not like Tara. My throat jammed.

His chest vibrated against me, and his breaths quickened.

I waited for his breathing to slow. Over the years of our

friendship, I had learned to read him and interpret his body language. When we were younger, he used to explode like a hidden landmine in a hostile desert. Seemed he used whatever skills he possessed tonight.

With his slow nod, our gazes locked, and I shared my experience. Every second … except for the kiss. My stomach curdled. No more people could know about that shameful moment.

A tidal wave of expressions flooded Keanu's face. Several tears escaped down his cheeks, dripping from the dimple in his chin, and sucker-punched me.

When my tears renewed, I clutched his shirt. Silent sobs shook my body and reverberated off the mass of bone and muscle cradling me.

"I …" His soft voice wavered. "I'm so sad right now."

"I know the feeling." I sniffed and wiped my nose along my sleeve. "But now you know, I need you to help me find my way back. You gotta make me feel normal again." The familiar tightness ramped up in my chest. "I need normal."

He planted a tender kiss on my head. "You got it. Normal, but with a twist."

"What do you mean?"

"You need to get outta the house, yeah, but need to do it with confidence."

I narrowed my eyes. "And how d'you plan on accomplishing this? I'm more nervous than a romance reader reaching the final quarter of an awesome novel. Whenever I contemplate walking out the door, I …" I wiped my wet cheeks. "An activity that's remotely normal … frightens me."

"That's okay because the next time ya step outta the house, I'll be with you."

I had made the right decision inviting him over tonight. "Thanks, K-Man."

"Anytime. Now, let's get you cleaned up so we can go out."

The air in my lungs stuck to my ribs like thick molasses. "W-what? Now?"

A dimple appeared in his cheek, and his eyes sparkled. "Outta those trackie daks and into something semi-sexy. We're going out. I'll wait downstairs with the chocolate mousse I stashed in the fridge. A little dose of comfort food, then we're off to work." With a kiss on my temple and a push forcing my feet to the floor, Keanu exited my bedroom.

I stared at the closed door, my heartbeat thundering. I turned to my wardrobe and stared at my outfits. A cute purple long-sleeved top called to me, so I matched it with hip-hugger jeans, boots, and my favourite trench coat. My insides eased when I settled at my mirrored chest of drawers and applied a light layer of foundation, mascara, and lip gloss. I smacked my lips together and smiled at my reflection. "You can do this, Diana Nicole. You can do this by the grace of God."

After a final inspection, I headed downstairs to Keanu and what I hoped to be a fear-free future.

I shifted my legs along the bed and stared at the open page of my novel. Just over a week had passed since Keanu forced me out of the house and into the familiar sounds and smells of his second home. While we stuffed our faces with chicken tenders and fat potato wedges at Benanu's, Keanu and I had formulated a plan toward becoming "normal Diana". Step one, to leave the house, was ticked off straight away, lifting my spirits at the microscopic progress. Next step was to find a part-time job, earn a little cash, and expose myself to interactions with different people in the safety of a workplace.

I closed the book and sighed. I had made three calls in the last six days for casual jobs I found online. Not the effort I expect Keanu had imagined.

He had offered me a job waiting tables at Benanu's, but having witnessed the odd inebriated client squeeze the buttock of a waitress in times past, I had drained the last of my hot chocolate, dabbed my lips with a stiff napkin, and shook my head. No thank you.

"Sissy Di-Di!" Jasmine's footsteps echoed along the upstairs floorboards.

I rose from my bed, exited my room, and caught my little sister. "Yes, Jazzy Bear?"

She widened her eyes to irresistible puppy dog size. "Park?"

Victoria's chuckle carried up the staircase where she stood on the bottom step. "The Little Miss needs some fresh air. I thought a trip into town for a visit at the park and a quick grocery shop was in order. We'd love to have you join us."

The park, I could do. But the shopping? I blew out a breath. "Can I stay in the car when you go shopping?"

Victoria's aquamarine eyes examined my features. "Of course."

"Yay!" Jasmine wriggled until I released her and toddled down the stairs.

I slipped on my runners, grabbed a warm hoodie, and helped Jasmine into the car.

Twenty minutes later, I pushed Jasmine on the same swing set I had used since I was a child. Apart from a fresh coat of paint and a new layer of tanbark, the playground had scarcely changed in twenty years.

"Higher! Higher!" Jasmine's giggles brought a smile to my face.

Victoria chuckled from the bench behind us.

I indulged in the sweet little darling's request until she tired ten minutes later.

Victoria unbuckled her toddler. "How about Mummy takes you on the spinner?"

"Yay!"

I glanced at the old metal carousel and scrunched my brow. "That thing still safe?"

"Was the last time we came here. I'll sit on it and hold her."

"Spin!" Jasmine grabbed her mother's hand and pulled her toward the carousel.

I moseyed to the bench nearest my family and peered around. A few mothers with prams jogged in a group along the shared walking-and-bike path. I sucked in lungfuls of chilled country air tinged with eucalypts and wood smoke. My mind seemed less jumbled. Calmer. I grinned at the change a little fresh air could do.

Jasmine's giggles filled the air, her buoyant laughter just the medicine my heart required.

I twisted on the seat for a better glimpse of her beaming face when I noticed an approaching jogger.

A man with auburn hair, a taut grey T-shirt over his washboard abdominals, and black running shorts, tread the pavement.

I gasped. *No.* My throat narrowed, and my lungs suspended their life-giving function.

Powerful tanned arms swinging on every step.

My eyes bulged, my chest desperate for air.

The man blurred, my heaving drowning out his footsteps.

I grasped the seat, balancing on the edge, frantic for oxygen. My vision darkened. *Breathe, Diana!*

"Diana?" Victoria's voice called from somewhere in the distance.

Heat flooded my body, accompanied by tremors. I closed my eyes and dropped my head between my knees, my pulse walloping my ears.

"Diana!" Victoria's voice broke through the clamour in my head.

A toddler's cries undulated.

The rising pressure in my chest reached its peak and dropped a degree. Chills permeated my body.

Victoria's warm hand rubbed my clammy back. "Breathe, sweetheart. Just take a breath."

Air entered my lungs, and my tears dislodged. I breathed, my tense muscles easing while my stomach raged. Why would I think he was alive? Pierce was dead.

Jasmine stared up at me with tear-stained cheeks and pressed my knees with her little hands, her quiet post-cry hiccups stabbing my heart.

How long would it take for me to heal and no longer grieve my family? I slid my pinkie over Jasmine's pudgy fingers, determined to do better.

CHAPTER FOURTEEN
Blowout

"It's a bust." I sighed against my mobile phone, tucked my resume-filled folder under my arm, and walked down the street to Victoria's car.

"Surely it's not that bad," Keanu said through the earpiece.

"Uh. It is." My body ached, my brain drained after several hours of resume-dropping at several retail establishments in Robinvale. "No one seems to be hiring at the moment." I neared the vehicle, opened the door, and flopped into the little Mazda. "Thanks for being my cheer squad. I'll call you later."

"Chin up. It'll all work out."

"Bye." I disconnected the call and tossed my phone in the cup holder. After all the effort I had spent mentally preparing for today's activity—despite last week's setback at the playground—had there been much point to this exercise? Other than a great smile-muscles-and-leg workout?

I buckled and pointed the car in the direction of home. Now that our house was located fifteen minutes out of Tellarine, I lived halfway between Tellarine and Robinvale, which gave me double the chance of finding a job to fill in some of my time-out from university.

Almost three weeks had passed since Keanu forced me out of the house, and what did I have to show? A big fat nothing. Did Tara face similar struggles? If only she would reply to my messages.

I focused on the long stretch of road and mulled over Keanu's latest suggestion. Self-defense classes at Tellarine Community Centre. Last night he had shown me a few moves, and Victoria had stepped in with her thoughts, techniques, and skills she learned over the years from work-related short courses. I noticed her eyes flicker when Keanu reminded me to be on guard whenever I was alone with anyone, especially a man. Thoughts of her ex-husband, Jude, came to mind. Victoria's self-defense classes had not offered her much assistance standing against the wallop he had given her face.

A loud boom snapped me from my thoughts, and the car shuddered.

I screamed and stiffened.

Tension zinged through my veins, unleashing a torrent of memories. Flashbacks of another loud bang.

With my mind ambushed with images, Victoria's car swerved onto the opposite side of the road.

I shrieked, my voice strangled and chest burning. I squeezed my thighs and anchored my adrenaline-fuelled arms on the steering wheel, directing the vehicle back across the broken white line. Regaining control over the wayward machine, I guided the car to the muddy shoulder of the road and pulled over.

My arms vibrated, and I clenched my jittery fingers until my knuckles whitened.

Minutes passed, and my breaths slowed. Once my pulse eased and my hands no longer shook, I stumbled out the door and inspected the damage.

The back of the car sloped toward the adjacent fenced pasture, one rear tyre now flatter than a deflated pool ring. My stomach dropped, and I groaned.

I staggered to the driver's seat, closed the door, retrieved my mobile phone, and dialed Dad.

He answered on the second ring. "Hey. You okay?"

I released a long sigh. "I'm stuck on the side of the main road from Robinvale with a flat tyre."

Dad groaned. "Sorry, Princess."

I cleared my throat. My voice wavered. "I know you taught me how to change a tyre last year, but—"

"It's okay. I'd love to help."

"I don't feel comfortable getting an RACV guy out here, and who knows how long that might take anyway."

"Of course. I'll probably be … hmm, twenty minutes or so. Sit tight in the car, and I'll be there soon."

Tears welled in my eyes. "Thanks, Daddy."

"See you soon."

I locked the car before cracking open the driver's window a slither. My arms ached, and I slumped against the seat back. I switched on the stereo and located my favourite For King and Country track, *God Only Knows*. I cranked up the volume, closed my eyes, and uttered a silent prayer. Tears slipped down my cheeks.

God knew what I had been through, and I was thankful He was with me. Although still early days in my healing journey, I knew His love would anchor me through every flashback, nightmare, and unexpected trigger. God's love and the unconditional love of my family.

Fresh tears welled in my eyes. The support and understanding Dad and Victoria had shown me since I arrived home was indescribable. I thanked God each and every day for the blessing my parents were to me.

I opened my eyes, grabbed a tissue from the glove box, and wiped my face. The song changed, and I lowered the volume, my attention focused on my surroundings. The tarry length of deserted highway stretched as far as I could see out the front and rear windows. A few tall trees swayed in the gentle breeze on the opposite side of the road, but this section of highway lay vacant from the usual bushy shrubs. Acres of pasture filled the remaining space, a spattering of sheep and cows in various paddocks. Other than my music, the area held a peaceful quietude.

A charcoal Ford Mustang approached. I straightened and drank in the sight. Big front grille, sleek fastback body, and understated rear GT badge. Sexy. My chest warmed, and a soft smile crept to my lips as I imagined myself behind the wheel of a similar beast. Maybe in blue or a deep maroon-red. Charcoal was hot too.

I leaned against the headrest and peeked at the rearview mirror. The Mustang completed a U-turn and pulled up behind my vehicle. My breaths quickened and throat tightened.

A tall, bronze, dark-haired man stepped out of his vehicle and inspected my deflated tyre.

I snapped the music off and prayed, my words stuttered and incoherent. My stomach churned. I gripped my thighs and pressed against the impending panic.

Slow, crunching steps amplified the closer he approached.

My heart thundered, and my chest screamed.

The man cleared his throat and leaned closer to the window gap. "Excuse me, miss. I see you're in need of assistance and would love to help."

The deep timbre of his voice awakened butterflies in my belly. Alarm bells clanged in my head, and I leaned away from the window. My gaze flickered to his chiselled face and away, back to his dark eyes, and down to my lap. My chest rose and fell in quick succession, my skin clammy and hot.

The Good Samaritan stepped back a fraction. "I didn't mean to frighten you. All I want to do is help change your tyre. Nothing more."

I opened my mouth to speak, but nothing happened. Sucking in a deep breath, I focused on the collar of his shirt. "Th-thanks, b-but my dad'll be here any minute now." If this man was here for less than honourable reasons, I hoped the imminent arrival of Dad sent him away.

He turned, glanced at his silver wristwatch, and eyed my face. A kind smile laced his dark lips. "It's almost four on a Friday. Why not give your old man a break and let me change your tyre?"

No such luck. I squeezed my fingers together. The man spoke reason, but he was still a stranger. My last experience alone with a strange man had not gone well.

Understatement of the year.

I lifted my gaze to his strong jaw and full lips. This guy could be a handsome serial killer, adept in locating helpless women stranded along country roads. Vibrations shook my body, and my mind swirled with extreme scenarios. No way would I give this stranger any opportunity to harm me.

His eyebrows drew together, and his sable eyes looked through the window crack. The Good Samaritan stepped backwards. "I give you my word I won't harm you. I just want to help. No strings attached."

Proverbs three verses five and six jumped front and centre in my memory, followed by a radiating tranquillity in my body and soul.

Trust God.

My skin cooled, and my chest eased. The laborious breaths from moments ago were forgotten in the presence of peace. I could do this by the grace of God.

I blew out a breath and nodded, grasped my phone, and unlocked the car.

The Good Samaritan stepped clear of the door.

I inched it open, popped the boot, and secured my feet onto the dirt.

His footsteps crunched away.

I breathed deeply and closed the door behind me before walking the length of the Mazda. With fisted hands and a straight back, I stopped a few paces from the car boot and crossed my arms.

The man returned from his vehicle with a shiny red jack in tow and dumped it on the ground next to the punctured tyre.

While he rifled around in the boot for the space-saver spare wheel, I studied him. Taller than my six-foot height, he reminded me of Dr. Suresh from *Heroes*, albeit with straighter hair and several shades lighter in complexion. Dad had been a big fan of the TV show and had introduced me to the series a few years ago. He and Dr. Suresh were the two main reasons I watched the show. Only Anna knew what a huge Hollywood crush I had on that actor.

The Good Samaritan lifted the spare tyre with effortless ease. His muscled arms flexed with each movement but lacked the corded pop of veins from strain.

I stared, mesmerised by his strength. Our gazes met, and I dipped my chin to study the muddy gravel below me, but I caught a glimpse of his soft smile and kind eyes before I looked away.

He stepped back, tyre in hand.

I rounded the end of the car, leaving a generous gap between us.

He positioned the jack with precision, raised the car within seconds, and loosened the first wheel nut.

"Wow." The word tumbled from my mouth without thought.

He paused and turned, and a boyish grin stretched across his face. "This is easy for me. I raced against my brother from age nine. The first to change a tyre safely went for a ride with Dad for ice cream."

I smirked. Clever father. "Did you ever beat your brother?"

"Every round from age eleven." He unfastened the remaining wheel nuts, removed the punctured tyre, and replaced it with the temporary spare. "I trust you know not to exceed eighty kilometres with this temp on? Do your best to get the puncture repaired or tyre replaced as soon as you can."

"Thanks."

Gravel crunched, and Dad parked his HiLux in front of the Mazda.

I released a breath, and my shoulders sagged.

Dad engulfed me in an affectionate squeeze. "I see you outsourced the job." He kissed the top of my head, released me, and approached the Good Samaritan. "Anything I can do to help?"

With a final grunt tightening the last nut, our helper shook his head and stood. He wiped his hands on his jeans before he looked up at Dad. "All done … Mr. J.! It's good to see you, sir."

Dad embraced the man with a hearty back slap, and they laughed.

I stared, mouth agape.

"Jonathan! It's been a long time. I heard you returned home after another promotion. Congratulations. I didn't get to say so at the funeral." Dad nodded in my direction. "So you've met my Diana?"

Jonathan's eyes widened. His attention fell on me before returning to Dad. "This is Diana?" He turned and appraised me.

My skin prickled under his scrutiny.

"When did you grow up? The last time I saw you was at school when I visited Principal Marsden the year after I graduated. I think you were in Year Seven?"

I peered at Jonathan and scrunched my brow. "You went to Tellarine Secondary?"

"Tellarine born and bred, like my dad. I'm twenty-six, so several years ahead of you in school."

I stepped forward and stretched out my hand. "Pleased to meet you."

He enveloped my cold fingers in his large, warm, yet slightly gritty hand. "Likewise."

I pulled away from his grip but not before his fingers brushed my palm, skittering shivers up my arm.

No, no! Heat stabbed my cheeks, and I turned to Dad. "What's the plan? Do you want me to drive home via Pete's to get the tyre fixed?"

Dad pursed his lips. "How about you drive my ute and I'll look after the puncture." He turned toward Jonathan and lowered his voice. "Your old schoolmate Danny Thompson's back working with

Pete. I wouldn't let him set foot a hundred metres near Diana." He growled his final words.

Jonathan's warm, pleasant demeanor evaporated, replaced with cool steel. "We were … reacquainted last week on my second day on the job." His stony expression eased, but the hardness remained, ageing him to a man older than twenty-six years. "I'd better get going. It was great to see you Mr. J." He nodded toward me. "Miss J."

I smiled and watched him return to his Mustang, jack in hand. When I faced Dad, he raised a brow. "What?"

Dad tapped a playful finger on the tip of my nose. "Nothing."

Jonathan reversed his Mustang on the gravel near us.

"Yeah. Right." I threw a hard punch at Dad's chest.

He reverberated with laughter, grabbed hold of me, and kissed the top of my head.

The back of Jonathan's sleek vehicle disappeared down the road.

"He's a good kid. You've met his parents, the Harrises, at church."

"The middle-aged couple who started attending two years ago?"

"That's them."

I sucked in a sharp breath. "Didn't they lose their son recently? S-so Jonathan's brother just died?"

Dad's expression sobered. "Damien. Yes. Good kid."

A heavy weight pressed against my chest.

He patted my shoulder and nodded toward Victoria's car. "Let's get this tyre fixed before Pete closes up shop."

I extracted the keys for the Mazda from my pocket.

Dad tossed his set of keys to me.

I climbed into the cab of Dad's ute and drove home, my mind filled with images of heavy tyres hoisted by muscled arms, red jack levers pumped with effortless motion, and two deep pools of chocolate-for-eyes. A smile teetered on my lips, almost happy my daydreams consisted of a smoking-hot Samaritan with a tender heart and an enviable caramel complexion very different to my peaches-and-cream skin. No glimmer of dark-hazel and blue-ringed eyes reverberated around my mind today.

Progress.

8 August

I'm doing a little better, Mum. Still no job, but I start self-defense classes in two weeks. Maybe I'll make a connection there and get a job through word of mouth? But, surely, something will happen soon, right? I mean, I put myself out there today, traipsing around Robinvale in search of work. And to be honest, I appreciated the distraction. When will his vibrant dark-hazel eyes ringed with sapphire cease to bring me to tears?

I'm done with the sadness weighing my shoulders like a heavy jacket, the sharp pains stabbing my chest. I know deep down I couldn't have done a thing to stop him from pursuing his intended course. But I still wonder. What could I have done differently? Other than leaving the shop the moment unease pressed against me.

I need to forgive myself too. I wish you were here to help me through it.

CHAPTER FIFTEEN
Fighting One's Battles

I stared at the scarred wooden door of the community centre and fought against my quickened breaths. Adrenaline fired through my veins, and I pressed my palms against the heavy door.

I pushed, inhaled a deep breath, and travelled across the worn psychedelic carpet. Weaving past a treasure-trove of novice art displays and contemporary sculptures, I approached a large multipurpose room, its conspicuous sign declaring self-defense classes for women. I could do this.

I clutched the brass handle with my slick palm, pulled the door, and slammed into a warm wall of muscled flesh. I strangled a cry.

Two large hands steadied my shoulders and held me against a firm chest.

I stiffened, my limbs heavy and chest tight. My breaths shallowed, and light-headedness fogged my every move. I blinked and focused on a familiar face with a familiar smile.

"Good afternoon, Miss J." Jonathan's husky voice penetrated the mist in my brain.

My pulse increased for a different reason. "J-Jonathan. What're you doing at a women's self-defense class?" The last time I had looked—and now knew for certain pressed against his rock-hard chest—he was no woman. Magnificent, almost breathtaking even, but there was nothing feminine about this man.

Jonathan released my shoulders and stepped back. "I'm volunteering my services." He cocked his head. "What're you doing here?"

He was teaching this class? I hugged my arms around my waist. "I'm here to learn."

"Good to hear. Why don't you take a seat, we won't be long."

I bit my lower lip, stepped away from the door, and found a vacant seat in the large semicircle of foldout chairs. I recognized a few mums from my schooling years but no one I knew by name. Apart from myself, the women in the room appeared to be over the age of forty. I smiled and pulled down the hem of my T-shirt. Knowing older women were interested in defending their personal safety comforted me somehow.

Most of the seats filled within five minutes, and the buzz of quiet conversations drifted around me. An attractive buttery-blonde with piercing brown eyes and a smooth, short ponytail raised her hands at the front of the room. Average in height, she wore a flattering light-blue tunic top over a pair of navy leggings and new-looking white-and-navy running shoes.

"Good afternoon, ladies." Her melodic voice silenced the chatter. "I'm Constable April Dennigan, and I'm here to teach you some self-defense strategies should you ever be found in the unfortunate situation of needing to defend yourself or your loved ones." She motioned toward Jonathan, and her lips upturned, eyes bright. "I've asked my partner Senior Constable Jonathan Harris to help me out today."

My mind and stomach swirled in tandem. Jonathan was a police officer? No wonder he coaxed me from the car in a calm manner. How many deranged criminals had he talked down off the proverbial ledge? A lump formed in my throat. His penchant to serve had spurred his kindness to stop and help, not any particular interest in my specific welfare. I balled my hands in my lap. *Of course it had nothing to do with me.* And his rank? Pretty impressive for an officer in his mid-twenties. He had to be good at his job to be a Senior Constable, or so I assumed from Uncle Steve's past comments.

I stared at the graceful woman standing in front of me and pouted. Constable Dennigan appeared to be a few years older than me. The way she smiled at him. Her partner. Something stabbed my chest, and I straightened. I imagined two police officers could find commonality at work and fall into a companionable relationship outside the job. I noticed the absence of an engagement or wedding ring on her petite hand. With different surnames, Jonathan and April were either dating or cohabiting. I huffed a breath.

Blondes are better. Too bad for you. I clenched my jaw and focused on my instructors.

Jonathan now stood next to Constable Dennigan with a friendly yet professional smile on his handsome face. They seemed comfortable with each other. A power couple.

His powerful gaze settled on me.

A flurry of butterflies loosed in my belly. I forced a polite smile to my lips.

Constable Dennigan launched into her session, emphasising the importance of vocalisation and pushing against an attacker before doing anything else.

I rubbed my jaw, thinking back on my experience. I could have yelled, "Back off!" at the top of my lungs, but to what end? With no rescuers nearby and untrustworthy men outside the bathroom, yelling might have hurt me more than helped. Would screaming have helped Tara escape?

Constable Dennigan discussed the most effective body parts to strike. "Jon, why don't you stand here so I can demonstrate."

Jonathan stood tall and flexed his muscles. He winked to his audience, and a titter of laughter filled the room.

Please.

Constable Dennigan feigned gouging, scratching, and poking Jonathan's eyes with her fingers and knuckles before demonstrating ways to strike in defense by ramming the heel of her palm into his nose and kicking the sides of his knees. The Constable then showed a way of using her knees, elbows, and head as a weapon against an attacker, similar to what Victoria had mentioned during our impromptu session.

Jonathan played the role of human punching bag with enthusiasm and received hearty applause when the mini demonstration concluded. The attendees were then paired up, and we practiced our mock punches while our instructors walked around the room, watching.

I partnered with the sprightly woman in her eighties sitting beside me. "Hi, I'm Diana."

She clutched my hand in her wrinkled one. Her vibrant blue velour tracksuit complimented her sky-blue eyes and her blue hair rinse. "I'm Dawn. A pleasure, love. How about I practice the moves on you first and you can see if this old bird has it right."

I stifled a laugh and grinned at the senior citizen. "Let me have it.”

Dawn thrust her wizened hands in my face, seeming to take great joy from faux-slamming her palm against my nose. By the time she jabbed me in the crotch with her knee, she puffed soft breaths. “Phew! Next session I think I’ll leave the girdle at home. It’s difficult to fight back when I’m crushing my attacker along with my gizzards.”

I burst out laughing. “I can only imagine. I’m not the girdle-wearing type myself.”

A deep laugh resonated behind me. “Good to know, Miss J.”

My foot faltered, and I barely dodged Dawn’s palm aimed for my jaw.

Jonathan stepped between us. “Looking good, Mrs. Inglebar. Don’t forget to let Diana have a turn.”

Stretching on her tiptoes, Dawn laid a wrinkled hand on Jonathan’s cheek and patted it. “I’ve missed you, Jonny darling. You haven’t changed a bit. If I were forty years younger, you wouldn’t stand a chance.”

Jonathan leaned and kissed the top of her head. “You know what they say about boys and their babysitters, Mrs. Inglebar. I may’ve been infatuated with your cookies as an eight-year-old.” He grinned and winked. “Did you bring me any today?”

Dawn chuckled, her laughter bubbly and light. “Not today, love.” She turned to me. “You take note. A boy will chase you for your cookies no matter how old he gets.”

Heat bloomed along my skin, setting off more laughter from my aged friend.

“Tell you what, dear, I’ll give you my recipe so Jonny here can harass someone younger with her beauty still intact. I’m getting too old for all this innuendo.”

Jonathan’s eyes glittered, and his lips twitched.

My cheeks burned. I turned to Dawn with a small smile. “Thanks. My dad loves cookies too.”

She narrowed her eyes and cocked her head. “Hmm, your father, you say?” She thumbed her chin. “You look like that scrumptious electrician whose wife died years ago. Now that’s a strapping man I’d stay up all night baking for.”

I suppressed a snort. “Sounds like my dad. Mum died when I was six.”

She tut-tutted and patted my hands. "Such a terrible tragedy. The knitting circle made a purple crochet blanket for you when we heard. You poor darling."

My eyes widened. "That was you? I still have Snuggles and use him often."

A bright smile spread across her face, a matching smile lighting up Jonathan's features.

Had I just admitted I had named my blanket? Heat upon heat layered my cheeks and spread down my body.

"Well, dear, that's the most wonderful thing I've heard today." She sniffed and wiped under her eye. "Enough of this mushy stuff, come and smash my face for a bit."

Jonathan stepped away.

I relaxed my shoulders and practiced the processes with Dawn for a few minutes. When I pretended to elbow the side of her head, Jonathan's strong hand touched my back on my third try, and I froze.

His warm breath caressed my ear. "Use the force of your body to strike," he said in a gravelly whisper.

My breaths laboured, and I focused on Dawn's head instead of the firm hand searing a hole through my long-sleeved T-shirt. Using the weight of my body behind my elbow, I thrust forward and jabbed the air near Dawn's ear.

"Much better. You've the potential to inflict a lot of pain with that elbow of yours."

I glanced sideways and nodded, noting the warmth in his eyes. I forced coolness into my own expression. I was not an old lady thrilled by husky murmurs and gentle touches. Jonathan was far too friendly for a guy in a relationship. "Thanks." My voice oozed civility. I stepped away, extracting myself from his hand.

Dawn and Jonathan shared a look.

A piercing whistle shrilled.

I turned toward the sound, where the Constable directed women back to their seats, and I hurried to my spot.

"Great work, ladies," Constable Dennigan said. "If my willing assistant would come back for another beating, I want to show you how to de-escalate a few common everyday scenarios. Next week we'll pull the floor mats out and get a little more physical in our training."

My awe for Constable Dennigan grew each scenario she took

us through. From talking down a drunk, handsy co-worker at an office party or slipping a wrist from the tight grip of an attacker, through to banging and screaming against the car window to scare away a potential assailant from opening the car door, she held my attention while she revealed simple tips on how to extract oneself from difficult situations.

No wonder Jonathan was enamored with her.

She dismissed the class, inviting us to return next week.

I gave Dawn a quick hug and promised to attend next week's session. Before I could escape through the classroom doors, an average-sized young woman with fiery-red hair and good posture touched my arm.

"I'm sorry to stop you, but I just wanted to say hello." Her emerald eyes sparkled. "My name's Kortney. Are you planning to return next week? Cos it appears we're the youngest people here, and I wondered"—she rubbed a hand across her freckled chin— "whether you're coming back?"

I glanced back to where Constable Dennigan and Jonathan tidied up front. "Yes, I plan to come back." I offered a small smile. "I'm Diana."

Kortney flashed a wide grin. "I'm relieved to hear! I won't keep you any longer."

"Thanks. See you then." I slipped from the room and headed to Victoria's car.

"Wait up, Diana."

I turned and stilled.

Jonathan closed the gap between us. His eyes flickered, his intent focus piercing my armour. "Just checking you're okay. You seemed a little ... detached earlier." He stepped closer.

I breathed in the intoxicating scent of spice. Oh boy.

His hair was tussled from "fighting" with Constable Dennigan, and a red splotch blazed under his chin stubble where she had connected to his face during one demonstration.

I shook my head and straightened. "I'm fine, thanks."

He cleared his throat. "Will you be attending next week's session?"

I scanned his dark eyes and nodded.

He rubbed a hand across his chin and flinched. "Good."

I waved, turned, and departed.

I placed the washing detergent into the final cloth bag and glanced at the monitor. "That'll be one hundred and forty-two dollars and eighty-five cents, please." A Tellarine IGA manager had offered me a casual position last week, and I worked my first shift three days later.

The middle-aged woman with bleary eyes and red lips counted out her notes.

I smiled and returned her change. "Have a lovely evening."

"You too." She pushed her trolley toward the exit.

Working at this country IGA was different to the supermarket back in Melbourne. Scanning and bagging groceries was the easiest part of the job, chatting with elderly shoppers the most pleasant part, and ignoring rude teenagers and their inappropriate whispers in the after-school rush topped my list of difficulties. A stark contrast to the hipster shoppers at the small Melbourne store.

I glanced at the register clock. Three minutes until shift end.

"Wow, hi!"

I turned toward the beaming face of the young lady I had met at self-defense on Monday night. "Hi …" What was her name again? Cathy? Kelli?

She placed a loaf of bread and a punnet of blueberries on the conveyor belt. "Diana, wasn't it?" She glanced at my name tag and grinned.

Great, she remembered my name. My cheeks flushed. "Yes, Diana. But it seems I forgot your name, sorry." I scanned her items.

She pressed a hand to her chest. "Kortney with a K, that's what I always say." She giggled. "Wish I grew up with a beautiful name like Diana. No one could misspell it!"

I smiled.

Kortney tapped her credit card.

I handed her a shopping receipt. "Are you new around here?"

"Grew up out past Robinvale." She gathered her items. "Well, it was lovely seeing you again. Catch you on Monday!"

"Bye."

Keanu walked up to my checkout with a few groceries in tow. "Good evening, Lady Checkout Chick. How was yer day?" He placed a few items on the conveyor belt.

I turned to Keanu with a tired smile, huffed at the smirk on his face, and commenced scanning. "Good, apart from the unsavoury comments from those testosterone-laden boys."

"I was itching to come down here the moment you messaged, the little punks."

I had sent him a quick update during my break. Perhaps not my grandest idea.

"If ya ever see them at Benanu's, point them out. I miss playing Hulk on your behalf."

I scanned the last of his purchases, biting my lip to hold back a smile. "Will do. Okay, pay up so we can get some dinner. I might even be up for a game or two of pool. I feel the need to crush your tender soul."

Phyllis, a brunette teenager on the next shift, nodded to me.

Keanu chuckled and scanned his credit card. "Feel free to crush me anytime. I'm man enough to take it."

I smiled at Phyllis, logged myself out of the system, and stepped away from the checkout.

Phyllis slipped behind the cash register.

I turned to Keanu. "I'll be back in a moment." I strode to the staff lounge, slipped into my coat, grabbed my bag, and hurried back to Keanu, sliding an arm through his.

"I'm proud of you," Keanu said through a dimpled smile.

We dodged smushed dog excrement on the footpath. "So am I. Oh! Forgot to tell you, I went to my first self-defense class on Monday."

He squeezed my interlocked arm. "I know. Mrs. Inglebar told me this morning."

I stopped and almost tripped, saved by Keanu's quick hands. "You know her?" Had my voice squeaked?

He released my shoulder, and we continued the short walk to the bar. "She's one of our regulars. We order root beer just for her. I'm her favourite. She bakes me cookies … and tells me everything."

I glanced at him. "Everything?"

A passing overhead street light highlighted the devilish look on his face. "Everything. Like the way a certain tyre-changing knight took a shining to ya."

I groaned. I had told Keanu about meeting Jonathan the moment my foot had hit my bedroom floor after driving Dad's ute home. I had wanted to share how I had taken a step of faith leaving the car but had ended up gushing about my handsome rescuer. Keanu had peppered me with questions, and I had stupidly answered them all, digging a hole for myself. He was going to milk this for all it was worth.

"Did Mrs. Inglebar also mention how said sizzling tyre-changing knight was only there to help his partner, the attractive blonde Constable Dennigan?"

Keanu pushed open Benanu's front door and chuckled. Chuckled!

A rush of warmth from the heated room impacted my face and warmed my skin. The familiar sounds of muffled music, conversation, and laughter danced through the building, unsettling me.

"Sizzling? You really have a thing for Officer Harris."

My chest tightened. Too many people. I headed toward the back office and shrugged out of my coat with Keanu's help.

He unlocked the small office door, draped my coat across a desk chair, and closed the door behind him. "Ya didn't answer me."

"What's there to say? The man's spoken for. End of discussion." I stepped to the closest chair.

Keanu grabbed my arm with a loose grip, stopping me. He turned my face with his large fingers and captured my gaze with serious intent. "Not end of discussion. This's the first time you've hinted at any interest in a guy since Peter Tracy rescued the worm on the footpath in Grade Four."

"I crushed on that guy at youth—"

"He doesn't count cos he's a jerk." He growled.

My lips twinged.

"When you spoke about meeting Officer Harris, it was like talking with normal Diana." He sighed. "I miss her."

A shudder shook my body. "I know."

Keanu enveloped me in his arms. "Would it help to know April and Jon are partners of a different kind?"

I lifted my head and leaned back, creasing my brows. "What do you mean?"

"Can ya keep a secret?"

I nodded, stretched up, and leaned my ear near his mouth.

"Constable Dennigan's a remarkable kisser."

I whipped my head around. "W-what? You didn't …" My mouth slackened. "Keanu. Tell me you didn't."

A Cheshire smile graced his lips. "I did. She's a great gal. Tough as nails but soft as silk. And as single as an odd sock."

I scrunched up my face.

Keanu ran his index finger across my forehead. "They're partners at work. They patrol together."

Of course! How was I so dense? My chest eased, and I smiled.

Keanu grinned. "She bought a beer last week while I was bartending. Sat at the bar for three hours waiting for my shift to end. Doesn't seem fazed by our two-year age gap, either."

"That's great." I gasped. "For you, I mean." Heat stung my cheeks, and I ducked my head.

"Ah huh." He grinned and nodded toward the door. "Wanna eat at the bar or stay back here for now?"

I pressed my hands together and straightened. "I'm feeling braver than five minutes ago, so let's sit at the bar."

Keanu led me out to the bar. He grabbed himself a beer and a bottle of water for me.

I rocked on the bar stool, my legs wobbly. Senior Constable Harris was not shacked up with the leggy blonde bombshell. I pressed my palm to my chest. Why did my chest lighten at this thought?

"I found a booth near the pool table. Wanna sit there instead?"

"Okay."

Keanu pawed my hand and pulled me along to the booth.

My steps teetered. I held fast to his grip. "Why didn't you tell me about her sooner?" I slid along the cold leather booth seat.

"I don't tell you about every girl I kiss. Especially not after the mess with Gabby."

I winced.

Gabriella had strung Keanu along until she disappeared to study at NIDA, a dramatic arts college in New South Wales. None of us knew she had applied for the costume design course until she announced her move a week before she left. Last I heard, she was content working on her Bachelor of Fine Arts.

"Anyway," Keanu said, "I haven't heard from April in a few days, so I'm not holding my breath." He reached for a menu, scanned the page, then handed it to me. "Waddaya want? My treat."

I stared at the thick cardboard, deciding it was a steak-and-chips kind of night. My abdomen squeezed with hunger pangs, and I pointed to the scotch fillet on the menu.

Keanu shuffled toward the kitchen.

I sighed. How unfortunate I had zero interest in Keanu. After all, he had cute, sweet, caring, and protective down pat. And I trusted him. Perfect husband material.

Keanu was right, I had harboured the rare crush at school, unlike my friends and their weekly loves, and racked up male friends, not boyfriends. Guys like Andrew were sweet, but I never saw myself with any of them. As in never ever, no chance, being-stuck-on-a-desert-island-for-ten-years-would-not-change-my-mind ever. Even if I woke one morning with a wedding ring on my finger—like those awkward romance novels where a woman discovers a naked husband in her bed—I would simply annul the relationship.

Probably.

I furrowed my brow. If Keanu and I were still single in thirty years, I might ask him to marry me so I could waltz into the busy Benanu's kitchen and order a steak on demand. Real food for thought.

"Are you plotting to take over the world, Brain?" A deep voice drew me out of my machinations.

I looked up into Jonathan's dark eyes. "Narf."

He chuckled.

"Sorry, couldn't help myself. Mind you, I feel a little dumb now. Pinky says 'Narf' not Brain."

His smile warmed my insides. "I thought you'd be too young for *Animaniacs*."

"Mum watched it with her younger siblings. I think she introduced it to Dad, and he was adamant I watch a TV show Mum loved. Just a little something she passed on to me even after death." Like the inspiration for my journalism career I had put on hold.

I crossed my legs and tilted my head. "I don't think I've had the chance to say I'm awfully sorry to hear about your brother passing."

Jonathan's eyes clouded. "Thanks."

"Were you close?"

"I thought we were." His jaw ticked.

Oh. I pursed my lips. "Ah, you're welcome to join us for dinner if you like?"

Jonathan glanced over his shoulder and back to me. "Us?"

"My friend stepped away."

He pulled at his collar, shook his head, and stepped back. "No. That's fine. I was dropping something off to a friend. I'll see you Monday." Jonathan tipped an imaginary hat, pivoted, and launched toward the exit.

What a puzzle.

Keanu returned a few minutes later bearing delicious gifts.

I salivated over the steak he placed in front of me before he planted himself across the table in front of a large bowl of pasta.

I sliced through the buttery steak, inhaling its scent. So good. "I was thinking"—I chewed the scrumptious slab of protein—"if we're still single at fifty, do you want to get married?"

Keanu's eyes enlarged, and he coughed on spaghetti.

I poured a glass of water from the full bottle on the table and waited for him to get his breathing under control.

"What?" His voice squeaked.

"Marriage." I pointed a fat chip between us. "You and me. In thirty years." I shoved the chip in my mouth. Carbolicious.

He squeezed his eyes closed for a brief moment, shook his head, and stared at me. "That's what I thought y'said."

I raised an eyebrow.

He chewed and stared. "Why wait? Let's get married now."

I spit up my chip, coughing. "What!"

A sly grin eclipsed his face. "Why not?"

"Why not?" Air blustered from my lips, and my stomach dropped. "Uh, because I'm talking in the far, distant future. Not now." Thoughts of being *married* married filtered through my brain. My skin heated, and I spluttered. "No way. I'm not doing … uh …"

Keanu glanced at my lips. "Doing what?"

My face burned under his scrutiny. "You know," I whispered.

He chuckled softly. "Would that be such a bad thing? I can think of a hundred worse things than marrying you."

I stared at the food remaining on my plate. "You're like a … a brother to me. Or a cute cousin. But I … I wouldn't want to share a life with you … like *that*."

He busted out in laughter. "I was only pushing ya buttons."

I gaped at him.

He winked and waggled his eyebrows.

After I gulped a glass of water, I cleared my throat. And my brain. "Wanna play pool?"

Keanu stood, reached across the table, and wrapped his meaty arm around my shoulders. "We're still good, right?"

I leaned up and kissed his cheek. "Always. Now it's kick-Keanu's-butt-at-pool time."

He tickled me under my arms.

I yelped, ran to the pool table, grabbed my favourite cue, and prepared for battle.

CHAPTER SIXTEEN
Birthday Boy

September and October flew by without much to tell. I completed the six-week self-defense course while working at the IGA and babysitting Jasmine when I could.

Jonathan and I had exchanged phone numbers after the third self-defense session and fell into a pattern of sending silly photos to each other. The inside of a coffee cup. A close-up of Jonathan's nostril. Fluff from the dryer. My favourite was the lone flower in a brick footpath he sent me last week.

I slouched on the couch, scrolling through our recent messages and grinning at today's gem I had snapped. Jasmine's dark curls fuzzed like a lion's mane teased high on eighties hairspray. She had attacked me with her little fingers post-bath—tickling under my chin and messing up my hair—so I had retaliated whilst drying her hair.

Jonathan: NEW SHELTER/STRAY PET DOG?

Me: HA HA! NO, MY SISTER'S HAIR AFTER A BATH.

Jonathan: LOOKS LIKE SHE NEEDS ANOTHER BATH AND SOME DETANGLER.

Me: :-P

Yesterday, Jonathan's text had woken me at six o'clock.

Jonathan: GOOD MORNING, DIANA. IT'S A GREAT DAY TO SEARCH FOR KEYS.

I had squinted at an image resembling the underside of a vehicle and someone's foot and stifled a laugh.

Me: YOU WOKE ME FOR CAR PORN? YOU COULD AT LEAST GO FOR THE RACY UNDER THE HOOD SHOT. ;-)

Me: I'M A CAR ENTHUSIAST (BLAME DAD).

Jonathan: FUNNY. SEEMS THE FAMILY CAT PLAYED TAG WITH THE

DOG AND HAD AN ADVENTURE WITH MY KEYS.

Jonathan: THINK IT'S TIME TO GET MY OWN PLACE.

Jonathan: SORRY TO WAKE YOU, CAR LOVER.

Me: NAH, FREE FOOD AND HOUSING IS THE BEST.

Jonathan: TRUE. #THECHEAPLIFE

Me: #CHEAPSKATESANONYMOUS #IWAKEPRETTYGIRLSWITHCARPORN

Jonathan: YOU'RE A PIECE OF WORK. A PRETTY PIECE OF WORK. ;-) ENJOY LAZING AROUND WHILE I KEEP BAD GUYS OFF THE STREETS.

Me: WILL DO. SUCKS TO BE YOU. ;-)

Me: HAVE A GREAT DAY.

Jonathan: YOU TOO.

My chest fluttered, and I smirked at the screen. I loved our back-and-forth banter.

Last week's photo of an anthill had somehow spurned a faith-based discussion on the book of Romans. Jonathan was a lot of fun to message, but our one-on-one coffee meetings at the park before an odd IGA shift were my favourite.

Jonathan attended Tellarine Christian Church with his parents. Where my parents and I attended. Small world.

I opened the calendar app in my phone. Jonathan's twenty-seventh birthday was just around the corner, and it seemed he was a November baby not big on gifts or being fussed over. Although we were only friends, I wanted to give him something special.

I scrolled through my phone contacts and dialed the number of the man with a plan.

"Diana, to what do I owe this pleasure?" Sam Kono's voice purred over the line.

"I need some help."

"Shoot." Sam was Jonathan's best mate. Deep coffee eyes similar to my own, and jet-black hair. He had chatted me up the first time we met, and from the twinkling in his dark eyes, I had assumed he did so to provoke his best friend.

"You mentioned the other night Jonathan's into photography?" It explained Jonathan's ability to send beautifully framed photographs from his phone.

Sam's chuckle echoed over the line. "An understatement, but yeah. He's an avid photographer and brilliant at it. Why?"

"I want to get him a little something for his birthday next

week."

"Aren't you nice." He chuckled again. "What're you thinking?"

"Just some quirky but useful gifts."

"Like?"

"A *LensPen* cleaning kit? Or a smartphone macro lens band?" I tugged my bottom lip between my teeth.

"Don't think he's got either of those."

Yes! "Thanks. I won't hold you up any longer. See you arou—"

"Before you go, I'm having a bash at my place next Saturday. You interested?"

I furrowed my brow. "What kind of bash?"

"A celebratory 'We had the pool cleaned for summer and resurfaced the tennis court' event."

"Oh." Was I ready for an event with lots of people?

"It'll be casual and fun. Jonathan will be there. You could give him his gift."

"I'll see him at church on Sunday, so I'd prefer to give him his present a day early than almost a week late."

Sam chuckled again.

"Message me the details and your address, and I'll think about it." Maybe.

"Awesome. Bye, Diana."

"Bye." I tucked Sam's party into the back of my thoughts and switched over to my calendar app. At my urging—and lots of encouragement from Dad—Victoria now worked three days a week at Tellarine Secondary College. On the days she worked, I spent eight to nine hours travelling to parks, watching *Octonauts* and *VeggieTales*, and doing things an eighteen-month-old enjoyed.

I glanced at the week ahead. Thursday would be perfect for a shopping road trip to Mildura with Jasmine while Victoria worked. I launched off the couch with an extra bounce in my step.

I opened my eyes, stretched my arms, and grabbed my phone from the bedside table.

Jonathan: THANKS FOR THE CAMERA CLEANING KIT. I LOVE GADGETS! I'VE NEVER SEEN THIS ONE BEFORE. WORKS REALLY WELL

TOO!

Jonathan: SEE?

I glanced at the attached photograph of the display screen on the back of a DSLR camera. The camera screen revealed a photo of Jonathan, smiling a ridiculous over-the-top smile, holding a *LensPen* near his face.

I yawned and giggled. How adorably dorky to send me a selfie via his camera via the phone. It was the sort of photo you looked at and laughed, stepped away, looked at again, and ended up in stitches once more. I grinned at the photo of a photo and typed my reply.

Me: YOU'RE WELCOME, BIRTHDAY BOY! YOU'LL HAVE TO EMAIL ME THE ORIGINAL PHOTO AS IT'S CRACKING ME UP BIG TIME. YOUR FACE = PRICELESS.

Me: PERHAPS YOU SHOULD SEND THIS PHOTO TO MASTERCARD FOR THEIR NEXT ADVERTISING CAMPAIGN.

I sat up, listening for the telltale signs of Jasmine's wakefulness. Dad and Victoria had stunned me at dinner last night with the news of their surprise pregnancy. Although ecstatic to be a big sister again, I knew the littler "big sister" would tire Victoria, and I was conscious to help with Jasmine's morning routine.

When the house seemed still, I grabbed my Bible and went to today's passage. These quiet moments of reflection helped me think about the direction of my life.

Four-and-a-half months had passed since I walked into that sandwich shop. I rubbed my chest. Jonathan and I might not have crossed paths if I never came home and stayed. I blew out a breath. How amazing the way our lives were moulded, and how the trajectory of our world could shift on its axis with one chain of events. My chest flooded with warmth. *Thank You, God, for being in my court.*

An alert chimed on my phone, and I closed my Bible.

Jonathan: HAPPY TO SEND YOU THE PHOTO, ESPECIALLY IF IT PUTS A SMILE ON YOUR FACE.

Me: THANKS, YOU SEEM TO HAVE A KNACK FOR MAKING ME SMILE. :-)

Jonathan: READING YOUR WORDS IS THE BEST BIRTHDAY PRESENT OF THE DAY.

Me: WHAT? I COULD'VE SAVED MYSELF A DRIVE TO MILDURA AND SIMPLY SENT A MESSAGE?

Jonathan: YOU DROVE TO MILDURA FOR MY GIFT??

Jonathan: I WONDER WHO HAS THE BIGGER GRIN NOW?

My heart fluttered. Yikes, this man. Handsome, brave, smart, and kind. My heart was being pulled in a very dangerous direction. One I was still unsure I wanted to go.

Me: YOU'RE THE BIRTHDAY BOY AFTER ALL, SO IT'S PROBABLY YOU.

I lifted my eyelids when the echo of pitter-pattering on the hallway floorboards filled my ears, and a dark curly-haired mop of sunshine popped through my doorframe. "Come here, darling," I said to Jasmine.

She raced across the room and held her arms up for me.

I plucked her up and onto the bed. "How're you today, my sweetheart? Did you sleep well?"

With a sleepy yawn, Jasmine nodded, fisted her eyes, and snuggled up to me.

I kissed the top of her head and glanced at my phone.

"Sissy Di-Di?"

I turned to Jasmine. "Yes?"

"What Jon-than say?"

I smirked into her curls. She knew my morning routine well. "Just hello. It's Jonathan's birthday today."

"Ooooh! Bir-day! Do pho-fo?"

I tipped my head forward and caught her steady gaze. "You want to send Jonathan a photo?"

She pointed to my phone. "You an' me pho-fo."

I smiled. "Okay, let's send him a photo."

I positioned Jasmine on my lap, angled my phone in front of our faces, smiled, and captured our likeness. I attached it with my final message to Jonathan.

Me: JASMINE WANTED TO SEND A BIG HAPPY BIRTHDAY PHO-FO (PHOTO) TO JON-THAN FOR HIS BIR-DAY.

"Come on, kiddo, let's get you dressed and fed so Mummy and Daddy can have a little more sleep."

"Pancakes for breh-fast? Peeze?" Jasmine twisted around, unleashing her big puppy dog eyes and pouty lips.

How could I resist such a gorgeous face? And what would I do when there were two adorable faces ganging up on me in the future? I smiled and kissed her forehead. "Okay, Jazzy, pancakes it is."

"Yay!"

I winced and raised my index finger to my lips.

She covered her mouth with pudgy fingers.

"Hopefully Mummy slept through that." Smiling, I helped Jasmine slide off the bed and neatened the covers.

Jasmine pulled on my hand at the same time my phone dinged.

"One moment, darling." I grabbed my phone.

Jonathan: TWO BEAUTIFUL LADIES LOOKING COSY AND WARM. PLEASE TELL JASMINE THAT JON-THAN SENDS HIS THANKS AND WILL CHERISH THIS PHO-FO INDEFINITELY. CAMERA CLEANING KIT FROM MILDURA AND PRIZE-WINNING PHOTOGRAPHY = BEST BIRTHDAY EVER. :-)

My heart flipped. Jonathan Harris equalled a whole lot of trouble.

CHAPTER SEVENTEEN
Making a Splash

I unbuckled and turned to Dad. "Thanks for the lift."

Dad quirked his lips. "Happy to help. If Jonathan's shift is extended, give us a call and we'll come get you."

"Thanks." I leaned across and kissed him on the cheek.

"Have fun, Princess."

I lugged my overfilled, bright beach bag over my shoulder, closed the ute door, and followed the footpath to Sam's mansion of a house.

I stretched my neck at the triple-level modern mega-home. Wow. An oversized horseshoe driveway was filled with vehicles near two double garages. I surveyed the slate-coloured structure and weaved along the paved driveway toward a large metal gate bearing a sign, "Party through here."

Slipping into the yard, I admired the lush, manicured gardens and weedless grass and trekked along the path past a tennis court abuzz with players.

So many unfamiliar people.

I sucked in a stabilizing breath, hugged my bag to my chest, and scanned the nearby outdoor entertaining area. An oversized Grecian-style in-ground pool shimmered in the sunlight. Andrew Daley chatted with a redhead on the back deck.

Andrew? What was he doing here?

He caught my gaze, and his eyes widened before he waved. The girl turned and beamed. Kortney was here too?

I ascended the steps. "Hey, you two."

Kortney leaned across and hugged me. "I didn't know you'd be here!"

"Same." *Thanks, God, for the friendly faces.* I relaxed my shoulders.

"I wondered whether you fell off the face of the earth." Andrew smiled. "Glad to see you're alive and well."

I pressed my hands together. "Still around." I glanced at the partygoers and back to my friends. "Do you both know Sam?"

"Yeah. His brother's friends with my brother," Andrew said.

Kortney leaned closer and discreetly pointed to a shirtless guy in board shorts near the barbeque. "I'm here with that cute one."

"Ah, great."

"I'd better get back to him." Kortney smiled and descended the steps.

Andrew scratched the back of his head.

I nodded toward the tennis courts. "Want to play?"

He smiled. "Let's do it."

We walked to an empty court. Andrew raised a brow. "Been practicing since the last time we played mixed doubles at school?"

I dropped my bag, grabbed a racket, and bounced a furry green ball against the reddish-brown turf. "Haven't had time."

"You were always a reluctant player."

"I preferred being on the school swim team."

The next half hour passed in a mix of sweat, missed shots—on my part since Andrew was still a beast on the court—and laugh-inducing sledging. Mock insults, teases, and taunts were our "thing" during practice matches at school, and we both chuckled and reminisced over remembered insults from our school matches. Seemed tennis was a brilliant icebreaker.

I wheezed and raised a hand. "I surrender."

Sweat beaded along Andrew's brow, his face glowing with a beaming smile.

My lungs burned, and I rubbed my calves. "I'm out of practice. Drinks break?"

Andrew lifted the bottom of his T-shirt and wiped his face. "Yeah, let's do that."

After shouldering my bag, we ambled to the drinks table. I grabbed a bottle of water, poured a little on my face, and drank the rest. The refreshing, cool liquid hit the spot.

"How about a swim?" Andrew looked back at the tennis courts. "Think we lost our spot."

"Yes!" I headed to the nearest chair, stripped down to my purple swimsuit, tucked my clothes in my bag, and plopped my tote and towel on the chair.

I missed swimming. My last beach trip had been with uni friends last summer. I ogled Sam's sleek pool and its sparkling water, half-shaded by the overhanging deck ceiling.

"Ready?" Andrew stood with one foot balanced on a seat mid sock removal. He swept an appreciative gaze down my body.

Heat suffused my cheeks. Could I deal with other guys checking me out today? I clamped my right hand over my left wrist.

He pressed away the smile curving his lips. "I'll see you in there."

I walked to the deeper end of the pool and jumped in with an unrefined splash, enjoying the cool water caressing my body and tingling my skin. I rose to the surface and flicked my long plait over my shoulder.

Andrew bobbed in the water nearby. "How about a freestyle race?"

We swam to the pool wall, and Andrew asked some people to move across so we had access to the entire length of the pool.

A cheerful, busty brunette offered to officiate. She pulled herself out of the water and balanced on the pool edge. "On your marks … get set … go!"

I pushed off the wall like a cannonball volleyed into the atmosphere and swam hard. My rhythm returned after several strokes, and I front crawled through the water, my arms slicing water and air, my hamstrings, quads, and glutes building to a pleasant burn. My swimming instructor's voice counted in my head, and I glimpsed the end wall. My chest stung, and my calves ached. I touched the edge, inhaled deep breaths, and wiped my palms across my face.

Andrew touched the wall moments later. "You're still faster," he said between puffs.

"Beat you by half a body length." I grinned and squeezed my braid.

"Bet you can't beat me." A lithe, muscled blond in his mid-twenties spoke from the pool edge.

I smirked at Andrew.

He huffed a laugh and whispered, "Go on, show him who's

boss."

I glanced up at my challenger. "All right."

He and Andrew traded places.

I glanced at the blond. "Any particular stroke you prefer?"

His blue eyes blazed, and he cracked his knuckles. "Freestyle's fine."

We raced, and I beat him by three seconds.

My lungs burned, and I heaved my breaths. I waded to the middle of the pool away from another challenge.

Andrew swam over to me, grinning. "Looks like we're trendsetters. Got any other bright ideas?"

I pursed my lips and glanced around. A toddler jumped from the shallow edge into her father's arms. I dived under the water, swam back to the deep end, and perched on the pool edge. A boxy ledge protruded from the centre of the wall half a metre higher than the rest of the edging. I grinned.

Andrew emerged from the water, his wet mop of hair brushing my legs. "What're you thinking?"

I waggled my brows. "You might want to move back or go to the side."

I stood on the higher ledge and positioned myself with my back to the pool. Edging backwards onto my toes, I closed my eyes and inhaled, imagining a backward flip. I opened my eyes, checked no one had ventured into my diving area, then raised my arms, palmed my hands to a point, and launched backwards. My toes lost contact with the ledge, and the familiar rush of adrenaline ravaged my veins. I slipped into the silky depths and re-emerged to cheering.

"You hardly made a splash on entry!" Andrew said.

My limbs buzzed, and blood rushed under my skin. "I've still got it!"

"You sure do."

I climbed back into position on the higher ledge—this time facing Andrew—closed my eyes and imagined somersaulting. A challenge with my height but doable. I had often surprised my swimming instructor with my ability to tuck into a small ball.

I opened my eyes and double-checked the chlorinated depths for obstacles, zoned out the small crowd now gathered, and focused on the dive. I launched up and forward, rolled into a ball before extending my arms on entry. Water slapped my skin, stinging my face and arms, and my chest tightened. Sloppy entry. My stomach fizzled, and I emerged to loud clapping and whistling. My cheeks heated. I climbed from the water, rivulets of water cascading to the concrete.

"Impressive." Jonathan's deep, velvety voice triggered goosebumps along my arms.

I turned, and my mouth dried.

A pair of aviator sunglasses obscured Jonathan's ebony eyes but not his lopsided grin. He wore short-legged black board shorts with a thick white waistband and black drawstrings. A blue-and-red beach towel hung over his wide shoulder, hiding one side of his spectacular caramel chest.

Holy virtue on a stick. Warmth permeated my skin, and another round of goosebumps prickled my arms. I gawked, my attention drawn to the spattering of dark chest hair trailing downwards and disappearing into the waistband of his shorts. *Stop looking at his shorts!*

I snapped my gaze away, and my cheeks burned. "Th-thanks."

Jonathan stepped closer.

I shivered.

"Are you always one to put on a show at a party?" He tilted his head.

I glanced back at the pool and its inhabitants. "Only if there's a pool deep enough to dive." I shifted on my toes. "My audience awaits." I returned to the podium, closed my eyes, and controlled my breaths. It seemed the arrival of a certain gentleman had spiked my blood pressure. I blocked out the image of his butterscotch abs and wowed the crowd one more time. My pièce de résistance: a backward-facing armstand somersault.

Yeah, my awesomeness prevailed. I rose to the surface to the rowdy applause of my adoring fans and launched toward the pool edge.

"That was hot, Diving Diana."

I peered up from the pool depths into the deep-coffee eyes of the party host. "Diving Diana? Really, Sam?"

Sam stood on the pool ledge with a delightful grin. "Would you prefer Double D?"

I spluttered. "No!"

He stretched his hand toward me. "How'd you not hit my radar until Jonathan introduced us? I love women who're tall. Please tell me you're into Asian guys."

I held back an eye-roll and wiped my palm over my face. With his boyish features—baby-soft skin with not a hint of a five o'clock shadow—reminiscent of a younger version of Harris Edwards in *Salvation*, Sam looked like a typical ladies' man in his button-down shirt with rolled-up sleeves and straight-fit navy shorts, albeit ten centimetres too short for me.

I raised an eyebrow. "How about you fetch my bag and towel, and I'll grace you with an answer." I pointed to my things farther down the path.

Sam collected and placed them on a nearby table, returned to the pool edge, and extended his arm toward me once again, his elbow resting on his bent knee. "So?"

I grabbed his warm hand and pushed up, stepping onto the paved path.

His gaze scanned my body.

I pulled away. Maybe I should wear a wetsuit. I suffocated a snort, reached for my towel, and wiped my face. I turned around, and my cheeks warmed. I had offered the playboy a view he appeared to have enjoyed. I whipped the towel around my slender body and secured a corner above my breasts.

He tilted his head.

I scrutinized his frame. "I'd totally be into you if it weren't for the hundreds of women you already spend your time with. I'm not into men with a revolving bedroom door."

He barked a laugh. "I'd send them all on their way if I have a chance at"—he waved a hand near my torso—"this."

"Dad taught me better than that. Thanks for the compliment, though." I swiped my bag and fumbled with the edge of my towel.

He glanced past my shoulder. "How about I whisk you away before Jonno woos you from me."

I peeked over my shoulder, and the blasted butterflies kicked up a fuss against my ribs.

Jonathan's heavy gaze rested on me while his friends talked around him.

I turned back to Sam. "What'd you have in mind?"

His eyes flashed. "I've something inside to show you. All above board, nothing illegal or scandalous."

I eyed the path to the mammoth house.

"Shall we?"

I semi-trusted Sam. What could go wrong? I cleared my throat. "Okay."

Sam escorted me down the path into the house and to the powder room. "I need you dressed and relatively dry." With a final sweep of his gaze along my toweled body, he sighed. "A shame to waste the view, but necessary."

I ignored his comment and locked the powder room door. Years of public pool bathroom changes had prepared me for a speedy exit. I loosened my braid, dried, dressed, and tied my long hair into a messy updo before exiting the bathroom.

"I prefer the towel look, but the summer dress works almost as well."

I suppressed a groan. "Does your mouth always talk without your brain knowing?"

Sam chortled and escorted me down two long corridors to a heavy-looking wooden door. He extracted a key from his pocket, unlocked, and opened the door with ease.

My breath hitched, and I stilled.

A colourful sea of vehicles filled the expansive room hidden underneath the house. Meticulous paintwork of at least ten cars gleamed under the overhead LED lights.

"They're beautiful." I sucked in my drool and caressed the grill of what I guessed to be an early 2000's Aston Martin Vanquish. My insides zinged. What a beautiful collection. A Valencia orange BMW 1 Series caught my attention, and my chest seized. "You know how to get a girl's attention." I stroked the metallic paint and shivered. "2011 M-Sport manual?" Was my voice husky?

Sam strolled over and touched the driver's door handle. "The one and only."

I ogled the twisted black wheel spokes and curved body lines and turned to Sam, grinning.

"So I heard right. You *are* into cars." He leaned against a Monaco blue 7 Series BMW, arms and ankles crossed, and regarded me.

I turned and focused on another car. A Maserati perhaps? I squinted, unfamiliar with this particular vehicle, and inched toward the next museum piece. I examined the cars ahead and noticed a classic Ferrari in the far corner. Stepping closer, my heart quickened with each footfall. "Oh!" I squeaked and jumped on the spot. "Is that a Rossa Corsa Red 1986 Ferrari 328 GTS?" I spun around and slammed into Sam's chest.

He chuckled and held me upright.

I pushed away, gliding my hands across the grills on the 328's squared bonnet, and strummed the small yellow Ferrari badge.

"It is." His voice was soft, reverential. "You know your cars well."

"It's Dad's dream car. I'd know this supercar anywhere after hearing about it all my life." I closed my eyes, recalling Dad's words. "The last classic Ferrari V8, its power-to-weight ratio's almost one hundred and sixty and is now worth"—I popped my eyes open and gaped at Sam—"well over two hundred grand."

He nodded and crossed his arms.

"Bet it goes like the clappers. Zero to one hundred in five-point-nine seconds. I'd do almost anything for Dad to ride in one of these babies." I admired the immaculate black-leather trim through the pristine driver's door window.

Sam hip-bumped me aside, opened the door, and nudged me toward the seat. "Get in."

I shoved my bag at his chest and luxuriated on the cool leather—avoiding the headrest, aware my chlorine-riddled hair could tarnish this perfection—and handled the gear stick and steering wheel with soft strokes. I closed my eyes and breathed in the scent. The aroma of aged leather filled my senses. Dad would love this. My eyes dampened, and I glanced out the windscreen, smiling.

Sam squatted beside me at the open door, eyes bright. "You'd do almost anything to let your dad ride this beauty …?"

My mouth dried, and I scraped my teeth over my lower lip. "Y-yes?"

Sam leaned closer with parted lips and an intent gaze. "How much are you willing to pay?"

My pulse thundered in my neck, and I ran a hand across my messy updo. This would cost me dearly. I closed my eyes, counted three breaths, and reverted my focus to Sam, who still watched me.

I straightened my posture. "Name your price." My voice shook, and I ground my back molars together.

He chuckled through curved lips. "Not sure you can afford it," he whispered.

I stared back with even breaths and ignored the tempest building in my belly. "Try me." I impressed myself when my voice sounded strong and sure.

Sam's pupils dilated before he broke eye contact. He wobbled in his squatted position, stabilising himself with a hand on the polished concrete floor.

The pounding in my chest and along my pulse points thudded.

Sam cleared his throat and stood. He stepped back and plunged his hands into his shorts pockets.

My hands shook, and I bowed my head. *Thank God.* Sam may have a reputation with the ladies, but he was a gentleman. No wonder he and Jonathan were best mates.

I exited the 328 and closed the door with painstaking care. Looking into Sam's dark eyes, I shrugged. "What did you want?"

A sheepish expression veiled his face. He pressed his pointer finger on the smooth skin of his right cheek. "How about a kiss?'

I lifted an eyebrow. "That's all?"

"Yeah."

I smiled and leaned down toward his cheek. My chest lightened, and a sense of calm flooded me as I placed a feather-light kiss on his soft skin.

A throat cleared behind me. "You cruising for a bruising, Sam?"

CHAPTER EIGHTEEN
Slow and Steady

Sam broke away from my peck and blanched.

I turned around, my insides spinning and crashing.

Jonathan stood tall and tense, muscled arms crossed, his stubbled jaw clenched.

Sam stepped away from me.

I narrowed my eyes, my face heating. "I was making a down payment for a service Sam'll be providing."

Jonathan's mouth fell open, and he rubbed his forehead.

I pointed to the Ferrari. "This's Dad's dream car, and Sam's promised to take him for a ride." I wiped my clammy palms against my thighs. "I thought it was worth the price to fulfil Dad's dream." I turned to Sam.

His face had regained some colour, and his eyes had brightened. A sly grin slid across his features. "Totally."

I snuck a furtive peep at Jonathan, and his fists were now clenched. I retrieved my bag from Sam. "I'll message you about a time for Dad's ride."

Sam nodded, his gaze flickering between Jonathan and me.

Now what? Jonathan was my ride home, but I needed some fresh air. I stalked toward the exit, avoiding Jonathan, my chest easing when I reached the doorway.

A firm hand gripped my left wrist and halted me in my tracks. "Diana."

I halted, my eyes drawn to Jonathan's hand holding my wrist, and my breaths quickened. Trapped.

A flashback, of another large hand grabbing me, punched me in the gut. My vision blurred, and I trembled.

"I'll, ah, see you both later." Sam brushed past us in the doorway and disappeared.

Jonathan shifted me around to face him, my gaze still transfixed on his hand wrapped around my wrist.

My stomach plunged, and I swallowed bile. *Do not vomit, Diana!*

I sucked in lungfuls of air and blinked at the neighbouring yellow Porsche 911. Where was I? I raised my fuzzy head and looked into the face of my captor. *Not my captor.*

Jonathan furrowed his brow, tilted his head, and released my arm.

I shuddered a breath and clutched my hands to my chest, rubbing my wrist.

He narrowed his eyes, his gaze boring into my movements.

I stilled.

He leaned closer, and his eyes widened. His focus bounced between my hands and my face. "What's that mark on your wrist?"

I peered down and grimaced. Faint red lines encircled my wrist, and my chest tightened. Coldness slithered down my spine and along my skin. I closed my eyes.

The hard, cool door against my cheek. Sharp plastic jerking my skin. Tugging and burning.

"Diana?"

"Cable-tie scars," I whispered.

"Pardon?"

I looked into Jonathan's eyes, and tears blurred my vision. "Cable-tie scars. Two cable ties, actually."

A storm of expressions flooded his face. He stepped closer. "What do you mean cable-tie scars. Did someone—"

"Yes." The first tears slid down my cheek.

His features hardened, and his nostrils flared.

"The reason I deferred my uni degree."

"Someone bound you?" His level, controlled voice caught me off guard. It seemed I had invoked the serious police officer within. I supposed all officers had to detach from their work.

"Yes."

His jaw flexed like he was grinding his molars.

My heart seized. Perhaps I had imagined his earlier detachment.

"No wonder you were petrified when I offered to change your

flat tyre." His voice cracked, and he cleared his throat. Twice. "It …
it all makes sense."

My lips curved in a sad smile, and my chest lightened knowing
my secret was no longer hidden.

He rubbed his jaw and straightened. "Did they hurt you?"

I laughed. What an absurd question! "Of course, he did." I had
lived with the nightmares, and the physical and emotional scars, for
months. The deep wounds inside often seemed immovable. I sighed.
"But, no, he didn't beat me or rape me if that's what you meant."

"I'm sorry. I can only imagine an event like that would change
you." His penetrating stare regarded me. "Did they apprehend him?"

"I've already told the police everything. I'm not interested in
another interrogation." I turned. "Not feeling up to a party anymore.
I'll see you later."

Jonathan blocked the exit. "But I'm your ride home."

I stared at the doorframe behind him. "Dad said he's happy to
get me, so you can enjoy yourself here for longer."

He stepped closer and lifted my chin to meet his gaze. "Please.
Let me make up for my monumental screwup. I want to get you
home safely."

My tummy fluttered at his gentle touch and pleading eyes. I
sighed. "Yeah, okay."

Jonathan's fingers slipped from my chin to my upper arm.

Fire licked a path along my skin.

He assisted me out the showroom door and pulled it behind him
with a thud as the lock clicked into place, and we exited the house.

I waited under the eaves of the entertaining area while Jonathan
farewelled several friends, his brilliant smile disarming his
disappointed mates. Sam waved from across the pool.

I smiled and blew him a kiss.

Jonathan brushed his shoulder against mine. "You shouldn't
encourage him. I'd hate to break his perfect nose."

We proceeded through the front gate and trailed the footpath,
fragmented conversation dwindling with each step. Jonathan
removed his key fob from his pocket, and the taillights of his
beautiful charcoal Mustang flashed down the road. He opened the
passenger door for me, he eyes intense.

I slipped onto the sun-warmed seat and closed my eyes.

The engine rumbled, and the stereo blared for half a second

before it was muted.

I opened my eyes and clutched my hands in my lap, watching trees pass by. *Think of something to say, Diana.* I turned and studied Jonathan's side profile. "Would you really punch your best friend?"

He nodded, face neutral, his attention on the road ahead.

Seriously? I leaned back in my seat. "Why?"

He slowed the vehicle at a T-intersection and turned onto the main road home. "He's my best friend, isn't he? So he should know to steer clear. Plus, I'm not sure I'd trust him with you."

Heat stung my cheeks and infused my chest. What kind of best friend threw his buddy under a bus like this? I slowed my breathing. "You don't trust your own best friend? Sam seems trustworthy to me."

He scoffed and overtook a slow van. "I'd hardly call asking a girl to kiss him a trustworthy trait."

I glared at him and crossed my arms. Girl indeed. "Whatever you say."

Jonathan's jaw twitched.

I stared out the passenger window.

"Diana."

I turned and met his softened gaze.

"Sorry. I …"

"What?" Silence stretched between us, and I swallowed a growl. "You what? Enjoy acting like an overbearing big brother to the pitiful *girl* I am?"

He flexed his fingers around the steering wheel. "I am … *not* … your brother."

"And I'm not a little girl."

"I noticed." Jonathan's gravelly tone vibrated down my spine.

I pressed hard against the seat back.

He rubbed his hand along the stubble on his chin.

My stomach knotted, my chest still inflamed with irrational heat. "Glad we have that sorted because incest's illegal."

He shot a wide-eyed glance at me before returning his attention to the road.

Why on earth had I opened my mouth and said *that*? Lord, have mercy on me.

"Can't imagine your father would be too pleased with your conversational skills." Jonathan's voice lowered. "You sure know how to charm a guy with your innocent Christian-girl talk."

I stared out the windscreen, fisting my hands. "Innocent Christian girls aren't typically abducted." My lungs burned more than my throat. "I apologize for allowing you to live under the pretense I'm anything close to the Proverbs thirty-one woman every Christian expects me to be."

I swiped a tear from my eye, turned my back to him, and stared out the passenger window. A sob shuddered my chest, and I focused on the trees whizzing past. "I was an A-grade student, but I've failed abysmally when it comes to life. I've wondered often if I'd feel differently if he'd beaten or raped me. I think I'd feel more justified in my feelings if he had."

A dampening hush clouded the car the rest of the trip home. My tears welled up and over. I had so much further to go in my healing journey.

Jonathan parked the car and turned off the ignition.

I glanced at the house. "Thanks for driving me home," I whispered. "Sorry you had to witness one of my … melted-brain moments. The self-loathing isn't as bad as it was a few months ago." I reached for the door handle.

"Wait."

I turned and noticed his drawn features.

"May I pray for you?"

I nodded.

He grasped my hands in his and prayed.

More tears jettisoned off my chin with each compassionate word. "Thank you."

He released my fingers and shifted in his seat, his face now closer to mine. "If there's anything I can do to help, tell me." He met my gaze. "And I apologize for the interrogations." A soft smile tugged his lips. "My mother says I've always been this way, even as a child. Says I care too much, and in your case, I know it to be true." He brushed my cheek, tucking aside loose strands which had fallen from my messy updo.

Butterflies trembled inside my abdomen.

His stare lanced me.

Heat bloomed across my skin.

"Do you feel similarly?" His velvety tone lowered.

"Guilty as charged, officer."

He smirked and removed the keys from the ignition. "You always this witty?"

I pursed my lips, meeting his gaze. "When confined in vehicles with handsome, young men."

He beamed. "So this's common practice for you?"

My eyes widened. "No! The last guy to drive me home ended up having a one-on-one conversation with Dad. I was sixteen at the time, so I'm out of practice … or never in practice to begin with."

"Don't start now unless you'd like me to confine you to a small cell at the station."

"Threat of arrest, Senior Constable Harris?" I clasped my hands together and pretended to swoon. "How romantic."

Jonathan grinned and shook his head.

I grabbed my bag and exited the vehicle.

We shuffled to the front gate with lazy steps and stopped. Jonathan sidled closer and brushed his soft lips across my forehead.

My pulse quickened, and I breathed in his unique scent. If a kiss on the head overstimulated my heart, could I withstand a kiss on my mouth?

Another kiss from another time edged into my mind. *Not now.*

My breaths shuddered.

Jonathan nudged my shoulder. "I'll call you next week. Hopefully you've a night free so we can go out for dinner?"

I blinked to clear my mind and smiled. "Think so. Just don't take your time. Otherwise, Sam might beat you to it."

A mischievous grin flitted across his face. "Not if I confiscate his mobile. One can't guarantee his phone wasn't bought with dirty money until it's thoroughly investigated."

I laughed and opened the gate. "Note to self, don't cross the hot cop. See you at church tomorrow." I half-bounced into the house straight to my bedroom, where I lay on my bed, closed my eyes, and dreamed of a better future.

✐ ✐ ✐ ✐ ✐ ✐ ✐

13 November

I did it, Mum. I went to my first party with lots of people in attendance. Well, you know, my first since … him. I was glad I had already arranged a lift home with Jonathan (who's such an amazing guy) because it meant I didn't have a car nearby to turn back and flee the moment I saw how many people were attending. So you can be proud of me for not wimping out.

Anyway, a few things happened (like finding Dad's favourite car!) and now Jonathan knows about what happened to me. Only the essentials. He was upset, which is natural, but he's a police officer so he asked questions I didn't want to answer. It kinda rubbed me the wrong way. I don't like the prying. I just want to forget and move on. I wish I could forget.

He also asked me out for dinner. I think it was dinner. His lips against my forehead seared my brain … and then I remembered the other kiss and couldn't stuff it inside quick enough. I'm not sure I'm ready to kiss a guy yet, Mum. I know Jonathan's different, but … I'm still feeling weird about everything. Am I ready for a boyfriend? Is it wise, considering I'll have to return to Melbourne next year?

I really like Jonathan. I wish you were here to help me talk this out. Sometimes I wonder what it would be like having these conversations with you instead of Victoria. Don't get me wrong, I love that petite woman and everything she's done for me and Dad, but you'll always be my mum. I hate that I've missed so much with you.

CHAPTER NINETEEN
A New Opportunity

Victoria captured my hand, mid-air. "Leave your hair alone. It's perfect." She squeezed my fingers and placed my hand on my vibrating knee.

I bounced on the kitchen stool, currents of electricity charging my veins and turning me into a human version of the Energiser Bunny. Would I survive my first-ever date?

Victoria cocked her head. "I think that's a vehicle."

I stilled. My heart jackhammered, sending a rush of blood to my ears. I squeezed my denim-clad knees and practiced my breathing.

A knock echoed at the front door.

"Want me to get it?" Victoria curved a brow.

"N-no." I closed my eyes, inhaled and exhaled, and returned her gaze. "I've got this."

She beamed a smile. "I'd better check on Jazzy. Have fun, sweetheart."

"Thanks." I stood on shaky legs, clutched my jacket and bag resting on the entryway table, and stared at the wooden barrier. I could do this.

Affixing a smile—which I hoped appeared friendly—I opened the front door and looked up at Jonathan. "Hey."

His Adam's apple bobbed. "Hey. You look really good."

"Thanks." I fingered my hair behind my ear and closed the front door.

"Ready?"

"Yeah."

Jonathan nodded toward his beyond-sexy Mustang. He strode

to the passenger door and opened it, his dark eyes tracking my approach.

My inner flutters reignited. I concentrated on each step, thankful Victoria had suggested I stick with casual flats instead of the small heels I had selected. My stomach flipped the closer I stepped toward my striking date, with his bright smile, unbuttoned shirt collar, and rolled-up sleeves. I now understood Victoria's obsession with forearms. Ee-chee-wa-maa!

Jonathan gestured to the passenger seat.

I brushed past him and slid onto the cool leather.

He closed the door and rounded the vehicle while I inhaled every atom of cologne trapped in the car with me. Intoxicating man. He buckled and aimed a lopsided grin my way.

My insides fizzed like a freshly opened bottle of soft drink. Why would this beautiful, brave cop be into a mess like me?

We drove to Benanu's and grabbed a booth away from the crowd. He ordered the salmon, and I ordered the eye fillet. My steak was almost as scrumptious as the company in front of me.

Jonathan grabbed the upright menu jammed near the salt and pepper shakers. "Any space for dessert?"

"Barely."

His focus flitted between my eyes and lips. "We could share?"

My breath caught. "Uh. Sure."

We perused the menu, and someone near our table cleared their throat.

I glanced up and smiled. "Keanu!"

His face shone. He nodded toward Jonathan—who offered him a wary smile—before returning his bright-eyed gaze to me. "Sorry to interrupt, but I just stepped out of a management meeting." Keanu would strain a muscle if he smiled any bigger. "We might have a job you'd like. Free tomorrow morning to go over the specifics?"

I gasped and clutched the table edge. "Really?" All I had tomorrow was my eleven o'clock checkout-chick shift. "Yes! What time? The earlier, the better."

Keanu puckered his brow and reminded me of a young Columbo about to crack his next case. "I'm opening tomorrow morning, so how about ya rock up around seven and we can have breakfast."

"Deal."

He smiled and extended his thumbs. "Night, Jacobsen."

"K-Man." I chuckled and returned to the menu. When I looked up, Jonathan's gaze pierced me with a steely stare. My smile wobbled. "What's the matter?"

"Do you think it appropriate to breakfast with the owner's son?" His voice was as cool as his eyes.

I scrunched up my face. "It's just Keanu. We've been friends since Grade Two."

His lips flattened into a line.

I pressed my hands in my lap and eyed my date. "He's like a brother. Cute and sweet but not my type."

Jonathan rested back in his chair, the edge of a smile creeping onto his face. "Okay." He eyed the menu. "What're you thinking? The dark chocolate cheesecake looks good." His satiny words launched a barrage of shivers along my skin.

I stared at his mouth. Could I kiss him one day? My cheeks warmed, and my abdomen squeezed away any appetite for dessert. "On second thought, I don't think I've enough space." I bit the inside of my mouth.

He scrunched his brow. "You okay?"

My pulse hitched. I looked away from staring at his full lips—again—and cleared my constricted throat. "Yep. Great."

His shoulders relaxed. "I might have a latte. Would you like a drink instead? I know you don't like coffee." He glanced back at the menu. "Tea? Hot chocolate?"

Goosebumps covered my arms. How on earth was I to contemplate dating this man when his every word ignited full-body tingles? I inhaled a short breath. "No. I'm fine. You have your latte."

He raised his head and captured my gaze.

Breathe, lungs! My stomach flip-flopped, and I wiped my clammy hands along my thighs.

Jonathan surveyed the contours of my face before gazing at my lips.

A flush crawled up my neck. "Coffee?"

A soft hue darkened his caramel cheeks. "Right. Coffee." He captured the attention of a nearby waitress. "Can I get a latte and the bill, please?"

"Right away, sir." She headed toward the bar.

Had I affected him as much as he affected me? I shifted in my seat and savoured the sensations.

♥ ♥ ♥ ♥ ♥ ♥ ♥

Keanu leaned against the doorframe of my small office, arms crossed, face prickled with fresh fuzz. Seemed Keanu's Christmas gift to himself earlier in the week was to grow a beard. "You finished the stocktake already?"

I glanced up from my computer monitor. "Not yet, took a break to chase up the New Year's Eve order."

He raised a brow. "That's why I dropped by, to see if you'd heard back from the supplier."

"Give me a sec." I scanned the email and attached invoice. "Everything's confirmed and will be delivered at six A.M tomorrow." I squinted and met my boss's gaze. "Did you contact your friend covering the live music?"

He scratched his beard. "All organized."

"Great."

Keanu nodded toward me. "Isn't it about time ya left for the day?"

"Soon. I've only one more shelf to check at the bar before Dad picks me up after his joyride."

He chuckled. "Isn't this the second time Sam's taken him out?"

"Third." Dad and Sam caught up every other week to talk cars and take one of Sam's father's vehicles for a spin. Dad came home buzzing like someone with a litre of coffee flowing in his veins.

"Guess it's a good thing yer dad gets along with him."

"Yeah." Dad's approval bode well for my friendship with Sam.

"And how's the preggo?"

I snorted and lifted my face. "Victoria might slap you if she heard you talk about her like that." I stood and tucked my chair under the desk.

Keanu's eyes sparkled. "She knows she's still my favourite teacher."

I rotated my neck and shoulders. "She's tired. It's a long way off until baby arrives in June." I grabbed the computer tablet from my desk, which I had used for stocktaking, and stepped toward him. "I babysat for Victoria's birthday last week and practically had Jazzy tied to my hip over Christmas and Boxing Day. While school's on break, I'll nag Victoria to give me custody of Jazzy whenever Dad's home or she just needs a break."

He arched a brow. "And you'll call if ya need to shift workdays."

I nodded toward the hallway. "I try not to rock the boat if I don't need to."

Keanu narrowed his eyes. "This's the whole point of the flexible gig. To make things easier for you and Mr. and Mrs. J."

I huffed a breath. "I know."

"Good." He stepped aside and walked beside me down the hallway toward the dining area. "And Officer Awesome? Haven't seen him much the last few weeks."

"He's spending his day off work today testifying in court. I had an inkling but really no idea how busy he'd be." I bit the inside of my mouth and clutched the tablet to my chest. "So long as nothing disastrous happens in town and he doesn't pick up extra shifts, we should be going out tomorrow night." Our last date was almost two weeks ago. We had missed the Twilight Christmas Carnival in Robinvale last week, so I was looking forward to visiting their local Christmas lights before everyone pulled their decorations down.

Keanu opened the door leading to the restaurant. "Other than discovering the pitfalls of dating a cop, is everything between you two good?"

Warmth dusted my cheeks, and I bit back a grin. "Yeah. Jonathan's amazing." I stepped behind the bar and entered the tablet password.

He scuffed his toes against the rough carpet. "Mum said she watched a morning talk show program earlier in the week which talked about living with an enforcement officer." He rubbed his chin. "Want me to download a copy?"

"That'd be great. Thanks."

He shoved his hands in his pants pockets. "See ya tomorrow?"

"I'll drop by early in case you need help."

"Thanks." Keanu nodded and disappeared around the corner.

I opened the cupboard and recorded the liquors we had on hand. "Diana?"

I straightened and turned. "Hey, Kortney."

"I thought it was you." She leaned against the bar. "You work here too?"

I returned a bottle of whisky to the shelf. "No longer at the supermarket."

"How opportune for me." Kortney flashed a bright smile. "I'm writing a piece on young women in the workplace."

My eyes widened, and I stilled. "You're a journalist?"

"Yes. I work for a local paper."

Wow, what a small world. "I study journalism."

"Really? How exciting! Where are you studying?" Her enthusiasm sparked a part of me I had ignored since the attack.

"RMIT in the city. I'm on leave at the moment."

"Oh." Something crossed her features and disappeared in a breath. "I hope everything's okay?"

I plastered a smile to my face. "Yes, all good."

She leaned closer and raised a brow. "When you complete your studies, do let me know. I can put a good word in for you at the paper."

My chest warmed. A real job at a local paper would be a wonderful start to my career. I should message Tara and tell her about my new friend. Tara had sent the occasional short, friendly message in recent weeks.

Kortney pressed her lips together. "So, would you be interested in sharing about what you do here and incidentals like that for my article?"

"It sounds like a great opportunity for me to learn from you, so, yes. I'm in!"

She beamed. "Great. Now I know where to find you, I'll get in contact." She nodded toward a nearby table where the guy she had attended Sam's pool party with currently lounged. "I'd better get back. Talk later."

"Have a great night." I returned to the final bottles needing to be checked, completed my task minutes later, and padded to my office.

An email from Keanu marked 'urgent' awaited me.

To: djacobsen@benanustellarine.com.au
From: keverton@benanustellarine.com.au
Subject: TV segment

J-Bird,
Here's the video I mentioned. Runs for about five mins.

Go home already,
K-Man.

I chuckled and forwarded the file to my personal email address. An alert beeped on my phone seconds later, followed by a different message tone. I scrunched my brow and grabbed my phone.

Jonathan: CALL ME WHEN YOU CAN.

My chest tightened, and I dialed his number.

"Hey, gorgeous."

"Hey." I closed my emails and other work programs. "How'd you go today?"

"Did what I needed to do." He cleared his throat. "Tell me, you up for an early dinner? I've been called in to cover the overnight shifts for tonight and tomorrow."

A heaviness squashed my lungs, and I sagged against the chair. "Oh. Yeah, s-sure. I'm at work waiting for Dad to pick me up."

Static buzzed over the line. "I'm a few minutes away. Can you call your dad?"

"Okay. See you soon." I sighed and dialed Dad.

"Princess! I haven't forgotten you." Dad sounded far too happy, like he was high on something. Petrol fumes, no doubt.

"Hey, Double D!" Sam shouted through my phone.

I groaned.

"Double D?" Dad's voice disappeared behind an odd shuffling scratchy noise before the distinct sound of Sam's laughter tolled.

What were those two up to?

"Dad?" I switched off the computer.

He laughed. "I'm here, sorry."

"Jonathan's been called in to work, so we're having an early dinner tonight. You're off the hook, so feel free to play at your friend's house longer." I stifled a laugh. How had the tables turned in our relationship?

"Oh, okay. Have fun, Princess." His voice lowered. "Not too much fun, though."

Sam's chuckles echoed through the earpiece before he shouted, "Say hi to lover boy for me!"

"Tell him yourself!" I laughed, said goodbye, and grabbed my bag.

I locked my office door, traipsed the long corridor to the

restaurant area, and spotted Jonathan leaning against the bar conversing with a uniformed officer.

Jonathan's gaze zeroed in on me, and his eyes brightened.

My heart performed its usual pitter-patter whenever I captured his attention, and I smiled.

Jonathan strode toward me, his black fitted slacks highlighting taut thigh muscles.

My mouth dried, and I ripped my focus from his pants to his handsome face.

He wrapped me in his arms, enveloping me with his comforting cologne. "Hey."

I tucked my face into his neck and breathed in the delicious scent before pulling back and grinning. "Hi."

"Want to eat here or go somewhere else?"

I furrowed my brow. "How much time do you have before you need to go home and change?"

He glanced at his watch. "A little under two hours."

"That's not going to leave enough time for you to drop me home."

"It'll be fi—"

"No." I fumbled for my phone in my bag.

"Diana, I've got this."

I squinted at Jonathan, shook my head, and dialed Keanu's office number.

"Home yet?" Keanu asked.

"I'm having dinner here with Jonathan, but he's been called in to work. Can you drive me home later?"

Jonathan's brow crumpled.

I pursed my lips with another head shake.

"Sure. Find me when you're ready."

"Thanks." I ended the call and eyed my slightly miffed boyfriend. "I'm not wasting a minute with you tonight. This way I'm with you longer."

His eyes softened. "Okay." He slipped his warm fingers between mine, and tiny shivers danced across my hand. "Let's find a table."

We weaved around diners to the corner table Jonathan preferred. He pulled my chair out, and I settled before he claimed his seat, his back to the wall. Although Jonathan was attentive, I wished he met my gaze more often when we dined out. Instead it seemed he surveilled the room more often than not. Was it a Jonathan trait or a skill drilled into him?

"I hope you're not too disappointed about me having to cancel our date tomorrow night."

I glanced at my hands and the fine lines encircling my wrists, the scars noticeable in the bright overhead light. Familiar memories drifted to the surface, and I pushed them aside. "I'll survive." I peeked up and noticed Jonathan's dark eyes considering me. My chest squeezed. I shifted in my chair and offered a small smile.

His scrutiny intensified. "One of the cons my job brings to a relationship."

Tell me about it. "I get it. Dad's been on call for as long as I remember. I'm used to being flexible." Even if I disliked being the sole person in this relationship needing to be flexible. Relying on myself had become second nature a long time ago. When I had not been such a basket case.

Jonathan nodded and glanced around the room. "Great."

Uh huh. Great.

CHAPTER TWENTY
The Downsides in Life

I lay in bed and stared at the paused video on my phone. My pulse jogged, and I bit my bottom lip. The TV segment shed light on many things I had not understood about Jonathan. Until now.

Two men and three women discussed the realities of living with a law enforcement officer. Everyone on the panel agreed with avoiding the "How was your day?" question. I cringed, knowing I asked this question often.

"Trust me," a petite blonde had said onscreen, "it's one of the worst enquiries to make because the answer's not something you want to hear. Who in their right mind wants to be reminded of the dangers their spouse faces on a daily basis?" She raised her brow. "I know I don't. And I know for certain I don't need to know how many criminals my hubby's arrested or how many abused children he extracted from a volatile home." Everyone onscreen nodded and murmured in agreement. "They're conversations best left unsaid."

I exhaled a long breath and pressed Play.

"Being aware of my husband's mood after a long shift has been a marriage saver," a middle-aged brunette said. "Many officers struggle to unwind, especially after a long, physically and emotionally taxing shift. We all deal with trauma differently, but our heroes face these situations on a daily basis, and it's up to us to be their support system."

A redheaded man nodded. "My partner prefers to sit and read in quiet for thirty minutes post shift."

"My hubby plays a video game or works out in our home gym," the petite blonde said. "The long hours compounded by hours of mind-numbing paperwork after an arrest or disturbing incident is a lot to detox from."

I paused the video again and ran my fingers through my hair. From what these experienced people suggested, I needed an abundance of patience, understanding, and flexibility to marry a police officer. *Marriage? Hold your horses, Diana.*

I leaned against the bedhead and closed my eyes. Jonathan was marriage material—this I already knew since Dad instilled in me years ago to only date a potential husband—but the idea still turned my stomach in loops. I prayed I was worthy of such a position … when I was ready for it.

My phone vibrated in my lap. I opened my eyes and clicked on the message app.

Jonathan: FAVOURITE VIEW OF TONIGHT'S SHIFT.

A brief video followed, and I pressed Play. My heart stuttered.

The screen revealed a computer monitor where images of myself flashed across the screen in a montage of photos. Some were new—Jonathan had shown me his favourite hiking track a few weeks ago, where he had snapped a selfie of our sweat-beaded, beaming faces—and others from church group outings when we had started hanging out together. Jasmine's sweet smile filled the screen on the final image where she was strapped to my front, mid-wave to "my Jon-than."

I sighed and replayed the video, my cheeks warming to match my heated insides. What was this man doing to me?

I fluffed my hair, switched to my phone camera, and snapped a selfie. The photo was a tad grainy, but my smile shone. Perhaps the spaghetti-strapped tank top I wore with its low scoop neck could be interpreted as a little risqué, but too bad. I looked pretty.

Me: ANOTHER ONE TO ADD TO THE COLLECTION. XX

Jonathan: NOT A CHANCE. THIS GEM STAYS ON MY PHONE WHERE I CAN STARE AS LONG AS I LIKE AND NOT MAKE YOU UNCOMFORTABLE.

My cheeks warmed, and I fanned my face.

Me: I DON'T MIND IF YOU STARE.

Jonathan: I THINK YOUR DAD WOULD IF I LAY IN YOUR BED AND STARED AT YOU ALL NIGHT.

My body flushed, and my heart drummed against my ribcage. Holy cheese balls on sesame crackers. Perhaps my skimpy summer pajamas had not been the wisest choice. I re-read his message, mulling over how to respond. I snapped another photo, this one of the ceiling where shadows and light from my salt lamp intermingled in a mesmerizing fashion.

Me: I EXPECT YOU'RE RIGHT. WHAT ABOUT THIS ONE?

Jonathan: SWEET. GIVE ME A FEW HOURS AND I CAN SEND YOU A PHOTO OF THE COFFEE CUP TOWER.

The coffee-cup tower? I snickered.

Me: WHERE'S THIS? ARE THEY DISPOSABLE CUPS?

Jonathan: STAFF KITCHEN. CERAMIC MUGS AND WHATEVER PEOPLE CAN FIND. IT'S A RUNNING JOKE BECAUSE THE FRONT DESK TEAM STACK THE DISHWASHER EACH MORNING.

Me: HOW MATURE. :-P

Jonathan: GOTTA BLOW OFF STEAM SOMEHOW. THE DAY CREW GET A LAUGH AT THE FACES FRONT DESK PULL, SO IT'S WIN-WIN.

Gotta blow off steam somehow. I rubbed my chest, my breaths quickening. Police officers needed to have fun too. A juvenile yet innocuous prank fit in with the things the panel had spoken about.

I rubbed my eyes and yawned.

Me: ENJOY YOUR COFFEE TOWER CHALLENGE. I'D BETTER GET SOME SLEEP. MESSAGE ME TOMORROW WHEN YOU WAKE UP?

Jonathan: SLEEP WELL, BEAUTIFUL. I'LL MESSAGE YOU TOMORROW. NIGHT. XX

Me: NIGHT. XX

I watched the final minute of the TV talk show segment, plugged my phone into its charger, switched off the light, and snuggled under the covers.

I reclined on my bed with my gaze glued to Mandi Blake's latest Christian romance ebook. A message flashed at the top of my phone screen, and when I caught the sender's name, my heart skipped a beat.

Jonathan: YOU STILL AWAKE, MY DELIGHTFUL DIANA?

My pulse raced, and anticipation shot through my veins.

Me: YES, MY JOVIAL JONATHAN.

Me: OKAY, THAT WAS PATHETIC. YOURS WAS BETTER.

Jonathan: THERE'S NOTHING PATHETIC ABOUT YOU OR YOUR SUBPAR ADJECTIVES.

I squeaked a laugh, and a snort shot out of my nose.

Me: YOU JUST MADE ME SQUEAK-SNORT-LAUGH.

Jonathan: WHAT! I MISSED AN ADORABLE SQUEAK-SNORT-LAUGH ERUPTING FROM THAT CUTE NOSE AND THOSE LUSCIOUS LIPS OF YOURS?

Heat crawled across my skin, and laughter bubbled in my lungs.

Me: YES?

The chorus of Casting Crowns's *Courageous* pierced the quiet—the ringtone I had downloaded for Jonathan—and I swiped the screen mid-laugh.

"Still squeaking over there, beautiful?" His velvet baritone oozed down the phone line, dancing goosebumps along my arms.

"Kinda."

Jonathan chuckled. "I love it when you laugh. I love making you laugh."

"Even when I shoot juice out of my nose?" I smirked.

His rumbled laughter filled my ears. "Especially when you snort juice. You fared much better than the people I come across on the job snorting other substances."

My stomach clenched. Another reminder of the dangers of his heroism. "No doubt, but it still hurt a lot!"

Earlier in the month we had met at Benanu's for an after-work drink. Jonathan had cracked a hilarious joke, and I had laughed mid-sip, sucking the juice up an airway. A painfully cold, bubbly stream of liquid soon shot through my nose into my lap, and Jonathan's eyes had bulged before he boomed with laughter, tears streaming down his face.

"At least I won't need to call an intervention for your addiction to sparkling apple juice." Jonathan chuckled.

"I do like me some sparkling apple … just preferably down my throat and into my belly." I performed my best Homer Simpson impression. "Mmm, spark-liiiing aaaaa-pple juuuuuuuuuuuice. Aaaaaaaaaaahhhhhh."

Jonathan's laughter sounded again, triggering another round of warm and gooey feelings inside me.

"So, what's up?" I furrowed my brow. "Thought you were working?"

"I wanted to hear your voice." He sighed. "Had a rough domestic violence situation, and I'm taking a break in the staff kitchen."

Heaviness weighed upon me. What a huge challenge for him to deal with. "I'm sorry to hear, and at this time of the year too. After the things Victoria told me about her ex-husband, I can only imagine."

"Wasn't pleasant, but it's especially difficult with children involved."

"Oh." I inhaled a shallow breath. "Are the children okay now?"

"Depends on your definition of 'okay.' Surviving hefty beatings and appalling parental neglect is hardly okay in my books, but they're out of the situation now. With relatives."

Tears stung my eyes. "I … I …"

"I know," he whispered, his voice almost strangled. "Sorry. Even the barest of details is hardly conducive to a late-night conversation. I should've held my tongue. I hope you sleep okay."

"I'll be fine." I rubbed my wet eyes. "I'll say a prayer for those children."

He cleared his throat. "Me too. It's nights like these I wish I had someone to go home to."

"I wish you were coming home to me," I whispered, my voice choked. "I'd give you all the hugs in the world."

"I know, beautiful, but it seems Sam'll score all my hugs from now on."

I withheld another sudden snort. "You're going to be roomies?"

"Yeah, we finally pulled the trigger, and we're moving into a three-bedroom place in two weeks."

"Awesome." I stifled a yawn. "I'd better sleep if I'm going to be at work at six. Be safe."

"Sleep well, Diana."

"Night."

I clicked the virtual bookmark in my ebook app, placed my phone next to my bed, and prayed for the children impacted by Jonathan's heroism this evening.

"Thank you, God, for making such a remarkable man like Jonathan and sending him to help this family like he has helped me."

✒ ✒ ✒ ✒ ✒ ✒ ✒

2 January

Happy New Year, Mum. Sorry I didn't write yesterday but it's been a crazy few days. Was up late reading then chatting with Jonathan last night, then got up at 5AM for a 6AM start. Yeah, I regret it too. Well, not really. You instilled a love of reading into me, so I can blame you for my love of books, reading, and writing.

I've been learning about Jonathan's world. Why he does the things he does, and what I can do to make things easier. I feel like I'm the one to "compromise" my schedule and plans more than he does, but I guess that's just how it is? Did you feel similarly when Dad received an urgent callout? Were your date nights interrupted too?

I wish you could share some of your experiences.

I love you, Mum.

CHAPTER TWENTY-ONE
Moving Day

"Diana? Can you come help?" Sam yelled from somewhere down the hallway.

I glanced around Jonathan's work-in-progress bedroom in his new house and slid another neat pile of folded T-shirts into his half-filled chest of drawers. "Just a sec!"

Apart from the large furniture items Jonathan insisted he help unload at the crack of dawn this morning, Sam and I had handled most of the grunt work with their move. Sam's flexible work schedule accommodated days like this. Fancy-pants IT guru.

Before Jonathan had headed off to work, he insisted I not organize his "personal attire." I had giggled when I spotted a pair of Batman jocks amongst the tops and tees I had folded into his drawers and chuckled at the amusing array of printed T-shirts with sayings like "Fun Police," "Off Duty, Save Yourself," and "Loading … Police Officer." Batman undies and a Fun Police T-shirt? I pressed my hands against my warm cheeks and stepped toward the open doorway.

"Diana!" Sam sounded panicked.

I launched out of Jonathan's room, past boxes lining the hallway filled with Jonathan's photographs, and found Sam flat on his back in his bedroom, his legs splayed over a box.

Sam's fingers were white-tipped, clutched around another large box which pressed his chest. How had he ended up in this position?

I stifled a laugh and traipsed into the room. "What can I do for you?"

"Help me up?"

I quirked a brow. "How'd you end up like that?"

Sam attempted a shoulder rotation and cried out. He gritted his teeth. "Box. Off. Please."

I relocated the box pinning him to the floor—lifting it with more ease than expected—and reached out a hand to pull Sam up.

"No. My back!" He wheezed. "It spasmed. Can you help me roll to the side?"

I dropped to my knees beside his chest and stretched across his torso so I could reach his other side. I grabbed his hip and was about to pull him toward me into a side-lying position when something growled behind me. I whipped my head around.

"What're you two doing?" A dangerous-looking Senior Constable stood in the doorframe, arms crossed and jaw set tight. Jonathan's dark eyes and penetrative gaze impaled my heart.

I jumped up, my cheeks burning and chest pounding. My throat closed, unable to speak. I stared back, helpless, and clasped my wrists.

"Back. Spasm." Sam coughed. "Help?"

The ice facade melted from Jonathan's face. He brushed past me and kneeled to help his friend. "You pull a muscle again, Masami?" His tone had mellowed.

Masami?

Sam grunted. "Uh-huh. And … don't. Call. Me. That."

"Yes, I know. I'm not your mother." The hint of a smile lifted Jonathan's lips. He assisted Sam onto the bed with more finesse than I expected.

I squeezed my hands together, my stomach roiling. How could I help? I racked my brain. "D-do you need something, Sam? Painkillers? A heat pad?"

Sam closed his eyes. "Jon knows the drill."

"Oh." I inhaled a tremulous breath. "Guess I'll get back to arranging clothes."

I exited Sam's bedroom on wooden legs, my veins still flooded with adrenaline. My hands trembled, and I rubbed them against my thighs with each step to Jonathan's room. Whatever the heck had happened back there had set my entire body on high alert.

I vacillated my shoulders, counted several breaths, and returned to sorting boxes of clothing. The man owned more outfits than I did, and his shoe collection doubled my own. Admiring a blue-and-white dotted silk tie, I rolled tie number thirteen and slipped it into a narrow walk-in-robe drawer.

Someone cleared his throat behind me. "Diana?" Jonathan's soft voice echoed in the small space.

I reached for another tie and glanced at him. "Yes?"

He fidgeted with the belt clip on his tactical pants, and he met my gaze. "I want to apologize. For before."

"Before?" A lump clogged my throat, and I coughed. "When you assumed I was behaving inappropriately with your best friend? *That* 'before'?" Heat suffused my cheeks, and I turned to the ties, blinking away tears. I rolled and slotted the silk tie into place with shaking hands. My eyes burned.

Jonathan grazed my arm and turned me around. He lifted my chin with his index finger, his dark eyes wide. "I'm sorry for jumping to conclusions."

I nodded, dislodging tears down my cheeks.

He cocooned me in his strong arms, my nostrils imbued with his signature scent. "It was a rough shift, and I was feeling pretty dour before I walked in the door." He rubbed my back.

I nestled my wet face against his neck.

"Seeing you on the floor over Sam?" His chest heaved. "It pushed a button I'd normally be more resilient to."

The panel on the TV segment had spoken about this issue. Mood swings and how being a support during tough times like these made all the difference.

"I understand." My voice quavered. "But what do I need to do to help you trust me?" I pulled away from his firm wall of chest and traced a finger along his jaw. The scratch of his five o'clock shadow tingled the tip of my forefinger, a tingle which spread and ignited a low thrumming burn through my torso. The air thickened, my gaze drawn to the ebony depths of his intense eyes. I inched closer, my breaths quickened, and angled my chin up.

His mouth crashed down on mine, his lips as warm and supple as I had imagined. He tasted like his favourite spearmint chewing gum.

Better than peppermint.

I forced the remembrance away and fisted his shirt front.

He drew me closer, his anaconda arms wrapping my back, deepening our off-the-charts-spectacular kiss.

This. This was what I had feared, yet in the moment our lips touched, I was not afraid. Love, not fear, now engulfed my heart. A deep, burning love for this man with one of the toughest jobs on the planet.

Jonathan severed our connection in an unexpected string of gentle kisses to my lips, cheeks, and nose. He rested his forehead against mine, and our erratic breaths steadied. "I love you."

My thumping heart skipped a beat, I was sure of it. A smile inched to my lips, and I bit my bottom lip. "I love you too." My heart cried the words though they slipped out a whisper. "Batman underwear and all."

He leaned back with wide eyes before they narrowed. "Thought I told you to stay away from my personal attire." He huffed, wielded his weapon-like fingers, and tickled me. Relentlessly.

I squealed and snorted. "Stop!" I pealed with more laughter. "I can't help it if … B-Batman got lost … on the way t-to the … Bat Cave!"

"An unlikely story." His grip loosened.

I stepped back and caught my breath. "It's true," I said. "I found him holed up in a pile of your admittedly funny T-shirts. Perhaps he was on assignment to find the fun police?" I winked.

Jonathan chuckled. "That's Sam humour for you. He buys me printed T-shirts."

"Did he buy the Superhero underwear for you too?"

"That's all me, baby," he grinned and waggled his eyebrows.

I chuckled, my cheeks sore from too much laughter. "What am I going to do with you?"

He stepped closer and grabbed my elbows. "I know one thing you could do with me." His husky voice fired heat straight to my insides. Pulling me gently toward him, he looped his arms around my waist. His breath tickled my ear. "What do you say?" He murmured into my neck.

"One kiss," I whispered, my throat dry. I licked my lips.

His pupils dilated, his attention fixed to my mouth.

The heat in my belly spiraled. "Then it's back to work for me," I said, breathless.

A salacious smile slid to his face. "Anything you say, beautiful."

His smooth lips descended on mine, and my breath hitched in my throat. I savoured every new guilt-free touch and sensation.

Kissing Jonathan was like slipping into a warm pool of minty syrup. Cloying, heady syrup I wanted to drown in, its intoxicating deliciousness almost overwhelming. No wonder Dad and Victoria constantly sucked face. They were strong people in their own right but undeniable in their addiction to each other. An addiction I wanted for myself with this man.

"Mmm." I croaked and pulled away from the magnetic force emanating from the scrumptious man a breath away from me. "Time for work before I melt into a puddle."

His body shook, his laughter hijacking his frame. "We can't possibly have that happen. The last thing I need is your dad breathing down my neck because of your state of puddlement."

I laughed. "Dad's pretty scary when he needs to be."

Something flashed in his eyes before he stepped backwards. "I'd better check on Sam, see if the Valium and ice are helping." With a final lingering look in my direction, Jonathan departed with a huge chunk of my heart.

February and March flew by, and Victoria's girth expanded each week. I now worked from home one day a week where Keanu and I troubleshot the online work portal. Sometimes he visited instead of making multiple phone calls. His reason? To check I was working. I suspected my little sister had a lot to do with it.

Today he exhibited his powerful limbs performing push-ups with Jasmine balanced on top.

"Up!" Jasmine slapped Keanu's back.

I snuck a peek—what was a girl to do?—and smirked.

Jasmine adored her personal set of human indoor-play equipment. His strong back and arms delivered a multitude of piggyback rides, airplane trips, and freestyle swinging before he flopped on a dining chair and bounced her on his leg or knee while we talked shop at the dining table. Jasmine particularly enjoyed the raspberries Keanu blew on her neck, her pudgy hands slapping his ears in glee.

Keanu caught me mid-glimpse. "Like what ya see?" His voice teased. He crouched for Jasmine to slide off his back.

She plunged off with a giggle.

"It's not a bad look on you. The baby factor." I raised a brow before rubbing my palms over my tired face and reverting my attention to my laptop.

"My baby!" Jasmine said before returning to her blocks on the floor.

I chuckled and opened a spreadsheet.

"That's also an easy fix."

I raised my head. "What is?"

"The B-A-B-Y." He grinned.

"Sure thing," I deadpanned. "Will you tell Dad you're the father to my illegitimate child?"

"Not a chance. That's definitely your job," he chuckled. "I'll be living in our secret house in another country, waiting for ya. No way on earth I'd tell yer dad something like that."

I poked out my tongue and focused on the screen. "Ever the responsible party. Doesn't bode well for our marriage in thirty years."

His laughter reverberated in the air.

My phone rang. Kortney's name lit the screen. "Hey."

"So? What did you think?" Kortney spoke with exuberance. "I thought it was a pretty decent draft."

I clicked to the email she had sent me last night, which I had read several times before falling into bed. Her article triggered goosebumps down my arms, the beautiful flow of language and solid writing skills swelling my chest. Maybe I could one day accomplish a similar feat. Tara seemed to think I could.

I smiled. "It's only a draft? I think it's a great piece! Really inspiring for me. I'm almost champing at the bit for July to hurry up so I can get back to my studies!" Although it had taken some time, my excitement for my career had grown since I discovered Kortney was a journalist.

She chuckled. "That's what I like to hear. Us journos have to stick together."

"I'm not there yet."

"You're there in spirit," Kortney said. "I mean, I only graduated just over two years ago, so you're not far behind."

"Well, I think you did a marvelous job. Well done."

"Thank you. I'll leave you to your busy day. Catch up later."

"Bye."

Jasmine ran back to Keanu and jumped, her arms raised. "Up, up, Keman!"

I smirked at her nickname for him. The first time Jasmine had addressed Keanu as "Keman," we had both squinted at each other and shrugged. Days later, Keanu had taken Jasmine on a round-trip flight of the kitchen, and I had called for K-Man from where I worked in the dining room. Jasmine had giggled and shouted, "Keman!" and we had burst into laughter.

"Yes, Keman, uppety-up for my little Jazzy," I said, laughing at their cute antics.

He grunted and lifted her high. "I won't need my gym membership if I spend time picking up this little midget. She may be small, but she's keeping me fit."

A knock sounded at the front door, and I rose from the table. I opened the door and was greeted by a familiar set of almond-shaped eyes. A huge smile stretched my face.

"Hey, beautiful," Jonathan said.

A squeal reverberated behind me, followed by the deep timbre of Keanu's laughter.

Jonathan's face hardened. He straightened, his posture now rigid. "Am I interrupting?"

My chest tightened. This again? I stifled a sigh and plastered on a smile. "Not at all, just working from home. Keanu's entertaining the little princess while we go through gremlins in our online system. Want a cup of tea?" I opened the door wider and stepped back.

"Tea sounds great." He sighed, ran his fingers through his hair, and stepped across the threshold, closing the door behind him. Fatigue lines indented his smooth forehead.

How could I hold his jealous reactions against him when he worked tirelessly to protect our town? My past friendship and family struggles paled in significance to his daily life difficulties.

I massaged his shoulders. "Another tough shift?" My fingers dug into his tight neck tissue. I loved touching him and hoped to have a legitimate reason to one day touch the firm skin underneath his shirt.

"Hmm, mmm." He grasped my hands and pulled me around to face him, brushing his lips against my knuckles.

His light kisses sparked flames of heat inside me. My abdomen tightened.

"You know how to improve my day dramatically."

"I'm glad." I pressed our joined hands against his chest, leaned forward, and fused my lips to his.

Jonathan's mouth devoured mine with firm, satiny kisses. His hands escaped my grasp and slithered to my lower back, pressing me closer. Confidence exuded from his touch. Our mouths worked overtime, our bodies against one another, the closeness almost too intoxicating.

My hands slipped up his hard chest into his thick hair, and I massaged the back of his head to a rumble of throaty growls.

Jonathan ended our kiss, his breathing erratic like my own. "We'd better have that tea before I forget my manners and devour you on the spot," he whispered.

My skin radiated more heat at such illicit thoughts, and I nodded before stepping away. Each encounter with Jonathan added another layer of difficulty when it came to keeping my wits about me. His hungry, possessive lips were an addiction, and each kiss inched us closer to the clear lines we had drawn in the metaphorical sand. Perhaps we needed to have another discussion. I refused to fail God or my parents by sleeping with Jonathan before we shared lifelong vows.

Taking his hand, I walked him into the kitchen. "Why don't you sit, and I'll see if the troops also want a drink."

I found Keanu and Jasmine cuddled up on the couch, Jasmine's eyes fluttering closed. I glanced at the wall clock and gasped. How was it after two already? "Oh, Jazzy, I'm sorry, darling. I completely forgot the time. You're late for your nap."

Keanu chuckled and stood with Jasmine curled against his chest. "I knew the time but hoped you'd forget."

I reached for my little sister.

Keanu stepped back. "Nuh-uh, I'll carry my favourite heat pad to bed."

I smirked and followed them through the kitchen toward Jasmine's room.

Jasmine opened her eyes. "Mita Saysee's here." She waved at Jonathan.

He returned her wave with a raised eyebrow.

Mita Saysee? I arched my brow. "You mean Jon-than, darling."

"No. He Mita Saysee!" She huffed and flashed her not-so-sleepy eyes at me.

"Okay. Why don't you say bye-bye before you go to bed?"

Jasmine wriggled in Keanu's arms and pointed at Jonathan. "I kiss Mita Saysee."

Keanu chuckled and approached Jonathan. "Yes, ma'am, bestow yer kisses on Mita Saysee."

A broad smile lit Jonathan's features. "It would be an honour."

Jasmine padded her pudgy hands over Jonathan's stubbled jaw. "You scratchy like Daddy." She scrunched her sweet little nose, pulled his face to her, and planted a sloppy kiss to his lips.

Jonathan's eyes widened.

I suppressed a giggle while Keanu boomed a laugh.

"Bye-bye!" Jasmine waved from Keanu's arms as they disappeared down the hallway.

"I'll be back soon." I ascended the stairs, bounded into Jasmine's room, and assisted Keanu.

We returned to the kitchen minutes later.

"What was that about?" Jonathan rubbed the back of his neck.

I filled the kettle. "The kiss?"

"Yeah."

I set the kettle to boil. "She doesn't like kissing Dad when he's scratchy, so she typically plants one on his lips. Apologies for not giving you the heads up."

He smiled and shrugged. "It was cute … just unexpected. And the name?" He creased his brow. "How'd she get Mita Saysee from Jonathan? I've been racking my brain but can't see a link."

I pursed my lips. Hmm, Mita Saysee. Mita Saysee. My eyes widened. Oh no! Was it possible she was saying Mr. Sexy? Heat spread across my face and neck. Mr. Sexy was my private nickname I used for Jonathan outside adult company. I supposed Jasmine heard it too often. My skin flushed again, and I peered between Jonathan and Keanu.

Keanu glanced up and squinted before returning my gaze. His eyes sparkled, and he laughed. "Is it what I think it is?"

I gasped when he said the two words I hoped he never guessed. Trust Keanu to understand Jasminese.

Jonathan turned to me, his eyes seeming to dance. "Mr. Sexy, eh?"

"Trust Jazzy to throw me under a bus," I muttered. "Fine. Yes, okay, it's your nickname I use in the privacy of my home when my parents aren't around. Guess I need to remember snooping little ears in future."

Jonathan wrapped his arms around my waist. "Any other secrets you need to confess before Keanu and I interrogate Jasmine?"

Keanu laughed. "Hey, don't drag me into this."

Jonathan turned to Keanu, eyes bright. "She's a minor. Thought you'd be willing to sit in."

Keanu nodded and rubbed his beard. "Makes sense. When're we doing this—"

"Oy, you two! No one's interrogating my little sister." I pushed out of Jonathan's hold, crossed my arms, and summoned my fiercest mock glare.

The men laughed.

Keanu slapped Jonathan's shoulder in a friendly guy way. "On that note, I'm heading out. See ya Thursday, Jacobsen."

"See you." The closing front door sounded moments later.

Jonathan studied my face. His eyes darkened. "I'm glad my friends won't throw me under a bus for the things I might've said about you."

My breath shortened under his potent stare. "What have you said about me?"

A slow smile upturned his lips, and he pulled me against his chest. "Lots of good things … and perhaps a few I really shouldn't say," he whispered.

My pulse quickened, and my throat dried. "Like what?"

"Like how I'd love to fast track our relationship as you're the biggest temptation known to man."

My breathing shallowed in the wake of his confession. Were we doomed to fail? Or was it possible to keep our clothes on for the rest of our unwed relationship? I prayed we would surf these treacherous waves of attraction and avoid a wipeout.

I pressed my lips together. "Good thing Dad had the chastity belt installed a few years back."

Jonathan's shoulders bounced with laughter. "What a clever father you have."

"Most definitely. Dad took no chances. Apparently chastity

belts are all-encompassing these days, like body armour."

Jonathan wiped a happy tear from his eye. "Glad we have that sorted. Tell me, does your dad still know where the master key is?"

I shrugged. "If he's lost it, my husband can jimmy the lock. There's nothing you can't find on YouTube these days."

He rumbled a loud laugh.

I smirked. My heart lightened, and I sighed. Maybe we could keep our promise to wait until marriage. With God's help, how could we not succeed?

Jonathan kissed the tip of my nose. "You free tonight? I've a late start tomorrow, and a few of the crew want to go out. Up for another crazy night? I may be able to twist Sam's arm to have him join us."

I retrieved my mobile phone and scrolled through to my calendar. No babysitting duties or church appointments. "I'm free. What's the plan?"

Jonathan shrugged. "Not exactly sure. We'll probably end up at April's aunt's pub out past Robinvale." He leaned down and kissed my forehead. "I'm heading home for a nap since I've been up since three. I'll call when I know the details."

"I'll be ready for you."

His gaze caressed my face, and he cupped my jaw. "You really are beautiful."

My chest squeezed, and heat radiated from his hand. "You're no plain Joe yourself."

Jonathan smirked and released my face. "Think I'm a bit all right?"

I grinned. "You're more than a bit all right, Senior Constable Harris. The stuff of dreams."

He lidded his eyes and brushed his lips against mine. "So are you. I love you."

"I love you too," I whispered.

CHAPTER TWENTY-TWO
Tilting on One's Axis

Jonathan switched off his beast of a vehicle, leaned over, and brushed his lips against my cheek. "Don't be nervous."

I inhaled a breath—the air still warm from our wintry drive to his parents' place with the heater blasting—and peered into his calming rich-cocoa eyes. What a handsome face. I pressed my palm to his jaw and offered a weak smile. "I know. It's just a little … full-on. Being invited to your parents' house for lunch with my parents? It makes everything feel so …"

"Perfect?" Jonathan grinned. "My parents have heard so much about you, and Mum's been bugging me since the beginning of April to invite you and your parents over for a meal. I finally acquiesced last week."

I stared at him. "Your mum's been bugging you for two months?"

An indulgent smile stretched across his face. "She's excited. She's admired you from afar for years."

"Huh." Being excited to see me was unexpected. Bolstered with this new information, I smiled with a little more confidence. "Okay, let's get this show on the road."

"That's the spirit." Jonathan laughed and unbuckled his seatbelt. "You'll do just fine. In fact"—he turned back to face me—"you'll do better than fine. You'll wow my parents, and then you'll be sorry."

I raised an eyebrow. "Why will I be sorry?"

He smirked. "You'll unleash the 'I want grandbabies' side of her, and Mum'll be arranging our wedding before you know it."

I burst out laughing, my chest vibrating on each breath.

"Thanks for the heads up."

Jonathan exited the car and opened my door.

I seized his outstretched hand, spluttered a lungful of cold air, and stood. We walked to the front entrance, where Jonathan opened the door and announced our arrival.

"In the kitchen, love," a sweet, accented voice said. Mrs. Harris.

Jonathan's mother originated from Kolkata. Her family had immigrated to Australia, and from the brief conversations we had shared at church, Mrs. Harris's Bengali intonation was enchanting.

Jonathan's fingers pressed against mine as we walked into a large kitchen infused with colour and a lingering swirl of delicious, heady spices.

"My darling boy."

"Amma." Jonathan bent and kissed his petite mother on the cheek, then pulled me closer to his side.

Without warning, Mrs. Harris caught me in a firm hug. "Wonderful to see you in a more personal setting, Diana."

"You too, Mrs. Harris."

Footsteps neared. "Farhana, dear, let the girl go. You're making her nervous." Mr. Harris's soft voice crooned from behind me.

"No, I'm not, Henrik. Am I, Diana?" She released me and arched a brow.

I blinked, wide-eyed. Was this what "deer in the headlights" meant? "Ah, no, Mrs. Harris."

She patted my hand. "Good, good. Come, let's have some tea while we wait for Nick and Vicki."

I cringed and smoothed my facial features into a pleasant smile. The many nicknames my parents garnered disturbed me. Dad would always be Nicholas, and Victoria, well, Victoria. Nick and Vic were my least favourite versions, especially when their names were slurred into one quick Nickanvic or Vicannick. And the abhorrent "Nicky and Vicki"?

Ugh.

"Tea sounds wonderful. Thanks."

Mrs. Harris lifted the lid of a pot bubbling on the stove. Steam billowed, and a delicious scent of masala spices wafted to my nose. "Do you like chai tea, Diana? I brewed a special batch of my amma's recipe, passed down several generations. Masala chai is indisputably the best."

Jonathan nudged me and winked. "It's delicious."

I nudged him in return and addressed his mother. "I enjoy a cup of chai now and again. Yours smells wonderful."

Jonathan directed me to a stool at the kitchen bench, and his mother handed me a cup of tea.

I inhaled the rich flavours and sipped the sweet, malty, creamy chai brimming with flavour. My throat and chest warmed, and I savoured the taste. "Wow, this is really good, Mrs. Harris. Care to share your recipe one day?"

She beamed, her eyes bright. "Of course, dear! You marry my boy, and I'll give you the recipe as a wedding gift."

I coughed the tail end of my sip, covered my spluttering mouth with my hand, and sucked in spiced air. My cheeks heated, my wide-eyed gaze aimed at Mrs. Harris's back as she stirred a different pot on the stove.

A barrel of deep laughter rumbled from Jonathan's father. His warm amber eyes twinkled under his blond eyebrows. I glanced at Jonathan, and he mouthed "told you" before he grinned a broad smile.

The doorbell rang, and Mr. Harris disappeared, returning with my parents. Victoria's swelled belly almost hurt to look at. *Hurry up, little baby!* With less than a month until I returned to RMIT, I wanted as much cuddle time as possible.

"Nick! Vicki!" Mrs. Harris bustled around the bench and embraced them. "Where's your other little one?"

Victoria palmed her back. "We left Jasmine with Nicholas's mum. She insisted we enjoy a childless outing before this one arrives."

I mock pouted. "Childless? What am I then?

Laughter filled the air.

Victoria grinned. "You're my big kid."

I hugged my parents. "Have some chai, Victoria. It's delicious."

Lunch rivalled a banquet with vibrant flavours and mouth-watering fare. A mish-mash of Indian, European, and what I would call Australian cuisine, which everyone dug in to with delight. I enjoyed a helping of paneer masala curry with coconut rice, steamed greens, and honeyed carrots followed by a small spoonful of a creamy meatball dish with mashed potatoes and thinly sliced pickled cucumbers. There was also roasted lamb with accompanied roasted vegetables plus enough pickles, chutneys, and mustards to start a condiment store.

Conversation at the dining table—which was located in the family room and not the dining room—was friendly and amicable. Both sets of parents spent most of their time talking while I answered a few questions. I spent a majority of the meal sneaking glances at Jonathan and tapping my toes on his foot when he said something cheeky. A few unintentional leg bumps and brushes with him under the tablecloth added to my rising warmth, but I hoped the spicy curry hid any giveaway signs of a blush.

"How about we retire to the lounge room for tea, coffee, and some of Henrik's childhood favourite rosette biscuits," Mrs. Harris said.

We stepped away from the table with a chorus of chair legs scraping the tiled floor. Jonathan and I cleared the table and stacked the dishes near the kitchen sink, then ambled into the lounge room, where I explored my new surroundings.

A comfy grey cloth three-seater couch with cream-and-gold throw cushions lay along a wall with a mahogany coffee table separating a matching two-seater. Two cream armchairs filled the space against another wall, completing the U-shape configuration. Near a window facing the street stood a long buffet with doilies, vintage-looking knickknacks, and a few old photos.

I admired the low cupboard and spotted a photo of very young versions of Mr. and Mrs. Harris on what I assumed to be their wedding day. On either side of the frame stood much older photos of two different sets of newlyweds.

Jonathan brushed my arm and pointed to one of the outer frames. "These are Dad's parents on their wedding day, and these"—he pointed to the other photo—"are Mum's parents. Talk about worlds colliding."

His grandparents' wedding photos were a stark contrast to each other. Apart from everyone's smiles, their outfits were polar opposites. Mr. Harris's parents were dressed simply, in a plain suit and basic wedding gown. Almost Amish in nature. But Mrs. Harris's parents looked like they had stepped off the set of a Bollywood film.

I grinned. "A striking contrast between the couples. How'd your parents meet?"

Jonathan rubbed a hand along his chin. "This is actually Dad's second marriage. His first wife died of an eclamptic fit after she fell in the shower and hit her head a week after my brother was born."

I gasped and shot a glance at Victoria. My heart twinged. "How awful."

"Dad was widowed at twenty-two and needed someone to help look after Damien. Grandma Harris assisted a few days a week, but Dad needed more help and posted an ad on the church bulletin board. Mum applied for the job and worked around her university timetable, spending the majority of her free time obsessing over an adorable baby-and-handsome-father duo, or so Mum's always said."

"How romantic."

Jonathan scratched his chin. "I guess. They married about two years after they met. Good thing, too, or I wouldn't be here." He waggled his brows.

"An extremely good thing. I'd be pretty sad if you didn't exist."

Jonathan laughed. "You wouldn't know the difference if you never met me."

I shook my head. "You're wrong. I'd know deep inside I was missing something. Or someone in my life."

He reached out and intertwined his fingers with mine, kissing my knuckles. "You're gorgeous."

"Okay, you two lovebirds, come sit down," Mrs. Harris said from behind us, near the couches.

We walked hand-in-hand to the two-seater, and I noticed more family snaps on the wall above the armchairs. A photo of an auburn-haired boy with a cheeky grin hugging a dark-haired toddler caught my attention. The little toddler looked like how I imagined Jonathan had looked as a little tyke. I leaned closer to the picture and realized the hug looked more like a headlock.

"Is that you being held in a friendly headlock?" I held back a laugh.

A smile slipped to Jonathan's lips, and he stared at the photo. "Yeah. That's me and Damien."

"You're chalk and cheese," I said. "He totally missed out on the caramel complexion."

"His mother was a redhead with pale skin and freckles." He smirked. "Maybe Dad decided to change it up when he married Mum."

"Now, Jonathan, don't disparage my Damien's heritage." His

mother's voice quavered from behind us.

Jonathan and I turned.

A tear fell down his mother's cheek.

"Amma, I wasn't criticizing him …"

"I miss him so much." Mrs. Harris sighed. She was now wrapped in a hug with Jonathan on the couch, her husband holding her hand on her other side.

I noticed Dad's sombre face and Victoria's wet eyes. Thank God Grandma Joan had offered to look after my sister for the afternoon. Jasmine would not enjoy seeing all the upset adults.

"I miss him too," Jonathan whispered, his broken voice pulling on my heartstrings.

"He was a beautiful boy, Diana." Mrs. Harris smiled with glassy eyes. "So cheeky and a handful at times, but I fell in love with him before I even loved Henrik."

"He was a great kid," Dad said. "A hard worker with a great work ethic."

I scrunched my brow. "How'd you know him?"

Dad rubbed the back of his neck. "He was my apprentice many years ago. You probably don't remember him. You were only seven or so when he finished working with me."

I vaguely recalled Dad's apprentices over the years, but they rarely met at our home. Dad preferred to collect the guys for work if they had no other means of transportation. "I can't recollect anyone in particular."

"Henrik," Mrs. Harris said, "why don't you find the lovely photo of the boys at Jonathan's graduation from the Academy to show Diana."

I glanced around the room and realized I was the only person standing, so I claimed one of the armchairs when Jonathan's dad stepped from the room.

"Gone too soon, my Damien." Mrs. Harris shook her head.

Mr. Harris returned clutching a wooden frame. He deposited it into the outstretched hand of his wife. "Here he is, my darling."

I rose and approached Jonathan.

His mother turned the frame so the photo faced me.

A lovely shock of auburn hair. Dark-hazel eyes edged with a ring of sapphire blue.

No.

I gasped and shook my head. "Pierce?"

The last thing I recalled before everything went black was this unchanging fact: Jonathan's brother was my attacker.

CHAPTER TWENTY-THREE
Blindsided

I blinked, closed my eyes, and squinted. A faint lavender scent filled my nostrils, and my eyelids tore open. My heartbeat doubled.

I twisted my fingers in the soft bedspread beneath me and rotated. An oversized pillow ruffle blocked my view, and I flattened it with my palm. A wall and an unfamiliar set of closed floral curtains. I rubbed my eyes. Where was I? And how had I ended up on this bed? I sat up, closed my eyes, and shook my head.

"You're awake," Jonathan said from somewhere nearby, his voice grim.

I gasped and turned toward an overstuffed floral armchair, where he perched near the closed door. Memories swamped me, and my throat tightened.

Brothers. My attacker and Jonathan were brothers. How had I missed this ridiculous piece of the puzzle?

My eyes adjusted to the darkened room. I noticed the small lines marring Jonathan's forehead.

He rubbed his jaw, his eyes unreadable in the shadows.

How could they possibly be related? Was this a distasteful prank someone had planned? My pulse thudded. Had Jonathan known all along? Were we dating because of some sick obligation to compensate for his dead brother? My chest clamped, and I struggled for air.

"Diana?"

I slowed my breathing and cleared my constricted throat. "Wh-what happened?"

"Other than discovering my brother's the monster from your

past?" His voice sounded tense and weary.

"Other than that," I whispered.

He leaned forward and rested his elbows on his knees, hands clasped. His fingers fidgeted.

I ripped my attention from the distracting movements to stare at his taut jaw. Were their chins similar? I squeezed my eyelids trying to recall the shape of *his* face.

"You started shaking, saying, 'It's him, it's him,' over and over. Then you looked at me, and … I knew." His voice cracked.

I opened my eyes, and my vision clouded.

"You garbled something indiscernible, shaking your head." He closed his eyes, sighed, fluttered them open, and stared at me. "Then you stilled and collapsed on the floor."

A shuddering breath escaped my body. "I … I'm sorry." Fresh tears stung my eyes.

His sardonic laugh caught me off guard. "Don't."

I bristled at his acerbic tone and straightened. What was his problem? I had been served the crappy victim card, not him. Had his brother abducted him? Scarred his wrists or splattered his brain all over his face? I gritted my teeth.

"Tell me what happened." Jonathan narrowed his eyes, and his jaw flickered. "Everything."

This was a demand, not a request.

I fisted the cottony doona and sucked in a large breath. "Must I rehash everything? How will this help?"

"It helps." His biting tone matched his clenched jaw.

My stomach curled.

He closed his eyes for a second. "Sorry." He blew out a breath and dropped his gaze. "It helps me grapple what's happening."

I cricked my neck and sagged. "Okay." Jonathan needed this interrogation, and I would comply. Because maybe somewhere underneath lay the man I loved. I shook my head. Once loved. *Still loved?* I squeezed my palms against my thighs. How could I love a man whose brother was my abductor?

"But first, why did you call him 'Pierce'?" Jonathan rubbed the bristles along his jaw. "No one calls him by his first name."

"That's the name the police officer gave me when I asked." I squinted at him. "Why don't you call him by his first name?"

Jonathan shrugged. "It's a weird thing on Dad's side of the

family. They call everyone by their middle names."

My pulse increased. "Is your middle name 'Jonathan'?"

"No."

My chest unknotted.

He huffed a breath. "Mum demanded I be called by my first name. Lucky for me."

"Why?"

"Doesn't matter." He straightened in the chair. "I'd like to hear the events from your perspective. The basic police report I accessed only contained the essentials."

I closed my eyes, inhaled a stabilizing breath, and uncorked everything inside. The fear, the humiliation, the struggle of my instant attraction and juxtaposed disgust of a man with the power to break me. I recounted every step and touch, and the kiss to finally steal the last ounce of my innocence. Tears streamed down my face.

Throughout my retelling, Jonathan's features remained hard and unreadable. But when I shared about the shameful kiss we shared in the ute, he winced.

My heart shattered, and I sobbed. I would be disgusted by me too.

"Is that everything?" Jonathan's cool articulation chilled me.

I nodded.

A gentle tap sounded on the closed door.

"Yes?" Jonathan said, loud and sharp.

The door opened, and Victoria peeked through the crack. "We heard voices." She turned to me. "You okay, sweetheart?"

"Yep." My throat ached.

"Mumma Joan just called. Apparently Jazzy fell off the swings and grazed her knees. She's pining for us, so Dad and I were thinking of heading home." She turned to Jonathan. "Are you able to drive Diana home?"

Jonathan leaned against the chair back. "Yes."

She smiled. "Thank you. Can I pop in for a quick hug before I go, Diana?"

"Please."

Victoria slipped into the room, lowered to the bed, and wrapped her arms around my waist.

I clung to her like a small child, or what I imagined a small child would do with her mother. Yet another thing taken from me.

Victoria rocked to and fro and kissed my temple.

I relished every moment of her comfort.

She squeezed my hand before she stood. "I'll see you later, sweetheart."

"Okay."

The door closed, and a hush filled the room. The first awkward silence I ever recalled experiencing with Jonathan.

My chest ached, and my head pounded. What was to become of us?

"Jonathan," I whispered. "Tell me what you're thinking."

He leaned his elbows on his knees and covered his face with his hands. His muffled, strangled sob broke the stillness.

My heart cracked. I slumped, the hefty weight on my shoulders too great to withstand. I stared at the hardwood floor, shuffling my feet against the floorboards. Life sucked.

"I don't know what to say." His voice trembled.

Tears pricked my eyes.

His gaze collided with mine, and the pain etched on his face knocked the air from my lungs.

I stilled my feet.

Jonathan stood and paced the short length of the room. "What am I supposed to say in this type of situation?" He spat a bitter laugh. "No one's prepared for a scenario like this!" His eyes enlarged, and he cupped the back of his head with his hands, running his palms back and forth. "There's no training for this at the Academy." He stomped a foot and collapsed on the armchair.

I wanted to reach out and take him in my arms or wrap his strong arms around me. But his brother stood between us. Even months after his death, he screwed up my life. I wanted to scream at the injustice. Instead, I counted my breaths.

"I should take you home."

What? I scrunched my face. "But we need to—"

"What? Hash this out? What's left to say?"

My heart rate increased, and I narrowed my eyes. "We haven't *said* anything yet."

His dark eyes captured my gaze, piercing my soul. "Can you honestly look at me right now and not see my brother?"

"I ..." I glanced at the ceiling. "I, ah—"

"Diana."

I pressed my lips together and then sighed. "It's still fresh, and—"

"You think you'll change your mind?" His gruff voice grated against me.

I sat forward. "I've come this far, haven't I?"

He shook his head. "You weren't dating my brother."

I crossed my arms. "And you didn't abduct me."

"But he'll always be my brother, even in death."

"I know." I rubbed my forehead. "It's too difficult to see things at the moment."

He blew out a long breath. "I … can't."

I furrowed my brow. "You can't what?"

He pointed between us. "Do this."

I opened my mouth, exhaled, and closed it again. Could I?

"My brother lived with me and shared my life, then chose to step out and end it all, dragging you along for the ride." His chest shuddered, and he growled.

I stared. What could I say?

"He did this to you."

"I know." I counted six breaths.

"At least his final message makes sense."

Huh?

Jonathan's bitter laugh filled the canyon between us. "His final text to me said, 'I hurt her and I hurt you. I'm sorry.'"

My eyes burned, and I stifled another sob. "I'd like to go home now," I whispered.

With another heavy sigh, Jonathan stood and extended a hand.

I accepted his assistance but slipped my fingers from his warmth once upright.

My body ached, and I travelled on precarious footsteps out to his Mustang.

I padded the familiar cracked concrete path bundled in my flannelette pajamas, winter coat, and old, scruffy Ugg boots. Pre-dawn shadows heightened the creepiness of Tellarine Cemetery, but with little cloud cover above, the sun would soon rise and heat my freezing face.

I wiped the cool dampness from my cheeks. Ugh, stupid tears. My footsteps echoed in the eerie quiet, and my shoulders eased when I spotted Mum's simple gravesite plaque. I squatted on the icy grass and blew Mum a kiss. "I know it's been months since I visited, but I really need to talk."

I shoved my hands in the warmth of my jacket pockets, and my fingers touched metal. I hoped Victoria forgave me for borrowing her car without permission. Considering Dad refused to let her drive with that basketball she housed, I figured I was in the clear.

I stared at Mum's plaque. Heaviness weighed my chest. How could this have happened? And now an ocean of pain and sorrow separated Jonathan and me. Had our relationship ended? I dabbed my eyes with my pajama collar. We were over. Even if I loved him.

"I love him, Mum. I love him." I covered my mouth with my hand and allowed the inevitable sobs to rack my body. My chest burned along with my eyes, nose, and throat.

If blasted Pierce, uh, Damien—whatever his name was—were still alive, I would slay him with the boulder crushing my chest. Would serve him right for destroying more than his own life.

FORGIVE HIM, AND YOUR HEAVENLY FATHER WILL FORGIVE YOU.

I stilled although my mind ran at full pelt. Forgive him?

Was this humanly possible? I had come to terms with and even accepted *that man's* actions in a way. But was this forgiveness?

I groaned. No. Forgiveness existed on a separate echelon above anything I could do.

But with God, all things are possible.

My heart raced. I knew this tiny passage of Scripture by heart and believed it. Yet deep inside, did I?

Did I truly believe all things are possible with God?

I retrieved my phone and opened my Bible app. If by God's grace I forgave Jonathan's brother, Jesus's love was powerful enough to help me see Jonathan through new eyes, free of his brother's stain. A stain which would cease to exist once I forgave.

I sighed.

Was this possible? Could I still have Jonathan in my life?

My hands shook, and I scrolled through verse after verse about the love of God and the love of His Son, as early morning light filled the heavens and brightened the area around me. Tears coursed down my cheeks, dripping off my chin. "If God is for me, who can be against me? I can do all things through Christ who strengthens me, including forgiving a dead man." I wiped my face with my coat sleeve, and the first smile since I viewed Mrs. Harris's photo slid to my lips.

My hip buzzed, and a blearing ringtone rent the air.

I scrambled for my phone. "Hello?" I croaked and cleared my throat.

"Where are you? Did you take Victoria's car?" Dad's tense voice vibrated down the phone line.

Uh oh. "Ah, yeah. Sorry."

"You didn't think to leave a note or message one of us?"

I grimaced at the rebuke in his tone. "I wasn't really thinking. I'm sorry I worried you."

"Frantic would be a better word, Princess. Especially after yesterday afternoon." He sighed. "Where are you?"

I watched soft light bathe the tops of gangly evergreens. "Visiting Mum."

"Victoria's in labour."

I shot to my feet, wiped my nose, and sucked in cool air. "I'll be back as soon as I can."

CHAPTER TWENTY-FOUR
Let's Call the Whole Thing Off

Jonathan: YOU HOME?

I stared at the new message as I rested on the couch rubbing tiny Elijah Matthew's back.

Victoria had popped him out at nine yesterday morning and was home by dinnertime. Dad seemed shocked by how fast everything happened.

Victoria rested in her armchair guzzling water. She drained her water bottle, wheezed, and nodded to my phone. "Is that him?"

I re-read the message, heat and opposing chills swirling inside my chest cavity. "He wants to know if I'm home."

She extracted Elijah from my arms and patted his back. "Didn't you say minutes ago you wanted to see him and try to work things out?"

I nodded.

She touched my shoulder. "You can do this. We're here to help, but you need Jonathan on board with the plan."

"I know." I bit my bottom lip and shrugged. "Guess I'm waiting for that injection of courage."

"Take one step at a time." She squeezed my knee and stood. "Message him. We're heading upstairs for naptime, and with Jasmine staying at Mumma Joan's, you won't be interrupted."

"Thanks."

Victoria carried Elijah from the room.

Me: YEAH. WANT TO COME OVER?

I jiggled my foot as the minutes passed. A message flashed on the screen, and my stomach cramped.

Jonathan: BE THERE IN 15

I stretched my arms and rotated my neck. Better. After a few lunges and squats, I pulled two mugs from the kitchen cupboard, boiled the kettle, and flicked the coffee machine switch. A small tray rested on the drying rack. I pulled it out and arranged several of Victoria's shortbread fingers on a plate.

While I waited, I prayed. Peace descended over me like a warm blanket, and my breathing eased. My belly settled soon after.

The front door vibrated with Jonathan's firm knocks.

I rushed to answer it.

"Hey," he whispered, devoid of his usual smile.

"Hi." I stepped back. "Want a drink?"

"Coffee would be great. Thanks." He walked in, but his gaze never reached mine.

I motioned to the lounge room. "I'll bring it in soon."

I prepared his coffee and my hot chocolate—this discussion called for some serious comfort food—and carried our afternoon tea to the lounge.

Jonathan filled the armchair, not his usual position on the couch.

I held back a sigh and affixed a polite smile. So it was like this. I lay the tray on the coffee table with his mug closer to him.

"Thanks." Jonathan sipped his coffee.

"You're welcome." I occupied the closest couch cushion, pivoted toward him, and tucked my legs underneath me.

I reached for a shortbread. "Victoria had her baby yesterday."

His eyes widened. "Really?"

A smile tugged at my lips. "I have a little brother. Elijah Matthew."

"That's great news. Congratulations." He offered a polite smile. "Mother and baby fine?"

"Yeah. They're napping upstairs." I chewed the biscuit, disappointed the baked good seemed tasteless today.

We sipped to the tune of the wall clock and several birds chirping near the window.

"Listen. Diana." Jonathan angled toward me, his shoulders straight and chin high.

I placed my mug on the table, tilted my head, and met his stare.

"I don't think we should see each other anymore."

Whatever air resided in my lungs evaporated, and I heaved.

"But why? I … I don't understand?"

His inky gaze intensified, and he rubbed his hand over his mouth and chin. "I haven't changed my mind since our last conversation." His hands balled on his knees. "I can't do this and don't see any future."

Heat pricked my eyes. "But I do. I want to move forward." I leaned closer. "We can do this together."

He squeezed his eyes and shook his head. "It's not possible."

My hands trembled, and I pressed them against my thighs. "All things are possible to those who believe." My voice quivered. "We can do this."

"No." He stood, and his eyes glistened.

I scrambled to my feet, my vision blurred.

"I can't separate you from him. No matter how hard I try, when I look at you, I see my brother and what he did to you. I can't live life playing happy families."

I reached out and touched his arm, my pulse roaring. "You had no control over what happened, and I choose not to hold this against you. We can't change the past, but we can deal with this situation and focus on the future."

Jonathan stared at my hand on his arm and lifted his head, his watery gaze seeking mine. "You're missing the point. The future doesn't exist with this hanging over my head."

"B-but I love you." Tears tumbled to my chin. "I choose to love you." How could he not see the price I was willing to pay for us?

"And I love you. But I don't know if I'll ever get past this." He sighed and stepped back, my hand now unable to reach him. "Sorry, beautiful."

The echo of his brother's words pummeled my skull, and I jerked away.

Blaring pulsations slammed between my ears, and my stomach lurched. I toppled on the couch.

Jonathan kissed my forehead and disappeared from my watery view.

A new buzzing sound filled my ears. I stared at the vacant doorway, tears spilling over my cheeks. The persistent buzzing increased in volume. My phone!

I lunged for the small handset on the couch and answered without looking at the caller's name. "Jonathan?"

"It's Sam."

"Oh." I curled myself against the couch cushions and closed my damp eyes.

"What's going on with you and Jon? He's been a mess the last two days. What the heck happened at your family dinner?"

Too much happened.

"Di?"

I sniffled. "We broke up."

"What!" I had never heard Sam shriek this loud. "What do you mean you broke up? Are you serious?"

"Yep."

Silence permeated the phone line.

Had we been disconnected?

"It's … it's not possible," he whispered.

"Believe it." *Yes, Diana, believe it.*

Sam sighed. "But, why?" Caution sounded in his tone.

I opened my eyes and exhaled a sigh of my own. "You'll need to ask him. He decided it was the only way forward."

"B-but it doesn't make sense!" He lowered his voice. "I've not seen him like this before. I thought you broke up with him?"

An involuntary squeak escaped my throat. "He can't deal, so we're done."

"Deal? He can't deal with what?"

I rubbed my tired eyes. "Like I said, you need to talk to him. I'm happy to share my side of the story, but his side's entangled with mine, so if he tells you … then he tells you." My nose tingled, and the backs of my eyes commenced their telltale burn. "I've gotta go." Before I blubbered like a baby.

"I'm sorry, Di." His voice sounded pained.

"Thanks," I whispered between stilted breaths. Wetness trailed my cheeks. "Bye." I turned toward the couch back, shoved my face into a cushion, and allowed the waterworks to fall.

CHAPTER TWENTY-FIVE
Reunion

My mobile phone rang. I swiped it from my bedroom desk and stared at the screen. Kortney. I blew out a breath. "Hey, you."

"How're you keeping?" Kortney's sweet voice soothed me.

"To be expected." Almost a week had passed since I spoke to Jonathan.

"Just wanted to make sure you're okay." She chuckled. "And let you know my latest article was a hit with the editor. Thanks for brainstorming ideas with me."

I smiled. "You're welcome."

"Want to hang out this afternoon?"

"I'd love to, but my bestie from uni is visiting me today." Images of my last heartbreaking meeting with Tara filled my vision, and I blinked them away.

"Really?" A frisson of an unknown something buzzed in her voice. "She's not in classes?"

"No." I paced in the hallway near my bedroom door. "We both deferred for a year."

"Both of you?" Kortney's voice vibrated with … anticipation? The front doorbell rang.

My pulse thumped. "I've gotta go, Tara's here."

"Have fun. Chat soon."

I ended the call, shuffled along the second-level landing, and jogged down the staircase. "I'll get it!" I called to Victoria, who, I assumed, was in the lounge.

"Okay," Victoria said as I passed her and Elijah in her armchair.

My insides somersaulted, and I yanked the door wide. "Knew it was you. No one around here uses the doorb—"

Tara slammed against me, wrapping her arms tight around my waist.

A warbled cry escaped my throat.

"It's so good to see you," Tara said.

My throat clogged, and I swallowed a lump. "I've missed you."

She cricked her neck up and grinned. "So glad Mum and my therapist suggested we meet face to face."

"So am I." I had missed her dazzling smile. Tears burned the backs of my eyes.

Tara's formerly long blonde hair now lay at her shoulders, with a layered fringe draping her forehead. A natural-looking sheen covered her lips, her blue eyes less pronounced than I remembered. Signs of fatigue peeked through a thin layer of foundation, a huge change from her usual made-up face. She appeared younger—almost innocent—without layers of cover-up, mascara, and lipstick.

I nudged her inside and closed the door, escorting her to the lounge room.

"Hi, sweetheart." Victoria waved from her armchair, where Elijah suckled at her breast.

"Hi." Tara zeroed in on my brother, and her eyes clouded. "He's beautiful."

"Thank you." Victoria looked down. "He's my special surprise."

Tara pressed her lips together, blinked, and turned to me. Her smile returned. "Can't believe I'm here."

"Perfect timing after the awful week I've had." I nodded to the couch, and we dropped to the soft cushions.

Tara pressed my hand. "Another reason I wanted to visit. Breakups blow."

Jasmine ran into the room, spotted Tara, and skidded to a stop. Her eyes widened, and she glanced from Victoria to Tara and me.

"Come here, Jazzy," Victoria said. "This is Sissy Di-Di's friend, Tara."

"Hi, Jasmine." Tara smiled. "I've heard so much about you from Diana."

Jasmine scurried to Victoria, palmed her brother's head, and turned back to Tara. "Hullo," she said, her voice soft.

"Can I get either of you a drink?" I grabbed Jasmine's water bottle from the coffee table.

She extracted it from my hand with her little, wiggly fingers.

"Water would be great, thanks," Tara said.

"Me too, please." Victoria tossed a burp rag over her shoulder and rested Elijah on top. "I forgot my water bottle, and you know how much water I need to drink these days."

I glided to the kitchen, filled three tall glasses with filtered water, and returned to the lounge.

Victoria chugged the entire glass.

Elijah boomed a frog-like burp.

"Good boy."

Jasmine giggled, and Tara and I snickered.

Victoria stood. "Come, Jazzy, let's let the ladies chat while you have lunch."

I glanced at the time and squinted. "Need any help?"

Victoria shook her head. "Jasmine needs an earlier nap so she's awake when Nicholas gets home for their special outing this afternoon." She eyed her son. "Hopefully they'll both sleep, and we can eat a little later." She bustled from the room, Elijah gurgling in her arms and Jasmine in tow.

A hush descended on the lounge room.

Tara fiddled with the hem of her T-shirt, sighed, and turned to me. "I'm sorry it's taken me almost a year to see you. I really hoped I'd have made progress sooner, but the thought of seeing you was associated with the past, and"—I touched her knee—"I'd spiral into a panic attack." She now played with the fringed edge of a couch cushion. Her misted gaze met mine. "I hated how you were a trigger for me, especially when you also suffered." Her chest heaved. "You were my best friend, and knowing I couldn't spend time with you because of the memories … losing you suddenly, in a way, did a number on me."

Was this how Jonathan felt? Heaviness squished my lungs.

I stilled Tara's fidgeting fingers and held her hand. "It's okay. You went through a heck of a lot more than me."

Tara huffed a breath. "We both suffered. Our experiences may've been different, but it still counts." She raised a finger. "And my therapist didn't coach me, either. I knew this from the beginning."

Tears clouded my vision, and my heartbeat heightened. "Will you finally tell me what happened? I know from the hints at the police station you were … sexually assaulted."

She flinched and nodded.

I squeezed her hand. My throat constricted. "I don't need to know everything, but I need to know how to navigate the coming months and years without overthinking my words … so I don't keep triggering you."

She sighed, and her shoulders drooped. "I can give you the rough story. My therapist's helped me break it down in a way I can rattle off the events and not feel hostage to the situation."

I wrapped my arm around Tara's shoulder and pulled her against my side. I needed this reconnection more than I let on. Pushing aside thoughts of anyone else—okay, someone in particular with soulful ebony eyes—I listened to the soft ticking of the wall clock and the erratic breaths Tara appeared to be slowing.

"Long story short, I was raped many times, mostly by one particular man, but a few times by three or four at once."

I gasped, and tears clouded my eyes.

"They held me in a cold, dark room tied naked to a four-poster bed. I struggled to sleep because of hunger and the cold." Tara's breaths laboured.

I kissed the crown of her head.

"During those three days, I-I think I was untethered maybe four or five times for a bathroom visit devoid of privacy. A man stood by and watched my every movement." She sniffed. "My main captor spoon-fed me soup or porridge twice a day but only after I p-performed for my food."

Tears trailed my cheeks. "I'm sorry," I whispered before a loud sob in my chest bubbled to the surface. How had she endured it?

She scooted away, twisted toward me, and grasped my hands. Her wet eyes focused on mine. "The police said you're the reason they found me sooner." She pressed her lips together and swiped away more tears. "Thank you."

I dropped my chin and looked at our joined hands. "I feel almost … guilty for the time it took me to get over my fairly harmless experience."

Tara squinted and cocked her head. "He blew his brains out all over you. No one gets over that quickly."

Jonathan crept into my thoughts, and I choked back a sob. "He's Jonathan's brother."

Tara furrowed her brow and palmed her damp eyes. "What?"

"My abductor slash rescuer. He's Jonathan's older half-brother."

Her eyes widened. "But … how?"

I shrugged. "He moved to Melbourne for work a few years ago, and Jonathan let him crash with him. Apparently he got caught up in the wrong crowd—"

"Obviously." Tara huffed.

"And must've thought this was his only way out?" I scratched my cheek.

"And this's why you broke up?" She laid a delicate hand on my shoulder. "Cos he's Jonathan's brother?"

And because I disgust him. I wanted to tell Tara about the kiss—I never felt brave enough to tell her in the past—but how could I now, knowing all she's suffered? My twisted experience might push her away.

I sniffed. "Yeah. J-Jonathan broke up with me because of—"

"The guilt." Tara rubbed my shoulder and pulled away. Her top lip curled up. "I hate Zeus."

"Huh?" I scrunched my face.

"The guy who told me about the sandwich shop. That pervert must've been in on it."

My stomach convulsed, and I squirmed. "I never thought about that."

"I have. Countless times." Tara slid away and wrapped her arms around her knees. "If I'd not listened to him, we'd never—"

"Stop. Look at me." I poked her shoulder.

She twisted her neck and eyed me.

"You are *not* to blame."

She blinked her shiny eyes.

"Those men are at fault. The guys in the shop and wherever they held you." I siphoned a breath. "The faces you'll never forget." My voice cracked. "They're to blame. Not us."

Victoria entered the room. "You two ready for lun—oh, sweethearts. Let me get you some tissues." She returned moments later with a tissue box. "Take your time. Come through to the kitchen when you're ready. I'll have my lunch now. Elijah's sleeping."

I extracted a wad, handed the box to Tara, and wiped my eyes. "Thanks, Victoria. Take some time out while you can. We can always look after the little man if you need to nap."

Tara bit her lip and dropped her chin.

"Thank you." Victoria smiled and disappeared through the archway.

I glanced at my friend. "You don't mind, do you?"

Tara raised her head. "Mind what?"

"Watching the baby. I'd do all the work anyway."

"Oh. No, I mean yes, that's fine. Sure." She blew her nose. "Ah, gross. Sorry."

I chuckled and wiped my eyes and nose. "Have you seen me? I'm snotting everywhere!"

"You're as pretty as usual." Tara's smile slid away. "I, ah, also wanted to apologize for something else."

I creased my brow. "What for?"

She fingered the tassels on the cushion. "My therapist's helped me deal with a lot of guilt about stuff not just related to my abduction." She twisted the threads until they looked like rope. "I'm sorry if I ever made you feel uncomfortable with your life choices."

My life choices? I arched my eyebrows and shifted on the seat.

She released the tassel and rubbed her lips. "I know I'd pick on you for not wanting to have sex, but …" She sighed. "I'm sorry. It was mean, and I never understood why until my choices were taken from me."

I laid a hand on her shoulder. "It's okay."

A tear slipped down her cheek. "Our body's like a gift, and we should be able to decide who unwraps it. I-I just wanted you to know. You were stronger than anyone I knew, sticking to your convictions."

I smiled. "I appreciate you saying that."

A small smile slipped to her face. "Who knows, maybe your inner goodness could rub off on me."

Inner goodness? A disgraceful kiss with my ex-boyfriend's dead brother pointed to a lack of "good" inside my heart. "Maybe." I hugged my friend, holding her close. "I'm always here if you need me, and you're always in my prayers."

"Your prayers are always welcome."

My chest lightened, and I smiled. Tara had never been this receptive before. "Can I pray for you now?"

She nodded, and we clasped hands.

I prayed a quick prayer for freedom, peace, and safety, then glanced at the clock. "Feel like eating?"

"I could eat."

We gathered our collection of soggy, crumpled tissues and disposed them in the kitchen.

The buzz of customers filtered down the hallway through my open office door. Friday afternoons were good for business.

My mind swarmed with thoughts, and I glanced at my mobile, tugging my bottom lip between my teeth.

Sam: IS JONATHAN STILL INVITED TO YOUR 21ST?

I rubbed my face and flexed my shoulders.

Me: REALLY, SAM?

I shook my head and blew out a long breath. How could Sam even think Jonathan was invited? My lungs heaved, and I blinked back tears.

When would the pain stop? Before I returned to Melbourne in three weeks? I huffed a laugh at the impossible idea. I hoped to be doing better by the time I left Tellarine than I was now.

I swiped the phone screen, promising myself this was the final interaction until the end of the work day. Keanu paid me for a reason, which was not to chat with my friends.

Sam: I'M SORRY. I JUST WISH YOU TWO WOULD TALK. YOU'RE SO PERFECT FOR EACH OTHER.

Sam: I MEAN, YOU'RE BETTER THAN BRANGELINA OR BENNIFER.

Sam: YOU'RE DIANATHAN!

I snorted at the portmanteau. Typical Sam.

Me: YOU REALISE YOU'RE REFERENCING TWO FAMOUS COUPLES WHICH BROKE UP, RIGHT?

Me: JONATHAN'S NOT INVITED BECAUSE I'M SICK OF CRYING AND IT'S MY PARTY, SO I DON'T WANT TO CRY (UNLIKE THE OLD SONG). PLUS HE PROBABLY WOULDN'T COME. :-(

Me: I REALLY HOPE HE TALKS TO ME BEFORE I RETURN TO MELBOURNE, BUT THERE'S NOTHING I CAN DO TO CHANGE HIS MIND OTHER THAN PRAY. I NEED TO GET BACK TO WORK. TALK LATER.

I tucked my phone away in my handbag, spun on my chair a couple of times, stretched my fingers, and focused on the work in front of me.

"You busy?"

I glanced up at Keanu in the doorway.

He thumbed in the direction of the restaurant. "Kortney's at the bar and wants to speak a moment."

I raised a brow. "You want me to slack off at work?"

He crossed his arms. "You work hard, so take a break."

Maybe a break would allow me time to calm.

"Go see yer friend."

"Yes, boss." I poked his shoulder on my way past and hustled to the dining area.

I waved Kortney over to an empty table. "Hey."

She squeezed my shoulder and plonked on the chair. "How you been?"

I huffed a breath. "Busy. With only a few weeks until I leave, it's all a bit crazy."

"I've always wondered why you went on leave." Kortney blinked several times.

I scrunched my face. "Some stuff happened …"

"To you and Tara?" She raised a brow. "Cos you left at the same time."

"Yes. We did." My skin prickled. "But I'm excited to be back soon." Then I can get back on track and make you proud, Mum.

Kortney's gaze intensified. "Yeah? Whatever happened has passed? Ended?"

I narrowed my eyes. "W-why?"

She shrugged. "I'd like to know you'll be safe when you return. So you must feel safe to go back."

Not entirely. "I suppose so." I forced a smile. "I know self-defense, so there's a start."

She pursed her lips. "True. And how's Tara feel about returning to the city?"

I pressed my hands against my thighs. "Fine, I assume." This conversation felt more like an interrogation than a friendly chat. I glanced at the wall clock near the bar. "I'd better get back to work."

"Of course." Kortney's eyes brightened. "I'll see you next weekend for your big birthday bash!"

"Yep."

We stood and parted ways.

CHAPTER TWENTY-SIX
Adulthood and Anguish

Kortney: HAVE A FABULOUS TRIP! I'M GOING TO MISS YOU IN HEAPS! CALL ME ANYTIME, JOURNO BUDDY.

I smiled at her words, thankful the last wisps of strain in our friendship had floated away. Her push for information had to come down to her journalistic training. Like Jonathan and his penchant to investigate.

Oh, Jonathan.

Me: THANKS. LOOK AFTER YOURSELF AND FOLLOW THOSE STORIES! XX

"Ready to go, Princess?" Dad's voice travelled along the hallway through my bedroom door.

"Almost!" I cracked the door and nosed the small gap. "Give me a few minutes."

"I'll meet you downstairs."

I closed the door and scanned my room for the tenth time today. Had I left something unpacked? I hoped not. My gaze fell to my mobile resting on my handbag, and my chest compressed. Now or never.

I shook out my arms and bounced on my toes, whispered a prayer, and dialed Sam's number.

His comforting voice answered on the third ring. "Diving Diana, you on the road yet?"

"About to leave." I rubbed the ache blooming along my chest. "Is Jonathan home?"

Sam cleared his throat. "Yes."

"Can I … can I talk to him?" I clenched my free hand against my thigh.

"I'll ask."

Half a minute passed, enough time for me to pace my bedroom floor three times.

"He's asked for more time and"—Sam half-sighed, half-growled—"would prefer not to speak with you."

Over a month had passed since I saw Jonathan in the flesh, smelled his intoxicating cologne, or shivered to his deep, resonating voice. Scratch that. Over a month had passed since we shared *any* interaction on any level. Here I was set to catch a Melbourne-bound bus—on the date Jonathan and I had discussed in length—and had hoped he would have at least said goodbye.

Apparently not.

I resumed my room pacing. "Can you put me on speakerphone then, please?" I hoped my pleading tone would force his hand.

"Of course."

My moment of truth. I inhaled a deep breath, employing the monologue I had practiced in my head the past few days. "Jonathan, I understand you don't want to hear or see me, but I need the chance to say goodbye."

The call stayed connected, and no one yelled on the other side, so I claimed the small victory and powered on.

"So here it is … goodbye. I'm sorry you're hurting as much as you are, because, believe me, I get it. I totally get it. But what I don't get is why I'm once again bearing the brunt of another fallout in a Harris explosion, with circumstances I never controlled, dictating my life a second time." I gripped the phone tighter. "I stopped wishing he'd shot both of us a while ago, and now I'm getting on with the business of living … with or without you."

My eyes misted, and I slowed my pacing steps. "I love you. I've nothing but good thoughts for you and your future. A future I want to share in but…" I stilled, and my throat constricted. "I'm sorry I'm not enough for you." My vision blurred, and tears dripped down my face.

A rending sob vibrated over the phone in the background, a matching cry building inside my chest.

Sam whispered my name, and I disconnected the call.

I swiped several tissues and wiped my cheeks. Counting my breaths, I straightened my shoulders and flexed my hands. Time to move on and become a better me. Life was too short for wallowing, and Victoria had already proved one could move on regardless of the gaping hole inside.

I shouldered my suitcase, palmed my handbag, and slipped from my clean and organized bedroom. How long until I walked these hallways again?

I stopped in the kitchen, where Jasmine grabbed my legs. Enveloping her in a big hug, I sniffled, my eyes wet. "I'm going to miss you, Jazzy. Be good for Daddy and Mummy, okay?"

Jasmine placed her pudgy hands over my cheeks, her eyes oddly sombre. "Okay, Sissy Di-Di. Love you." She planted a kiss on my nose, pulled back, and launched into Victoria's arms.

Victoria wrapped her free arm around my waist, her glassy eyes and watery smile stinging my chest. "If you need anything at all, call. You've got a house key, so come home anytime you want." Her smile widened. "Elijah needs to be reminded of his brilliant big sister as often as possible."

I leaned into the softness of my stepmum and bottled the feeling of her embrace for another day. I loved this woman more than I had dreamed possible. God had granted the prayers of a motherless young girl. "Give my baby brother extra kisses when he wakes up."

"Okay, Princess, let's get this show on the road," Dad said, his voice low and throaty.

Planting one more kiss on Jasmine, I retreated from the warmth of my loved ones to the cold interior of Dad's new Toyota HiLux twin cab ute. His previous ute coped with one car seat but not two. Considering I was twelve when he bought his previous vehicle and he had racked up three hundred thousand kilometres, it was time to beat another ute into submission.

Dad secured my suitcase in the ute tray.

I opened the passenger door and settled on the fabric seat.

He slid behind the steering wheel. "Sorry I can't put your suitcase in the cab anymore." He chuckled. "A lot's changed in the last twelve months."

I glanced at the back row, teeming with baby gear. "Pretty funny to think this is a work vehicle." I laughed. "You planning on upgrading Victoria's car anytime soon? I think she's in need of a nice SUV to make the spare seat in the back row more comfortable for those one-off passengers."

Dad drove in the direction of Robinvale Railway Station. "We discussed it prior to Elijah's arrival."

I smirked and turned to him. "I suggest you revisit the conversation."

We spent the remaining journey listening to Christian music. I surveyed the familiar countryside, my breaths shorter with each kilometre. The scenery and atmosphere in Melbourne were incomparable to the bright, clear skies, fresh country air, and rustling eucalypts of home. Colourful city lights dulled the stars, and each night I glanced out my South Melbourne bedroom window, I craved the heavenly luminosity of a Tellarine sky.

Dad parked near the V-Line bus stop outside the small, abandoned train terminal and retrieved my bag. We lowered to a creaky metal bench seat under the eaves of the cream weatherboard and rusty-red corrugated iron roof of the building.

I retrieved my pre-purchased ticket from my wallet and checked my watch. Ten minutes until the coach's expected arrival.

Dad cleared his throat. His tense expression communicated his question before he spoke. "You sure you're going to be okay?" His voice rasped. "You don't have to go if you're not ready."

I stared into his soulful dark eyes and glanced at his strong jaw. Grey hairs peppered his chin and collided with the dark hair at his temples. When had this happened? I smiled at how distinguished Dad now appeared despite the pressures of a bonus baby. Funny how the hardest times in life brought about unexpected positives. God's promise in Romans—all things working for good for those who love Him—in action.

"I know." I leaned against his side. "But I'm going to be okay. If God's for me, who can be against me?"

Dad wrapped me in his arms, those all-encompassing limbs holding me just as close as he had when I was a six-year-old child mourning my mother. My strong tower. A physical manifestation of what I imagined God would be like if He rested on a metal bench seat on a cold July afternoon waiting for His daughter to be whisked away to her life away from Him. Dad was the hands and feet of God in my life, and I cherished him.

Dad kissed the top of my head and released me from his hold. "Remember, you're always in my heart and my prayers."

A tear slipped down my cheek. I shoved it away. "I know. Thank you for loving me."

Minutes later, I waved from my semi-comfortable position on the coach headed to Swan Hill, where I would catch a ride to Melbourne with Tara. Melancholy pressed against my chest when the bus maneuvered and Dad disappeared from view.

✎ ✎ ✎ ✎ ✎ ✎ ✎

14 July

I'm back in Melbourne, Mum. It's almost hard to believe a little over twelve months has passed since my world upended. But this next twelve months, I'll spend my time with my new roomie by my side. Tara's staying at the Morgans' with me, and I couldn't be happier. Our friendship weathered a horrible, gut-wrenching storm, and we're closer for it in many ways. But there are some things I haven't told Tara yet, and I'm certain she hasn't told me everything, either … and I'm okay with that.

Despite kicking study goals (I made it to today's lecture on time and stayed awake through the drivel!) and feeling stronger each day, I miss Jonathan. I miss his smile and his strength. How he would keep me safe. And his belly-warming kisses. Now my heart grieves a loss for the man I love. Is this how you felt when you left us? Or was it just us left behind who suffered this pain? Maybe I should talk to Dad and Victoria cos they've dealt with their fair share of grief, and then some.

Be proud of me, Mum. Regardless of my wounds, I'm determined to make it.

I love you and miss you.

CHAPTER TWENTY-SEVEN
Ambushed

Erin: Hi, Diana. Can you please call me? I really want to talk to you about something which would be better said over the phone than over text.

I shifted, where I stood on the tram with one hand wrapped around the vertical metal poll and the other holding my mobile, and squinted at my phone screen. I sort of hung out with Erin at the city church I attended although this was my first-ever message from her in over two years. What did she want? I had seen her at church yesterday, but she never approached me with a burning need to chat.

Tara leaned against my side. "Who's Erin?"

"A girl from church here in the city."

"You gonna call her?"

I glanced around the busy tram carriage. "Now?"

Tara nodded out the window. "Our stop's next, so call her then."

"You don't mind?" Answering a call while walking with your friend was one thing, but making one seemed rude.

She waved her free hand in the air. "Seems like a good use of your walking time."

Since returning to Melbourne, it had only taken me a month to form a decent routine of study, online office work, Morgan family life, and weekly personal training sessions. If only other parts of my life functioned well. Jonathan often strayed to my thoughts, my brain bent on replaying his final rejection. When would I be okay, Lord? My heart squeezed.

The tram halted, and we dismounted the low-floor transportation.

I adjusted my backpack straps and dialed Erin.

"Hello? Diana?"

"Hi, Erin. Is this a good time for you?" I passed a loud group of tourists and pressed the handset closer to my ear.

"Yes, now's good." Erin cleared her throat. "I, ah, wanted to talk to you about one of your passing comments you made yesterday. About clubbing and dancing?"

"Okay?" What was happening here?

"Meg, Jane, and me discussed it yesterday afternoon, and I'm reaching out on behalf of everyone."

I snuck a furtive glance at Tara striding beside me.

Erin cleared her throat again. "We urge you not to return to the lifestyle you lived before your stint away."

Return to my lifestyle? "What do you mean?"

"Well … before you left, you went out to pubs and clubs with your uni friends and …"

My pulse clopped. "And …"

"And real Christians refrain from mixing in cesspools of sin and debauchery."

Excuse me? Heat infused my cheeks.

"Don't get me wrong. We know you don't drink, and you wear modest outfits, so we assume you're chaste, but with your friendly demeanour and the natural intimacy associated with dancing, we're afraid men will take advantage of you."

What the flibbertigibbet. "Uh." I glanced at Tara. Could she hear this?

"You're such a lovely person, and we'd hate to see you travel such a sin-filled path."

I clenched my empty hand against my side.

"Diana? You still there?"

"I'm just … digesting your message." I stopped under a tree on campus.

Tara mouthed, "See you inside."

"Oh, good." Erin's voice brightened. "Well, that was all we wanted to say. See you at church on Sunday!"

My throat pinched. "Bye."

Heat bubbled inside my seething chest. I inhaled cool air, pushed the conversation aside, and traipsed indoors to where Tara waited outside the lecture theatre doorway.

She raised a brow. "All good?"

No. "Yeah."

We slipped into the familiar seats several minutes before our ten o'clock session. I propped against the semi-comfortable seat back, sighed, and retrieved my laptop, notepad, and pen. Call me old-school, but I sometimes enjoyed jotting notes by hand.

The sends-a-girl-to-sleep lecturer commenced his class, and I chided myself for not packing toothpicks or a Taser to keep myself focused throughout his prattle.

Tara bumped my shoulder. "You never said what you thought of my idea to go dancing."

So she *did* overhear my conversation with Erin. I cringed.

Tara elbowed me. "Well?"

I turned toward her and bit the inside of my cheek. "Ah, maybe? But it's just for us, right? For fun? Not like the pub crawls we used to do before …"

"Just for fun." She dropped her gaze. "My wild streak's officially been tamed."

I nudged her arm. "I noticed. Without meaning to sound haughty or make you feel bad, it's refreshing seeing you speak genuinely with guys at uni."

She lifted her chin and met my stare. "Yeah?"

I smiled. "Yeah."

She snickered. "I suppose I did have a propensity to make out with a guy within five minutes."

I stifled a laugh.

She leaned closer and lowered her voice. "I haven't slept with a guy since … then."

My eyes widened. "Really?"

Tara nodded, and her shoulders vibrated. Had she shivered? "Th-the therapist promises I'll, ah, regain that particular appetite down the track." She shrugged. "But I kinda like this new 'me.' The trauma sucked, but I think I'm a more considerate person."

"You are." I leaned against her. "You're doing amazingly. Just as I've prayed."

"Thanks."

Friday and Saturday nights soon became our "dancing" nights. We clubbed at The Albion or visited a pub with a few uni friends. Nothing which pushed our comfort zones, and the moment any guys showed overt interest, we walked away. My city church friends shunned me when they found out I had disregarded their advice. How could dancing cause such a rift between friends? I never flirted with men. I danced! Who wanted to spend time with faultfinders anyway?

I enjoyed dancing and meeting new people, and over time I became the driving force of our little group. When I danced, my skin tingled, and my chest expanded. I gravitated to an almost other-worldly high of movement. The swirling bodies and vibrating, dank atmosphere of sweat-infested clubs blocked the memories I needed to push aside and created new remembrances which I hoped smothered ones I no longer wanted to recall.

Like intense dark-chocolate eyes and luscious caramel skin. A smooth, strong, determined jaw. Warm, velvety lips curved in his quintessential smile. A tailored navy-blue uniform enhancing the sculpture beneath.

"Here's your drink." Tara handed me a water bottle.

"Ta." I guzzled half the bottle and secured the lid.

"I found a few people from uni lingering near the bar. Wanna chat?"

I panted and wiped my brow. "Why not." I followed Tara through the swarm on the dance floor to the bar, where I recognised several faces. One in particular. My eyes widened.

"Diana!" Lacey beamed at me, her sweat-slicked forehead glistening under the bar lights. "I haven't seen you in ages! How are you?"

I smiled and caught my breath after my invigorating workout. "It's great to see you, Lacey." And here of all places.

She sipped from her water bottle. "So, what've you been up to?"

I scuffed my ballerina flats against the sticky floor. "I actually took a year off and recommenced my classes at the beginning of this semester."

She furrowed her brow. "Is everything okay?"

"Better than it was." Well, in some ways, but not in others.

She tapped her closed bottle against her thigh. "Well, I know the Christian Union guys would love seeing you again."

"Thanks." With Tara now living with me, I had focused on doing activities I knew she preferred. "You must be reaching the tail end of your degree by now?"

Lacey nodded. "I finish at the end of the semester, but I intend staying local because I love my church and don't want to move." She chuckled.

What would it be like to attend a church which welcomed me?

Something warm and hopeful bubbled in my chest. "Which church do you attend?"

"A large inner-city one with lots of young people, great music, and great times catching up with friends our age once a fortnight. They even host some events at RMIT."

Giddiness filled my lungs. *Calm your farm, Diana!* "Maybe I should check it out sometime."

Lacey's smile widened. "That'd be great!" She told me the church name, website, and the service she attended.

I sipped my water. "Do you club often?"

"Nah. I come along now and again with friends."

I wrapped my free arm around my waist.

She arched her brow. "Honestly? I love dancing, but I prefer dancing at church."

"You dance at church?" Clapping was an extravagant expression of worship at the church I now attended, which had been difficult to adjust to from the clapping and swaying of my home church in Tellarine.

She laughed, and her eyes glowed. "The praise and worship music's loud like this, and once the beat hits"—she shrugged—"I can't help but move."

My lungs loosened, and I breathed with ease. "That's why I enjoy clubbing. I usually dance with Tara, or alone, and enjoy the moment to myself." I rubbed my fingers along my jaw. "I suppose it'd be better to dance with abandon to church songs than these ones."

"Totally!" She glanced over my shoulder. "Well, I'll see you at uni if not before." She smiled and slipped past me.

I finished my water and caught Tara's attention, giving the signal to leave. We walked to Tara's car. "I think I might've found a new church at attend."

She unlocked the car. "Hopefully it's kinder to you that those self-righteous morons at your current place."

"Be nice." I clucked my tongue and buckled my seatbelt.

"I was."

I snorted. "Think I might check out her church tomorrow. She says there're lots of young people, music, and stuff like that."

"Cool." Tara started the car and headed toward home.

I squeezed my hands together. "You think you might like to visit with me?" My stomach fizzed.

She glanced across at me. "I dunno."

I raised my palm. "It's okay. No pressure."

"Maybe another time?"

"You're on." I grinned.

I dabbed on a final sheen of lip gloss and smacked my lips together at my ensuite mirror. "That'll do."

Tara peeked around the doorframe. "If they don't accept you for who you are, they can all go to—"

"Maybe don't finish that sentence." I grabbed my bag from my bed. "Not sure when I'll be back from church, but if you need me, call."

She flopped back on her bed. "Have fun while I snooze."

I blew her a kiss, closed our bedroom door, and shimmied down the stairs. The lower level was quiet, so I assumed the Morgan clan had attended the early service at their church. I double-checked the note board in the kitchen—which no urgent communications adorned—while I buzzed a fruit smoothie and sipped my delicious breakfast through a wide metal straw.

After cleaning up, I tucked my phone inside my bag, shouldered the strap, and opened the front door. Something on the internal door handle stuck to my fingers. I wrinkled my nose and released the gooey metal handgrip. After a cautious sniff of my sticky digits— strawberry jam with a hint of peanut butter—I popped the deadlock, stepped backward onto the front step, and pulled the door shut. Now to find a tissue.

Weird snapping sounds filtered through the air behind me, followed by footsteps.

I turned and faced Kortney and a guy with a camera. "Kortney?"

"Diana." She smiled, but her usual bubbliness seemed muted, tamed. "Lovely to see you again." She stepped away from the camera guy and glanced at her phone. "I'd like to ask you some questions."

I furrowed my brow. "What are you doing here?"

"Following a story like a wise friend once insisted I do."

I stared at her, my gut prickling.

"It's about a current trial where I've heard some interesting information." Her eyes narrowed. "Although the names of the sexual abuse victims related to this case are sealed, I've been informed that a gentleman hailing from your hometown was the big breakthrough for the police."

My legs seemed to have fused to the front step.

"A man who, over twelve months ago, abducted a young woman and suicided in North Melbourne."

No. My hands trembled, and I pressed my back against the firm door.

Her eyes flashed. "What I'd like to confirm is whether Pierce Damien Harris truly abducted you, or whether you just have a taste for Harris blood?"

My lungs ached from my laboured breaths.

Her mouth twitched. "Did Officer Harris know of your relationship with his brother?"

My vision blurred.

"And is Tara one of the assault victims? Will she testify at the trial?"

My chest burned, and I inhaled exaggerated breaths.

"How has this experience changed you? Do you see yourself—"

"Stop!" I coughed and sucked in air. "Just stop."

Kortney stiffened. "This story is my big break. I need th—"

"Leave me alone." I peered down at my twitching hands. House keys.

"I'm doing my job. Just answer the questions."

I fumbled with the keys in the lock. "Go away!"

Kortney clamped her hand on my shoulder.

My self-defense skills kicked in—thank the Lord Almighty—

and I pushed back. "Leave me be!"

Kortney glowered at me, straightened her shirt front, and whispered something to the photographer.

Had he been snapping pictures of me the entire time? What if they leaked my photo and story to the masses? How could I live and study in the city with my personal struggle up for public consumption?

I cupped my hands against my rioting abdomen. "Get off the grass, or I'll call the police."

Kortney huffed. "Make me. I'll get this story one way or another."

"Go!" Sickening currents vibrated through my limbs, nauseating me. I bent and braced my palms on my knees.

The front door flew open, and Aunt Stacy stepped out in her robe. "What's going on?"

Tears burst from my eyes, and I fell against her.

She thrust her arms around me and pulled me behind her. "Why are you harassing my family?"

My entire body trembled, and whatever conversation occurred was lost to the wham of blood pounding inside my head. How could Kortney do this to me?

Aunt Stacy slammed the door behind us and escorted me to the family room. She raced for a tissue, sneezed, and blotted her nose. She squatted in front of me and patted my knee. "Steve'll be home from church with the kids in about ten minutes. I'll update him, and we'll arrange an intervention order against that crazy woman."

I stared at her until she disappeared in the haze of my tears.

An hour later, I pressed closer to Tara where she embraced me on the family room couch. "Did you know they were on trial?"

"Yeah. The police said there was a chance I would be asked to testify, but they believe they have a strong case and our witness statements may be all they require." Her hollow voice stabbed my heart.

"I've never thought about it, even with the police saying the USB contained everything they needed for prosecution." I shrugged. "It never crossed my mind."

"You have closure." Her arms shuddered. "Your attacker's dead and can't come back to hurt you."

No, his original hurt still had the power to level me and the ones I loved.

"But I don't have that. The men who hurt me?" She sighed. "They'll probably get jail time, but for how long?"

What would I do if I faced the same reality? Without God, the situation seemed impossibly overwhelming.

"But that's a concern for another time." Tara pulled away and scooted back against the couch, wrapping her arms around her knees. "Would it be wrong to pray they're all murdered in prison? Or suffer heart attacks? Or maybe get mutilated by fellow prisoners and left incapacitated?"

The backs of my eyes burned.

"Or is that wrong? Because I never want to see them again," she whispered.

I encircled my arms around her. "The Bible says to love your enemies, but ... I think I'd struggle with similar feelings to you." And live with the guilt of wishing death and destruction on my enemies when I knew otherwise.

"How could she do that to you? How could a friend say the things she said?" Tara fisted her hands.

"I don't know." Was Kortney's behaviour the norm in journalism? Would I be subjected to similar expectations to perform and get the story? I shuddered. Why was I even studying journalism? Was I cut out for it?

Tara growled. "I'm almost angrier at her than I am the men who destroyed my life ... and that's an insane thing to admit."

I rubbed her back. "It is what it is. Just ... don't give in to the hatred. You're better than that. You're a survivor and destined for more than wishing death on others."

She relaxed her fingers. "So I can't sew up a collection of voodoo dolls?"

A smile broke out on my face. "No voodoo dolls."

"You're no fun."

I chuckled.

She leaned against me. "But I love you anyway."

"Ditto."

25 August

I know I write this almost every time I journal, but I wish you were here, Mum. Today was wretched. I discovered the men who hurt Tara are on trial. Maybe it's a pretrial, I dunno. I might live with a barrister, but I don't listen to half the stuff she says. Heh. Anyway, the men are facing charges (as they should!) but I'm worried about Tara. She knew about the case but never said a word. That omission says a lot. And Kortney? My "friend" and esteemed colleague harassed me about the attack and things related to Tara. Can you believe it? What friend would do that to someone?

The panic when she started offloading her demands, wanting information, was astounding. But somehow, I stayed upright and strong. I used my self-defense skills and techniques, which brought April to mind. And we both know who she's inextricably linked to in my brain.

I miss him, Mum. I know I should be moving on, and don't get me wrong, because I am. The ache inside is slowly but surely drifting away whenever I think of him. But I'm not sure when I'll ever be ready to date again.

I'm also not sure about this journalism thing. There, I said it, and I'm sorry if this disappoints you. Maybe I got it wrong? I'm just not sure I'm cut out for the cutthroat world of chasing leads and making headlines. Do you think I can do it? Do I have the moral fortitude to work in the media? I want to do this, Mum. I want to make you happy.

I love you.

CHAPTER TWENTY-EIGHT
Camaraderie

The following Sunday—after an exhausting week filled with court appointments related to the personal-safety intervention order the police initiated and the court approved—I stepped into a modern-looking church building filled with hundreds of people, young and old. My tummy flipped multiple times, and I pressed a hand to my abdomen.

The greeting team welcomed me, like I had welcomed others many times at the church entry in Tellarine, several smiles aimed my way.

I wandered the foyer and spotted Lacey with another girl near the auditorium door.

She turned and grinned wide. "Diana!" She rushed toward me. "So good to see you! Want to sit with me and my friend?"

I smiled, and my shoulders relaxed. "Yes, please."

We located seats, and I hummed a prayer while congregants filled the remaining chairs. The live music began, and my ears seized from the song loud enough for the deaf to hear. I grinned, enjoying every second of freedom. My tears overflowed when a song called *Through it All* blared from stage, shooting straight into my pain-filled heart, and shocking it with a comforting dose of God's love. In the sweet moment, surrounded by hundreds of people singing these heartfelt words to Jesus, my confidence in myself and in Him restored. God loved me. He was with me and would continue to be with me throughout everything life threw my way. I was wrapped securely in the safety of His hand.

After the service, Lacey introduced me to a few of her friends, and we decided to head over to the South Melbourne Market for lunch, a mere five-minute walk away.

We travelled in smaller groups befitting a busy city footpath. Lacey stepped around a muddy patch. "Did you enjoy the service?"

I stuffed my hands into my coat pockets. "I loved every minute of it."

She squeaked. "I'm glad. Think you'll come back?"

"Definitely." I glanced ahead and was distracted by a guy five metres ahead with a thatch of sandy hair and broad shoulders. The guy turned to his mate and laughed.

I almost squealed when Andrew's laughter reverberated through the air. "Andrew!"

He halted and turned, stopping the flow of humanity on the path. His eyes bulged and a huge smile spread across his face.

I ran and punched his arm. "What's up, Daley?"

He rubbed his bicep and chuckled. "Not much. What about you? Haven't seen you since Sam's party last year. You been hiding on campus or something?"

My smile faded, and I rubbed my chest. "Some stuff happened, and I took a leave of absence the past year. Just started back this semester."

He dipped his eyebrows. "I'd no idea. I thought you were home on break like me." He rubbed his smooth chin. "Must've been some serious stuff for Miss Brilliant to take a twelve-month break?"

"It was," I whispered.

He rested a hand on my shoulder and met my gaze. "More than happy to be a sounding board or serve some justice with my fists."

I chuckled, freeing the building tension in my torso. "Thanks."

We chatted while we traipsed the covered market. Andrew pulled me toward a pie stall and joined the queue. "Best pies in the area. You'll thank me later."

I smiled and relaxed, comforted by his familiar face. After pondering the menu, I indicated to Andrew my pie preference and turned to observe passers-by.

An attractive guy in his mid-twenties approached us in the queue. He wore a New York Knicks cap, a deep-blue bomber jacket, and dark jeans. His grey eyes twinkled, and he settled his gaze on Andrew.

I leaned toward Andrew and gave him a not-so-subtle nudge. "You know this guy?"

Andrew peered over my shoulder and smiled. "Tom!" He waved the stranger over, and they shook hands in the odd manly way some guys do.

I arched a brow.

"This is my cousin Tom." He nodded to me. "Tom, this is Diana."

Tom stared, wide-eyed.

My face warmed under his scrutiny.

"Dreamy Diana?"

I smothered a nervous giggle and extended my hand. "In the flesh, apparently. Pleased to meet you."

Tom grasped my hand, lifted my knuckles to his lips, and planted a gentle kiss. "The pleasure's all mine." Did I hear an American edge to his Australian accent?

I retracted my hand and elbowed Andrew. "What on earth have you been telling him?"

Andrew chuckled. "Only the truth."

The customer ahead of us departed, and we stepped to the counter.

Andrew smiled at the sales lady. "I'll have a chicken-and-leek pie, and a Moroccan lamb for the lady. Tom?"

Tom scanned the overhead menu. "Lamb and rosemary, thanks."

Andrew paid, and we stepped aside to wait for the pies.

I opened my wallet and withdrew some cash, holding it out for Andrew. "I'm more than happy to pay, you know."

"Not on your life. I've waited nine years to buy you lunch." He grinned.

I covered my mouth to hide my snort-laugh.

Tom slapped Andrew's back, laughing, and turned to face me. "Andy's been talking about you since the first day he laid eyes on you. Our school holiday catch-ups were filled with 'Diana this' and 'Diana that.' I dubbed you Dreamy Diana to tease Andy, but he liked the name … and that's who you've been ever since." He flashed his straight white teeth and leaned closer. "I thought you were a figment of his imagination."

I quirked my eyebrows. "Why?"

His eyes softened. "You sounded too good to be true."

My cheeks and neck heated like a fast-spreading rash. Was he for real? I stared at the two men in front of me. "I'm far from perfect, so either Andrew's embellished his stories, or you heard incorrectly."

The men boomed with laughter. "Told you. Self-deprecating to a T," Andrew said.

Our pies were deposited on the counter. Tom grabbed all three, and we wandered to a nearby seating area.

The first bite of buttery pastry and hot, flavourful Moroccan lamb slid down my throat and spread warmth through my torso. I savoured each delicious bite. My final mouthful arrived too soon, and I brushed crumbs from my fingers. "So good, Andrew. Nice call."

He stuffed his final bite of pie into his mouth and gave me a thumbs up.

Tom crumpled our empty brown paper bags and discarded them in a nearby bin. "Anyone feel like some dessert? I passed a Patisserie earlier."

I licked my lips and grinned. "Did they have any snot-blocks? Or chocolate eclairs?"

Andrew rubbed his hands together. "I could go for a snot-block right about now."

Tom wrinkled his nose. "It's a vanilla slice, guys. Van-ill-a slice." He shook his head. "Not sure I feel hungry anymore."

Andrew and I laughed.

"You always had a sensitive stomach, Tom," Andrew said.

Tom glanced at his watch, and his eyes widened. "Wow, didn't realise the time. What're you two up to this afternoon?"

Andrew and I shrugged.

Tom chuckled. "Well, I'd love to crash your well-thought-out plans, but I'm due back to church. Helping set things up before the next service."

I smiled and nodded. "Lovely meeting you."

He tipped his Knicks cap in my direction. "The pleasure was all mine, Dreamy Diana." He cuffed a playful whack on Andrew's shoulder and sauntered away.

"So that's your cousin."

"That's him."

I scrunched my brow. "Am I imagining he has a bit of an American twang?"

Andrew shook his head. "His family relocated to the States for five years when I was in Primary School. Tom's five years older than us."

"Makes sense."

Andrew scratched his chin. "But his accent's quite pronounced today. He returned a few days ago from a month-long work thing over there."

"Oh." And once again my mind drifted to Jonathan. How the rare word or two he spoke carried a similar intonation to his mum. I shuddered a breath and shook my head.

Andrew raised a brow. "No dessert?"

I rubbed my churning stomach. "Maybe not today."

We stood, and I walked alongside him. We passed more tables on our way to the street, and Lacey waved. "See you, Diana!"

"Bye!" I turned to Andrew at the pedestrian crossing. "Any chance you could give me a lift home, please?"

"Sure." He extracted his keys. "Where to?"

I recited my address and fell into step with his pace.

He cleared his throat. "You planning on going home anytime soon?"

"I don't have a car, so it becomes a bigger event than I'd like with trains and buses, then someone having to come out and meet me." I sighed. "I'd love to hug the kids every weekend, but with work and study … I usually save up my trips for semester or mid-semester breaks." I shuffled around a puddle. "What about you?"

Andrew shrugged. "I have the car, but with my double degree, there's a lot of study involved. Spending so many hours driving one way only to do it again the next day feels like an inefficient use of my time." He approached a late-model Holden and clicked the key fob.

"I get it. I have my licence but don't really enjoy the long drive." I opened the passenger door and buckled.

He twisted in the driver's seat and faced me. "If you ever feel homesick, let me know. We might be able to work something out."

A comforting warmth filtered through my chest, and I smiled. "Thanks."

He started the ignition. "That's what friends are for."

♥ ♥ ♥ ♥ ♥ ♥ ♥

"It's so good to see you here!" Lacey squeezed me in a fierce hug inside the church foyer after the Sunday evening service.

I vibrated with silent laughter. I had arrived late and missed seeing anyone I knew until now.

She lifted her head. "What? Can't I be excited?"

My chuckles reverberated in my chest cavity. "I admire your enthusiasm." None of the girls at the other church had welcomed me with similar abandon. Conditional love and qualified acceptance seemed to be their way of life.

She dropped her arms and stepped back with a grin. "I've always appreciated your gentle spirit, and I like hanging out with you."

"So do I," a rich, accented male voice toned behind me.

I turned toward Tom, my heart beating faster. "Hey."

"I've seen you around, but I don't think we've officially met." Lacey extended her hand toward Tom. "I'm Lacey."

"Tom. Pleased to be officially introduced." He flashed a grin and glanced past my shoulder. "And the knucklehead coming our way is my cousin Andy."

I turned and waved.

Andrew nodded mid-stride, waved to a few guys near the open auditorium doors, and stopped beside his cousin. "How're you doing, Lacey?"

Lacey smiled in a bashful manner. "I'm good, Andrew. You?"

I narrowed my eyes. Had she not thrown herself at me in a bold hug moments before? I glanced at Lacey and Andrew, then snuck a peek at Tom.

He stared back with a pleased grin.

Andrew focused on Lacey. "Is the gang heading out somewhere for dinner?"

A soft pink blush dusted Lacey's cheeks. "That's the plan."

I snuck closer to Tom. "Does it look—"

"Indeed it does." He winked, touched my elbow, and pulled me a few steps away. "Which works in perfectly for me."

Electricity snaked along my arm from Tom's brief, light touch. Uh oh.

A few other people crowded nearby, chatting, and Tom seemed to loom even closer than before.

A guy in a casual T-shirt and jeans bumped my shoulder as he walked past. He paused, leaned in, and said, "Sorry," then kept walking.

I froze. Dreaded memories slammed into me with sudden force.

My breathing laboured, and my mind fogged. What was happening?

My stomach roiled, and flashes of heat prickled my skin. The world tilted, and I lost my footing.

Tom grabbed my shoulder and steadied me. His grey eyes widened, and he furrowed his brows. "You okay? You're very pale."

"Uh." I palmed my forehead, my skin clammy.

He pressed a hand to my back and led me to the visitors lounge.

I wilted against a plush couch.

Tom handed me a cup of water and squatted in front of me.

Waves of nausea crashed inside me, and I sipped the cool water, the plastic cup misshapen under my firm grip. What had set off my attack?

I breathed in deeply.

His cologne. That guy was wearing *his* cologne.

"You've a little colour in your face now." Tom's facial expressions oozed intensity. "Want to tell me what that was about?"

"Just feeling faint." My limbs seemed to vibrate even in this seated position. I closed my eyes and practiced my breathing exercises.

Slow breaths in and out.

I pressed my hand to my tummy and willed the pancakes I had eaten for a snack dinner with Ella and Toby to digest and not make a grand entrance. I murmured quiet prayers. With each passing breath, the nausea dissipated.

"Does this happen often?"

I opened my eyes and met Tom's profound gaze. "Thankfully, no." How could a scent memory trigger such a powerful response?

A new groove wrinkled his forehead. "Do you need a lift home?"

Was he always this considerate? I shook my head, more to clear my new thoughts than in answer to Tom's question. "I should be okay." I showcased my best smile, my heart now plodding at normal pace, and stood.

Tom rose. "Speaking of needing a lift home, Andy mentioned

something about mid-semester break coming up?"

"That's right." I pursed my lips.

He flanked me on our short walk back to the foyer. "I'd be happy to offer my services as driver."

I halted. "Really?"

His features relaxed. "I enjoy the long drives and am always happy to visit family."

Wow, benevolence exuded from this guy, just like Dad.

Andrew shouldered his cousin. "What's going on?"

"Tom's offering to drive us to Tellarine next week," I said.

Andrew smirked. "Of course, he did."

Flutters multiplied in my midriff. Better than fainting spells and nausea.

Tom eyed his cousin. "The offer stands. Let me know what you both think."

"I'm in." Andrew nodded to me. "You?"

Almost two months had passed since I left home. There were more people in Tellarine I wanted to see than not. "Okay, count me in."

Tom grinned and aimed his grey gaze on me. "It's settled then."

I returned his smile, but the sensations affecting my pulse were far from settled.

CHAPTER TWENTY-NINE
Glimpses of Home

The early spring afternoon sun streamed through Dad and Victoria's lounge room windows, warming my front where I lazed on the couch opposite my parents. A whiny squawk crackled over the baby monitor which rested on the coffee table.

"My turn." Dad kissed his wife's forehead and zipped through the archway.

Victoria laughed. "Your father's enjoying his daddy duties now Elijah's more responsive. The little mister rolled over last week and is trying his hardest to bunny-hop. That's pre-crawling motion!" She shook her head. "Only a Jacobsen would insist on moving about at three months. The funny little man."

I plucked my water glass from the coffee table and consumed the cool liquid. "Wasn't Jazzy about five-and-a-half months when she started to crawl?"

Victoria nodded. "It took her over a month to get to that point, so Elijah has a long way to go." She stretched and yawned.

"Can I help with anything?"

An indulgent smile crossed her lips. "We're fine, thank you. The nappy bag's packed, and we're set to leave as soon as Jazzy wakes from her nap."

On our trip from Melbourne, Andrew, Tom, and I had decided a night out for dinner would be better for my semi-exhausted parents than having them play host and slave over a meal. I had made the arrangements for an early dinner at Benanu's, then the boys and I would hang out with Keanu and play some pool.

"Okay. I'll finish off some office work so Keanu can't haul me over the coals about it later." I walked upstairs to my bedroom and completed my final spreadsheet.

Jasmine tumbled through my doorway. "Sissy Di-Di, is time to go!" She bounced in a pink-and-purple dress-and-leggings outfit, dancing her little fingers in the air.

"Okay, bubba, let me put this away, and I'll be down." I switched off my laptop and gathered my things.

We bundled the little ones into Dad's ute, and I squished myself between the two car seats in the rear row. My backside and hips slept most of the way to Benanu's.

Andrew and Tom waved from a larger table. "Hi, Miss Burke, ah, I mean, Mrs. Jacobsen," Andrew said, his cheeks tinged with pink.

"Mr. Daley!" Victoria shifted Elijah on her hip and wrapped Andrew in a one-arm hug. "You've grown! It's been a while. And please call me Victoria."

"Victoria." Andrew greeted Dad, then turned to Tom. "This's my cousin and the wheels for our trip this week."

Tom extended a hand to Dad. "Tom Chirnside. Pleasure to meet you, Mr. Jacobsen."

Chirnside? Why had I thought he was a Daley? I bit my lower lip. What kind of friend was I not to know a guy's surname? My insides twisted. I knew little about Tom despite our interactions at church. Maybe Dad would interrogate him. I suppressed a grin and realized everyone else had claimed a seat. I slipped into the remaining chair beside Tom.

"Uh, Diana, is this normal?" Victoria fiddled with Jasmine's high-chair straps, but no matter what she did, they refused to budge.

I tried to work out the issue without success. "Let me find another one." I dumped Jasmine in Dad's lap and carried the faulty highchair to a back room, returning with another feeding chair. We ordered our drinks and meals.

Dad leaned an elbow on the table and dangled his car keys for Elijah's enjoyment. "Andrew, Victoria tells me you were one of her diligent students. And Diana mentioned something about aerospace engineering and business management. Do you have plans to take over NASA?"

Andrew laughed. "In a nutshell, yes. I'd love to work in some capacity with the Australian Space Agency, especially in light of their partnership with NASA on the Moon to Mars project. That'd be my dream job."

Victoria gathered Elijah in her arms, rested his little head in the crook of her elbow, and discreetly breastfed him. "Where's the Agency located?"

"Headquarters are in Adelaide, but they work with different teams and organizations nationwide, so I could end up anywhere. I'm only halfway through my five-year course, so I've plenty of time to work out what I really want to do."

Dad sipped his beer, then turned to Tom. "What about yourself, Tom? What keeps you busy during the day?"

Tom smiled. "I'm a lawyer at a firm in the city."

Dad seemed impressed by this revelation.

As was I. Why had I never asked Tom about his job? I crossed my legs and jiggled my foot. Was I so self-absorbed I failed to ask basic, caring questions?

"What's your specialty?" Dad helped Jasmine with her cup, which she thought too fun to spill.

"I've my Masters in intellectual property. You know, patents, trademarks, copyright law. Well, it's a drop in the ocean of what my area of expertise encompasses, but I don't want to bore you with details." Tom glanced at me before turning to Dad. "Diana mentioned you're a sparky? Sometimes I wonder why I didn't choose a more hands-on career."

Dad chuckled. "It's not as glamorous a job as this current generation seems to think, but it pays well most of the time and is quite fulfilling."

Our food arrived, and our conversations carried us through dessert until Keanu arrived with the bill. I had warned the guys on the futility of paying for dinner, and Dad handed over his credit card with a victorious grin.

He and Victoria bundled the children, hugged us, and departed.

"Your family's great." Tom leaned close, his pleasant cologne wafting toward me. Earthy and woody, with a citrus note.

Whoa. My breath hitched. How had we dined beside each other without me catching a whiff sooner? I scooted from the booth toward our reserved pool table, where Keanu waited. "Thanks. I think they're pretty awesome."

We meandered between tables. "It was nice being officially introduced to your dad," Andrew said. "I've seen him over the years but was petrified to approach him. His height's imposing, and I can't imagine any girl's father being partial to meeting a boy whose sights are set on his daughter."

I chuckled and inspected the billiard cues against the wall. "Especially when it comes to my dad."

Keanu grunted.

I eyed all three men surrounding the pool table and raised my eyebrow. "You boys ready to be beaten by a girl?" I set the colourful balls into the triangular rack and positioned them on the table. "Who's up first?"

Tom chalked the end of his cue in rhythmic swirls. Tiny particles of powder billowed into a dusty blue cloud near his fingers. He glanced at his cousin, shrugged, and turned to me. "I volunteer as tribute."

Keanu and Andrew pressed the fingers of their left hands to their lips, raised their left arms in a three finger salute, and burst out in laughter.

I clamped my lips together, shook my head, and executed a legal break shot for our first game.

Feeling a little rusty after studying non-stop for six weeks, I indulged in a few rounds to get in the swing of things but was soon back to my usual competitive self.

Keanu called a drinks break after forty minutes. Andrew bought the first round and Tom the next. By the time my turn to shout arrived, the guys were tired of "losing to a girl," so we found a table and ordered some snacks.

"I've been practicing my cocktails, Di. Wanna try one tonight?" Keanu asked.

"Maybe some other time." I still needed to resolve my issues with alcohol. One day.

We followed Keanu to the bar so he could fix our drinks.

I glanced over my shoulder mid-laugh—Tom cracked far too many jokes for a lawyer—and almost stumbled into Andrew.

Jonathan's dark-brown eyes zeroed in on me from where he slouched at a small table.

"You okay?" Andrew gripped my shoulder, bracing me.

My heart had stopped beating for half a second, and my skin pulsed. "Ah …"

Keanu glanced over my shoulder, inhaled a sharp breath, and

grabbed my other shoulder in what seemed like a protective move.

Jonathan nodded to Keanu before redirecting his focus back on me.

My chest squeezed, and I gasped for air. What had happened to the man I loved?

He clutched a half-drained double-walled latte glass in his unsteady hand, his usual styled hair unrecognizable in its disheveled state. His crumpled T-shirt reinforced the impression he had slept on a park bench, or perhaps not slept in a long while. And his bloodshot eyes? Streaked and enflamed yet held a thousand times their intensity from our last meeting.

My chest shuddered, and my heart tore.

"What happened to him?" Andrew whispered.

"Me." Shrugging hands off my shoulders, I absorbed a deep breath and approached Jonathan's table. "Hey." My voice croaked, and a small smile touched my lips.

"Hey." His rough tone clogged my throat.

I swallowed the lump. "D-do you mind if I sit a moment?" *Please say yes.*

He stared for longer than comfortable.

My pulse accelerated.

He nodded strands of hair into his eyes and brushed them aside with shaky fingers.

My chest heaved, and I held back the desire to fist-pump. I glanced over my shoulder and nodded to Keanu, who pointed to a nearby table where my friends now sat and talked. I returned my focus to the man seated in front of me and occupied the chair. *Lord, give me the words to speak.* "So … how're you doing?" Would he be truthful in his response or hold himself back?

Jonathan shrugged. "Okay, I guess. You?"

I raised my shoulders. "Yeah, okay."

He sipped his coffee, and his eyes glossed over. "You're as beautiful as ever," he whispered.

My insides melted, and a blush heated my cheeks. "Th-thanks. You look …"

"Terrible." The hint of a smile ghosted his features.

"Working too hard, Senior Constable Harris?'"

A genuine smile slid to his features. "Guilty as charged."

I sighed and caught his potent gaze. "You need to look after yourself. You can't catch bad guys with debilitating fatigue. You need more sleep."

He rubbed a hand over his face. "No time to sleep when work needs to be done."

An onerous weight pushed on my ribcage. "You need to refuse extra shifts and get some rest." Heat and pressure amassed in my chest. "You're no good to anyone if you're dead." My stomach curdled, and I pressed my hand to my torso.

"That's debatable."

Tears stung my eyes, his appearance blurring while he finished his coffee. "Haven't your parents suffered enough losing one son? Your recklessness and excessive risk could deprive them of another." I wiped my eyes. "You're worth more than this," I whispered. "Get back on God's timetable for your life, and live life to the full. Do it for your parents if you can't do it for yourself." How could I get his worth through to him? "Do it for your friends on the force, for Constable Dennigan. For Sam." I stood. "For me."

His jaw tensed, and he rubbed a hand across his eyes.

I spun and approached my friends' table, all eyes aimed at me. My legs shook with each step away from Jonathan. I wilted on the unoccupied seat—my body now weighed a ton, and all energy disappeared—and guzzled some water, my superhuman ability shining through when I failed to spill any liquid. My heart bled for my broken ex.

Keanu wrinkled his brow. "How about we call it a night and I drive ya home?"

I nodded, said my goodbyes, and climbed into his twenty-year-old ute. I clutched my hands together, counting breaths.

Keanu reversed out of the parking bay, and the quiver in my limbs slowed on the main highway.

I relaxed in the seat. "When're you going to replace your ute?" He loved his old beaten-up Toyota HiLux.

Keanu chuckled. "I'll probably leave this to my grandchildren."

I glanced at the dashboard and laughed. "You've already clocked three hundred and twenty thousand kilometres. You think this'll run another million?"

"I bought this with my hard-earned money five years ago with two hundred and fifty thousand kays on the dial. These utes are built to last. My mate has a similar-aged HiLux with over four hundred thousand clicks, so I figure"—he tapped the steering wheel—"she's got a few hundred thousand left in her."

I snickered, my final interaction with Keanu on our trip home. A choice I soon regretted when the lull brought Jonathan back to mind.

Why had he allowed himself to give up? All I could do was pray God would keep him safe and bring him to a place of peace.

Keanu pulled into the driveway and idled.

I unbuckled.

He peered at me. "You gonna be okay?"

"Yeah, all good. Nothin' prayer can't fix."

Keanu grinned. "My poor grammar's rubbing off on ya. You'd better return to Melbourne and get some smarts back in yer head."

A genuine laugh broke free from the heaviness inside my chest cavity. "Yeah, nah. If my journo gig goes down the dunny, I can always be a garbo," I said in my best ocker drawl.

Keanu's deep laugh reverberated through the ute cabin. "You're crazy."

My matching chuckle quaked my shoulders. "I know."

Keanu wiped his big fingers under his leaking eyes.

I smiled. "That's why you love me and want to marry me in thirty years."

"Too right." He beamed and clasped my arm, pulled me close, and planted a kiss on my temple. "Sleep well," he said against my hair.

"You too." I dismounted from the ute and padded to the front door, welcoming the sanctuary of my family home as I slipped inside its walls and left the world behind.

"I enjoyed the service." Tom glanced around Tellarine Christian Church's small auditorium.

"Me too." Andrew sighed. "Wish I'd found this place when I was living here. I prefer it to the traditional church Mum's gone to since before I was born."

Tom smirked. "You mentioned checking out Diana's church years ago, but I counselled you not to, remember?"

Andrew laughed and shook his head. "That's right. You said it'd make me look like a stalker, and I didn't want to ruin my chances in Year Eight."

"I don't think I'd have thought you were a stalker … maybe." I grinned at Andrew.

"But Madison would've said so for sure!" Andrew burst out laughing.

"So true." I looked across the room and stiffened.

"What's the matter?" Tom followed my gaze to where Mr. and Mrs. Harris chatted with an older couple.

"Jonathan's parents." I licked my dry lips. "I haven't spoken with them since we broke up."

"Oh." A reassuring smile slid to Tom's face. "You've got this, Diana. Just be your wonderful self, and they'll be enamoured with you like the rest of us."

Blood flooded to the surface of my skin, inflaming my face and neck. I turned back to the Harrises.

Mrs. Harris waved and trotted toward me.

I fidgeted with the cuff of my long-sleeved top.

"Diana." Mrs. Harris wrapped her arms around me in a quick, firm hug.

"Mrs. Harris." I swallowed, hard. I forgot she was a hugger.

She held my hand. "Dearest girl." Her long sigh filled the space between us.

My muscles tightened.

She patted my hand as Mr. Harris slipped an arm around his wife's waist. "Dearest, dearest girl."

Mr. Harris nodded to me.

My burning cheeks kicked up its intensity. Words failed to sprout in my brain or on my tongue.

Mrs. Harris relinquished my fingers and tutted.

I clamped my arms at my sides.

"I'm sorry about what happened with you and my boy." Mrs. Harris wiped a finger under her eye. "I thought you would be the one to have the Marsala chai recipe."

So had I.

"You really were so good for my boy," Mrs. Harris said, her voice hinting at tears.

Were so good for my boy. Even his mother admitted our relationship was over. I glanced toward Tom and Andrew, my insides flipping on turbulent seas.

Tom's back met my gaze, his lean body angled toward Andrew, offering me a skerrick of privacy.

Air siphoned from my lungs. I met Mrs. Harris's eyes. "I saw him last night."

She tilted her head. "My Jonathan?"

I nodded. "He's not looking very … happy or healthy."

Several tears trailed her cheeks. "We're worried about him, aren't we, Henrik?"

Mr. Harris bobbed his head. "That we are. He's working long hours and—"

"He's not attending church." Mrs. Harris sniffed and retrieved a handkerchief from her cleavage. She dabbed her eyes. "It breaks our hearts."

I blinked against the heat of tears and issued a scant smile. "I'll keep your family in my prayers."

Mrs. Harris clutched my fingers and squeezed. "Thank you, sweet girl."

I stepped back. "It was lovely to see you both."

Mr. Harris smiled, but his eyes reflected a hefty seriousness. "Look after yourself in the big city."

Did he carry guilt because of his eldest son's actions? My chest pinched. "I will." I glanced between Jonathan's parents. "All the best."

"You too, dear." Mrs. Harris pressed into her husband's side, and they stepped away.

I sighed, turned, and slipped in beside Tom.

"You okay?" Tom's grey eyes beseeched me.

Uncertain my voice would remain steady, I nodded.

Tom touched my arm. "Your dad said lunch was at their place, then we'd be free to travel home."

Tellarine is home, not Melbourne. My heart twisted. After all that had transpired here, Melbourne might be the best place for me. I repelled the thoughts and smiled. "Sounds great."

Andrew, Tom, and I exited the church for our final afternoon with my family.

CHAPTER THIRTY
Triggered

I trundled down the staircase to the Morgans' expansive kitchen, where my eyes were assaulted by the tail end of an amorous lip-locking session.

Uncle Steve held his wife wedged between the kitchen bench and his firm frame. Their soft moans released into the atmosphere.

A memory pricked at my mind: Jonathan pressed against me, his warmth permeating my shirt, the kitchen bench at home in Tellarine digging against the backs of my thighs.

I shook the remembrance away, abruptly turned, and cleared my throat. "You're definitely related to Victoria." I shook my head. "Is it safe to turn around?"

Uncle Steve's deep chuckle pervaded the room. "Give me a few more minutes, then I should be done."

"Steven! Behave yourself." Aunt Stacy's tone wavered, probably more to do with the after-effects of her husband's kisses than any faux outrage on her behalf.

I turned toward the lovebirds—why were the adults in my life obsessed with swapping spit?—who glanced at one another with lovey-dovey eyes, and suppressed an eyeroll. Ugh!

I caught Aunt Stacy's gaze. "I saw you have a work function marked in Google Calendar for tomorrow afternoon, but I promised to help Andrew and Tom at church all day." Would she appreciate my forethought?

Uncle Steve released his wife, turned, and tilted his head. "Work function? On a Saturday?"

Aunt Stacy pursed her lips. "We're meeting the Dubois at chambers so I can leave some documents for the clerk and then go out together for dinner." She turned to me. "Are you able to cancel?"

I scrunched my face. "I committed to this before I visited Dad, and it's been in the calendar for several weeks."

Aunt Stacy nodded. "Will Tara be available?"

"She's visiting her mum this weekend."

"Oh."

I bit my lower lip. I wanted to spend more time getting to know Tom, but the Morgans were my priority. I presented my most pleasant smile. "But I could cancel?"

Uncle Steve scratched his chin. "Can Amber look after the kids overnight?"

Aunt Stacy's eyes widened. "That's an idea. I'll call her now." She bustled from the room, murmuring something about promising to be more organized.

I poured myself a glass of water, conscious of Uncle Steve's scrutiny.

"Everything okay with you?" His serious police officer tone filled the quiet. "You've been unusually reserved since you returned from Tellarine last week."

I suffocated a groan and projected a smile. "Yeah, I'm fine. Had some things on my mind is all." Living under the same roof as a switched-on police sergeant was downright annoying at times. No wonder Jonathan responded to situations the way he had when we were dating.

Uncle Steve crossed his arms and lifted a thick eyebrow. "Things like a young Senior Constable?"

I dropped my chin and sighed. "We kinda bumped into each other." I bit the inside of my cheek.

"And?" His interrogative tone lilted in his voice.

"And if someone made a movie starring a homeless zombie, he'd look the part."

Uncle Steve winced. "That bad?"

I nodded.

He leaned against the bench cupboards, arms crossed. "If you ever need to talk, you know I'll keep our conversations confidential."

"I know." Uncle Steve had already proven as much in the past. "Did you know ... back then?"

Uncle Steve creased his brow.

"About Jonathan and his brother?"

He shook his head. "I'm sorry I didn't pick up on it, though."

"Same."

Aunt Stacy re-entered the kitchen and smiled at her husband. "All done. We'll have lunch with Mike and Amber on Saturday then collect the children on the way to church on Sunday." She wrinkled her brow. "What a way to fill your weekend off."

Uncle Steve shrugged.

Aunt Stacy turned to me. "Will you be home for dinner? Feels like weeks since we all dined together."

"I should be." I placed my empty glass in the dishwasher, avoided Uncle Steve's heavy stare, and returned upstairs.

Tara threw her suitcase into the boot of her car. "I'm kinda looking forward to seeing Mum. I think our time together while I … recuperated …was good for our relationship even if the circumstances were crappy."

I opened the passenger door. "I'm glad, because I know you've hinted at some past tension. It's great you were able to draw closer."

"Yeah."

We drove to uni and lumbered into the Screening Politics and Economies lecture. I claimed my usual seat next to Tara.

Professor Yong strolled inside, his usual beaming smile filling his somewhat small face. He deposited his black laptop bag on the lectern and sorted through his things. "Morning."

A murmur of greetings filled the room.

"Right, before we get back into our topic from last session, I want to address a big news article in today's papers." He set his laptop on a table next to the lectern and plugged in a few cables connected to a nearby panel. "This is a prime example of how an international human-trafficking ring will not only affect the economy of our nation but many surrounding Asian countries." Clicking buttons on his laptop, Professor Yong displayed a news headline from a local digital-news site. "I can only imagine the blockbuster movies being inspired by the events leading up to and including the trial. Anyone see this gem this morning?"

I glanced at the large screen behind his head, and my chest

constricted.

The headline read, "Twenty Found Guilty During Black Dagger Trial."

My stomach and head spun faster than the words on the screen. Memories flared like a flash drive downloading information, and my breaths quickened.

My eyesight blurred.

I swiped my trembling fingers across my cheeks, swiveled to face Tara, and inhaled a sharp breath.

Wide, wild eyes and tear-stained cheeks betrayed Tara's thoughts. Was she reliving her three-day nightmare?

I reached across, clasped Tara's clammy hand, and stared straight ahead.

Tara squeezed back.

Professor Yong had been replaced by the haunting eyes of Pierce Damien Harris, his bloodied, whiskered jaw on full display. Luminous eyes flickering with pain, the shiny gun barrel inserted in his mouth.

I jammed my eyes shut and shook my head.

Please, brain. Stop this torment.

After several breaths, I cracked my eyes open, but this was all too much for me.

Tara sniffled.

I stuffed my laptop back into my bag and assisted Tara with her things.

We stood and hobbled from the room without apology or explanation, burst through the large doors, and ran for the exit.

I needed fresh air. Stat.

We stumbled to the closest park area and plonked under a tree.

"It's different being the story instead of writing it," Tara whispered.

I rubbed my neck and studied my friend. "Are you going to be okay to make the drive to Swan Hill?" The last thing I wanted was a phone call from her distraught mum saying Tara's car was wrapped around a tree trunk.

Tara blew her nose. "I'll be fine but think I'll skip the rest of today's classes and catch up online." Her blue eyes searched mine.

A faint smile shadowed my lips. "I'll be fine too. You go home. I'll tram it back to the house and have a quiet day."

After a long hug, Tara and I parted ways. I bumbled to the tram stop and prepared myself for a day of prayer. Because no matter what happened, I knew God was on my side.

The hot sting of a syringe jabbed into my neck. Cool liquid crippling my motor functions and adrenaline hammering my veins. Shallowed breaths, blurred eyesight. Animalistic growls and meaty hands clutching my breast. Extreme, numbing burns in my wrists. Warm fingers against my thigh. Radiating heat and glazed dark-hazel eyes edged with sapphire. Wet, warm peppermint, and fireworks behind my closed eyelids. Unreadable dark eyes glinting with disgust.

I awoke with a start and fell off my desk chair onto my side. "Ow!"

My heart thundered and my thigh ached. I gripped the seat of the chair, rested my ear against its soft cushioning, and counted my breaths. When had I fallen asleep?

I rubbed my banged-up thigh and closed my drooping eyelids.

Tara's wide, wild blue orbs and tear-stained features morphed into sallow, pale skin and vacant eyes. "Oh, Tara." Bandages coiled her neck and wrists.

I opened my eyes, and tears dripped onto the seat. I lifted my arm and traced my finger along the faint white lines encircling my wrists. My eyes shut of their own accord, and I dropped my arm.

Anyone see this gem this morning? A smiling Professor Yong materialized.

Not again.

I whimpered and clung to the chair.

Fiery red hair billowed like a riotous ocean around the professor, conjuring Kortney's piercing gemstone eyes. *I'll get this story one way or another.*

"Go away!" I screamed and burst into fresh tears.

I'm doing my job. Just answer the questions. Kortney's words reverberated through my head and into my heart.

A journalism career now seemed farfetched.

I glanced at my bedside clock. Two hours since Tara messaged. Was that long enough for her to debrief with her mum?

I rose, grabbed my phone, and dropped onto the foot of my bed.

"You checking up on me again?" Tara laughed on the other end of the line.

"No. I … need to ask you something." I lay along my bed.

"Ask away."

I puffed a breath. "I'm thinking of booking in to speak to someone at RMIT. A career advisor."

"Why would you do that?"

"I'm not sure I'm cut out for this journalism thing." My mouth dried.

"Nonsense." Tara huffed. "You're a natural. What happened today doesn't reflect on your ability and passion to work in this field."

I sighed. "I can't be like her."

"Her?"

"Kortney," I whispered.

A soft growl filtered through the phone. "You don't need to be like her. You can be yourself—a woman of moral integrity—and still wow your readers."

I stared at the ceiling. "You really think so?"

She chuckled. "I know so. I mean, c'mon, I'm still chasing this dream despite all the stuff I'm dealing with."

"So you're not thinking about switching to something else?"

A noisy huff irritated my ear. "Why would I do that? No way am I giving up on accomplishing this degree, especially because of *them*. Even if I'm still unsure about my future, I enjoy the study and spending time with you. I'm not going anywhere."

Something settled inside me. "Okay. Thanks."

"Anytime."

✒ ✒ ✒ ✒ ✒ ✒ ✒

20 September

I'm so weary of it all, Mum. The crying, the ache in my chest. Flashbacks and thoughts activating memories and igniting my fears. What am I meant to do when my past continues to torment me? Will things change? I feel the moment I grab hold of God's peace after a setback like today, these emotional blows spark concerns for my future.

When will it end?

I messaged Tara about fifteen times while she drove home. On the one hand I didn't want her to reply because, hello, it's not safe to text and drive. In fact, it's been illegal to do so since you died. But on the other hand, I needed to know she was safe. After I had arrived home and cleared my head, I spent the afternoon kicking myself for letting her leave. Tara must've been shaken, and hours behind the wheel couldn't have been good for her fragile mental health. But I forgave myself once she sent me a photo of herself standing outside her mum's place. "Proof of life," she had written.

Sometimes I wonder what my life would look like if you'd survived your injuries. Whether I'd be studying journalism at RMIT or perhaps jet-setting somewhere else to learn and create. Today's news article brought Kortney's transgressions to mind too. Yet again I hunkered at my little desk in my shared room and wondered … am I cut out for journalism? Would I have chased a story like Kortney? Or be happy attending court sessions to report the ugliness of humanity to my readers? Would compromise follow me while I trekked this path? Something inside me is "off" when it comes to my career.

After suffering at the hands of my dead attacker and an ex-friend all afternoon, I called Tara, and she oozed love, chatting me off the fence. I'd like to think it's something you would've done for me.

I'll stick with my studies because I love writing, and I also love you, so I'll run the race set before me.

Thank you for loving me. I miss your smile.

CHAPTER THIRTY-ONE
Floored

A hazy fuzz eclipsed my consciousness and the eighties tune *Get Outta My Dreams, Get into My Car* occupied the space around me. Billy Ocean serenaded me on a tossing sea of senselessness. The tide drew me closer to the shore and the brightness it possessed.

I opened my eyes in the darkness. Sam's ringtone. I stretched in the direction of my bedside table, yawned, swiped the screen, and peered at the clock.

Two in the morning.

"Thank God." Sam rasped over the phone. "Thought you'd never answer."

Another yawn escaped me. "What do you want?" I croaked, sleepiness coating my vocal cords.

"I need you to get out of bed, walk downstairs, and open the door."

"Huh?"

"Get out of bed, Diana, and let me in."

With my brain still on autopilot, I slipped from my bedroom, tiptoed down the stairs to the front door, and cracked it open.

Sam looked at me with huge eyes and mouth agape.

I widened the door opening.

"There is a God," he whispered, surveying me.

"Why're you here? It's two in the morning!" I hissed, my tired state shrouding all politeness.

Sam stepped close with a sly smile. "Seriously, I think I want to marry you." He winked.

I shook my head and squinted. "What?"

"I come to your house in a state of distress, and I'm met at the door by a sexy goddess in satin." He chortled. "You made my night."

Distress? My hearing seized, and my chest pounded. "What happened?" I whispered, my throat tight.

Sam's face transformed into an unfamiliar seriousness. "I'll tell you inside. But first, I need a permit-parking pass." He nodded toward his car parked under the closest streetlight. "Do you have one? Or should I move my car?"

"Oh. Sure. Wait here." I tiptoed to the kitchen, retrieved one of the two plastic permit-pass cards we used for guests, and scurried back to the door. "Here."

Sam grabbed the card and returned to his vehicle.

A cool breeze skimmed my calves, and I shivered.

Sam reappeared, ushered me indoors, and led me into the lounge room.

"I think it'll be better if you come hide out in my room." Hang the house rules. The last thing I needed was an overprotective police officer pouncing before asking questions.

"Lead the way, Princess."

We snuck up the staircase, along the hallway, and into my bedroom. I closed the door behind us and plonked on the edge of the bed, weariness restricting my movements. My neck ached. I massaged a knot and caught a glimpse of myself in the wall mirror. *Oh no.*

I blinked my slow, sleepy lids. My favourite short silver satin nightie had dipped low in the front, hugging my curves, and my dark, semi-messed bed hair cascaded my shoulders. A sight I never intended to share with a guy I was not married to. No wonder Sam's eyes had bulged when I opened the door.

I scampered to the foot of the bed for my lightweight dressing gown, slid inside its cool cotton, and nestled cross-legged on my bed.

Sam stood halfway between my bed and Tara's, head tilted, and hand grazing the back of his neck. He glanced between the furniture. His brows buckled, and he pressed his lips together.

I patted the mattress next to me. "What's going on?"

Sam lowered to the bed. His body dipped the mattress.

I fell against him.

He touched my lower back and sighed, his chest heaving. "Jon's been hurt." A sob shuddered in his chest.

"Wh-what?" The air in my lungs sucked out, my breaths tenuous and stingy. "When? How?" My fingers trembled, and I restrained my hands against one another.

Sam's breathing seemed to quicken. "He was shot on duty."

"What!" How could this be? I squeezed my eyelids closed.

A gunshot I had heard many times before ricocheted in my ears, and I covered my mouth. The echoes of searing ear pain followed, and tears stung my closed eyes. Skin sensations prickled like the warmth of splattered matter. But this time, a new face surfaced in my mind. Jonathan's.

My stomach roiled, knots upon knots twisting my insides. No. *No!*

Sam rubbed the small of my back.

I met his gaze.

"He was working highway patrol at a breathalyser site for drug-and-alcohol testing. It's dangerous but nothing more than the usual for him. He stopped a driver who grabbed Jon's holstered firearm and shot him."

My eyesight hazed in the dim room, my hearing now tunneled and obscured. I furled my hands. My fingernails bit into my palms.

Jonathan was injured, shot at close range. With his own gun.

Heat prickled my clammy skin, and I clenched my jaw. A gun!

My body twitched, igniting a shivery trail along my limbs. Tears splattered my nightdress. "Wh-where was he shot?"

Sam's body quaked. He whimpered, the sound building to a guttural moan. "The side of his head."

Shot at point-blank range.

I slammed my face against my pillow and screeched, my heart bulldozed. My muffled, heated breaths suffocated me, and my knotted stomach tumbled faster than any rollercoaster I had ridden.

I sprang up, launched off the bed, and stumbled to my ensuite. The soft glow of Tara's nightlight lit my path to the toilet bowl, and I purged my late-night snack, heaving undigested food. Bile burned my throat, and mucous dripped off my nose.

Not my Jonathan. Please, God, no.

I collapsed on the adjacent shower mat and sniveled a torrent of tears. Coldness bit my side, the mat too thin to shield me from the frigid tiles. I shivered all over, fear and faith colliding in my head. Muttering words only God could perceive, I balled into a fetal position, my face slick with moisture.

Sam's warm body curled behind me, drawing me against his front, and cocooned me in his arms. His consolation triggered an immediate sense of solace within the turbulence I endured. He kissed my hair although I heard his soft, puffed breaths more than I felt them.

I hiccupped, reached behind my head, and placed my hand on his smooth cheek. "Where is he now?" I whispered between hitched breaths.

"St. Vincent's."

I shuddered. The last time I had entered that hospital, I bore fresh scars on my wrists and my soul. I pushed against the flash flood of images splintering my brain.

"They flew him down here, and he's currently undergoing surgery. They've one of the best plastic-and-reconstructive-surgery departments in Victoria." Sam rubbed my arm. "Mrs. Harris called me thirty minutes after the incident, and I jumped in the car and headed straight for you."

More tears dribbled across my face. "Thank you." I sighed. "I …"

"I know."

We lay together a few minutes longer on the ensuite floor before Sam suggested I get some sleep, and we helped each other up. He remained fixed to my side while I dragged my drained body back to bed.

I flopped against the soft sheets, lay on my side, and watched Sam untie his sneakers where he perched on Tara's bed.

He removed his jacket and lay it at the end of her bed, then reached for the covers.

"Sam?"

He turned, weariness lining his features. "Yes?"

"I don't want to sleep alone tonight."

Sam nodded, stepped to the end of my bed, and crawled in behind me. We resumed our bathroom-floor positions, and I fell asleep enveloped in the warmth of Sam's arms.

♥ ♥ ♥ ♥ ♥ ♥

"Diana? Diana darling?"

I grumbled when someone shook my shoulder. Light punctured the darkness, and I fluttered my heavy eyelids. Aunt Stacy.

Her brow was wrinkled, and her wide-eyed gaze darted around my face.

"Aunt Stacy?" My husky morning voice bleared in my ears.

"It's nine-thirty," she whispered. "Andrew and Tom are downstairs to collect you."

My heart rate spiked, and adrenaline galloped through my system.

Saturday morning brunch, then work at church. What had happened to my alarm? And why did my head hurt?

I blinked, hoping to dislodge the woolly slowness in my head. "Oh, I …"

Something toasty pressed against my back.

I stilled. Who was—no!

A sudden rush of memories flooded my mind, and tears burned my eyes. "Jonathan." Would I ever see him again?

Aunt Stacy kneeled and caressed my face. "What's going on? When did Sam get here … and why is he in your bed?" Not a trace of accusation hinted in her tone.

I appreciated the small mercy before my throat constricted. "Jonathan was shot last night."

Aunt Stacy's eyes widened. Something deep and haunting flashed within them before they softened.

Had Uncle Steve ever been injured on duty?

"Sweetheart. I'm sorry."

I ground my molars in a desperate attempt to ward off another load of tears and cleared my throat. "S-Sam arrived at two and broke the news. I … I couldn't sleep alone."

She compressed her lips. Her eyes misted. "Is he stable?"

"I don't know. He was in surgery the last Sam heard." I turned and glanced at Sleeping Beauty behind me. "I should wake him and see if he received any more information." I sought Aunt Stacy's gaze. "Are you able to apologize to the guys for me? Please?"

She nodded. "How about I let them know you'll update them later."

"Thanks."

She slipped from the room and closed the door behind her.

I rolled and stared at the defining features of Sam's face, spoke his name several times, and patted his arm.

His long dark lashes lifted, and a quirky smile slipped to his lips. "Am I in heaven? What a way to wake up." Sam winked and stretched his arms.

"Would you please check for any updates on Jonathan?"

He yawned. "My phone's in my jacket pocket on the other bed."

I crawled from underneath layers of cosy linen, re-tightened the waist tie around my rumpled robe, and searched Sam's jacket pockets until I located his mobile. Plonking atop the warm covers, I delivered his phone and waited. *Please let there be good news.*

Sam scrolled and read, and a large smile filled his face.

I inhaled a breath.

"Mrs. Harris messaged at seven, said she hoped I made it to your place safely and that Jon had just come out of surgery and is stable. She said to call her when I woke."

My lungs flooded with oxygen, and I laughed.

Jonathan was stable. Thank You, Jesus!

Sam tapped the screen and spoke to Mrs. Harris.

I prayed for Jonathan, my heartfelt whispers excavating past sentiments.

"Okay, we'll see you soon." He disconnected the phone call. "Jon's doing remarkably well. She's expecting us in the next hour, so you'd better scoot that delicious booty of yours off the bed and get dressed."

I punched his arm.

He laughed. "I threw a bag together but left it out in the car, so how about you shower while I talk with your family downstairs. I'll knock before walking back in." He waggled his eyebrows, pushed me across the mattress, scrambled off the bed, and disappeared, shoes in hand.

I showered and dressed—my nasal passages clear and skin no longer vibrating—plaited my heavy, damp hair, and trod downstairs. I flopped onto the sole vacant seat at the kitchen table and filled my plate with a buttery toasted bagel, crispy bacon, scrambled eggs, roasted tomatoes, mushrooms, and sliced avocado.

Sam and Uncle Steve discussed Jonathan's condition in low tones while I stuffed my face. Somehow my appetite thrived in the midst of this calamity.

Sam slung a bag over his shoulder and departed in the direction of my room.

I sipped my orange juice and watched Ella squish avocado with her fork.

"If you're finished, Ella, you may climb down and choose some clothes," Aunt Stacy said from the kitchen sink, where she scrubbed a soapy tray. "I'll be up shortly."

Ella climbed down and ran from the room.

Toby carried his plate to the dishwasher. "When's Tara home?" He asked his mother.

Aunt Stacy glanced at me. "Tomorrow night."

A sweet smile stretched his still-chubby cheeks. "Oh good. She promised to read with me at bedtime." Toby left the kitchen.

Aunt Stacy and I exchanged smirking looks. We suspected Toby had a little crush on Tara. The way he talked with her, admired her with puppy dog eyes, and wanted to play games with her, fuelled our suspicions.

Uncle Steve cleared his throat and looked at me, intensity kindled in his eyes. "You doing okay?"

Was I? Jonathan's brush with death had frightened me to the core. And reawakened emotions and desires I had tried to suffocate for months. Even after all the pain behind us, could we have a chance? Would a brush with death change his heart?

And was I prepared to risk my heart again? Still?

I pushed back in my chair, closed my eyes, and shook my head.

Chair legs scraped the kitchen floor, and Aunt Stacy's arms enveloped my front, followed by a bulky-muscled set around my back and shoulders.

I inhaled Aunt Stacy's sweet perfume, Uncle Steve's cologne wafting from behind. A Morgan hug sandwich.

How I loved this family.

Someone cleared his throat.

I opened my eyes and met Sam's melancholic gaze.

The three of us separated—once Aunt Stacy administered several kisses to my cheek—and Sam and I set off to the hospital.

CHAPTER THIRTY-TWO
Stalemate

I tapped a rhythmic beat in my leather boots, seated alone in the small hospital waiting room.

Sam had phoned Mrs. Harris while we strode through the car park, and she had met us at the hospital entrance with tears and hugs. We were whisked into a private waiting room and ten minutes later, Mr. Harris had asked Sam to accompany him.

I glanced at the wall clock. Over twenty minutes had passed. The longer I remained alone, the faster my heart walloped.

Footsteps echoed in the hallway.

I stilled.

Two medical personnel ambled past the open doorway.

My lungs clamped. I rubbed my hands along my thighs. Had Jonathan refused to see me? Would he push me away again? My breaths hitched. What if his sight or hearing was marred from the attack? A cold chill quivered through my bones, and another round of tears pricked my eyes. None of Jonathan's family had shared the full extent of his injuries.

I stood and paced the room, praying and meditating on Bible Scriptures, drawing strength from within.

"Diana."

I lifted my head and tracked the grim lines on Sam's face.

The hint of a smile lifted his lips for half a second. He opened his arms.

I thrust myself into his embrace. "How're you holding up?" My voice quavered.

"Been better." He kissed my forehead. "Jonathan was awake for a few moments. He even offered a weak smile, but I could tell he was disappointed it wasn't you."

How could he tell?

I swallowed a lump in my throat. "Did you … did you tell him I'm here?"

"Yes." His chest vibrated against my torso.

"And?"

"And … a flood of emotions crossed his face at the mention of your name, then he uttered a broken no."

I pushed back and looked Sam in the eyes. "What?"

Sam drew me back against his chest. "He's in a lot of pain, possibly high on morphine. Could mean anything. Or nothing."

It could mean anything. From "No, I never want to see her again" to "No, I messed up and need her back in my life."

I needed to know which one. "When can I see him?"

Sam shrugged. "Mr. Harris will come out for you when the time's right." He rubbed my back, released me, and led me to a chair. "Jon's been sent to ICU for close observation post op, but his vitals have been better than expected, so he may be moved sooner than planned. As it stands, only a few people can visit at a time. Constable Dennigan's glued to his bedside. She was on shift with him at the time, and she refuses to leave."

Constable Dennigan. April's beautiful dark eyes and smooth blonde locks surfaced in my memory. Her soft laughter echoed through my skull. Had their friendship grown since I had left? Had she consoled him in her arms, offering her sacrificial lips to her broken-hearted partner? Enticed him to revoke his stance for purity and seek an ounce of solace in her bed?

I shook my head and rebuked the torturous thoughts, reminding myself of the godly man Jonathan was in his actions, not only in speech.

"Diana?"

I shifted in the seat and looked up into Mr. Harris's exhausted face.

Deeper wrinkles and lines blemished his forehead than when I last saw him.

"Mr. Harris."

He slumped in the chair next to me and sighed. "Seems my son's still acting dense and asked me to make sure you returned home safely."

I shook my head and wiped my leaking eyes. "B-but why?"

Mr. Harris dropped his head forward and shrugged.

Sam wrapped his arms around me.

My chest heated. "If he's going to be pig-headed, then so will I." I huffed a breath and stretched my fingers.

Mr. Harris chuckled. "Atta girl." He scrubbed his palm over his face and stood. "I'll let him know when he wakes."

"Please do. Tell him I refuse to leave until he grants me visitation." I smirked and imagined Jonathan's response to my peaceful protest.

Sam snickered.

Mr. Harris's laughter grew. "It may be a few more hours until he's able to see you."

I shrugged against Sam. "I can live with that."

Mr. Harris shuffled through the exit, out of sight.

Thoughts thumped around my head, and a question burned inside me. I faced Sam and blurted, "Is April his girlfriend?"

Sam stared at me. "Pardon?"

I bit my lower lip. "Are they more than just work partners now?"

Sam narrowed his eyes. "Why would you think that?"

I shrugged, ignoring the cloying sensations in my chest. "She's gorgeous and clearly cares for him. Maybe she comforted him after he pushed me away?"

A slow grin spread across his face. "My, my. The green gremlin strikes." He chuckled.

I poked his chest and glowered. "What am I supposed to think when she's glued to his bedside?"

He raised an eyebrow.

My throat constricted. "He threw me aside like a worthless toy, so maybe he decided to … to …"

"Decided to what?"

Heat invaded my face. "Well, he may've decided to, um …" No matter the crazy things I had imagined, voicing said crazy ideas churned my belly.

Sam tilted his head and smirked. "He's not sleeping with her. You think he's me now?"

"Are you sleeping with her?"

His lips twitched. "Not this week."

I slapped his shoulder. "Really, Sam." My chest loosened. "I wish I knew how to get through to him. After all the heartache, I still want to be part of his life … even if it's just friendship." A complicated, heart-tugging friendship.

Sam wrapped his arm around my shoulder. "I know."

"When will he know?" I leaned against Sam's chest, inhaled his aftershave, and closed my eyes, indulging in a needed power nap.

The pungent tang of coffee filled my nostrils. I opened my eyes, stretched, and glanced around the room.

Sam stood by the window, drinking coffee, gazing at the setting sun.

How long had I slept? I croaked his name.

Sam turned, his face beaming a secret grin. "Hey, Miss Sleepyhead. You've the most gorgeous snuffly snore when you sleep upright."

I clutched my chest. My cheeks heated. "Don't lie."

He chuckled a husky rumble of laughter. "I have recorded proof on my phone." He smirked.

I stiffened against the seat back. "What! Delete it!"

His laughter amplified. He reached into his jeans pocket, extracted his phone, and swiped the screen a few times before stepping closer. His mobile emitted soft rumblings of what sounded like a kitten impersonating a sewing machine.

My eyes widened, and I reached for his phone. "That's … that's not me."

"Afraid so." He turned his mobile screen toward me.

I choked on an inhaled breath at the image on display. Me sleeping with my mouth ajar, lips curling up and down on every breath. I covered my eyes with my hands. "Turn it off. Please. Have mercy and delete it."

He leaned and kissed the top of my head, moved my hands away from my eyes, and lifted my chin. "Sorry, no can do. This'll be used as white noise when I sleep."

What an infuriating man! I wrinkled my nose. "I don't like you."

"No, you love me. We slept together after all."

I fisted my hand and punched his abdomen.

A satisfying "oof" met my ears.

"Yeah, well, I don't recall a thing, so you weren't very memorable."

He boomed with laughter. "You know how to hurt a guy's ego."

I crossed my arms. "You asked for it, saying stupid things like that."

He chuckled, shook his head, and disappeared. He returned a few minutes later with a hot chocolate and sandwich for me.

My stomach grumbled my thanks—no way was I thanking him after his prank!—and ate. We soon fell into our usual conversation and chatted about cars, the cost of petrol, the blandness of hospital food, and where to buy the best dim sims in Tellarine. Our unanimous vote was the local fish 'n chip shop.

We settled on the chairs and played a few rounds of *Words with Friends* against each other—I know, such an old-school mobile game, but I liked it—and when I was close to thrashing Sam for the fourth time, Mr. Harris poked his head into the room.

"The king seeks an audience with you both." He winked.

My midriff tightened, and nervous energy crackled along my arms. I stood, grabbed a hold on Sam's hand, and followed Mr. Harris on shaky legs through to Jonathan's cordoned-off space in ICU.

I could do this.

My heart pounded. I counted my breaths and readied myself for a terrible sight, whispering prayers under my breath as we entered the room.

Jonathan lay propped up in the bed, awake, and not even a little reminiscent of the battle-weary bloody characters in the World War II movies I enjoyed. Stark white bandages swathed his right eye, ear, cheek, and parts of his hair. A dark splotch shadowed his unbandaged left eye. The rest of him appeared unharmed. Cords ran from neighbouring machines down the front of his hospital gown, exposing a few dark chest hairs. His eye tracked me from across the room, his expression neutral.

"Hey." I smiled and stepped closer to his right side. Somewhere along the walk, Sam had released my hand.

"Hey," Jonathan whispered. His expression flickered, and his intent stare pinned me in place.

I held his hand and filled the unoccupied chair next to the bed. Glancing the curtained space, I realized we were alone. Constable Dennigan was able to leave his bedside after all.

"How're you feeling?" I swirled my fingers over the back of his hand. My fingertips tingled. Was I really touching him? After all this time?

He studied our joined hands, then returned his attention to my face. "Like I was kicked in the head by a horse."

"Thankfully, you were only shot." I huffed a wry laugh.

The hint of a smile tweaked his lips before his expression flattened. "Why're you here?"

Heat ignited in my chest. Why must he be so stubborn? "Because I care." I pressed my lips together. "I care you could've been killed." My throat constricted. "I care about you and am here for you."

He pulled his hand away and avoided my gaze. "It's over between us."

I creased my brow. "What's that got to do with my caring for you? And our friendship?"

He blew out a long breath. "I don't want to lead you on …"

I straightened, trying my hardest to suppress the growl in my tone. "I received your message back in June loud and clear."

He blustered a breath. "It's just … I … I can't get past the kiss you shared." He closed his eye.

The memory of Jonathan's revolted expression slapped me across the face.

I pressed a hand to my cheek and wilted against the chair. What a despicable and repulsive person I had been to draw pleasure from his brother's kiss. No wonder Jonathan thought it impossible for us to be more than friends. Or even friends at all.

What else had I miscalculated? My career? Was Tara wrong? Could her faith in my abilities and talents be misplaced? Maybe Mum once held this dream for me, but I had been a happy, innocent child back then. Now a shard of darkness twisted inside me.

Help me through it all, please, Jesus.

My chest compressed, and I fought back tears. "You know what?" My voice quivered, and I cleared my throat. "Perhaps it's best I leave. The last thing I want is to jeopardize your healing. Clearly I'm upsetting you, and I'm sorry I came." I choked on my words and stood.

He opened his eye, and it glossed over. "Diana," he whispered.

"Please just … reconcile with God," I whispered. "We weren't designed to carry the weight of the world on our shoulders." I sniffed. "I'll continue to pray for you, that you'll finally be freed from the bondage of your brother's actions." I turned to the door. "I decided to forgive him. It's time you did too."

I returned to the small room where Jonathan's parents, Sam, and Constable Dennigan waited.

Sam's hopeful gaze met mine.

I shook my head.

He scrunched his face and opened his arms wide.

I crumpled onto his lap.

"I'm sorry," he whispered.

I sobbed in his neck. How could my heart still hurt this much? My cries reverberated in my ears, my throat strained.

Sam's arms banded tighter around me.

Why had I allowed myself a slither of hope? My snot and tears soaked Sam's collar. I needed to forgive Jonathan—and myself—and move on. Truly move on, not live in denial. I was not enough for him.

My diaphragm muscles twinged from crying, and I counted my breaths. Time to let go.

"Let me take you home," Sam said into my hair.

I leaned back and surveyed the gummy dampness on Sam's shirt. "I'm sorry about the mess. I can wash it."

Sam shook his head and wiped tears from my cheeks. "You can cry me a river any day of the week." He glanced across the room and shifted me to my feet. "See you tomorrow," he said to the Harrises. "Let's go."

With each step away from the waiting room, it seemed a section of my heart ripped apart. Again. I leaned against Sam, while we walked, and prayed, throwing up another lifeline to help not only me but the broken man lying in the hospital bed upstairs.

CHAPTER THIRTY-THREE
Trivial Moments

Sam: I'M IN MELBOURNE FOR WORK NOVEMBER 11– 15. ANY CHANCE YOU'LL BE AROUND TO SHOW A GUY A GOOD TIME? YOU HAVE A MONTH TO PREPARE A SPECTACULAR NIGHT FOR ME. I'LL PAY TOP DOLLAR. ;-)

I snorted, compressed my lips, and peeked around the large lecture theatre. *Phew.*

Tara nudged me and raised a brow.

I showed her Sam's message.

She snickered and returned to her notes on her laptop. Something I should be doing.

I sighed and tucked my mobile aside. Sam could wait a few hours. I readjusted my position in the undersized, uncomfortable seat. How was Jonathan?

Three weeks had passed since I saw him at the hospital. The familiar ache bloomed in my ribcage, and I rubbed my chest a little harder than necessary. I sighed and focused on the middle-aged woman in her business attire touting her journalistic accomplishments. And something to do with ethics. *Focus, Diana!*

"And while we all enjoy roasting certain infotainment publications"—the guest speaker chortled—"we also need to eat. Beware the high and mighty journo with unrealistic expectations. Don't be surprised when they shoot and eat their own horse to survive." The students around me snickered. "These ethical issues are ever-present, and I still wrestle them twenty-eight years down this path."

Twenty-eight years! Could I wrestle with the same ethical dilemmas over and over "to survive" in this industry?

Kortney's face came to mind, and I fisted my fingers in the hem of my purple T-shirt. Had Kortney intended to exploit me from the get-go? Or had she sold me out in order to survive?

I shuffled in my seat. Would I ever become so desperate as to turn on a friend or a confidential news source? My stomach squeezed.

The room erupted in sudden applause.

I startled, my heart hammering against my ribcage. I glanced around the room and clapped.

Tara leaned closer and smirked. "Awake now?"

"Uh huh."

We gathered our belongings and trailed the other students from the room.

Lacey stood in the corridor and waved me over. "How're you doing?"

I smiled and tightened my grip on my backpack. "Good. You?"

"I'm great. You coming to Trivia Night on Friday?"

I had tried to convince Tara to come with me, but she still hesitated about any activities held in a church building. "I should be."

She beamed. "Awesome." She nodded toward the exit. "Better get to my next class. See ya."

"Bye."

Tara sidled next to me. "A few of the guys wanted to do lunch on campus. You interested?"

I retrieved my phone and checked the time. "Not today. I promised I'd have a document ready for Keanu before five."

"Thought so, but was worth a try. See you at dinner." Tara waved, and we walked in opposite directions.

I caught the next tram home, settled in the half-empty carriage, and re-read Sam's message.

Me: ANOTHER COMPUTER GEEK CONVENTION? ;-) WHEN? EXAMS START IN FIVE WEEKS SO MY FREE TIME IS SLIM.

My pocket vibrated halfway between the tram stop and the Morgan residence.

Sam: NO JOKE, IT GETS SCARY SOMETIMES AT THE BIGGER TECH GATHERINGS. TOO MANY SMART PEOPLE IN ONE ROOM.

Sam: I'M FREE THAT MON-THUR ANYTIME AFTER, SAY, 5:30PM? EVEN IF IT'S HALF AN HOUR. JUST WANT TO SEE HOW YOU'RE DOING.

I laughed, scuffed my shoe on the concrete footpath, righted myself, and dodged a bush.

Me: COME OVER FOR TACO TUESDAY, THEN WE CAN HANG OUT AT THE LOCAL BAR. REMINDS ME OF BENANU'S.

Sam: PERFECT. LOOKING FORWARD TO SEEING YOU.

Me: SEE YOU THEN.

I unlocked the front door and shucked my shoes, toting my bag to the kitchen. Uncle Steve shifted his attention from the paperwork he perused at the kitchen bench.

I arched an eyebrow. "You're home early."

"Covering an emergency overnighter tonight." He lowered his gaze and flipped a page.

I glanced at the work rosters on the fridge and cross checked the whiteboard notes below with our Google Calendar. Aunt Stacy had a court case the next three days. "Need me to do anything extra tomorrow while you sleep?"

"Can you drop Ella at Mrs. Jennings' after breakfast? Stace said she should be able to drop Toby at school on her way to work, but it'll be a stretch for her to stop twice."

"Of course, happy to help." I filled a glass with filtered water and grabbed a banana. "I can message Tar and see if she could do the school run instead?"

Uncle Steve glanced up, and a beaming grin lit up his face. "We know how much the big guy loves Tara." He chuckled. "Sure, won't hurt to ask."

I sipped some water and typed a message. Multitasking for the win.

Me: UNCLE STEVE'S BEEN CALLED IN FOR AN EMERGENCY OVERNIGHTER, AND AUNT STACY'S IN COURT TOMORROW. THINK YOU COULD TAKE TOBY TO SCHOOL WHILE I DROP ELLA AT THE SITTER?

I peeled the banana and chomped a chunk of fruit.

Tara: MORE TIME WITH MY HANDSOME LITTLE BUDDY! FO' SHO! ALWAYS HAPPY TO HELP.

I chewed and swallowed. "Tara says she's happy to help."

Uncle Steve raised his head and caught my gaze. "Thanks. Stace and I appreciate everything you two do."

Warmth spread through my chest. "We love helping and appreciate the sweet deal we have here." I wolfed the rest of the banana, grabbed the chicken Caesar salad I had prepared this morning, and topped up my water glass. "Make sure you have a nap before the children come home from school and kindy."

Uncle Steve grunted.

I chuckled. "I'll be upstairs working if you need me."

"Thanks."

I traipsed upstairs to the communal study area, set up my laptop and lunch, and launched the new Benanu's accounting software. Seemed less clunky than the previous program. Nice. I nibbled a piece of chicken and scrolled the last two days' worth of linked bank-statement data dumps. Keanu had texted early this morning about an email, so I checked my inbox.

To: djacobsen@benanustellarine.com.au
From: keverton@benanustellarine.com.au
Subject: Reduced hours

Miss Jacobsen,
Dad's happy with the new accounting program, and pleased with our progress. With the new automated processes, we're spending less time in the office. You've done well.
Thanks for the hard work, now step back for a few weeks. I know we discussed you'd take leave during exams (which is still in place) but we'd like you to cut back to two days a week (same pay) until your leave kicks in. Email me a list of things you don't get to and I'll cover it each week.
Now get back to work,
Mr. Everton.

I squinted at the laptop screen and re-read Keanu's email. Same pay but less work? How could this be?

Me: I READ YOUR EMAIL. NO COMPRENDO.

I stuffed dressing-slathered lettuce in my face, enjoying every bite. So good.

Halfway through my salad, my message app toned.

Keanu: THE SYSTEM SAYS YOU'RE CLOCKING TOO MANY HOURS. DAD SUGGESTED WE MAKE THIS ARRANGEMENT IN LIEU OF YOUR UNPAID WORK. TAKE THE GIFT FROM THIS HORSE'S MOUTH AND FOCUS ON STUDY.

My cheeks warmed, and I palmed my heated skin. I forgot I left a digital footprint each time I logged in. I sighed. Maybe more time to study was a good thing. I had to push aside the distractions and my inconvenient career doubts and focus on remembering my course material.

Me: I think you're mixing idioms, but I understand and accept your gift. Please thank Mr. E. xx

I settled against the chair back, my heart lighter and mind clearer than it had been in months.

"Your first Trivia Night?" Tom's low, accented voice—which I had secretly labelled "Austramerican"—gravelled behind me in the large room at church used for Young Adult functions.

I turned and grinned. "Should I run for the hills?"

His laughter vibrated the space separating us. "Only if you hate trivia."

I scrunched my nose. "No idea if I'm any good at it."

He stepped closer, his eyes twinkling. "I'm sure you'd do just fine."

"How's this work?"

Tom pointed to the front of the room where a large electric whiteboard was set up. "We pair up, get issued a number, and form smaller groups. Even though the people in your group are competitors, it's easier for conversation flow within the larger group setting."

"Makes sense."

"As a small group, we discuss and give our answer, but the team inside the group who answered first wins the point." He leaned closer, unleashing his delightful cologne.

I inhaled a furtive sniff. "Still not sure if I'll be any good at this."

"I'm confident in your abilities," Tom said. "I'd like to team up with you."

A pleasant heat infiltrated my chest. "How can I doubt such bold assurance? I'd love to partner with you." My eyes widened. "In trivia." My skin flushed with rapid heat.

Tom concentrated on my face. "Trivia's a great start." His gaze dipped to my lips.

Was this happening? My pulse tripped.

Tom stepped back and cleared his throat.

Andrew and Lacey bounded into the room mid-conversation. Andrew slapped his cousin on the back.

Lacey embraced me. "Glad you made it."

"Me too."

"Want to team up?"

I glanced at Tom. "I'm partnering with the hotshot lawyer."

Andrew eyed his cousin, and a silent dialogue transpired between them.

I leaned closer to Lacey. "Why don't you team up with Andrew?"

"Ah." Her cheeks dusted a pretty pink.

"Sounds great to me," Andrew said.

We mingled with the other attendees before breaking into smaller groups. Andrew, Lacey, Tom and I played with four other people.

I spent the evening laughing and talking with everyone in the group, yet one hundred percent aware of Tom's presence beside me. The moments we leaned closer and whispered answers to each other heightened my senses until my blood thrummed. Was there hope of a future without grief? Could I have that one day with a man like Tom?

"I completely understand. It's a thrill when you know exactly the career you want to embrace," Andrew said to someone in the group.

What had I missed?

He turned to me. "Diana's always known she wants to be a journalist, haven't you?

I stilled. Have I? Not in recent months. "Um, I guess?"

Lacey sighed. "I kinda envy people who know what they want. I struggled to decide my preferences when I started uni, but I'm happy I chose education."

"That's great," the guy next to Andrew said. "If you're not dedicated to your studies now, you'll have a difficult time when you step into related employment. That's why I switched majors halfway through university. Never looked back."

I sighed. Would I ever reach a place when I no longer wrestled with my future plans?

18 October

So much is rattling inside my head at the moment, I don't know where to start, Mum.

Journalism. I'm struggling to come to terms with this career path I've chosen, but with a little over a year left in my course studies, does it even make sense to change? I wish you could help me work this out once and for all. I don't want to disappoint you.

Tom. Wow, I'm perturbed by him and the zaps of electricity he elicits. The feelings are unexpected and frightening. Am I ready to enter a new relationship? I'm not even sure I'm reading his signals correctly because he's not asked me out yet. Maybe it's all in my head and I'm reading too much into this. Either way, I'll take it a step at a time. A slow step. Cos my heart is still bruised.

Jonathan. I still wish we could talk. I miss his random photos and conversation. Sam sends me updates, although I try not to ask for information anymore. Apparently his first two weeks post-surgery were difficult, and I wished I could've been there for him, even as a friend. A daily hospital drop-in wouldn't have affected my schedule too much. But a friendship is just not meant to be. And that hurts the most.

Love you, Mum.

CHAPTER THIRTY-FOUR
To Dip One's Toes

Sam and I stepped from the crowded bar which reminded me of Benanu's and wandered down the footpath. The late-spring evening breeze caressed my bare arms.

I slipped on my jacket.

"Bit cooler out here than inside." Sam shoved his hands in his pockets.

I nodded.

We travelled in the semi-dark, overhead streetlights bathing us in luminescent circles every hundred metres. Our footsteps echoed in the muted surrounds, fuelling the occasional growl or yap from the fenced pets we passed.

I looked up and sighed. Even with little cloud cover, the glow from the city dimmed the skies above.

"I miss the stars too." Sam nudged my shoulder. "I'll take a pic when I'm home again and send it to you."

I smiled. "Thanks." Our steps slowed, and I inhaled the beautiful floral scent wafting from an adjoining garden.

"You haven't asked about him yet. I'm impressed."

I turned and peered at Sam. "I'm trying."

He heaved a deep breath. "Wish it weren't necessary."

Same.

"He's getting there. The last two weeks have been an improvement in his physical and mental health. He's definitely chirpier. Mrs. H. seems to be coping better now the huge bandages are off."

Improvement. Chirpier. Jonathan seemed to be doing just fine.

I balled my hand and counted my breaths. A vision of Tom

flittered in my brain. Yes, Tom was a better fit for me.

We plodded down the road I lived on, and I emptied my brain of thoughts to do with men. "That's great."

"You truly okay?"

I slowed beside Sam's car. "I'll get there."

"I know you will." He bopped my nose like Dad had done many times in my lifetime.

I grinned. "Thanks for visiting. Everyone enjoyed your company tonight. Taco Tuesday won't be the same without you."

He chuckled and pulled me into his arms. "I had fun and hope to do it again sometime." Sam stepped back, lowered my chin, and met my gaze. "Message me night or day. I've got your back, Double D."

I melted against his chest. How had such a repulsive nickname become so endearing? The power of Sam in action. I stepped back. "Until next time."

Sam kissed my cheek. "Get some rest." He saluted me and sauntered around the car to the driver's door.

I trod to the house and waved from the front step.

"You can't be serious!" I studied the barely there Christmas outfit Tara held out from the clothing store rack we scoured and shook my head. Christmas was a month away, and several party invitations had already landed in our inboxes, inspiring Tara's shopping spree. I suspected she would attend parties here in the city in the coming weeks even though I would be back home in Tellarine.

"What? It's sexy and will look cute on you." Tara turned the short dress around.

"I'm not going for a stripper Santa's Helper vibe." I pushed the costume away. "I like the red but need more coverage."

Tara resumed browsing the clothing rack and zoned in on another outfit. "What about this?" She held up the dress for my perusal. "It's a more relaxed body-con fit than the previous one, without the slutty vibe."

I shrugged. "It's still a bit tight. But it's super cute with the fluffy white hemline and wrists." Covered wrists were always a win in my playbook.

Tara shoved the outfit into my hands. "Please try it on for me?"

"Fine." Trudging into the change rooms, I removed my shorts and T-shirt and slid into the soft, stretchy knit fabric. I zipped and pivoted on the spot, spying all the angles in the mirror. The long-sleeve red dress was pretty cute and a winner with its high neckline. The fluffy hem rested just above my knees, and the body-con style suited my tall, slim, not-much-cleavage body shape.

I eyed myself in the mirror and tilted my head. A smile slipped to my lips. Had Tara found a dress style which enhanced my shape and gave the illusion I possessed a set of decent-sized breasts? I stifled a grin, opened the cubicle door, and waltzed to where Tara waited.

Her eyes widened, and a grin spread across her gorgeous face. "Yes! This's definitely the one. Gosh, you look hot in an elegant, yet cute, kind of way. Paired with two braids or pigtails and a Santa hat, you'll be the envy of everyone at the party."

I fidgeted my fingers, rocking on the spot. "You think?"

"Totally. And Tom will love it."

My cheeks warmed. Since the first Trivia Night we paired up together, Tom and I had called and texted each other often. No crazy photos, just pleasant, adult conversation.

Tara smirked. "Now I've gotta up my game with what I'm going to wear."

Was I brave enough to wear this in public? The big university bash was set to explode my calendar next weekend. A horde of students were gathering for a Christmas slash end-of-year get-together. After another year of completed studies, many of Tara's and my friends had graduated and wanted a bigger celebration. The undergrads in our current classes mixed well with our previous classmates, so the gathering had opened for people far and wide. Andrew had invited Tom which saved Tara from having to drive.

We wandered back to the change room.

I squizzed the outfit one last time.

Tara waggled her brows.

I laughed. "Okay, I'm buying it."

"Yes!" She fist-pumped the air, jigging on her toes. "Find me when you're done. I need to find a smoking-hot dress."

I laughed, fastened the door lock, and studied my figure in the mirror. What a hot look. I rifled amongst my things on the floor, found my phone, and snapped several photographs to memorialize this moment in time. As I thumbed my phone lock, I noticed a message.

Tom: DREAMY DIANA, WHEN YOU HAVE A MOMENT WOULD YOU PLEASE GIVE ME A CALL? I LOOK FORWARD TO HEARING FROM YOU.

My pulse quickened. I needed to get out of this dress before the sweats erupted.

After one last peep at my image in the mirrors, I wriggled out of the clingy fabric, and re-dressed in my lightweight clothing. I loved our summer Christmases. How had Tom survived years of cold Christmases in America? I shuddered and rubbed my upper arms. The hotter, the better.

A few minutes later I paid for my new outfit. I returned my wallet to my bag, where my phone buzzed. Tom again?

I thanked the older lady behind the counter and stepped away.

Victoria: JAZZY AND ELIJAH ARE READY FOR YOU TO COME HOME FOR CHRISTMAS. YOU FINE WITH SOME SQUATTERS?

I quirked a brow, opened the attached photo, and snorted a laugh. My little sister and brother hid underneath the covers of my bed in Tellarine, their cheeky little faces the only parts of them visible.

Me: TELL THEM ONLY EIGHT MORE SLEEPS THEN I'LL BE WITH THEM FOR THREE WHOLE MONTHS! SO EXCITED! XXX

I had wanted to return home the day classes had finished, but Tara had requested—begged on her knees—I stay for next weekend's party, and had held off my return home. I was not *that* excited about the party, but I loved Tara and wanted to support her. We were sisters. Plus, I liked the idea of seeing Tom a little longer.

Another phone message chimed, disrupting my thoughts.

Victoria: JASMINE HAS TWO ADVENT CALENDARS THIS YEAR. ONE FOR JESUS'S BIRTHDAY AND ONE FOR WHEN DI-DI COMES HOME. SHE'S BEYOND EXCITED.

Victoria: BTW, DID YOU AND TARA FIND OUTFITS FOR YOUR CHRISTMAS PARTY YET?

My insides warmed, and I smiled. Ever the thoughtful lady, Victoria often remembered what was happening with me.

Me: MY CLEVER MUNCHKIN!

Me: JUST STEPPED AWAY FROM THE STORE COUNTER AFTER MY PURCHASE! BOUGHT THIS LITTLE RED NUMBER YOU'LL THINK IS CUTE

... JUST DON'T SHOW DAD AS HE'LL BLOW HIS TOP. IT'S NOT INDECENT BUT IT GIVES ME BOOBS ALMOST AS CLEAVAGE-LADEN AS YOURS. ;-) LIKE IT?

I attached the photos I had taken in the change room and pressed Send.

Tara tapped my shoulder. "Wanna see what I bought?"

"You already bought it?" I peeked inside the plastic bag. "Is that a furry blue-and-white mini skirt?" I lifted the fabric and pressed it against Tara's waist.

"Yeah, I feel ready to flash my legs off for once."

"That's great." Real progress for her. I tucked her purchase into the bag.

We weaved our way to the tram stop and caught the next one headed to South Melbourne. Tara pointed to two vacant seats, and we claimed them, tucking our shopping bags between our feet.

I checked my message app.

Victoria: NICE! I WON'T TELL IF YOU DON'T. :-)

Laughing, I showed Tara the thread of messages with Victoria.

She snorted a laugh. "I love your stepmum. She's awesome."

"Yeah, Victoria's pretty awesome. She's wonderful with the children, and Dad's besotted. Mr. Mushy Man. I love my daddy, but I especially love seeing his soft side with Victoria and the babies." I typed my reply.

Me: ANOTHER REASON WHY I LOVE YOU. XX

I glanced back at my phone, and Tom's message seemed to glow on the screen. I turned to Tara. "Do you mind if I make a call?"

"Go ahead."

I breathed in and out and dialed his number.

"Dreamy Diana." Tom's voice sounded deeper over the phone. Oh boy.

"Thanks for calling." Something shuffled in the background before a loud click toned which ushered silence. "That's better. The guys in the office are a bit noisy today."

I pressed a hand against my thigh. "What's up?"

"I'll get straight to the point. I like you. A lot. And I want to take you out on a date."

My insides squeezed and stirred.

"Is this something you'd be interested in?"

"I … ah." I bit my lower lip.

"I wanted to talk to you on Sunday but never found the opportunity to pull you aside." A shuffling sound crackled over the phone connection. "I sensed a mutual … interest… but it's completely fine if you'd prefer not to."

"You did. Sense it." I covered one of my hot cheeks with my hand. "But …"

"It's okay. We don't have to—"

"No, I just … can I have some time to think?"

"Of course. No pressure." Tom blew out a breath. "Take your time."

"Thank you. I'll … let you get back to work." Ugh, could I sound any more awkward?

"See you Sunday, Diana." Tom's voice crooned my name.

Shivers danced along my spine. "Bye."

Tom liked me. I sucked in several calming breaths. He wanted to date me!

Tara nudged my shoulder. 'Was that Tom?"

I gaped at her. "Did you hear everything?"

She smirked. "Does it matter?"

I shook my head. It was probably better for me not to have to form extra words at the moment.

"He's gorgeous and totally into you. And his Aussie-American accent's the cutest thing I've heard." Tara waggled her eyebrows. "He's sweet, confident, listens when you talk, has a great sense of humour, and is into all the God stuff you're into."

I chuckled. Tara knew how to highlight the things I liked.

"If I was looking to date, I'd totally go for him apart for his thing for Jesus and all." She wrinkled her nose. "Don't think I'm ready to get tight with The Man Upstairs, if you know what I mean. But I'm warming to the idea."

My heart exploded with happiness. "I'm so glad you don't think I'm such a crazy Jesus freak anymore."

She furrowed her brow. "I didn't say that. Just that I didn't mind you weirdo Christians as much. Those songs you sent me really comforted me on my darker days after … you know. I never thanked you for that."

"You're welcome." I kissed Tara's cheek and hugged my friend as her words sank in. Ripples pulsed inside my chest cavity. Not only had I sensed God lead me to send those YouTube links so long ago—

and I had forgotten about it, to be honest—but Tara's heart was slowly opening to the idea of God. Warmth filled my chest, and I ushered another prayer to the heavens for her salvation.

Maybe I would take her up on her advice about Tom too.

♥ ♥ ♥ ♥ ♥ ♥ ♥

"Oh, my goodness." I closed my eyes and choked back a moan in the dining area of the swanky inner-city restaurant Tom had reserved. Rich, velvety dark chocolate, coconut, and strawberry flavours coated my tongue and glided down my throat. A far cry from my first date at Benanu's with Jonathan.

Tom's chuckles reverberated across the white linen-covered table we occupied.

I grinned at him. "Wow. I need to tell Victoria about this place. She'll love it." And Dad would love all the food-loving moans his wife rendered.

Tom raised a stemmed glass to his plump lips, sipped the last of his white wine, and smiled. All the while, his gaze remained fixed on my face.

My pulse doubled.

Tom dabbed a thick white napkin against his mouth. "You sure you don't want a coffee or hot drink before we go?"

I wrinkled my nose. "No thanks, not a fan of coffee, and I think I've reached my chocolate limit."

He squinted. "How do you charge through your busy schedule without coffee?"

I swallowed the last of my scrumptious dessert and blotted the corners of my mouth with my linen napkin. "I believe I do less charging and more clomping through my busy schedule."

Tom's deep laughter stirred something inside my chest.

My mouth dried. I sipped the last of my water to wet my parched throat.

"Ready to go?" Tom dug inside his navy dress-pants pocket. Mr. Lawyer Man exuded a quiet confidence wearing his tailored suit. His relaxed features added to his handsomeness.

An image of Jonathan wearing his police uniform snuck to the edges of my mind.

I pushed the appetizing memory away. "Okay."

Tom unearthed his wallet, caught the attention of the wait staff, and paid the hefty bill. Jonathan had preferred to pay our bills too.

I pushed the thought away, looped my dainty handbag over my bare shoulder, stood, and tucked in my chair. "You're sure I can't contribute?"

"Certain. I invited you out, so it's my treat." Tom extended his arm in front of him.

I nodded and stepped ahead. "If I haven't already said so, thank you for a wonderful evening."

Tom leaned close and opened the restaurant door from behind me. Heat radiated off his chest against my back.

And his cologne? Wowzers.

He steadied his penetrative gaze on me. "The pleasure's all mine."

We sauntered along the uneven city footpath toward the underground car park where Tom's late-model Lexus waited. The summer evening air, which had cooled somewhat—I no longer perspired in my white-and-purple floral halter-neck dress like I had during our walk to the restaurant—licked my bare arms and calves. The clear, dusky sky showcased a magnificent exhibition of pinks, oranges and a hint of purple. What would twilight in Tellarine look like tonight?

Tom's quiet laughter recaptured my attention.

I turned and quirked an eyebrow. "What's so funny?"

"While you admired the sunset, four men strolled past and checked you out."

What men? "You must be mistaken."

Tom smirked. "One guy almost tripped when he noticed you."

Really?

"Just watch this guy up ahead."

An older man walked beside a middle-aged woman. When he noticed me, his focus stuck like glue.

I dropped my head as a flushing heat saturated my face.

Tom pressed against my side as the couple brushed by, his quiet laughter easing the discomfort in my chest. "See?" he whispered. "You're gorgeous, and everyone knows it."

I peeked across to him. "And this doesn't bother you?"

"That men ogle my beautiful date? Not at all."

Would I feel the same if a herd of women drooled over Tom?

I pressed my lips together. *You reacted when you thought April and Jonathan were together.* A phantom dagger twisted in my gut.

"Does it bother you that it doesn't bother me?" Tom's question pulled me from my self-accusations.

"Oh. No." I brushed my arm against his shirt sleeve.

We entered the car park and sidled to Tom's sleek black Lexus ES.

He opened the passenger door. "Want to do this again?"

I covered his hand where it held the door open. "I might." My portion of happiness was long overdue.

"What if I let you pay and women ogled me?" He winked.

I laughed. "How can I say no to that?"

CHAPTER THIRTY-FIVE
On The Brink

"Knock knock." Aunt Stacy leaned in our ensuite doorway, her eyes alight. "I have a handsome Christmas Pudding and Candy Cane waiting downstairs for you both."

Tara and I peered at each other in the mirror and burst into laughter. "I bet Andrew's the pudding. He loves cake." I laughed and applied another layer of mascara.

"They're happy chatting with Steve, so no need to rush. I'll see you ladies downstairs." Aunt Stacy tapped the doorframe and disappeared.

Tara applied the final touches to her makeup and packed her lipstick into her clutch purse. "You done?"

I checked my hair. "Think so." I gestured to the full-length mirror, where we admired our outfits.

"You look amazing, Mrs. Santa." Tara stuck her bottom out and viewed it from different angles, her grin melding into a pensive expression. "Do you think my bum's okay in this?"

I raised an eyebrow. "Your butt's a sculpted work of art in that sultry elf ensemble."

She bit her lower lip. "Is it too much?" Her gaze trailed her reflected image. "It's the first mini-style outfit I've worn since …"

I cupped her shoulder and brushed my thumb against the soft fabric. "If you feel confident enough to wear it, then wear it. It's classy sultry, not scungy. You look gorgeous. Besides, Andrew promised to stay close to you tonight."

A mischievous gleam flickered in her eyes. "I heard." She pressed her lips together before a smirk snuck to her face. "Since he wants to give his cousin a little space with my bestie."

Tom. A combination of thoughts roiled inside my head, and I shuddered a sigh. Tom's body language, eye contact, and those little things a girl notices screamed how into me he truly was. And apart from a tiny niggle of hesitance in my heart, I was on-board with us dating, especially after our first date a few nights ago. The man was what I needed in my life.

"Hmm." I grabbed my phone, credit card, and driver's license and slipped them into a secure, secret pocket at the top of my left boot. "Ready?"

Tara shimmied on the spot. "Ready!"

We slunk downstairs to the kitchen, my stomach twisting in knots with each step. I glimpsed Candy Cane Tom.

His eyes seemed to bulge beyond their natural parameters before his pupils dilated. Electricity thrummed through the air. His Adam's apple bobbed, and a nervous smile appeared on his face.

A wolf whistle sounded to my right. "Well, how do you do, ladies? You both look mighty fine." Uncle Steve's teasing tone triggered my laughter.

Aunt Stacy slapped his arm. "Oh, don't mind him. You look lovely, girls. Very festive."

Toby waltzed across to Tara. "You look beautiful, Tara." He extracted her hand—and several girly giggles—and kissed her knuckles.

I suppressed a laugh and eyed Toby's parents, who both appeared stunned.

Tara smiled down at the little Romeo. "Thank you, Toby."

I fisted my hands on my hips and tapped my foot. "What about me, Tobes? Don't I get a kiss?"

Toby scrunched up his sweet little nose. "I can't kiss you. We're related!"

The adults burst into laughter.

I smiled at the mini man. Not a millilitre of our blood shared any genetic connection, but explaining this fact would confuse the kid, so I high-fived him instead.

We waved our goodbyes to the Morgans at the front door, and Andrew and Tara stepped outside.

Tom leaned close to my ear. "I'd be more than happy to kiss you if you like, Dreamy Diana."

Another first kiss? Amber-ringed eyes and soft lips. I dropped my head and inhaled.

Go away.

Dark eyes and disgusted features. My breaths constricted and pained my torso.

Breathe.

"Maybe one day soon." Before Tom changed his mind about me. I lifted my head.

Tom's grey eyes darkened before his gaze dropped to my lips. "I'll be sure to remember," he whispered. He ushered me to my seat in the rear of his Lexus.

Tara slipped in beside me. Her eyes glittered, wide and bright, and she motioned toward the driver's seat then leaned close. "I've no idea what you two said to each other back there," she whispered in my ear, "but it was seriously hot to watch. Go get him, babe." She winked.

I pressed my hands against my warm cheeks. My stomach thudded with nervous energy the entire trip.

Tom parked in a parking garage and opened my door. He assisted me from the vehicle with a soft smile. His hand brushed my wrist in a slow, deliberate manner, igniting warm tingles along my skin.

I looped arms with Tara, and the four of us crossed the street. The dull drone of thundering music permeated the space around us, and we followed the signage to the thumping party.

Bright colourful lights flashed overhead, concentrating on the DJ platform, and dance music blasted through large black speaker boxes scattered about the huge room.

"Let's find some familiar faces," Tara said with a raised voice.

I gestured a thumbs up, and we located some friends in a cosy corner filled with comfy couches sheltered from the excessive noise. We chatted and laughed, and I enjoyed the freedom from study.

Sometime later, a song I recalled from the clubs ripped through the air. I swayed with the music, my cheeks sore from excessive smiling.

Tara stepped close. "You look like you need to dance. Want to venture out with me?"

I grinned, grabbed her hand, and rushed onto the dance floor. We shimmied to the tune, screeching the lyrics in a semi-melodic fashion and laughing at intervals. Several songs played, and we danced and laughed.

Another song ended, and Tara's heavy breaths dusted my cheek. "Let's take a break. I'm thirsty."

My lungs ached. "Okay." My scratchy throat needed hydration.

We returned to the couches, and I reached for my almost-empty bottle of water. I guzzled the remaining liquid, the coolness soothing my strained vocal cords. I leaned against Tara's clammy arm. "Think we need to rest from the over-the-top singing." I cupped my throat. "I'd like a useful voice in the morning."

She smirked. "So you can have a long conversation with Mr. Sweet Tooth?" She nodded to my left.

I wrinkled my brow and turned. My insides simmered.

Tom's grey eyes stared at me, burning with a new level of intensity.

I held his gaze and smiled.

Tara nudged my shoulder. "I'm telling you, the sparks between you are cray-zee."

I ducked my head from Tom's ridiculous attractiveness, even in his outlandish costume. How could a guy still be appealing in bold white-and-red stripes and a cane handle on his head? I glanced up, peered at him a moment longer, and arrived at the same conclusion. Absurd.

Tom excused himself from a conversation and stepped toward me, his pace relaxed and unhurried.

My pulse matched the overhead dance beat.

"Enjoying your evening?" Tom's voice purred through his grin.

I gulped for air. "I-it's been good." I bit my bottom lip, eyed his costume for the twentieth time, and broke into a smile. "And how've you enjoyed the life of a candy cane so far?"

He cocked his head. "It's a sweet but hard life."

I groaned. "Nice try, but dad jokes aren't allowed. Try again."

Tom pursed his lips, furrowed his brow, and glanced over my shoulder. All of a sudden, his eyes brightened. "My evening's been refreshing."

I huffed a micro-laugh.

"One of my mates told me he collects candy canes. Apparently they're all in mint condition."

I chortled, my chest spasming. "Still bordering on dad-joke territory but aren't too bad. Anything else?"

Tom's greys sparkled, and his lips curved into a lopsided grin. "When I walk into an Apple store, I feel like a kid in a lolly shop because I can't afford anything in there."

"You ning nong." I whacked his shoulder and chuckled. "And clearly not true, Mr. Brilliant Lawyer man."

"You shouldn't judge a book by its cover, nor a candy cane by its wrapper."

I convulsed in a nervous laugh as my cheeks heated. "I've no intention of judging you out of your wrapper, Mr. Candy Cane, so it's a moot point."

His eyes widened, and he emitted a choking sound. "I most definitely *did not* mean to proposition you. See, even lawyers say stupid things." He shook his head, and an adorable pink tinted his cheeks.

I stifled my giggles, my chest light. "It's okay, I know an intentional sleazy come-on when I'm faced with one. Yours was innocent and accidental, if not funny and decidedly inappropriate."

"Tell me about it." His smile slipped. "I really am sorry."

I waved my hand at him. "Don't think anything of it." I arched a brow. "Can we skip the awkward silence and move to a new conversation thread?"

Tom wiped his brow with the back of his hand, sighing with exaggeration. "I'm glad that's over." He winked. "Tell me, are you free for dinner before you head home for the summer?"

I blew out a long breath and squinted. "I planned on heading home first thing Monday morning, so there's really only tomorrow night."

A kind expression crossed his face. "Sunday night could work?"

"I still have packing to do, and Uncle Steve and Aunt Stacy wanted to do something with me and the children tomorrow night."

Tom nodded. "Not a problem. We'll be able to chat and message, and I might be able to travel north at some point."

"Really?" My gaze found his, and warmth dispersed along my skin. "That would be wonderful," I whispered.

Tom brushed a strand of my hair and tucked it behind my ear. "I'm glad you think so."

My mouth dried, and I lifted my water bottle to my lips. Ugh, empty. I spied the crowded bar in the distance. "I'm going to get another water. Would you like something?"

"No, thank you," Tom said.

"Okay." I stepped away, extended a bashful smile over my shoulder, and sashayed to the throng of people waiting to be served.

The modern bar comprised a similar but larger-scale set up to Benanu's, with black leather stools and elegant chrome hanging-light fixtures. A diverse selection of spirits and liqueurs lined the bar's back wall, and open shelving housed various shaped and sized glassware, tumblers, and mugs below. Two staff members manned the bar, working as an efficient team. Impressive.

Minutes passed, and I inched forward. Sweaty skin and accompanying smells assaulted my airways, and I scrunched my nose against one particular offensive odour and his far-too-close vicinity. *Give a girl some elbow room, guys!* The press of people almost suffocated me, but my lack of anxious shaking in the packed room pepped my smile. My thirst intensified.

Music beats vibrated my skin more than my ears, the sound drowned by close conversations. I studied the bartenders and their customers, praying the next few orders would be less elaborate than the bevy of cocktails filling a number of trays. Several cocktails caught my eye, and I thought of Keanu.

A familiar cologne wafted to my nostrils, stirring my senses. My mind wandered. How did I know this delicious fragrance? I stepped forward when the queue gap widened, scrunching my brow. Was it Dad's scent? Or Uncle Matt's? Before my memory recall powers answered me, someone brushed their toasty body against my back.

I straightened and inched forward. Heat brushed my back a second time, and I sighed and leaned forward. Could the guy behind me not take a polite hint? Did he need me to spell it out to him? A large hand gently pressed my lower back, and my chest tightened. *Back off, Mister, before I self-defense my knee into your groin!*

"I don't think Mr. J. would approve of your outfit, Diana, although it's certainly challenged my self-control the last twenty minutes."

I stilled at the heart-stopping, husky voice in my ear.

CHAPTER THIRTY-SIX
Atonement

I squeezed my widened eyes shut and sealed my gaping mouth. My heart pounded harder than any PT session had induced. Adrenaline overwhelmed my body, and dizziness followed. Was my brain playing tricks on me?

Only one way to know.

His exhales warmed my neck, his breaths even. Steady. Was Jonathan truly standing behind me? *Turn around, Diana!*

I trembled, and my throat thickened, my tongue now heavy and useless. I shuddered each breath, fighting the haze in my head, desperate to control my oxygen intake.

Count my breaths.

Anything to still the cacophony inside.

Why was he here? And how had he known my whereabouts?

My eyes pricked, and I raised my eyelids.

"Diana." Jonathan's pain hemorrhaged on each syllable.

How long had I wanted him to seek me out, say my name?

"I'm sorry." He rasped a breath against my ear.

A tear slipped down my cheek.

"It took much longer than I anticipated to get my head right."

I flexed my jaw. Too right it had.

"I was trapped in my mind, and I …" He sighed and his breath warmed my neck. "I couldn't save him or protect you. That's my job, and I failed."

What? How could he blame himself for what his brother did? I wiped a finger under my eye.

"I struggled to function. I felt … small … and undeserving of you."

How could he think such a thing? My eyes misted again. The only thing he had done to notch a mark against "undeserving" was pushing me away.

"When I saw you at the hospital, I wanted to pull you into my arms and never let you go, but … I couldn't." His voice cracked. "How could I trap you in a relationship which could destroy you?"

I heaved a soft cry.

"Even if I love you."

I covered my mouth with my palm. My clammy fingers trembled against my cheek.

How was I meant to respond? Jonathan had rejected me twice and broken my heart. Now I was with Tom.

Ice slithered along my veins. What about Tom? The thought slammed my gut and left me breathless.

The queue gap had widened, so I lurched forward.

How could I trust him again? What guarantees could he offer against the repeat of past mistakes?

I lifted my chin and inspected the bright lights flashing across the ceiling. *What should I do, Jesus? Please light my path.*

My pulse slowed, and heat prickled my skin. I sucked in a fortifying breath and whirled around, lifting my damp gaze to his familiar face and glorious caramel complexion.

Jonathan's eyes looked the same. Dark, deep, and intense. His inviting lips still fluttered my stomach. A smattering of whiskers covered his chiseled jaw, where I noticed the biggest change. Raised scarring lined the right side of his face.

I brushed a finger along the puckered seam. The cosmetic blemish added a brutish appeal to his excessive sexiness.

Jonathan's eyelids shuttered at my touch, and his breath caught when I stroked my fingertips along his damaged ear. Sam had messaged me before each of the three reconstructive surgeries, and I had prayed. Whatever the surgeons had done seemed to have worked. His earlobe shapes matched although the skin grafts were not as smooth as his undamaged ear.

I leaned close to his left ear. "What percentage of your hearing's been lost?" I skimmed my fingers over the crinkles of skin on his right ear before travelling to his jawline. My brain screamed, "Refrain from touching a man who is no longer yours!" but my fingers refused to obey.

A small smile lifted his lips, and his mouth brushed against my ear. "Forty percent in my right. Very mild ringing in both. It could've been worse."

I stepped back, wiped away another errant tear from my cheek, and glanced the swollen queue at the bar. Still a ways to go.

He had closed the physical divide again. "Can you forgive me, and we can talk this out?"

My throat clogged. I clenched my trembling fingers into tight balls. Knife-like stings shot from my fingernails. "I-I don't know if I'll survive another relationship with you."

He stiffened, then relaxed his shoulders. A pained expression flittered across his face. "I'm sorry."

I met his unreadable eyes, my heart barreling against my ribs. "I need time."

What a ridiculous situation I now found myself in. Needing time after I had waited so long and already given up on us.

Jonathan gestured behind me.

I glanced back, stepped closer to the bar, and crossed my arms. "You were so closed off. And then …" I shook my head.

He shuffled forward. "Then what?"

"Nothing. It's … nothing." My shoulders slumped. I lowered my arms to my sides and directed my attention to his tasteful shoes.

Jonathan's body heat radiated through my clothes. "Say it. Tell me, Diana." His graveled tone scraped against me.

I lifted my chin and met his stare, his face closer than I had expected. Peeking over my shoulder, I closed the queue gap for the umpteenth time and settled my breathing. "You recovered from your injuries and seemed … fine."

He raised an eyebrow.

"Sam kept me in the loop."

Jonathan grunted.

I lifted my chin. "I figured you'd moved on. So I determined to do the same."

"And have you? Moved on?" His voice cracked.

I tilted my head and stared straight into his eyes. My heart banged, each beat ringing in my ears.

Someone tapped my shoulder.

I swivelled.

"S'cuse me, sexy, but you're up next." An average-height guy in a black T-shirt winked up at me. He pointed to the bar, then back to the drink he held. "You're in line, yes?"

I nodded and stepped to the bar.

Jonathan's cologne wafted once more to my nostrils.

A blonde bartender leaned toward me and asked for my order.

I slipped my credit card from my boot, ordered two exorbitantly priced bottles of water, and swiped my card.

She handed me the bottles with a nod.

I spun around.

Jonathan ran a hand through his hair.

I escaped the waiting bar patrons to a quieter location—presumably with Jonathan trailing behind—stopped and guzzled several mouthfuls of water while I watched Jonathan.

He rubbed his unshaven jaw.

I glanced toward my friend group and unintentionally caught Tom's attention. Had he seen me speaking with Jonathan?

He grinned and waved.

My stomach plummeted, and bile scorched my throat.

"How long have you two been together?"

I whipped my gaze to Jonathan's stormy eyes. "Officially, less than a week." My voice squeaked. I swallowed acid and grimaced.

"And unofficially?"

I ground my molars. "I don't think it's in your best interest to ask questions about my boyfriend."

Jonathan winced. The same face he pulled when I had told him about the kiss.

I clutched my turbulent abdomen.

Jonathan shuffled on his feet. "I should leave. We can catch up another time."

"That's probably best."

"Will you be in Tellarine over the Christmas period?"

"At some point." The less details he knew, the quicker I could come to terms with whatever needed to happen to resolve our issues.

He stuffed his hands in his pockets. "May I message you?"

I furrowed my brow. "I don't know …"

He nodded. "I'll see you around." Jonathan pivoted and exited the large room.

I wandered to my friends, my jelly legs rendering the simple task of walking difficult.

Tom extracted himself from an animated discussion with two girls from the graduating journalism class. He squinted, and fine lines cratered the skin around his eyes. "You okay?"

I scrunched my nose, arching my top lip. "I'm not sure."

He glanced over my shoulder. "What happened?"

How could Jonathan blow my life up like this? I fisted my hands at my sides.

"Diana?"

Should I tell Tom what happened? Or share more once I grasped how I felt?

Tom lifted my chin. "What's going on?"

"Sorry." I blew out a breath and smiled against the desire to punch something … or someone … on his perfect caramel nose. Ugh! "It's … not important. What's important is whether you're having fun."

Tom stared at me for several beats before unleashing his brilliant smile. "It'd be more fun with you."

I slipped my trembling fingers between his solid digits. "Then let's have some fun."

♥ ♥ ♥ ♥ ♥ ♥ ♥

I stretched and rotated my neck whilst propped on my office chair behind my desk at Benanu's. Keanu could complain all he wanted about my long hours in the office this week. Work was far better a task to accomplish than the confusing turmoil of thoughts, feelings, and choices tossing inside my brain.

How had life become this complicated?

I removed my phone from my bag and re-read the text Jonathan had sent me this morning.

Jonathan: I HOPE YOU DON'T MIND ME TEXTING, BUT I SNAPPED THIS AND THOUGHT OF YOU.

The adorable curls of what appeared to be a dark-haired dog was reminiscent of the photo I had sent him eons ago—albeit Jasmine's curls were far more outrageous-looking at the time. I smiled at the snapshot, amazed Jonathan had remembered that particular exchange, considering we had swapped a plethora of photos.

I scrolled to my last text session with Tom and sighed. What was I to do about this quandary of men? Jonathan's rejection had cut deep into my soul—a gouge to match the one his brother had already inflicted—and my insides rankled at the idea of attempting round two if it led to the same outcome.

Tom was dependable. Sweet, kind-hearted, and … safe. I scrunched my nose. Would he be offended by my appraisal? He was handsome and stirred delightful feelings inside my tummy, but … was he the one?

Whether I married a lawyer or a police officer, I was assured of a future filled with a partner working long hours. They both also helped people, in different ways. Two items to be crossed off my list of pros and cons.

I rubbed my face and tossed my phone back in my bag. How could I make such a life-altering decision based on a list of checks and balances while the God of the universe loved me and wanted the best for me? I had one viable choice. To trust Him and rest in His peace. I leaned against the seat back, closed my eyes, and prayed.

"Napping on the job now?" Keanu's voice interrupted my post-prayer quietude.

I poked out my tongue. "What's up?"

He leaned against the doorframe. "Was wondering if you'd like to chat about New Year's Eve? Last year was one of our biggest earners, and I figured it'd something to do with all the work ya did, so maybe"—he shrugged—"you'd like to give more input to the ideas?"

I smiled at my friend and his uncertain expression. "I'd be delighted. But first I need—"

"Excuse me." Our latest hire—a sweet girl in her late teens who worked as a server—peeked her head around Keanu's shoulder.

"Isabelle." Keanu stepped into my office and turned toward her. "What can I do for ya?"

She glanced between us and settled her attention on me. "There's a woman at the bar who seems desperate to speak to you."

A woman? I creased my brow.

Keanu stiffened. "What does she look like?"

"Red hair, sad eyes, seems a little lost."

Kortney. My heartbeat increased. I glanced at my boss and the fire in his eyes.

I had told him everything that had transpired between Kortney and me—including the still-current intervention order—and he had punched a hole in his office wall. Well, I assumed he had because after I had dialed his direct office line from my bedroom in Melbourne and updated him with my latest drama, I had heard the loud crunch and noticed the patched-up wall the next time I visited.

Keanu growled.

Isabelle paled. "Should I—"

"Thanks for letting us know," I said.

She nodded and disappeared down the hallway.

Keanu focused on the ceiling for several seconds before returning his scrutiny to me. "One phone call, and she'll be charged with a criminal offence."

"I know." I chewed the inside of my cheek. Kortney knew the ramifications of approaching me. Why would she risk it?

Keanu stood in the doorway. "Get back to work, and I'll go deal with this."

I raised my hand. "Wait."

He stilled.

Something inside urged me to speak to Kortney. And the Lord knew I sought answers regarding her actions, especially after she had iced me out during court proceedings. Not that I had minded at the time while I grappled with her betrayal.

I sucked in a breath. "She's sought me here in a public place. Maybe I should hear what she has to say."

Keanu growled again. "No."

I stood, crossed the room, and laid a hand over his heart. "It feels like the right thing to do." I patted his chest. "In here."

His dark eyes flashed.

"You could escort her here." I pointed to the single chair at the front of my desk. "She can sit there while you stand guard over the proceedings."

His brows buckled, and he rubbed his hand along his whiskered jaw.

"Please? If things go south, you can haul her off to jail."

He sighed. "Okay."

I leaned up and kissed his cheek. "Thanks."

Keanu nodded and ducked out of the room.

I returned to my swivel chair and raised it to maximum height.

Keanu returned moments later with Kortney ahead of him. His

gaze never left her.

She hesitated in the doorway.

"Have a seat." I straightened and gestured to the empty chair on the other side of my desk. My arm trembled, and I lowered it to my lap.

Keanu stood in the doorway with his arms crossed. His dark expression shouted his displeasure.

Kortney perched on the furniture, back stiff with her usual perfect posture. Her focus darted between me and my bodyguard. "Thank you for seeing me. I know this places us both in a precarious situation, and I won't take long."

I nodded and crushed my hands together. *Stay calm and listen.*

"I've accepted a position in Western Australia."

What did this have to do with me?

"Your story was meant to be my big break. I needed a strong piece for a promotion out of the trifling, little local paper. I learned early on that the parent company of the newspaper owned major papers in all the city capitals." She peeked at Keanu. "So when I sniffed out a big story with you and your friend, I jumped on it."

"And you never thought how this would affect me?" I gritted my teeth and counted several breaths.

"No," Kortney whispered. She dropped her chin and stared at her lap.

Do not lose your peace, Diana. Let it go. I closed my eyes for a split second and nodded. "Then I wish you all the best."

She whipped her head up and blinked. "Th-thank you."

I smiled. Well, I hoped what my face displayed was a smile.

Kortney stood. She stared at me, glanced at Keanu, and nodded. "I also put in that good word with the editor I had promised."

She what? My breathing stalled.

Her lips twitched up. "Thank you for allowing me this opportunity to speak with you. All the best, Diana."

My throat squeezed. "You too, Kortney."

Keanu led her from my office with a grunt.

I stared after them.

Had this conversation really happened?

I drafted an email to the Morgans, asking how to cancel the intervention order.

Later in the evening, I reclined at my bedroom desk and stared at my laptop screen. How had Kortney chosen to exploit me as a means to an end? What drove her to this decision? Desperation? A desire to get the truth to the people?

Or the need to advance her career before cynicism kicked in?

I closed my eyes and rubbed my temples. How could she disregard our friendship and my mental health—of which I had no idea whether we were truly friends from the beginning or whether I was fodder from day one—for a promotion?

I arched my brow. The passion Kortney held for journalism was something I lacked. I enjoyed reading and writing. I found freedom in expressing myself and communicating with others through words. But to want something so much? Was I prepared to sacrifice my friends and family, my faith and my moral standards to get ahead?

I sighed and slouched against the chair. So, what should I do with my studies? I was back to this merry-go-round.

Although I wished to get off the ride, I needed to stick with it. What was the point of changing things up when I had one year of study left?

~ ~ ~ ~ ~ ~ ~

9 December

Did you ever think your daughter would grow up to be a disappointment, Mum? The thought crosses my mind more often than not of late. Not because of anything I've done wrong (although you can attest to that list being mighty long) but because it appears I'm not passionate about this journalism gig.

I know you wanted the best for me. I really do. But maybe I'm just not cut out to be the best. And I'm sorry I have to convey such sentiment to you. Regardless, I won't give up. Despite my failings, I'm not a quitter.

I love you.

CHAPTER THIRTY-SEVEN
Transformation

I padded down the back passageway of Benanu's offices, carrying a mug of hot chocolate in one hand and my phone in the other.

Jonathan: I TRUST YOU'RE WELL AND ENJOYING LIFE IN MELBOURNE. I SNAPPED THIS SHOT EARLY THIS MORNING AND THOUGHT OF YOU. SUNRISES WERE NEVER THIS BRILLIANT ON MY EARLY-MORNING CITY SHIFTS.

I gazed at the ethereal colours staining the horizon and tinting the cloud haze in Jonathan's photo. He knew how to capture God's sublime creation. But the Melbourne comment threw me. How could he not know I had been home for almost a week? I assumed once Sam knew, Jonathan would too.

I slipped behind my desk and placed my drink on my purple unicorn coaster. Why would Sam not tell his best friend? Was this a sign of his loyalty to our friendship? I scrolled through Jonathan's recent messages. Short and sweet, and not a hint of persuasion. As though he trusted me to decide for myself what to do about him. My heart stirred.

I blew at my drink and sipped. Smooth, silky chocolate glazed a path to my tummy, warming my throat and chest. Despite the warm temperatures outdoors, I enjoyed the sensations. A sugar hit to get me across my final hour of work for today.

My desk phone rang. "Hello?"

"Dreamy Diana. Glad I caught you," Tom said.

I rested my elbows on my desk. "You are?"

"I am." His voice deepened. "I wanted to check that you're okay and give you some news."

I wrinkled my brow. "Why wouldn't I be okay?"

Something scratched over the line. "You seemed a little distant the last time we spoke."

Oh. No surprises when I was still coming to terms with … everything. I cleared my throat. "I've had a lot on my mind."

"Anything you want to talk about?"

"Not yet." I cupped my cheek and leaned on my elbow. "But soon."

"Good, because this brings me to my news. Andy and I will be in town for Christmas."

My eyes widened. "Really?" I covered my mouth and winced. I had not meant to blurt that out.

"Yes." He sounded hesitant. Momentary static clung to our connection. "And I'd like to see you if you consent."

Ugh, I needed to keep my mouth shut sometimes. "Of course, I'd love to see you." Kind of. The hummingbirds in my chest wanted to see him, but the rippling unease in my midriff dampened any excitement I harboured.

"Great. We'll arrive on Christmas Eve and stay until my office reopens a few days into the new year."

Two weeks. I chalked the deadline in my brain and refocused on the call. "Looking forward to it."

"I've a client waiting for me. Chat soon?"

"Chat soon. Bye, Tom."

"Until next time, Diana."

I returned the handset to its cradle and stared at the blank wall ahead. Two weeks.

Keanu bounded through my door with hair sticking up and a frazzled, almost crazy glint in his eye.

"What's the matter?"

He shoved his fingers in his dark hair and pulled. "Just going mad."

I stood and approached him. "Can I help?"

He closed his eyes, puffed several breaths, and met my gaze. "If ya can. Please."

I touched his arm. "Anything. What can I do?"

"We're short-staffed." He flattened his unkempt hair. "I'm currently three people. And I can't do it all."

"Breathe." I rubbed his chest. "Tell me what to do."

He covered my hand on his torso. "We're catering a function at the Community Centre. It's a quick set-up, but I can't spare anyone to deliver it."

I smiled. "When do you need me to go?"

He squished me in a bear hug. "You're the best."

I chuckled against his chest. "That's me."

He dropped his arms and grinned. "Sure ya don't wanna marry me now?"

"Nope. The thirty-year plan stands." I returned to my laptop and packed my things.

Keanu provided me a brief rundown of whom to speak to, what to do, and where to go before he raced from the room.

I shouldered my laptop bag, locked my door, and strode to the kitchen.

♥ ♥ ♥ ♥ ♥ ♥

"Car park, car park, please, Lord, a car park." I circled the area nearest the Community Centre entrance in Victoria's little car. Sweat trickled down the back of my dress and pooled at the hem of my knickers. A wet patch near my butt was all I needed.

A familiar elderly lady tottered down the building steps.

I opened my window. "Mrs. Inglebar! Are you heading off?"

She squinted, smiled, and neared the vehicle. "My favourite punching bag!" She chortled and pointed to a car two spaces away from the entrance. "Just leaving. I bribe the big boss with baking, and he leaves an orange cone in my space every Friday morning."

I snorted with laughter. "Thank you for the space. I've a delivery from Benanu's."

She smiled and sighed. "I should stop by soon and give Keanu Boy some love while I get some of my drinks." She tapped the side of the car. "I'm off. See you soon, love."

"Bye." I reversed to give her ample space to exit and filled the vacated parking bay two minutes later.

Glancing at the time, I hustled the oversized plastic-covered tray of sandwiches, biscuits, and slices into the cool building. The room number was the same as the self-defense class, so I hurried along the familiar path and reached the closed door. I peeked through the rectangular glass windows slotted in the wooden door.

A meeting of some kind was in session. Everyone had their backs toward me.

I cricked my neck and balanced the tray on one hand. The long edge rammed my chest. I opened the door, slipped into the room without making a noise, and checked the door had closed properly before I loped to the back table. An urn, several water jugs, mugs, and tumblers covered one side of the tabletop. I slid the tray into position and cringed.

Perspiration adorned my head and hairline. Gross. With my back to the group, I untied my messy bun and ran my fingers through my damp hair.

Someone spoke amongst the group.

I froze.

Jonathan? What was he doing here? Using my long locks as a shield, I turned ever so slightly and listened.

"Many of you know my job is to help people and keep our community safe. But I didn't read the signs of my brother's struggles … until he was dead." His voice croaked.

I covered my mouth to silence my gasp.

"This group has been a godsend. To know you're all dealing with similar grief, shock, and guilt has helped me process my denial and find a new confidence."

What group had I stumbled into? Who were these people helping Jonathan pick up the pieces?

He cleared his throat. "As a few of you know, my situation became more complicated six months ago, and … I lost hope."

A ball of ice materialized in my gut. Six months ago. When he discovered I was the girl his brother had abducted. Tears leaked down my cheeks.

He sniffed. "Thank you for helping me."

Several people murmured their support before a woman stood and started sharing.

I rushed to the exit, slipped through the door, and leaned against an adjacent wall.

"Family of Suicide Victims Support Group" was written on the board near the door.

How had I missed the sign? I closed my eyes and counted to ten. My breaths slowed as my thoughts ran at triple speed.

Jonathan was getting the help he needed. Proof he was changing for the better. But to what end?

I opened my eyes and returned to the car park.

"Careful, Jazzy. Hold onto the swing while Andrew pushes you." I watched my sister and kissed the top of Elijah's hair where he slept against my chest in the baby carrier, his soft tufts of fuzz tickling my face. My baby brother was six-and-a-half months old.

I glanced at the park bench, where I had endured a panic attack so long ago and beamed. *Thank You, God, for getting me through that ordeal and helping me each day since.*

"You look remarkable with a baby strapped to you." Tom's low voice launched shivers down my spine despite the same tug-of-war wresting inside.

Over two weeks had passed, and I still had not decided what to do. Nor had I spoken to Tom about my dilemma or seen Jonathan since I glimpsed him at his support group.

I was a horrible, horrible person.

Tom nudged my shoulder. "Too forward?"

Yes and no. I feigned a smile and flopped Elijah's hat back over his head.

"Di-Di! Tell Andwew higher!" Jasmine yelled.

I snickered and wandered closer to the playground swing set.

Andrew met my gaze with wide eyes. "I thought this was high enough."

"No! Higher!" Jasmine giggled and kicked her legs.

I smiled and nodded. "You can go a little higher."

"Yay!"

Andrew pushed her swing a fraction higher until she squealed.

"Look! Doggy!" Jasmine wriggled in her swing seat and pulled against the buckles. "I wanna go down."

I turned and spotted a man jogging with a tall, dark-haired dog. I squinted.

"Down, Andwew. Peeze?"

The man seemed familiar. Was it—

"Can I let her down?" Andrew asked.

Air sucked from my lungs. Jonathan.

"Diana?" Tom touched my shoulder.

I turned. "Pardon?"

Tom chuckled. "The princess wants out."

"Oh, yes, unbuckle her."

Tom assisted Andrew at the swing.

I tracked Jonathan's progress, flutters batting against my insides a hundredfold. When had he committed to a dog? Weeks had passed since we spoke at the Christmas party, and now I imbibed the sight of his rippling muscles beside that sweet curly-haired dog. My palpitations multiplied.

His footsteps faltered the moment he recognized me.

Jasmine wrapped her arms around my legs. "Pat the doggy?"

I patted her hat-clad head. "If the owner stops and lets you touch his dog." I lifted my face and met Jonathan's eyes. *Please stop.*

He slowed on the path, ran a hand through his dark hair, and smiled. "Merry Christmas, Diana."

I adjusted my sun hat. "Merry Christmas to you, too, Jonathan."

"Pat the doggy!" Jasmine jumped beside me.

Jonathan chuckled and squatted next to the dog.

My insides melted into a puddle.

"Come give Loki a pat, sweetheart." Jonathan demonstrated where to scratch the canine.

Jasmine giggled and stroked the dog's curls.

My heart thrummed. "What breed is your dog?" My voice sounded husky.

"He's a curly-coated retriever. He's actually Sam's rescue dog, but I tend to take him for runs more than Sam." He angled his face up and pierced me with his soulful gaze. "Someone suggested that a pet-therapy pal might be beneficial, and the day after I mentioned it to Sam, he came home with this treasure." He chuckled.

My breaths caught. Pet therapy?

"Sam's wanted a dog for a long time and took this as a green light." Jonathan helped Jasmine scratch under Loki's chin. "He likes that. Good job."

The dog licked her arm, and Jasmine giggled.

Someone pressed a firm hand against my back.

I turned and glimpsed Tom's face. Tom's hand, not Jonathan's. Something inside me deflated.

Jonathan rose from his haunches, secured Loki's leash around his wrist, and nodded to my boyfriend.

Tom extended his right hand. "I don't think we've been officially introduced. I'm Tom."

Jonathan shook Tom's outstretched hand. "Jonathan." He nodded toward Andrew before looking at me.

Tom's hand burned my back.

"A pleasure to meet you," Jonathan said with a small smile.

I reached out for Jasmine. "We'd better let Loki get home for a drink."

She clutched my hand and waved with the other. "Okay, bye-bye, Loki. Bye, Mita Saysee." She remembered.

My hands shook. Of course she did. Jonathan was unforgettable.

I lifted my gaze and read the deluge of unspoken words oozing from Jonathan's mesmeric eyes.

He rubbed his chest. "Have a great New Year's, guys. Don't get up to too much mischief, because I'm on shift." His soft chuckle caressed my ears and slipped straight into my heart.

CHAPTER THIRTY-EIGHT
Setting Matters Straight

"Daddy! Mummy!" Jasmine raced from my lap—where I basked on the couch with Elijah and a storybook—and slammed into Dad's legs.

"Jazzy bear!" Dad scooped her high in the air, extracting dozens of giggles before returning her to the plush carpet.

"Thank you for looking after them again." Victoria kissed Jasmine and reached for Elijah. "It's been odd being away from this little one."

Elijah dribbled mid-babble, his face gleeful.

"Come, Jasmine, say goodnight to Sissy Di-Di and Daddy." Victoria offered her slobbery boy to Dad for a goodnight kiss.

"It's Di-Di, Mummy." Jasmine huffed and kissed my cheek. "Night, Di-Di."

"Night, Jazzy." I missed the "sissy" part of my name but was glad the "Di-Di" still stuck. For now.

Victoria exited the lounge with the children.

Dad lowered to the armchair closest to where I sprawled. "Good book?"

I glanced at the picture book in my lap and raised a brow. "Really, Dad?" A book from my childhood. I still recalled Mum reading it to me.

He chuckled and leaned forward in the chair with his hands clasped and elbows on his knees. His cheerful countenance morphed into the serious expression I had seen many times in my twenty-one years of life. "What's up, Princess? You've not been your usual self the last few days."

Was I that transparent? I expelled a long breath before meeting his eyes. "Did Mum ever mention certain aspirations she held for me?"

"Aspirations?"

I nodded. "You know, expectations she held as a mother? That I would someday hopefully meet?"

He rubbed his stubbled jaw and peered at the ceiling before looking at me. "Other than loving you and wanting you to be happy, healthy, and successful, I don't recall any specific aspirations."

I furrowed my brow. "What about my writing? She encouraged me often with the stories I wrote and the ones I dictated to her, which she jotted down. She said I should keep writing and that I could be a journalist when I grew up."

"She did?"

Of course, she did!

Dad tilted his head. "Debbie often laughed about the creative juices flowing through your veins. She loved how you could paint a picture with words like she did with a paintbrush." Dad narrowed his eyes. "But above all, she wanted you to be true to yourself. If that was down the creative path, great. But if you chose something different, your mother would've supported you, no matter what career you chose."

What? How was this possible? My chest loosened, and I blinked away a sheen of tears. "I wish I'd known sooner."

Dad sunk to the couch and wrapped his arm around me. "What's going on?"

"I …" My throat shrunk. "I'm struggling at school." My voice rasped.

Dad's arm tightened around me. "How so?"

I sucked in air. "I thought … I assumed Mum wanted this career for me, and I wanted to accomplish it because"—tears tracked down my cheeks—"I didn't want to disappoint her."

Dad tucked his finger under my chin and lifted my head. "You would *never* be a disappointment to me or your mother. You're a blessing, pure and simple, so get those lies out of your head."

I nodded and rubbed my hand across my wet face.

"You're loved. Very much. Be who God called you to be and live up to His expectations. When your heart follows Him, you'll never disappoint." Dad kissed my forehead and released my chin.

"What did I miss?" Victoria traversed the room. "Oh,

sweetheart, are you okay?"

"I am now," I said. "Thanks, Daddy."

"Anytime." He stood and enveloped Victoria in his arms. "Tea time?"

"Ooh, yes, please." She leaned up on her tiptoes and brushed a kiss against his lips.

"Tea, Diana?"

"Yes, please."

Dad nodded and ambled toward the kitchen.

Victoria dropped beside me on the couch. "You sure you're okay?"

In one area of my life, at last. I nodded.

"And how's Tom?" She raised a brow like she could see right through to my heart.

I pursed my lips. "He's … wonderful …" How could I answer otherwise? Tom was great. Everyone loved him, especially the Morgans. Pain etched my chest.

"But?"

I leaned against Victoria's side and closed my eyes.

She's going to hate me. Just like Uncle Steve, Aunt Stacy, and Dad would once they knew my thoughts and feelings.

My stomach dropped. Would they lose respect for me? Think I'm crazy? They had all dealt with the aftermath of my Jonathan fallout. But … what could I do?

I relaxed my taut jaw. "I think I might still love Jonathan."

Victoria's body vibrated against me.

I lifted my head and saw her holding back laughter.

She gripped my hand resting in my lap. "Sorry. You sound just like me over three-and-a-half years ago."

I furrowed my brow. "With Uncle Matt?"

She nodded. "Except I dated him much longer than you have Tom, all the while fighting my feelings for your father." She rubbed my hand. "But *I* ran away from your dad, as opposed to being pushed away like Jonathan did you."

I bit my bottom lip. "He came to Melbourne to apologize and tell me he was working through his grief and changing his ways. He asked for a second chance."

"When?"

"At the beginning of December."

Victoria narrowed her eyes. "What happened when he found out about Tom?"

I mulled over the memory of our conversation. "He seemed disappointed, borderline defeated. I asked for time to think, and he gave me space. Hasn't pressured me about my decision, didn't even hint at us getting back together when he ran by us at the park a few days ago."

"And what makes you think you might still love him?"

I closed my eyes, and a torrent of images flashed through my mind. The good times and the painful. But through it all, my heart refused to snuff the ember glowing for Jonathan. I opened my eyes. "Because he consumes my heart even though it frightens me." I turned to Victoria. "Do you think I'm a fool to go back for round two? He's changed. He attends a support group for families who've lost loved ones to suicide. He was gentle with Jasmine, like always, and kind to Sam's dog. I think the pet therapy's working because he seemed calmer. Didn't hint at playing the jealousy card when he saw me with Tom and Andrew. And …"

"And?" Victoria squeezed my hand.

"And when Tom pressed his hand to my back when he introduced himself to Jonathan, I … I wanted it to be Jonathan's hand, not Tom's," I whispered. "But I don't want to hurt Tom. A-and I don't know where to start with Jonathan."

Victoria thumbed the back of my hand. "I don't think you're crazy. God gives us second chances, time and time again." She dropped her gaze. "If Jude had committed to real change like Jonathan before I contemplated leaving Melbourne"—she lifted a shoulder—"perhaps I might have indulged him in trying to reconcile and wouldn't be here."

Whoa. Victoria's ex-husband had hurt her in more ways than Jonathan did me.

She shook her head and smiled. "But enough about me. Let's pray so you can step forward in peace."

Dad entered the lounge room carrying a tray. He lowered the drinks and nibbles to the coffee table before sitting on the armchair. "You doing better, Princess?"

"She's doing a Victoria." Victoria chuckled.

"Huh?" Dad creased his brow.

Here went nothing. "I'm dating Tom, but I think I might still love Jonathan," I said in a rush.

His eyes widened. "Oh." He nodded. "Okay. So, what's the plan?"

Dad was okay with this too? Wow.

I exhaled and shrugged. "Prayer and then see what happens next."

He rubbed his hands together before resting a palm over Victoria's hand, which still covered mine. "Then let's pray and believe God will help you sort this out."

I closed my eyes, bowed my head, and thanked the Lord Almighty for the most precious parents I could have ever wanted.

"It's beautiful out here." Tom surveyed the tall eucalyptus trees along the back of Dad and Victoria's property. Several birds chirped and twittered on the high branches.

A warm, earthy, scented breeze filled my lungs. "It is."

"A guy could get used to this life." Tom halted near a fallen log in the shade, crossed his arms, and closed his eyes. "Amazing how refreshing everything smells, even on a hot day like today."

The circus in my tummy must have been conducting a tightrope performance because I wanted to vomit. But I had to do this. Needed to do this. I inhaled menthol and lavender and touched Tom's arm.

He opened his eyes and smiled.

"Want to sit for a moment? I'd like to talk about something." *And potentially end our friendship with you hating me. And Andrew hating me again.* Bile singed my throat, and I covered my mouth with my hand.

An unreadable expression crossed Tom's face before he dropped to the rough lumber.

I lowered beside him and regarded him.

"What's up, Dreamy Diana?"

Oh, Lord, how could I be so cruel to hurt this wonderful man? I cradled my hands in my lap. "I have a confession to make."

He tilted his head.

"This has to be one of the hardest things I'll ever say." I dipped my chin. My vision clouded and insides tossed. *Do not vomit!*

"I'm a big boy." Tom blanketed my hands with his.

I stared at the wildflowers dotted in the patchy, clumped grass and sandy dirt. "It seems I never got over Jonathan."

The leaves chattered in the trees above my head.

"I see."

I raised my face. "I don't want to lead you on, Tom."

He nodded, stared at my lap, and separated his hand from mine.

"I'm sorry, truly I am." Tears slipped down my cheeks. I brushed my fingers along the wet tracks. "It was never my intention to hurt you." I huffed a breath. "I'd determined to move on and given up on him, but God never did. And now …"

"He's reclaimed your heart."

"Something like that," I whispered.

Three sparrows landed on the ground and commenced scratching and pecking. They hopped between the clusters of grass before flying away. Oh, to lead a simple life, never concerned about the necessities. Or which bird was the best partner.

Tom rubbed his palms along his thighs, stood, and extended his hand.

I grabbed his fingers, and he hoisted me to my feet.

He nodded toward the house, and we ambled down the sloped block. Tom chuckled and shook his head.

"What's so funny?"

"You sure know how to do a number on the hearts of Chirnside and Daley men. I'll have to warn future generations of the dangers of mixing with Jacobsens."

I pulled a face. "I deserve that."

His deep laughter complemented the birdsong above and the percussive crunch of our footsteps. "Andy is going to laugh so hard." He nudged my shoulder. "It'll be a great bonding experience. Comparing notes of our collective heart damage."

I cringed. "I really am sorry."

He halted and touched my arm. His grey eyes exuded the same kindness I had always associated with him. "I'd rather this conversation now than in a few months' time when I'd be too far gone and Andy would have to dredge me from the bottom of a whisky barrel." He smiled. "Guess I'll have to friend-zone you too." He winked.

I pressed a hand to my relieved torso and smiled.

One conversation done, one to go.

CHAPTER THIRTY-NINE
Resolution

I jiggled my foot under my office desk and stared at my mobile phone. Twenty minutes had passed since I texted Jonathan—my first reply to any of his messages since he had reached out to me. A monumental occasion. Would he ever reply?

I re-read my message to him.

Me: WOULD YOU BE FREE TO CATCH UP? I'M AT BENANU'S AND THOUGHT IF YOU'RE NOT WORKING, WE COULD CHAT HERE.

I returned to my laptop screen and scrolled through social media. I had knocked off work half an hour ago, but it had taken me all day to build up the nerve to press Send on my message to Jonathan.

My phone buzzed. I sucked in a breath.

Jonathan: SORRY, JUST WOKE FROM A NAP. ON EARLIES. MEET YOU IN 15?

Yes! My fingers trembled. I slowed my breaths enough to type a reply.

Me: PERFECT. SEE YOU SOON.

I packed up my laptop and rested it on my desk to collect on my way home, swiped my phone and credit card, and locked the office.

Wait.

The last time I had glanced a mirror was when I supplemented the bar stock before lunch. I re-entered the office, retrieved my bag, and scurried to the staff bathroom for a quick inspection.

Once I was satisfied with my appearance—relieved with the lack of sweat patches and associated horrid odours—I locked everything unnecessary in my office and ambled to the restaurant area.

The open tables were brimming with boisterous customers. I smiled at the scene, thankful this number of people no longer set my anxiety levels to critical.

"Finished work at last." Keanu leaned close. "Looking for a table?"

I should have planned this better. "Are any of the booths available?"

He nodded. "Want one?" He whipped a "Reserved" magnet from his top pocket. Keanu had designed a cute system where servers stored several magnets in their pockets and could snap one on the metal strip edging the wood tabletops at a moment's notice.

"That'd be great. Thanks." I peered at the front entrance.

Should I wait for him? Or rest my trembling legs?

"All done. Table fifty-three." Keanu wrinkled his brow. "Are ya meeting someone here? Cos I thought Andy and Tom went home yesterday?"

Would Keanu smash another wall when I told him what I had done? I tugged my lower lip between my teeth. "Well, the thing is …"

He looped my arm and transported me to my reserved booth. "Talk."

I plopped on the leather bench seat. "I broke up with Tom."

The ridges in his forehead deepened.

"I haven't updated you about … Jonathan." I fidgeted my fingers against the table edge. "Long story short, he came to see me in Melbourne, apologized, asked for a second chance, and then gave me the space I had asked for."

Keanu's dark eyes narrowed.

"And from what I've seen since coming home, he's changed. He's dealing with his grief, working on stress levels, and seems to be getting back to normal."

"I agree."

I creased my brow. "You do?"

Keanu nodded. "Since his brush with death, he's dropped the zombie vibe and started working on himself. He was quick to adopt the pet-therapy idea I'd suggested one night we chatted here."

My eyes bulged. "*You* suggested it?"

"Yup. I've a vested interest in you and also needed to de-stress myself, so I watched several videos like the one I sent ya and picked up some great tips. Was glad to share with him." Keanu glanced over my head and tapped the table. "I'm off. Call me if ya need me."

"Thanks." I poured myself a glass of water from the flip-top bottle on my table and guzzled half a glassful.

"Thirsty?" Jonathan hunkered on the seat across the table.

I nodded at his handsome face. Thirsty was a great description for the mess of reactions shooting off in my belly.

He grabbed the beverage menu. "Would you like a drink?"

I gestured to my empty glass. "Water's fine."

He rubbed his hand along his dark stubble and examined the menu. "Might stick with water too." He filled a fresh glass and topped up mine with water.

"Thanks." I balled my hands together in my lap. "I'm not really sure where to start."

"Then let me." Jonathan exhaled. "I don't know how to adequately express my remorse over the shambles I created between us. I hurt you, and it gutted me."

I chewed the inside of my mouth, rolled my lips, and lifted my gaze. "I forgive you."

He stilled. "You do?"

"Yes. But I need some … answers." To the hard questions bouncing inside my brain.

He bobbed his head. "Of course. What would you like to know?"

I straightened and ran a finger along my glass. "I understand you grieved over your brother before we even met."

He nodded. "I carried a lot of regret and responsibility."

Responsibility? "But you weren't to know he'd … do what he did."

"I might've been the younger brother, but I looked out for Damien." Jonathan rubbed his rough cheek. "After his apprenticeship, he floated from job to job. When he hinted at moving to Melbourne, I offered him the spare room in my apartment. I spoke with him most days yet didn't know the trouble he'd found himself in." He flexed his jaw. "I'm a police officer. It's my duty to help people. And he must've been in deep to collate all that information and … do what he did." His voice croaked. "Why didn't he tell me?"

"Maybe he didn't want to drag you into the fray? Or was protecting you?" I caught his attention. "We'll never know. But despite all of that … you seemed on top of it."

He grunted and sipped his water.

"So why did my involvement push you over the edge?" I scrunched my brow. "I mean, I get how shocking that revelation was. It was difficult for me too. But you seemed … incapable of believing we could move past it." Which had hurt. A lot. I examined Jonathan's pensive features.

"Deep-seated guilt? I couldn't save my brother, and at that point believed I had come to grips with reality, which I later realised I hadn't. To know you were traumatised by him and I never stopped it? My chest physically hurt with that knowledge because I loved you."

Loved? A sudden surge of nausea crashed inside me, and I curled my arms around my waist. Had I misheard or misunderstood Jonathan before Christmas?

Tom's face surfaced in my mind. No! Had I made a mistake breaking up with Tom?

"Diana? You've gone pale."

Breathe. I closed my eyes and counted my breaths.

"You feeling okay?"

I lifted my eyelids and sought his dark-chocolate eyes. "Yes."

Jonathan squinted. "Okay." He cleared his throat. "My brother had physically and emotionally violated the woman I saw myself marrying. And had the audacity to kiss her goodbye too."

I dry retched and covered my mouth with a napkin.

Jonathan's eyed widened. He tumbled the stainless-steel cutlery from its storage canister and thrust the container toward me.

I slowed my breaths. Tears stung my eyes. I would never get past this blasted kiss, would I?

"Are you sick? Do you need to lie down?"

Yes, sick for kissing your brother and liking it. Tears dribbled to my chin.

Jonathan stood and rounded the table, eyes wide. "Let me drive you home."

I shook my head. "Give me a minute." I needed to face this enemy once and for all.

He watched me breathe before returning to his seat.

After half a minute, I nodded. "Continue."

He huffed a wry laugh. "Trust my brother to have the last laugh. When you told me your side of events, I wanted to punch him, punch myself, and wallow in my guilt." He arrested my attention with his dark, soulful eyes. "But I'm moving forward. I love you and want to spend my future with you, if you deem me worthy."

"You still love me?" I whispered. "Even though I disgusted you when your brother kissed me?"

"What?" His eyes widened. "Why would I be disgusted with you?"

I blinked away my hazy vision. "Your face gave it away. You cringed when I told you."

Jonathan moved to the seat beside me. He twisted me by the shoulders to face him, then caressed my cheeks with his warm palms. "You've never disgusted me." A soft chuckle erupted from his chest. "You've turned me on plenty of times, but never grossed me out. Even when shooting juice out of your nose."

A tiny smile nudged my lips.

"I cringed because of my guilt about … everything. Not because you sickened me." He thumbed my cheeks. "Okay, beautiful?"

"Okay."

His gaze heated. "Can we kiss and make up now?"

My insides now tossed for a different reason.

The whites of Jonathan's eyes expanded, and he stiffened. "Or are you still spoken for?" He dropped his hands and closed his eyes. "I'm sorry. I should've asked about Tom."

I leaned forward and kissed him on the mouth. Soft, sweet, and filled with all the love I possessed despite being petrified to say those three little words again. Baby steps.

My lips tingled, and I pulled back. "I'd like to try again." I pressed my lips together. "But can we take it slow?"

His face split with a dazzling grin. He wrapped his arms around me and pulled me against his pounding chest. "What a marvelous plan."

✒ ✒ ✒ ✒ ✒ ✒ ✒

4 January

I can't believe I haven't written to you in weeks, Mum. Sorry! Well, maybe I can believe it, what with all the crazy things I've been thinking, feeling, and dealing with on the daily. You might like to make a cuppa (or whatever is the equivalent thing you do when you have downtime in Heaven and want to sit back and relax) because I suspect this might be a long one. Or not. Heh.

Where to begin? Kortney stirred up so many feelings when she visited a few weeks ago … as you'd already know from my earlier word vomit (I hit the angsty "woe is me" button on that entry, sorry!). I just couldn't get her out of my head. Or you, Mum. You know I love you and want to make you proud, but it seems I was wrong all this time. Not about wanting to make you proud. I hope I do that all the time. But Dad says you'd just want me to be happy in whatever I do. I believe him more than my memories of you. How could I have crossed so many wires in my life? Thinking I needed to be a journalist because of some expectations I fabricated in my head as a kid. I'm sorry for tainting your memory. You were always free and generous in your love for me, and I shouldn't have boxed myself inside a set of parameters I imagined on your behalf. So, I'm done with it all, and it's freeing. As for my studies, I'm still not a quitter (ha ha!) but feel unhampered and ready to find my course in life, journalism or otherwise.

You may or may not be surprised to know that I also broke things off with Tom (yep, it's been a big few weeks!). Gosh, he's such a sweet, wonderful guy. But I couldn't string him along while I worked out everything inside my head and heart regarding Jonathan. I thought I'd lose friends and family over this decision, but everyone's been supportive. I even called Aunt Stacy to inform her of what's transpired, and she was happy for me. Go figure. So, I reconciled with Jonathan today, and we're going to take things one small step at a time. Slow and steady wins the race, right? And I want to win this one, Mum. But I've also got another year of study to go, and by the time that finishes, I hope I'll have some idea of what to do career-wise. I enjoy my job at Benanu's, but I'd also like to keep writing. Maybe a job will pop up closer to home, but I suspect Jonathan and I will be doing this relationship thing long-distance for a while yet. And that's okay too.

I wish I could hug you and see your eyes sparkle. They're the memories I'll treasure now, not some feigned expectations. Because

you're my mum no matter what.
    I love you.

CHAPTER FORTY
Shalom

"Happy twenty-third, gorgeous!" Tara launched at me, wrapping her petite arms around my frame. Rays of light from the setting winter sun filtered through Dad and Victoria's backyard eucalyptus trees, accentuating the amber threads in Tara's blonde hair.

I chuckled and squeezed her. "I'm so glad you made it. Took you long enough to visit." This was only her second time to step foot on Tellarine soil.

She gifted me with an eyeroll. "You know how it is with the pig I work for. You'd think I'd wiped my bare butt on his precious car instead of asking for two days off work."

I smirked. "Still enjoying the delights of your non-journalistic job while your talents waste away?"

"Shut up, you." She nodded toward the house, where my family and friends congregated under the oversized covered deck, surrounded by outdoor heaters. "Nice work on Jonathan's part popping the question a week before your birthday." She wrinkled her nose. "Saves me asking for more leave."

I slung my arm around her shoulder. "You really should look into getting a new job."

"I guess."

"Speaking of jobs …" My insides burbled, and I grinned. "Guess who's writing a fortnightly column for the local paper?"

Tara's eyes widened. "You got the gig? No way! That's awesome! Congrats!" She squished me in another tight hug.

"Thank you. It's one thing to work occasionally with the online mag, but this is consistent work." I waved to Sam, who now ambled toward us. "The editor said he recognized my name from talking with Kortney nineteen months ago, so when my resume crossed his desk, I rose above the pack." I still marveled Kortney's recommendation had been to my advantage.

Tara blinked. "Wow."

"Yes, wow," Sam said. "You're both on the 'wow' scale." He waggled his eyebrows.

Tara slapped his shoulder.

Sam raised a brow. "Why're we huddled in the cold while the party's happening in the warmth?"

I pointed to the horizon. "I wanted to catch the sunset since it's been a clear day."

"And you can't do that on the patio with the conveniences of heat?" Sam scrunched his face.

"Nope." I turned and watched the sun dip below the horizon.

Tara looped her arm through mine. "C'mon, let's indulge the pretty boy and his sensitive skin."

We sauntered down the block toward the house.

Tara turned to Sam. "What're you going to do when this one"—she gestured to me—"and your bestie get hitched?"

Sam shrugged. "Dunno. I've been talking to a few mates to see if they're interested in renting a room."

Sam, Tara, and I reached the edge of the decking.

"Won't it still be a ways off?" Tara turned to me. "When's the wedding?"

Sam snorted. "Don't think it'll be a long wait now that Jon's finally got the diamond on her finger."

My cheeks warmed. I ogled the lustrous rock on my slender digit. "We're still deciding." I had moved home earlier in the year to focus on work at Benanu's and my writing craft. But now Jonathan and I were no longer long-distance, we both desired to marry sooner than later.

"We're still deciding what, beautiful?" Jonathan said from behind me. My brutish pirate of a beau slipped his arms around my waist and pulled me back against his chest. "You smell so good." He kissed the skin below my ear.

Goosebumps prickled my neck under his warm breath. "I was just telling Tara we've not decided when the wedding will be."

He rested his chin on my shoulder and his hands on my stomach and glanced at Tara. "Book leave for the first weekend in November."

"What?" I jerked from his hold and spun around. "That's four months away. I thought you wanted to wait until next year?"

He furrowed his brow and cradled the side of my face with his large hand. "I thought we agreed the sooner the better?"

"I assumed that meant January." Although I would marry him in a heartbeat.

His eyes twinkled, and a cheeky smirk slid to his lips. "I'd like to say in the future, I had sex in my twenties, so that'll give you a few days to pop my cherry before my thirtieth."

My cheeks heated. "Uh …"

Tara and Sam cackled with hooting laughter.

"What'd I miss?" Keanu joined the group, eyes narrowed. He glanced at the four of us.

"Jon's excited about the upcoming defloration ceremony," Tara said between giggles.

Keanu squinted. "The what?"

My face burned with the intensity of a thousand suns. At this rate my eyelids would melt off.

Jonathan dragged me back against his warm, broad chest.

"The joyous ceremony of deflowering his wife and vice versa." Tara grinned.

Keanu chuckled. "Got ya."

She batted her eyelashes. "You sure can."

Keanu's eyes darkened. "You must be Tara."

I snickered.

Tara stretched out her hand. "And by the looks of your mischievous eyes, that hair mop on your head, and your dimpled chin, you must be the boss."

Jonathan's quiet laughter vibrated against my back.

I wished I had some popcorn to nibble. These two were fun to observe.

"Okay, ladies and gentlemen, get your party on because Madison's in town!" Madison's loud declaration and subsequent whoop tore through the cool winter air. She was sandwiched between Grace and Anna.

"Well, looky here. Hello, ladies." Sam's voice dropped to what I called his "predator," flirtatious tone. A harmless predator, but a man on the prowl nonetheless.

Madison, Grace, and Anna slammed into me and forced a group hug, which Jonathan was an unfortunate party to since his arms still wrapped my torso with boa constrictor strength.

"Happy birth engagement day!" Madison slapped a kiss on my cheek and another on my fiancé's stubbled jaw.

Anna grinned up at me. "You doing well since I saw you all of four hours ago?"

I chuckled. "Really well."

Grace smiled. "It's so great seeing you, Diana."

"You too. Thanks for making the trek up from Melbourne." I nodded toward Madison. "I see you survived her driving?"

Madison scrunched her nose. "Whatevs."

"Mum apologizes and said they'll all be over later." Anna shrugged.

My shoulders tensed, and I pressed my lips together. "Is Mitch still looking after the music tonight?" Anna's younger brother had acquired some DJ'ing skills over the last few years and was pretty decent at it. But the last thing I needed was to spend the evening manning the sound system.

Jonathan nipped at my neck, his warm breath inciting chills along my skin. His arms still held me in place, and I relaxed into them.

Anna shrugged again. "I believe so? Although Grandma Jean still grumbles his music's loud when he's practising, so he might back out."

I chuckled, imagining my grandma getting upset with my cousin. "He better not, or Uncle Chris will have a strong word with him."

Anna snickered. "Mum's probably the one who'd have a go at him for cancelling on a commitment than Dad would."

Someone called my name, and Jonathan released me.

I turned and beamed at Lacey and Andrew. "How was the trip up?" I embraced Lacey. "Welcome to Tellarine!"

She laughed and pointed toward the side gate. "The drive was smooth. I left my bag in Andrew's car. Should I get it now or later?"

I looked at Andrew. "You sticking around?" Andrew had messaged me earlier in the day that his mum was unwell and he might need to leave early.

"For a bit. Might be best to get the bag now." He nodded to Lacey, and they disappeared around the corner.

Jonathan pressed his warm hand against my back. "Looks like my parents just arrived. Want to get the 'hellos' out of the way?"

I turned and kissed his cheek. "Of course. Lead the way."

He enveloped my hand with his and tugged me toward his parents.

"My dearest girl!" Mrs. Harris hugged and kissed me. "Happy birthday. We left our gift for you inside."

I smiled down at her sweet face. "Thank you."

"Where's Nick and Vicki?"

I searched the entertaining area and spotted Dad and Victoria chatting with Uncle Steve and Aunt Stacy. "By the barbeque."

"Come, Henrik." Mrs. Harris trotted off in my parents' direction.

I turned and pressed a kiss to Mr. Harris's cheek. "You well?"

"Always." He chuckled and heeded his wife.

I entwined my fingers with Jonathan's. "I should see if Victoria needs any help."

We joined the gathering near the barbeque where Uncle Steve and Dad shared the task of not burning things.

I touched Victoria's arm and waited for her to finish her conversation.

She rotated and smiled. "Hey, sweetheart. Having fun?"

I nodded. "Do you need any help?"

Aunt Stacy shook her head. "We've got it all covered. Enjoy your guests."

I arched my brow. "Where're the children?"

Victoria pointed toward the back door. "Inside with Matt and Be—"

The glass sliding door banged the wall, and a flurry of children raced through the opening. The four-year-old cousins, Ella and Jasmine, squealed and darted around Madison, Grace, and Anna, with my two-year-old brother on their heels, dragging soon-to-be eight-year-old Toby by the hand.

Aunt Stacy peered past my shoulder, her eyes alight with mirth. "Toby said to Steve that he'd like to dance with Tara tonight. Will there be dancing after dinner?"

I chuckled, and the vibration of Jonathan's laughter tickled my back. "I believe so."

Half an hour later, dinner was served. I luxuriated in the casual atmosphere of chatting with loved ones and eating fabulous food. Aunt Belinda, Aunt Stacy, and Victoria's cooking skills shone.

Mitch moseyed over a little after seven-thirty—my uncle, aunt, and grandma arriving moments later—and set up his wireless equipment. He donned his outgoing DJ "hat" and encouraged people to dance.

I nudged Jonathan's shoulder as we nestled together on one of the outdoor couches and pointed to where Toby approached our group of friends.

Toby's face was a picture of determination, with his creased brow and focus glued to Tara, who lounged on a nearby deck chair. He bowed and extended his arm toward my best friend. "Would you like to dance?"

Several titters and soft giggles filtered through the out-of-doors area.

Tara snuck a glance at me, winked, and showered Toby with her brightest smile. "It would be my honour, young man." She slipped her hand into his proffered one.

Toby's chest puffed out along with his cheeks—which strained under his abundant smile—and escorted her to the empty area closest to Mitch and his gadgets.

I caught Aunt Stacy's attention and grinned.

Keanu leaned forward on the opposite outdoor couch. "The kid's got guts, that's for certain. Not sure I'd be so brave."

Jonathan laughed and stood. "Toby's set a great example." He reached out for me. "Care to dance?"

I clasped his fingers and allowed him to guide me to the dance floor.

Jonathan scooped me close. His arm tightened around my back. "You're so beautiful."

I wrapped my arms around his neck and sighed. "I love you, Jonathan Henrik Amas Harris, and I'm so glad your mum didn't let your family call you by one of your middle names because"—I wrinkled my nose—"that'd be weird."

He chuckled and kissed my lips.

Swoon.

"I love you, Diana Nicole Jacobsen, and promise to show you

exactly how much over the coming weeks, months, and years."

I rested my face in the crook of his neck and breathed in his delicious scent.

We stood encircled in each other's arms, swaying to the music and the beating of our hearts.

I stood and wiped my brow with my hoodie sleeve, surprised to have worked up a sweat on a cool, partly cloudy spring day. Sucking in the fresh mid-morning country air, I stretched my back and kneeled in the garden bed. So many weeds! How had Dad allowed the now-vacated tenant to leave the garden—Mum's garden—in such disarray?

"Am I getting old, or are you feeling the burn too?" Jonathan chuckled from an adjacent garden bed, his delectable denim-clan backside front and centre for my viewing pleasure.

"You're not old. I'm a little achy too."

He leaned back and rested his yummy butt on his sneaker heels and stretched his arms above his head. A small gap appeared between his T-shirt and jeans waistband, showcasing a slither of caramel skin.

My mouth dried. A little over six weeks and I would be permitted a peek at the rest of him. *Help me get through the next month and a half, please, God.*

"You checking me out again?" Jonathan's sable gaze now met mine.

When had he turned around? I dropped a seedling weed into the collection bucket, rose to my feet, and removed my gardening gloves. "Maybe."

He stood and stretched his legs.

Holy cucumber sandwiches.

Toned thigh muscles baited me, endeavouring to propel me toward forbidden indulgence.

Not on my watch. I inhaled and pointed to the weeded, raised beds behind us. "We're more than halfway. Drinks break?"

"Please."

I unearthed our water bottles from my backpack, handed Jonathan his, and drained my container.

He tossed his empty bottle onto the ground near my backpack. "I've been thinking."

"Did it hurt?" I stuffed my water bottle in my bag.

He lunged for me and wrapped me in his arms.

I squealed and laughed.

"Someone needs to teach you a lesson on how to respect your elders." Jonathan's eyes twinkled.

I smacked his firm chest. "Enough with the age-gap comments. I've told you, I don't commit to marrying old men."

He chuckled and inspected my lips.

My insides bloomed with heat. I leaned up and met his warm, soft mouth with mine. Tingles rippled down my spine and shivered my skin. I disengaged—far too soon in my opinion—and darted my tongue across my lower lip.

Jonathan blinked, his focus pinned to my mouth.

I raised a brow. "You were thinking?"

He cleared his throat and nodded to my childhood home. "What if we rented this place from your dad? Once we marry, of course."

I stared at him, mouth agape.

"What do you think? Good idea or bad idea?" Jonathan then recited the whistling "Good Idea, Bad Idea" skit from *Animaniacs*. "The. End."

I snorted with laughter. "You're a nutter."

"And you still love me, so who's the real nutter?" He grinned and captured my gaze. "So? Want to live here? Or is that too weird for you … to move back into your childhood home?"

A warmth settled deep inside. Peace.

I pressed one hand to his chest and lifted my other to trace a finger along the ridge of the faint scar near his temple, a daily reminder of how blessed I was to still have him in my life. "I think it's an amazing idea. Thank you."

His chest shuddered under my other hand, and a slow grin eclipsed his face. "Now that we've had our drinks break, can we have a kiss break?"

I pressed a soft kiss to his mouth. "Still too much work to do." I scanned the garden and squinted. What was sticking out from the trunk of Mum's red standard rose plant?

I pushed away from my fiancé and strode to the rose section.

Protruding from the thick tree-like trunk, just below the old wood where the glossy green leaves and a few red roses flowered above, sprouted a thin, flexible green stem.

I furrowed my brow and leaned closer.

"How's that possible?" Jonathan stood behind me.

Was that …? I shook my head. A single purple rosebud hung from the green stem.

"I don't know," I whispered. "I know roses are grafted. Maybe this red rose was grafted onto a purple?"

"Fascinating. Purple's your favourite colour too."

"And Mum's," I whispered. I touched the fragile silken soft-purple petals and closed my eyes. The hint of a musky vanilla fragrance I recalled from my childhood tinged the air. I breathed in the comforting aroma before it disappeared seconds later. *I love you, Mum.*

"Back to work?" Jonathan's deep rumble stirred me from my reverie.

"Soon." I lay my head on his shoulder and melted against him, my chest light. I was finally at peace. With Mum and my career. Jonathan and his brother. Even random strangers no longer frightened me.

I closed my clouded eyes and beamed. My wounded soul was healing by the grace of God.

AUTHOR'S NOTE

I wrote the first draft of Diana's story in 2019, lay it aside, and spent 2020 focused on *Punctured Heart*. It wasn't until mid-2021 I picked up *Wounded Soul* again and reworked the manuscript.

Many of my beautiful readers know I live in Melbourne, Australia. Some of you might recall last year's heightened tensions between our community and Victoria Police. After months of witnessing unrest on our streets—during and between multiple lockdowns—I opened my work-in-progress… only to rediscover Jonathan is a Victoria Police officer! I had to laugh at God's wisdom as this project proved therapeutic for me, a reminder of the many good officers on the force.

For my Northern Hemisphere readers, our tertiary institutions follow the calendar year in a similar cycle to the Australian school year (as experienced in *Punctured Heart)*. University students enjoy longer summer (late November to late February) holidays than our primary and secondary school students, unless pupils enroll in a summer term.

Diana embraces her Aussie roots, and I didn't realize how many Australianisms I had written! Can you believe I replaced many words, halving the Glossary? Perhaps I'll be able to weave words like "yobbo," "bludger," and "budgie smugglers" into my next book. Or not.

Thank you for reading Diana's story. Her bestie Tara is now monopolizing my time with her heartbreaking tale…

ABOUT THE AUTHOR

Sheridan Lee is an Australian writer with a penchant for true-to-life characters who triumph over adversity.

When she isn't singing along to her favourite Christian artists or watching Hollywood actors named Chris in superhero and Star Trek movies, Sheridan is reading or writing—with at least one of her five daughters lounging on her—and wishing the dirty laundry would clean itself.

Learn more about Sheridan and her books at www.sheridanlee.com.

SUBSCRIBE to Sheridan's newsletter (and receive The Tellarine Series prequel chapter as a gift): www.sheridanlee.com/subscribe

SHERIDAN'S BOOKS:

The Tellarine Series

Punctured Heart

Wounded Soul

Fractured Mind

Broken Spirit *(releasing 2023)*